This is a work of fiction. Any similarity of events are purely accidental and are the results of too much free time and an overactive imagination.

Visit the Author's Website: www.myislandbooks.com

Author's email: a.c.humes627@gmail.com

Cover Design by Theandra Thompson: theandra.thompson@gmail.com

EPILOGUE

SOUL SEARCHING

As I hopped out of the SUV and headed to the ATM, I thought about what I had just told Nishka. Most of it was true, and most of what she said was also true. I had to admit, it's easier to have many women rather than one. You may not think so depending on whether you are male or female, and depending on your views on relationships.

Me: I'm complicated. I have one woman that I call my own, but I also have many on the side. You may ask why. Simple. I'm a playa. I don't feel as if one woman can satisfy all my needs at this time. Then why do I have Nancy? I'm trying to wean myself from trickin. It's hard. Extremely hard. Women make it difficult.

Every time I find a nice way to get rid of one, another one—sometimes two—pop into the picture. Women don't want single guys. They want men who are already taken. I guess they figure if a man's single, then something's wrong with him; how else do you explain no other woman wanting him.

Other men make it difficult for me to stop, too. A lot of men aren't taking care of business at home. The 'cum when I cum, or cum when I come back' shit isn't the way to keep your woman. Then we have those men that don't want women at all. You know the ones I'm talking about: the ones that are attracted to other men. It's these men that are really messing things up. For each one of them that go that way, they leave ten women man less. Let's not forget the ones that get caught up in the prison system.

You don't really want to fuck with those dudes' women; the consequences you can't—you shouldn't—put out of your mind. But then again, if the woman is sharp enough to keep her business from getting behind those prison walls, and she fine as hell, then I have no choice but to take up the slack. We're losing too many women to other women as it is. In order to keep our women straight, someone has to take care of their needs. Let's be honest, somebody's got to do it, so, why not me?

Now, as far as the women I see on the side, none of them could ever become the one woman that I decide to settle down with. Why? They're cheaters! Once a cheater, always a cheater! Look how hard it is for me to stop. Yes, people can change, but very few ever do. When it comes to cheating, there's too much temptation. And if you're good at it, then the temptation is even more attractive. The more times you cheat without getting caught, the more confident you get; the easier it becomes You stop giving a second thought whether to cheat or not. You stop thinking about the consequences. Why? Because you think you're not going to get caught. Simple.

Another reason why none of my sidepieces could ever be my main woman; there is no promotion for sidepieces. Once a sidepiece, always a sidepiece! If I were to leave my main woman, Nancy, all my sidepieces will remain my sidepieces—unless they decide to leave—and I will find another woman to fill that vacancy.

This might seem cold to some, but if you think about it, you will see the reality and logic behind it. My reason, in case you haven't figured it out: the side piece knows some—if not all—the tricks and games that I used to run on my woman to come and spend time with her. So, if a sidepiece becomes the main woman—even if I am not cheating and have indeed settled down—she'll always be suspicious of my every move. Her suspicions will lead to her cutting back on taking care of my needs. And, her constant probing and digging will eventually annoy the hell out of me and lead me back to cheating. If I can't be happy, comfortable, and get my needs tended to at home, I will find someplace to go where I will be welcomed, treated like a king, and get my needs and desires met...even if it's only for a few hours. The Bible says that there is nothing worse than a nagging woman at home. And, that's exactly what that promoted sidepiece will turn into: 'Where are you going? Who all's going to be there? What time are you coming back home?' You get the picture.

Now, to keep it real, no man...no matter how many women he's fucking, wants to even think about someone else getting a taste of the one pussy that he sets aside for himself. In my case, that would be Nancy: My woman: not our woman. Ain't no sharing her!

I don't care who's fucking Toya, Ashley, Monique...they're not my women. But Nancy! My Nancy, that's a different story. She's in a committed relationship with me. She said that I am the only man for her: the only man in her life. And you can bet your ass I'm holding her to that. If she ever breaks that commitment, she's gone. G. O. N. E. It's over. No ifs, ands or buts. It's finish. Over. I might still fuck her after a while, but the most her status could ever go to after that would be a sidepiece, a booty call.

I wouldn't be able to love her the same way I used to. Not with me knowing that some other man was digging up in her guts. Think about it, that's my sacred temple that another man defiled. It's a temple that I hold precious and dear to my heart.

I know you are probably thinking that I shouldn't feel that way since I defile other men's temples, but guess what, the other men don't worship and hold dear their temples like I do mine. They don't take care of their temples. I take care of Nancy's needs, her desires, her fantasies...she think it: I do it.

I know, you're asking yourself if I would expect Nancy to forgive me if she caught me cheating. The answer: yes. I expect her love for me to be strong enough for her to forgive me and give me another chance. You must understand; I'm meeting almost the full one hundred percent of her needs and desires. (No one can satisfy all a woman's needs, remember.) And remember, she has no clue of my indiscretions. I don't give her any reason to think I'm stepping out on her. If I have plans and she wants to do something, I cancel my plans. It's simple: she comes first. As far as Nancy's concerned, I am 99.9 percent faithful—she says all men have a lil bit of unfaithfulness in them.

Think what you want, I am a good man. And, we have an excellent relationship. She brags about it all the time. That's why I have to be so discrete about what I do and with whom I do it.

So now you're asking yourself: If Nancy's so precious and dear to me, why do I do it? I already told you; somebody's got to do it, so why not me?

Chapter 1

The Temptress

"How low can you go," I sang along with Ludacris as I dared Nishka to go lower.

Her dark eyes were locked on mine; they were sparkling from the reflection of the strobe lights. Her full red lips formed an orgasmic "O" as she dropped and shook her sexy ass to the sound of the pounding bass.

I brought the bottle of Dom Perignon up to my lips and took a nice, healthy swig to try and wash down the rising temptation of fucking my sister's best friend. She was making it so, so hard.

Nishka slithered back up my body, rubbing her firm mounds against me as she came up. She pressed her pelvis against my growing erection, then smiled, pleased with the effect that she was having on me. She knew exactly what she was doing. Nishka was just 19--eight years my junior, but she had me on the edge of the cliff. If she kept this up, she was definitely going to get what she was looking for: sister's best friend or not.

Nishka held my hand with the bottle of champagne and brought it up to her lips. As I tilted the bottle for her to drink, my eyes travelled from her juicy red lips, down her sensuous neck, then lower to her lush cleavage. My mouth filled with saliva as my eyes danced over her firm mounds. They settled on her pert nipples, which were stretching the soft fabric of her camisole top. I swallowed and heard a light giggle. I gazed into her glinting eyes, then her mouth distracted me as she let her tongue play around the rim of the bottle. I wanted to feel that tongue: taste her sweetness.

Then she stuck her tongue into the bottle. That did it.

Our eyes locked. Our bodies pressed harder against each other—moving as one. My head automatically started down toward her. Her lips parted as her head tilted up so that she would meet me somewhere in the middle. Her hand caressed my back, pulling me in closer...

"You two need to stop," my sister, Yasmine, said, appearing out of nowhere and pulling Nishka back far enough to put at least an inch of space between our bodies.

"What the hell?" I snarled, glaring at my sister.

Her eyebrows shot up and she smirked. "You're not going to get my best friend killed up in this damn club. Toya just walked in."

Toya is one of several girls I'm juggling. Don't get it wrong; they all know that I have a woman. Shit, most of them have a man—even if it's because they can't have me all to themselves.

Nishka continued dancing provocatively in front of me. Toya knew her. They all knew her and my sister; and she and my sister knew them all, too. But, this—what she had taken to another level tonight—wasn't finished. This has been going on ever since the two of them came to Florida for college and I started taking them to the club with me on the weekends: let's just say, they don't like staying on campus on the weekends. I figured if they were going to go out drinking and partying, it was much safer for them to do it with me. There are a lot of unsavory characters out there.

I spotted Toya as she wove her way through the crowd. Really and truly, the crowd parted to let her through. All eyes were on her—mine included. White breast hugging top with straps around her toned exposed stomach; white skirt, solid to the mid thigh, then see-through the rest of the way down to her ankles.

Her hair was bouncing as she walked. Her smile lit up her face as she spotted me. That throbbing erection that Nishka had worked so hard to construct...it now had a safe destination. I knew exactly where I was going to put it.

CHAPTER 2

CLOSET AFFAIR

"Hey, Nishka," Toya said with a dazzling smile. "Girl you rockin' that mini. You go girl!"

"Thanks," Nishka replied, sliding from in front of me and making room for Toya.

Toya reached up and touched Yasmine's hair. "Love the highlights, Sis. They suit you."

"You think?" Yasmine gushed. "Thanks."

"And you, I need you!" she sang as her other hand snaked around my waist. She tiptoed and placed a soft kiss on my lips. "Hey, Baby."

"Hey yourself. I wasn't expecting to see you in here."

"I had a few minutes to spare, so I decided to come and see you."

"What if I were here with someone?" I asked after I kissed her again.

"I would have said hello and kept it moving. I know the rules, Khristin.... Mmmm!" she cooed, pressing herself against my erection. "I sure am happy that you're so happy to see me."

"I'm always happy to see you."

"I can't stay long. He's home."

"Your loss," I smirked.

"Unn-unngh, I'm not going home without getting some of this," she sang, her Trinidadian accent slipping from beneath her Brooklyn accent.

Yasmine cleared her throat. "We're going to make our rounds."

"Don't get lost. Y'all know I'm flying in the morning."

"We know," Nishka replied, taking the bottle of champagne from my hand as they both turned and sashayed away.

As soon as they were out of sight, Toya grabbed my hand and pulled, leading me toward the rear of the club where the offices and storage rooms were. We slid through the door without anyone stopping us.

We entered a dimly lit hallway. Toya tried the first door; it was locked. She dragged me on, checking doors as we went. The next three doors were locked. There was one more door all the way at the end. The knob twisted in her hand. She looked back at me and smiled deviously as she pushed open the door, entered, dragging me into the dark room behind her.

Toya spun around to face me. She closed the door with one hand and started loosening my belt with the other. Her lips pressed hard against mine and she moaned as she parted her lips to let in my probing tongue. My hands caressed her firm ass, pulling her closer at the same time. She trembled under my touch. She kissed me hungrily as she fumbled to unfasten my button. My zipper slid down a second later. Her silky hands didn't take any time before wrapping around my hot, throbbing dick. Suddenly, she pulled away, freeing herself from my kiss.

Then she was getting low, real low. How low would she go?

Toya looked up at me deviously. Her soft brown eyes were shinning so bright that they looked like they were glowing in the dark.

Then just like that, the light went out. I felt like I was floating as she took me into her hot, wet mouth. Her hands slowly released me as her greedy mouth gobbled me up, inch by blissful inch, until she had all of me. Delightful murmurs tingled my shaft as they managed to escape from her throat. Slowly, she let her tongue lick and flick as she worked her way back toward the tip.

My hands ran through her soft hair and caressed her face. I fell back against the closed door, toes curling in my shoes, as Toya teased and stroked me. Her hand caressed my balls as she swirled and twirled her tongue around and across my mushrooming head. She let her tongue lead the way from tip down to base. I felt the condom ensheathe my head, then unroll all the way to my base. Her tongue didn't stop there: it continued down my sack. She tantalized me with her skillful tongue, then plucked both my balls into her mouth. My stomach muscles spasmed as her mouth made love to my jewels.

Toya stood up, pressing her body hard against mine, and kissed me passionately. She spun around, grinding her hips against my erection as she gathered and pulled up her skirt.

I kissed and nibbled on her nape and along her neck until I felt the warmth of my manhood rub between her bare cheeks.

Toya parted her legs, bent over and grabbed her ankles.

I flipped her skirt up over her back and smiled. No underwear. Gripping her firmly by the waist and spreading my legs so I could get up and under her temple, I stroked her slowly; just enough to let my bulging head glide back and forth between her wet lips. I started arcing up, letting my head bump and grind against her clit to bring it out of hiding.

Toya sucked in air noisily between clenched teeth in response to my teasing. She writhed her hips to try and get me to enter her: At the same time, I was making every attempt to torment her entrance. She got tired of the sweet torture. Toya reached up, grabbed my dick and thrust it into her.

With my back against the wall, I had nowhere to run as she backed up and wiggled her hips. I stood there as sensation after sensation ran through my body. Toya flexed her inner muscles, acclimating and savoring the feeling of complete and utter fulfillment. Slowly she bent forward until her hands were on the floor in front of her.

Now she had leverage. Her gyrations started out with small, deliberate circles: Smooth and passionate.

All I did was hold on. I bit my lips and my eyes closed involuntarily as her tightness pulsed around my dick. Then she started changing up her gyrations.

Toya knew how to use what I had without my help—well, that's how she liked to start off, so I let her. It was hard just holding on. It was even harder to watch her gyrating ass. It was dark, but I could see that round ass twerk—shake, roll, wiggle and jiggle. Then she started making it jump. That was my indication that she was almost there. I spanked her ass with one hand and grabbed her by the back of her neck with the other.

Toya's pace increased. Her back arched.

I started giving her a nice, slow grind as she humped and threw her ass back harder.

Her left leg started shaking. She fought to keep her grunts to a minimum, but it was a battle that she was destined to lose.

I spanked her harder and faster. My thrusts got faster and went deeper. She bit on her bottom lip as she exploded around my shaft. I had to wrap an arm under her stomach to keep her from falling, as well as to keep my balance so that I could keep stroking her until her orgasmic wave crested and ebbed.

Toya straightened up slowly as she tried to compose herself. She brought her legs together to steady herself as she turned her head so that she could lean back and kiss me over her right shoulder. The kiss was soft at first, increasing in intensity as her hunger grew. Her gyrations started back up again.

I spun us around, bracing Toya up against the door like I was about to frisk her.

Toya assumed the position, extending her hands up and against the door, then eased back and spread her legs.

I backed up—one hand on her shoulder, the other on her hip— and started pounding her with some long, hard, wicked strokes.

Toya gave back as good as she got. Her left leg started quaking. I threw in a few extra twists, and unorthodox strokes into the mix as I clamped one hand tightly on the back of her neck.

She liked to be choked—not too hard: couldn't leave any marks, and more importantly, she still wanted to be able to breathe.

I felt her fingers on either side of my shaft as it slid mercilessly in and out of her. I felt her body spasm when she started strumming and patting her clit.

I bent my knees and stroked up as hard as I could while putting downward pressure on her neck, making sure she got everything out of every stroke. The staccato of skin slapping against skin, as our pace increased was nothing compared to the pleasurable sounds that managed to escape from her lips.

"Come...come with me," she begged.

"I'm cumming," I said, tightening my perennial muscles and making my dick jump. I missed a stroke on purpose and grunted.

I released Toya's neck and gripped her by her tiny waist. I took out all the twists, jumping, and wickedness out of my strokes:

straight jackhammering.

Toya came cooing.

I didn't come. I pretended to.

As she panted and floated back down to earth with a satisfied smile on her face, I quickly pulled out a napkin from my pocket and used it to pull off the empty condom. I balled it up and put it in my pocket to discard later.

Toya fixed her skirt and ran her fingers through her hair. She walked to me as I pulled up my pants, and planted a sensual kiss on my lips. "I love you," she whispered as she pulled back.

I smiled as I buckled my belt. "I know," I chuckled.

She hit me playfully in the chest. "Would it hurt you to say it one time?"

"You know I'm not going to tell you what you want to hear. When I say it, I'm going to mean it."

"If you say it now, you're going to mean it. You know you love me."

"Come on, Toya. Let's not get into this tonight. We're both creeping."

"That's because we're both with the wrong people."

"Let's get out of here before we get caught," I said, ignoring her last statement.

"Okay. One more kiss."

A minute later, we were in separate bathrooms cleaning ourselves. I flushed the empty condom, shaking my head and smiling as I watched it disappear.

CHAPTER 3

HOME SWEET HOME

"Y'all ready to go?" I asked Nishka and Yasmine.

"Where's Toya?" Nishka asked.

"Gone home to her man," I replied with a smirk.

"I guess she got what she came for and left, huh? Damn! She carrying home sloppy seconds to her man," Nishka mumbled.

"What?" I asked.

Yasmine was laughing.

"Nothing," Nishka replied, laughing along with Yasmine.

"Let's go," I said, turning to head toward the exit. "Which one of y'all drivin?"

"Nishka," Yasmine shot. "Y'all could drop me off by Sean."

Neither Nishka, nor I bothered to reply.

When the valet attendant brought the Range up, I tipped him and slid into the back seat. Nishka drove.

Five minutes to get to the turnpike and my phone buzzed. I checked the caller ID: Toya. "Yeah?" I answered.

"I'm pulling through my gate now," she cooed.

"Cool. Don't forget to erase my number from your call log."

"I won't. Thanks for tonight. Love you," she sang as she ended the call.

I laughed, as I pressed end, then hit the speed dial for wifey: Nancy.

Nancy answered on the first ring. "Hey, baby."

"You sound as if you were sitting with the phone in your hand, waiting for me to call."

"I was. You on your way home?"

"Yeah," I replied, stretching out on the backseat. "We just have to drop this booty call off at her boyfriend's house."

"Don't call her that! If she's a booty call, then so am I. At least she's on her way from the club. I'm home—in my bed—fast asleep and had to set my alarm to wake me up to come out to you."

"You can stay in and sleep, you know."

"My monthly visitor is gone, and you want me to stay home! Yeah, right. I'm on my way. I'll see you in a few."

"Alright," I chuckled, ending the call.

I tapped Nishka on the shoulder. "Come on, Nish, we've got twenty minutes to drop Yas off and get home. Step on it!"

"Nancy," Yasmine said as Nishka stared at her. "They have it timed. It takes her between seventeen to twenty minutes to get to his house, depending if she catches all green or red lights after getting off the pike."

Ten minutes later, Yasmine was out the vehicle. I remained sprawled out on the backseat, and seven minutes later, we pulled into my driveway. I was out of there before the Range was in park.

"You better hurry," Nishka smirked. "Go wash Toya's scent off of your dick."

"That's not Toya's scent, it's yours. The way you were grinding on me...mmmm-mmm-mmmm! You should be ashamed of yourself," I teased, giving her a proper once over.

"You only wish I would give you some of this," Nishka shot back as we headed to the door. "You get some of this, you'll stop all this ho'in you doing."

"That right there is what does get you young girls in trouble. Y'all always believe y'all pussy soooo good that it'll change a man. Ain't no pussy that good. A man changes when he wants to change," I said, turning off the alarm. "And, if...no, not if, when...when I decide you're woman enough to handle me, you're going to be the one that'll change."

"See, that's where y'all old men get shit twisted. Y'all think a hard dick can tame a woman. It takes more than a hard dick. If it's only a hard dick we looking for, we could go to the toy store and pick out the size, shape, and color."

"If you think a toy is as good as a real dick, that just proves that you're not ready for me," I said, smacking her on the butt as we walked up the stairs. "Oh, just in case you run out, batteries are in the second drawer in the utility room," I shot as I scooted toward my room.

I heard her cursing as I closed the door behind me. I stripped quickly as I headed to the shower.

Two minutes later, the shower door slid open. "What woman's scent are you trying to wash off?"

I stepped under the shower to rinse the body wash off my face. I opened my eyes and smiled. "I don't remember her name, baby. Actually, I don't think I ever got it. She was all over me. I told you about letting me go out without you. Girls just can't resist me."

"Is that so?" Nancy replied. "I hope, whoever she was, she didn't wear you out. I didn't drive all the way up here for nothing."

"I thought you came so we could cuddle and watch..."

"Cuddle?" Nancy repeated like it left a bad taste in her mouth. "Oooooh," she crooned, rubbing her hand up and down my erection. "I guess she didn't wear you out after all."

I turned off the shower as she reached behind her and grabbed my towel. She continued to fondle me as she dried my skin. At the same time, I was undressing her. It wasn't much to take off; camisole and matching sleep pants. No bra. No panties.

While she towel dried my body, I wet her smooth, chocolate skin with soft, sensuous kisses, backed her into the vanity, scooped her up and sat her on its edge with the basin directly behind her.

Nancy opened herself to me. I caressed her breasts and ran my thumbs across both nipples until they plumped out and pointed up toward the sky. I got them hard enough to cut glass. My tongue was leading an expedition down her neck, between her breasts, over and under—not leaving an inch of her firm, succulent breasts untouched. I teased around her dark areolas, causing her to go giddy with pleasure. Her soft, delightful moans only goaded me on. I nipped, nibbled, sucked, teased and adored her nipples.

I like noise. I like to hear how I'm making my partner feel. And Nancy made all the right noises; all the right moves in response to my actions. That incited me to spend more time worshipping her breasts.

Her soft heels dug into the back of my thighs as she ground her pelvis onto my erection. She brought one leg up until it was around my waist. I could feel her juices as her wet lips lathered my dick up real good. I wanted to be inside her. I wanted to feel her. But, I needed to taste her nectar.

I slid down slowly, letting my mouth, lips and tongue run down her stomach, stopping to delve into her navel before nibbling on her sides. That made her squeal and try to get away from me, but I held her firmly in place as I traced along her pantly-less panty line, then nibbled on her pelvic bone with just enough teeth to make her clench her teeth and close her eyes. I let my nose graze lightly on her skin as I followed the landing strip all the way down to the apex of her temple.

Nancy's left leg came up and swung over my right shoulder, her soft heel gliding up and down my back. Catching the right leg, I nibbled on her calf, kissed and sucked gently on the soft spot behind her knee. I glanced up as I kissed her inner thigh and watched as her lips blossomed. I hungered to taste her.

I skipped the rest of the appetizers, choosing to go directly to the main course. My lips on her moist lips: gentle kisses with just a slight hint of tongue.

Nancy's hips started moving up and around; her head leaned back against the glass: her hands caressing her breasts.

I loved the way she tasted. I loved the way she smelled.

I loved the way her body responded to my skilled tongue. I parted her swollen outer lips, letting the small build up of her sweet nectar flow into my mouth. I lapped it up like a kitten laps up milk. My tongue slid between, then over every centimeter of her inner folds; slow and menacing were my tongue lashes. I felt a small tremor course through her body as I intentionally expelled air through my nostrils onto her throbbing pleasure knob. I let the tip of my nose brush gently on it as my tongue darted in and out of her pleasure chest.

Nancy moaned pleasurably. Her hand gripped my head as my tongue drove her to the brink of insanity. My tongue darted in and out, flicked up and down, then vibrated against her pleasure knob.

Nancy's moans and tremors increased. She was dying a sweet and torturous death: A death that I was doing my best to send her to.

The two-handed clamp on my head told me that Nancy was teetering on the edge. I concentrated my efforts on her pleasure knob: teasing and pleasing. I slid my index finger into her causing her body to spasm as her inner walls closed in and clamped down on it. In and out I worked it. Twisting. Turning. Then I curved it up against the soft, spongy spot at the front of her vagina.

Nancy bucked, swearing sweetly as I made come-here motions, literally calling her to ecstasy. Nancy followed my lead, humping my finger and mouth with fervor.

I pressed my tongue against her pleasure knob and vibrated it as hard and fast as I could. Her flavor burst into my mouth as her juices flowed freely across my tongue, filling my mouth. I drank to my heart's content.

I held a little of her juice on my tongue, saving it for her as I stood up and assisted her as she scooted directly to the edge of the vanity. I kissed her, giving her my tongue so that she may sample her own sweetness.

Her body was still resonating from her orgasm. One hand shot around my neck, the other grabbed my joystick and plunged it deep into her pleasure chest. Her legs came up automatically, allowing me to go even deeper. She tried to wrap them around my back: she wanted to restrict my motion, but I had something else in mind.

I caught her right leg in the crook of my left arm, grabbed the calf of her left leg with my right hand and held it up at shoulder height, opening and stretching her to her limits. She was at my mercy now.

I stroked her good. Left. Right. Side to side. Up and down. Then I changed it up...mixed it up a bit as I sucked on her toes and nibbled on her ankles. She began begging, pleading for me to give her the straight shots. The piston. The jackhammer.

Nancy's hands found a way to get around to my butt. She dictated the speed. Her body spasmed and her panting got harder and shorter.

I increased the speed of my jackhammering, alternating angle and penetration depth. I did the random misfire and stutter strokes that always drive her over the edge.

Nancy's body spasmed with a little more urgency than before. "Come with me, baby," she sang between pants.

Her inner muscles trembled against me with each stroke. I could feel the blood flowing through her most precious parts. I could feel every twitch: every tremor as she drew closer and closer to ecstasy. My own pressure was building. It was building quickly. This was going to be explosive.

Nancy's tremors grew exponentially. Her body spasmed violently. Her mouth opened and not one sound came out.

My mouth covered hers, devouring her. Nancy's tongue shot into my mouth enthusiastically. Our tongues danced their own erotic dance right until she started sucking my tongue. She sucked so hard that I had a difficult time deciphering whether it was pleasurable or painful. Then she began sucking my tongue to the same frantic rhythm of our stroking.

I felt myself swelling.

She had to have felt me growing inside of her. She kissed and humped me with increasing intensity. Ecstasy descended upon her with brute force. She bucked and shook violently.

My pressure built to where I couldn't hold it any longer.

I stroked faster and erupted on top of her orgasm. My hot lava flowed into her, sending waves of pleasure rippling through her body.

Her kiss softened as her orgasm and tremors abated. Our mouths separated. She sighed with a contented smile and as I released her legs, she whispered, "I love you, baby."

"I love you too," I replied.

We stayed on the vanity kissing and caressing until I went limp and stiffened again. Then we took it to the shower. Needless to say, I didn't get a minute of sleep before my 7:30 a.m. sign in. It didn't matter: it was just a fifteen-minute flight from Fort Lauderdale International Airport to Freeport, Grand Bahama. Besides, I had all day at the hotel to sleep.

CHAPTER 4

WEEKEND GETAWAY

My flight took off on time at 9 a.m. The flight was short and uneventful. By 9:45 a.m., the entire flight crew was strolling into the hotel in Freeport. Behind the front desk stood Monique: breathtaking smile, cute dimples and a body that would raise the dead. Her eyes lit up as I walked to the front desk. The entire time, I was praying that she had already taken her morning break.

"Just the man I was hoping to see," Monique beamed as she handed out room keys to the rest of the flight crew.

She didn't give me a key. That meant she had plans. "No room in the Inn for me?" I asked, teasing her.

Before she could answer, Chris stepped through the door holding up a key. "I have your room key right here. I wanted to make sure you pay up on that Lakers victory last night," he said, waving me down to the far end of the front desk.

When I got to where he was, I whispered, "What's up? You know we didn't bet on any game last night."

"Lakers didn't even play last night." He grinned. "Ashley's in your room. I went around there to let her in so Monique wouldn't see her," he said, shaking his head and grinning like a complete idiot.

"What you grinnin for, fool?"

"You should see the little dress she was wearing."

"I don't need to see the dress," I said, snatching my key from him. "I get to see that body with nothing on it but me."

"Lucky muddafucka!" he cursed as I turned and walked away. "Next!" he called.

"Mo," I said as I was passing. "I'm going to catch a nap, I'll call you when I wake up, alright?"

"Don't forget," she said, and winked. "I really need to talk to you 'bout something."

Sure you do, I thought, nodding to her. Ashley was in my room desperately needing to talk to me too.

I slid the card key into the door and opened it. The room was dark. Scented candles flickered on each side of the bed. Mary J. Blige sang, "Ain't nobody gonna love you better."

Ashley looked up nervously from the bed where she laid, hands and feet tied with scarves. She was dressed in a soft blue negligee that did nothing to conceal that tight little body of hers. Instead, it emphasized all her assets. It molded around her ample bosom and exposed her swollen lips that were pressing hard against her lace undies. The soft blue teddy matched her seductive blue eyes. She was spread out like it was a magazine shoot. Everything was arranged for maximum effect. Even her blonde hair was perfectly splayed on the pillow, making her look like an angel with a halo. It was quite a dramatic look. And—I must admit that it had a most desirable affect on me. I was no longer tired. I felt rejuvenated. I was aching to get into her.

"Who are you?" Ashley asked, then stuttered quickly, "I'm sorry, I thought this was my-my husband's room."

I was smiling on the inside. Role-playing. I felt a stirring in my loins. This is going to be good, I thought excitedly as I dropped my bags, locked and latched the door. I started stripping as I walked over to the bed. "Well, well. Look at what I found."

"Don't come near me...I'll scream. Untie me!" she cried.

"Untie you?" I said, climbing onto the bed right between her legs.

"Don't touch me or I am going to scream."

"Does your husband know what to do with all this?" I asked, squeezing her swollen lips. "Mmmm, you're nice and wet, too."

"Oh, God, what are you going to do to me?"

"Give you exactly what you want."

"I want my husband! I'm going to scream," she said.

"Look like I'm going to have to put something in your mouth to stop that from happening, then," I said, climbing up and over her breast. I held my dick with one hand, grabbed a handful of her hair, and lifted her head from the pillow. "Open your mouth," I commanded.

"What are you doing? I want my hus.... Aaargh."

I stuck my dick in her mouth, cutting off her speech. I loved the way my dick stretched her lips. I forced more of myself into her mouth until she gagged. "Suck this dick like this the sweetest dick you ever had in your mouth," I snarled as I started easing out of her mouth.

She looked into my eyes, terrified.

I could see the fright in her eyes.

It seemed to register to her that I was going to get what I wanted one way or the other. She started off tentatively: her tongue slowly licking up and down my shaft.

"C'mon, I know you can do better than that. Everyone's always raving about white girls being able to suck a nail from a piece of wood. Prove it. Suck the sap from my tree trunk."

Apparently, that's all she needed. She started swirling and twirling her tongue up and down my shaft, lubricating me. She twisted, adjusting her body so that she could get at me real good. She found a comfortable position and settled in.

Enough of my dick got out of her mouth so that she could polish my knob. Her tongue skillfully rendered me speechless. She wasn't just sucking my dick: she was applying polish, taking it off, and spit shinning it all at once. With no hands to help her, she pumped me with her jaws. Inch by blissful inch, she took me into her mouth. I watched, fascinated, as she took me all in. I felt my head slide against the soft tissue at the back of her throat. She must have been faking earlier, because she wasn't gagging now.

She was deep-throating me like a pro, and the pleasurable sounds escaping her lips told me she was enjoying every minute of it.

She let me slide out of her hot mouth, and began peppering my shaft with light kisses. Her thin lips felt wonderful. Then her velvety tongue traced the big vein all the way down to my sack. She handled my balls with honor and reverence. Then her tongue lashed lower.

"Oooooh...mmmmm! Girl, you nasty," I said, raising up just a little more so that she could really get to where she wanted.

Her tongue fluttered back and forth in the space between my ass and balls. My stomach knotted like I had done a thousand sit-ups. Her tongue ran circles around the rim of my ass causing me to squeal like a bitch. "Ooooiiii! Fuck! You...are...so- so...fucking...nasty."

Suddenly, her tongue breached my ass. Her tongue dipped in

and out. I wanted to jump up and run, but I also wanted to stay put. I felt violated, but it felt sooooo fucking good. My salad was being tossed...and it felt like heaven. My dick throbbed against my stomach. I spun around so that I could get access to her. She was terrifying me with her sinfulness. I wanted to return the favor.

I lowered my head and started kissing the inside of her thighs, letting my chin rub against her lips as they strained against the lacy fabric of her underwear.

She mumbled for me to rise up. I tooted my ass up. Her mouth ran back up my length to my head. Once again, her tongue dazed and confused me. Her tongue titillated and exhilarated me. When she took me back into her hot, wet mouth, I thought I was going to explode. A sudden animalistic urge surged through me. I grabbed her underwear on both sides of her pulsing vagina, and pulled.

The lace shredded, exposing her succulent pink flesh. I used my fingers to massage and spread her lips. The beautiful, fleshy inner folds called my name. My lips led the way, but it was my tongue that licked and slurped up her sweet elixir.

While I humped her mouth, Ashley humped my tongue and fingers. My lathered fingers massaged her lips, slipping in and out of her and adding to her pleasure. I slurped her protruding clit into my mouth, sucking and vibrating the tip of my tongue against it with just enough pressure to cause her to explode. I felt her body quake. Her humping made the headboard bang against the wall. Her grunts and groans vibrated against my dick as it slid in and out of her delicious mouth.

My pressure was building. I started humping her mouth faster. She squirmed as she bumped her pussy hard against my mouth.

I rewarded her with two fingers, working them in and out of her at random speeds.

She sucked harder and faster, still managing to swirl and twirl her tongue. She humped harder. She humped faster.

I slid one lathered finger into her buttonhole and she stiffened in mid air. Her hips and back were completely off the mattress.

Her body trembled, as her sweet elixir started flowing like a river.

Her mouth opened. She wasn't sucking anymore. She wasn't swirling and twirling her tongue anymore. My stroking was now free and unrestricted. She had her head tilted back, which allowed me to have my way with her mouth. I took full advantage.

With my own climax on its way, I fucked her mouth faster.

Deeper.

Harder.

She loved it. It made her come harder.

Come longer.

I continued to fuck her mouth. I felt my nut rising. I swelled in her mouth. My toes curled as the first shot exploded down her throat.

Ashley moaned in delight as she lowered her hips back to the bed. She started winding her waist again, small circles to begin with. She closed her mouth around me as I continued pumping into her mouth. She added a little suction and got every last drop out of my pipes. When she had drank all there was to drink, she cleaned my entire shaft, then polished my knob, using very little pressure. She was so good that my dick remained hard. She planted a kiss on the all Seeing Eye and said, "Since I'm already here, I might as well let you fuck me. My husband can't eat pussy like you, so now I'm curious to see if you can fuck as good as you eat."

I was deep in character mood as I got up from the bed and went to my bag to get my rubbers. I went into the bathroom and got a towel, wet it with warm water, then cleaned myself off before sliding on the French Tickler that I had chosen from my stash. I figured I would treat her to something special since she went out of her way to tie herself up to the bed...even if it was the wrong man's bed. I smiled, relishing the thought of someone actually being that ditzy.

Missionary isn't one of my favorite positions, but since she was tied up spread eagle, what the hell, I'll make the best of it.

Her pretty feet and pedicured toes looked right for sucking, but this is another man's wife, I reminded myself. I wanted to please her; not cause her to fall in love.

I climbed onto the bed between her opened legs. Her breast, firm and round, couldn't be ignored. My hands groped, fondled, and caressed them through the sheer, silky fabric of her top. Her nipples stretched the top, begging to be sucked. I pinched them and her body shook. I smiled as I let my mouth taunt each nipple in turn.

Her eyes closed. She bit her bottom lip. Her hips rose from the bed as she tried desperately for her pelvic region to make contact with my dick, which was purposely hovering just out of reach.

Since she was up, I got an idea. I released her captured nipple, raking my teeth gently over it as I did, and sat back on my heels. I slid my thighs beneath both of hers to brace her. I grabbed a pillow and stuffed it under her arched back and hips.

I massaged and spread her wet lips with one hand as I guided the tentacle-covered head from the French tickler up and down between her slick lips. When the tentacles were lathered enough, I let them dance over and around her swollen clit. I strummed her clit and outer lips until she was about to climax, again. Then I stopped. I didn't let her climax. I made her take deep breaths to suppress it.

I started teasing her opening with the mushroom head, just letting my short strokes barely penetrate her opening. The tentacles danced about her opening, driving her wild with pleasure. She was bucking wildly, trying her best to get more of me into her.

I used my hips to keep that from happening. I looked up at the pleading and longing that was written all over her face. I shook my head. "You know you shouldn't be doing this. You're a married woman," I said, pulling completely out of her.

"Just this once. Pleeeease?" she drawled, sniffling and sounding like she was about to cry.

I wanted to feel sorry for her, but she's a married woman. This wasn't right.

"C'mon. Give it to me. Just this once," she begged.

"There's no such thing as just once. If I put this dick on you," I said, slapping the head against her quivering pussy lips, "you're going to want to do this all the time."

She let out a big breath. "My husband doesn't have time to fuck me."

"That's a sorry excuse for what you're doing. If you put forth the effort, he'll make time to fuck your fine ass."

"Look what I had to resort to. I had to try and sneak in his hotel room to get him to notice me. All this," she said, using her eyes to motion around the room, "is for him. I just got the wrong room. And-and now, not even a complete stranger wants to fuck me," she said, letting a tear roll down her cheek.

Oh, she's good at this role-playing shit, I thought. I was amazed at myself as well. I was really feeling this character. And right now, my character was thinking she had a valid point. I had to fuck her. If I didn't, her self-esteem would be shot. Even out of character, I had to fuck her for her creativity and effort: pretending to get into the wrong room. I shook my head. If she were really as ditzy as she's pretending to be, she would have probably been at the wrong hotel as well.

I grinned as I forced myself into her stirring pussy. "Damn!" She's soaking wet, and her pussy is tighter than a muthafucka. "This some good-n-tight you have here. Ooooooeeeeeee!"

"Oooooh, this dick feels soooo...fucking...gooood. Oooooh! Show me how much you like this pussy."

The pussy was so tight, I felt like the rubber was desecrating her sacred temple. I almost believed that it was robbing me of some of the sensation. I was tempted to pull out, take off the rubber, and run up in her raw. But, I knew better. I had to let my big head control the little one; the big one has a brain; the small one is egotistic, self-satisfied, and just plain old vain.

My strokes, even though not hard, were punishing to her.

She's tight and shallow. I was hitting her back walls with every stroke. I tried to finesse the pussy, but she begged me to hit it hard. So, what was I supposed to do? I gave her fine, good pussy having ass exactly what she asked for.

The headboard banged loudly against the wall. But that was nothing compared to the noise she was giving me. I liked noise. It does something to my ego. It makes me perform better.

The more noise she made, the harder I stroked her, and the more creative I got with my strokes. I was pummeling her toward a violent explosion.

She wanted to explode. She was chanting for me to send her to paradise. She was like a suicide bomber; she was ready to go to paradise.

I gripped her waist as she stroked me back ferociously. She growled then stopped moving. "Oh...Fuck...I'm...cumming."

I held her waist tighter and stroked her as fast as I could, as slow as I could go, as tender as I could, as hard as I could.

The pressure from the suppressed climax added to this one.

It was powerful. The dam couldn't hold. The pressure was too much. She sang, sounding the alarm. Then the dam burst. Her hot, thick fluids flowed with tsunami like force.

I rode her wave of pleasure as she went soaring to paradise. Hot, thick juices pumped out of her as I continued to pummel in and out of her tightness.

The look on her face brought a smile to my face. As gorgeous as she was earlier, her face contorted into something almost scary as she came. And just as quickly, the beauty returned. She was glowing now. When her eyes opened, my heart went out to her. This was all she wanted; all she sought to garner from her husband.

He didn't have the time to give it to her, so she had to find pleasure from other resources. If he had taken care of home, I wouldn't have to do it. And, I wasn't finished. There was more work to be done.

Ashley hadn't come all this way for a quickie. Ashley wasn't returning to Palm Beach until tomorrow at three. And knowing her, she intended to get everything she needed out of me before then.

CHAPTER 5

HARD FACTS

"I thought I was going to have to circle again," Nishka said as I threw my roller onto the back seat.

I hopped into the front and closed the door. "You came early? You must have missed me," I said as she pulled back into traffic.

"I missed you like I miss my monthly cramps: when it's gone, I don't want it to come back, but I know it will."

"Damn! What did I do?"

"Nothin. I'm just teasin," she grinned.

"Where's my favorite sister? Sean's?"

"No. I dropped her back on campus. She had to meet with her lab partner to complete an assignment for tomorrow."

"Swing by the bank for me first," I said, directing her into the right lane. "I have to make a deposit." I pulled out the envelope from Ashley. I counted out fifty crisp hundred-dollar bills.

Nishka shook her head. "Ashley must have been to Freeport for the weekend," she chuckled. "Does she know that the same dick she's paying for, you giving away to other females for free?"

"She used to get it for free, too. She still is getting it for free. I was hitting that before she got married and got wealthy," I laughed, thinking back to when she couldn't afford to buy a pack of condoms for me to fuck her with. "She's not paying for the dick, she's paying for this Range Sport. She's the one that said she could picture me driving it, so she gave me the down payment, makes the monthly payments, pays the insurance and scheduled maintenance, and buys the gas," I stated. "She can afford it, thanks to me."

Nishka shook her head. "Tell me something, why do you do it?"

"Do what?"

"Ho."

"Because I am too much for any one woman to handle," I replied.

"Yeah, right. I think you do it because it's easier. It's easier to please a bunch of women because they're not around as much; you don't spend a lot of time with them as you would if you only had one woman. It's like taking a bubbling baby from its mother and playing with it. You get them when they're all happy and bubbly; then when they get miserable, hungry, bored, or need changing, you hand their cute little asses right back to their mother."

"Why are you saying it like it's a bad thing? That's a good thing for me, and for the woman: she doesn't have to deal with me too often either. We get together when it's mutually beneficial, satisfy each other's needs..."

"Physical needs," Nishka interjected.

"It's more than just physical: it's emotional too."

"Ain't no emotions involved."

"I beg to differ," I stated. "Emotions are involved. We care for each other. These women have deep feelings for me. What, you don't think Toya loves me?"

"Toya's crazy. She doesn't count. Besides, she has a man. Obviously, she loves him."

"Can't she love the two of us?" I laughed. "It doesn't have to be the same. She could love certain things about him; different things about me."

"She loves your dick."

"That too, but we have an emotional connection. She can be herself with me. She's comfortable around me. I listen to her talk. I advise her on how to keep her relationship going..."

"You sexin' her. How is that advising her?"

"You're not getting it. Okay, let's switch from Toya, 'cause for some reason you don't like Toya too much." Before she could offer a rebuttal, I pressed on. "Let's take Ashley for instance," I said, holding up the five grand. "I met Ashley years ago. I was only seeing her and one other girl at the time. Ashley was only seeing me, but she knew about the other young lady. She was okay with it at first, but after a while she started demanding more. She wanted me for herself. I couldn't give her what she wanted. At the same time, she met her present husband. She wasn't in to him. He was fifteen years older and he was trying to buy her attention. He sent her flowers, jewelry; day passes to the spa for her and two of her friends. The gifts kept getting more and more extravagant. He wasn't giving up. Eventually, she agreed to a dinner date. First thing that morning, he sent his personal assistant over. They spent the day at the spa and shopping. That night, he sent his Phantom to pick her up. They had dinner somewhere over the Atlantic in his private G-550, and desert as they descended into Paris, a place she had always dreamed of going. They stayed for the weekend; she was calling me the entire time and asking me what she should do. He took her shopping and with a little coaxing from me, she let him charm his way right into her pants. She enjoyed all the pampering, attention, and affection, not to mention being able to have anything she asked for. Only one problem, he had no stamina. He was good and attentive to her needs, but she was still left wanting more. Now, should she have given up all that...and I'm not just talking about the money. I'm talking his kindness, his genuine love for her just because he lacks the stamina that her body craves?"

"I think she should have left then."

"You're crazy."

"That's better than cheating."

"Is it? The next man might not have been as good, and she would not have been as happy and contented as she is now."

"So? Life's about taking chances."

"That's exactly what she's doing; taking a chance. She's sneaking out to get that sexual need fulfilled."

"What about his feelings?"

"What about it? If she's happy, he's happy. If she's sexually frustrated at home, then she's going to be irritable, and no matter what he does, she's going to make his life miserable. Anything he does is going to grate on her last nerves.

"So basically, you're telling me that if you decide to settle down with one woman, it would be perfectly all right with you for her to go out and find a man to satisfy whatever need she has that you left unsatisfied?"

"First of all, I'm not going to settle down with any one woman. You women are too hard to please."

Nishka laughed. "So you admit that it is easier to satisfy several women rather than one."

"All I'm saying is that you women want a man one way in the beginning, then once y'all get him, y'all start to change him so he could be more in-tuned to y'all feelings. Then once he changes to what y'all claimed y'all wanted, then y'all don't want him anymore: 'He's not the same man I fell in love with.'"

"Y'all do the same thing," Nishka countered. "No, we don't. We get bored because y'all want us to spend more time with y'all; stop hanging out with our boys, but then y'all don't want to keep us entertained at home. Y'all stop doing the things that attracted us to y'all ass in the first place."

"That's not true."

"Yes, it is. Y'all stop caring about how y'all look in front of us. Y'all stop dressing sexy and provocatively. Y'all want to walk around the house all day with y'all head tied up and cream on y'all face. Y'all stop all the hot, freaky sex...all the spontaneous sex. All those texts and calls begging for sex stops."

"Y'all stop taking us out. Stop sending us flowers. Stop calling us during the day to say 'I just couldn't stop thinking about you'. Stop paying attention to our sexual needs. Y'all come home, dick hard from drinking all night, wake us up, force y'all dick up in us dry, bust a nut before we even get wet, then y'all roll off and fall asleep leaving us horny and unsatisfied."

"So see, we're right back to square one. In order for relationships to last, you need a man like me to satisfy those sexual desires and needs that y'all men at home are leaving unsatisfied."

She laughed and shook her head. "You're good. I like how you brought that shit around full circle."

"It's true!" I laughed. "You just said so yourself: All those women not getting satisfied because their men become complacent. What you think would happen if they didn't have an outlet for their sexual frustration? How many arguments? How many fights? How many domestic violence cases? How many children would grow up seeing mommy and daddy fussing and fighting instead of laughing and loving each other?"

"So, what you're telling me...me, a woman, is that I'll never find a man to fulfill one hundred percent of my needs?"

"You can't fulfill one hundred percent of your needs," I stated. "You don't even know what you want, much less what you need. God is the only one that can fulfill one hundred percent of a woman's needs," I said, chuckling.

"That's not funny."

"Seriously, the best thing you can do is know what it is that you want and be willing to compromise."

"Why does the woman always have to be the one to compromise?"

"I didn't say that. Both partners have to be willing to compromise. There are good men out there. You can find one that meets most of your needs. Just understand that no one man can satisfy all your needs. Find one that satisfies your most important needs. One piece of advice: If you don't want to cheat, make sure you don't compromise in the sex department. If you do, you'll find yourself running to a man just like me," I said, glancing over to her, then added. "Maybe it will be me."

CHAPTER 6

FACING THE FACTS

Nishka watched as Khristin waited his turn to get to the ATM. She reflected on their conversation. Would she find a man to love her unconditionally: one that will satisfy her needs?

That was funny, because she didn't really know what her needs were. Or, would she end up running to a man just like Khristin? To be honest, Khristin wasn't so bad. He treated Nancy like a queen, even though he cheated on her. But, Nancy didn't know he was cheating. As far as Nancy was concerned, she couldn't ask for a better man. Khristin was good. He was extremely good at playing the game. In fact, he was too good at it for her to catch him.

Nishka shook her head. No, Khristin isn't that good. I know for sure I would catch his ass. Nancy was just young and naive: she actually trusted Khristin.

Nishka smiled and shook her head as Khristin stepped up to the ATM and began his transaction. Age didn't have anything to do with Nancy being duped; Nancy was the same age as she and Yasmine were. Love had Nancy blind. And, Nancy was just too damn trusting. Right then, Nishka promised not put all her trust in no man except the Father up above. She would not let love blind her.

Nishka grinned deviously at the thought that ran through her mind. If I can't trust any man, then I might as well sample what Khris has to offer. All his females think he's all that.

Right then she saw him walking back toward the vehicle. He sure is nice to look at. Then she remembered how good he had felt up in the club before Toya had came in. She felt a tingling between her legs. Suddenly, she no longer felt like driving. Nishka unbuckled her seat belt and motioned for Khris to come to the driver's side. Getting on her hands and knees, she took her time crawling over the center console.

Khris opened the door and caught her halfway across. "Look at that nice, juicy ass! Mmmmm-mmmm-mmmm," Khris sang. "I should just take a bite! Grrrrrr!"

Nishka hastened across and plopped down in the seat. "You's a freak, you know," she said, giggling and raising up a little to pull her shorts from biting into her crotch.

"That ting fat, eh," he said, staring between her legs. "Now that's a camel toe right there! That ting look like a juicy hamburger."

"You need to keep your eyes in your head," Nishka sassed.

"You the one that had all that ass up in my face when I opened the door. You could have slid across, but nooooo, you had to go doggy style across the seat."

Nishka kissed her teeth. "You could say what you want, you could look all you want; you ain't getting none of this. They say old men does give young women worms."

"Not worms, snake..." Khris stopped talking at the sound of Nishka's phone trilling.

She picked it up from the cup holder where she had it. She glanced at the caller ID and smirked. "This your favorite sister right now." Hitting the send button, she answered, "Hello."

Smack!

"Don't touch me," Nishka yelled, smacking Khris's hand as he reached across to pinch her camel toe.

"That thing too fat. You have to be spoon feeding that."

"Don't play with me," she said, turning away so that he wouldn't see her blush. "Yasmine, you need to talk to your brother. I don't know what's wrong with him," she said, then paused to listen.

A second later, she said, "Here, your sister wants to talk to you."

$ $ $ $

"Yo," I said, pulling out of the bank's parking lot.

Yasmine chuckled. "Hey. Why are you harassing my girl?"

"Have you seen the shorts she has on? Them things so short and tight, they're cutting her breath. I might have to give her mouth to mouth in a minute."

Nishka heard Yasmine and me laughing. She rolled her eyes and snarled, "Screw you and your sister."

Yasmine chuckled. "She know she like when you mess with her.

Did she tell you I cooked dinner before I left?"

"No, she didn't. What you cooked?"

"Pepper conch, white rice and cole slaw," she bragged.

"What got into you? If I had known you had cooked dinner for me, I would have put an extra hundred on your account."

"I'll be waiting when you come to drop off Nishka. I do take cash."

"Next time. I already deposited all the cash except for this lil two hundred I have for Nishka."

"Well, let me get mine before you change your mind," Nishka said, twisting sideways and sticking her hand in my face.

I smacked her open palm. "I don't pay before I play," I shot, sticking out my tongue at her.

"You wrong for that," Yasmine said, laughing as Nishka punched me, then rubbed her hand.

"Ouch, girl. I'm just playing," I said, grinning at Nishka. "I'11 give you half up front."

Nishka punched me again. "Give me my damn phone so I can talk to my friend," she said, trying to snatch the phone.

"We'll talk later," I said to Yasmine. "Your girl wants her phone. I hope she has money to pay the bill, 'cause she's not gettin a dime from me anymore. I'll call you later and tell you if I like your food." I chuckled. "Love ya."

"Love you too. Oh, hey, Mommy said to call her."

"Okay, I'll call her now," I said, then gave Nishka her phone.

I pulled out my cell phone, put in my Bluetooth earpiece and hit the speed dial for my mother.

The phone rang twice before she answered. "Hello."

"Yes, Mother Dearest. I heard you rang earlier."

"I'm glad you called. You picked up my suits like you were supposed to?"

"Yes, Ma'am, I sure did."

"Good. I want you to drop them to Sherice for me."

"Who is Sherice? And where is she?"

"You know Sherice. She works with me. Bowlegged Sherice."

"Ohhhhhh, that Sherice," I sang with a smile. "Where she at?"

"She's staying at the Marriott by Broward Mall. Call her. Get a pen so I can give you her cell phone number."

"What's the number? I'll put it in my phone."

After she gave me the number, she riddled off a list of other things that she wanted me to pick up from Target. When I hung up, I called and touched base with my baby, Nancy.

CHAPTER 7

RUNNING ERRANDS

It was almost six thirty when I got off the phone with Nancy. She and her mother were visiting her sick aunt up in Palm Beach, so that gave me the night to do as I wished. I glanced over at Nishka, still talking animatedly to my sister. Those legs sure looked sweet, I thought.

She caught me looking.

"What's wrong with you? You need to keep your eyes on the road," she said, pointing at the road ahead.

"I prefer looking at what you're showing me."

She rolled her eyes at me and spoke to Yasmine. "Please remind me never to wear these shorts around your brother anymore."

I stopped listening to her at that point. I had things to do, and I had no intention of letting it take up my entire night. What would I do first? Right then, an image of Sherice's bowlegs popped into my mind. Those bowlegs would sure look good wrapped around my waist. They would feel even better. Right then, I decided to call Sherice.

Sherice didn't answer; the call went straight to her voice mail. She must still be in the mall shopping, so I left a message with my number for her to call me as soon as possible.

I stopped off at Target to pick up the other items that my mother had requested. Nishka consulted with Yasmine and picked up some toiletries and cleaning supplies as well.

Nishka was standing directly in front of me while we were on the checkout line. We were cracking up on the way some people came out of their houses to shop. As we got closer to the register, I pulled out the two hundred dollars I had for her. "Here," I said, reaching around her waist to hand the money to her. "Now you can pay for y'all stuff," I teased.

She laughed as she leaned back and rubbed her body against mine. "Thank you," she cooed, looking back over her shoulder.

"Don't thank me, thank Ashley. Better yet, thank God for blessing me with the tool and skills I possess."

"Tool? Skills? Ha! Thank God for making Ashley crazy enough to be breakin' you off like she does, you mean."

"One of these days I'm going to make you eat those words," I said, then kissed her on the nape of her neck.

"Promises, promises," Nishka sang barely loud enough for me to hear as she used her butt to push me back.

I saved my response because it was our turn to checkout.

After leaving Target, I swung home to pick up my mother's package just in case Sherice called while I was dropping Nishka back on campus. I was hungry, so I asked Nishka to warm up my food while I took a shower and changed. By the time I ate, it was almost eight o'clock. Sherice still hadn't called.

I took Nishka back on campus and hung out with her and Yasmine and a few of the other co-eds that came through to holla. I hung out with them until shortly after nine. I fielded a few calls while I was there, but none of the females that called piqued my interest that night. Actually, I needed to rest. I wanted to spend the night in the comfort of my own home. Alone.

I was trying to stall some time before heading home, so that I could make the delivery before I turned in for the night. Once I went in, that was going to be it. There would be no more coming out tonight.

At ten o'clock, I decided to leave the girls and head to the crib. As I turned onto Glades Road, my phone rang: Sherice.

I smiled and answered. "Talk to me; I'll talk back," I chuckled.

"You haven't changed one bit, have you?" Sherice chuckled.

"I was told that I got better with age," I teased.

"Mmmm-hmmm. Your mother say you have some stuff she wants me to bring back for her. Me and my 'boyfriend' leaving early in the morning, so we need to hook up tonight. You at home, or on the road?"

"I'm just leaving FAU in Boca."

"You have the stuff with you?"

"Yeah, I have them. You want to meet somewhere?"

"We way down south, but we're heading up to Coral Springs to my boyfriend's sister."

"That's my area," I said.

"Oh shit, my minutes are going. I'm going to let her call you right back, and you can give her directions. We'll pick up the stuff from your house..."

The phone went dead.

Her boyfriend. Well, there go my plans of wrapping those bowlegs around my waist. I had tried to holla at Sherice about five years back, but she had told me that I was too young. She's about five or six years older than me, and since she worked with my mother, she had resisted my charms. But, I remembered what my father had told me all those years ago: "All the women in Nassau that you want to fuck and they playin hard to get, catch them away: they'll be throwing the pussy at you."

He had spoken the gospel then. It had been tested and proven.

I had hoped that would be the case with Sherice's fine, old ass, but she was with her man. I should have known something was up from our little conversation. Sherice is feisty. She has a sassy-ass mouth and a wicked walk to boot.

I was getting off the turnpike when the sound of my phone ringing brought me out of my trance. It was a 954 number, but I didn't recognize it. How silly of me. It must be Sherice's boyfriend's sister. I answered. "Hello?"

"Hi, Khristin, this is Sonia. Sorry for taking so long to call you back. I just pulled into Marshall's for Sherice to run in the store. She asked me to call you to get the directions to your house."

"With a voice sweet as yours, you can get directions to my heart," I replied even before I realized it.

"You always this flattering to women you don't know?" she giggled.

"Oh! Did I say that out loud? I'm sorry."

"You don't have to be sorry, you just need to be careful: I might have taken you seriously."

"Now why would you take a man that you don't know seriously?"

"Oh, I know you. You may not know me, but I know you."

"You know me? From where?" I asked curiously

"Yes. Fort Lauderdale. Aarti."

Only one Aarti I knew in Fort Lickerdale; Trini Aarti.

I laughed. "How is Aarti? I haven't seen or heard from her since she moved out to Cali?" I chuckled, remembering the freaky bouts of sex that we used to have. I made my first sex tape with Aarti.

"She's doing fine. She got married about two years ago. She has a little girl now."

"Yeah. That's good," I said, honestly. Aarti was a good catch. I just wasn't ready to settle down. Another good girl I let get away.

"Aarti was crazy about you. All she used to do was talk about you."

"How come me and you never met?" I asked.

"Aarti never trusted any woman around her man! Furthermore, I had a crazy-ass boyfriend back then. He never let me out of his sight. I was young and dumb back then. I took that shit for love. Glad I saw the light."

I chuckled.

"Anyhow, I'm going to be out in this parking lot for probably another half an hour, knowing them. Thank God the store is closing soon. It'll take us another half an hour to get up that way, so don't fall asleep before I get there."

"You sound like you know where I live," I teased.

"I heard Sherice say that you live up my way. Where do you live?"

"I hope you ain't a stalker."

"If I were, you would have to consider yourself lucky."

"You already got my phone number, so I guess I can tell you where I live..."

"Unless you want to wait until I get home and then come by me?" she suggested, cutting me off.

"Nooooo. When I go in, I'm going in for the night."

"You're not going out to the club tonight?"

"No. I'm planning on chillin. Probably jump in the hot tub and relax a bit."

"You got a hot tub at your crib?"

"Pool, too. Bring your swimsuit, if you wish." I threw that in there remembering that all the girls that I had ever seen around Aarti were fine.

"No woman ga kill my ass."

"You think I would let anyone kill you?"

She laughed. "That's slick! You didn't say that there wasn't a woman."

"Trust me, I would never knowingly put anyone in danger."

"Humph. You can dance good, boy. Well, dance round this. Do you have a woman living with you?"

"No, I live alone."

"You're good," she laughed.

"You were supposed to be being direct. Just ask me what you want to know."

"Do you have a woman?"

"Yes, I do. See how easy that was. So, since you want to be all up in my business. What about you?"

"I don't do women."

"Oh, you gat jokes."

"Be direct. Ask me what you want to know, Mr. Bold."

"Okay. If you come in the hot tub tonight, are you going to let me hit?"

"Boy!"

My laughter cut her speech short. "You said be direct...and you called me Mr. Bold."

"Mmmm hmmmm. I was just finna go off on your ass too."

"So, you have a man?"

"Something like that."

"That means you leaving the door open. Well, I ain't mad at ya. So, since you know me, tell me about you. Tell me how you look. And, don't lie, either."

She laughed. "I'll tell you the differences between me and Aarti so you can get a good visual. Two inches shorter; about a shade lighter; lighter eyes; fuller lips; just a little more meat in all the right places...and not to sound conceited, I'm just a little bit prettier."

"That's the good stuff; tell me the other stuff."

"That'll take a while."

"Oh shit! Sound like your medicine cabinet full with prescription pills."

"Boy, you crazy." She laughed.

"I think I'ma have to meet you on the corner," I said.

"I'm not on any prescription pills. Ain't nothing wrong with me."

"You may be in denial."

"Well, meet me on the corner, then. Your loss. And to think you had me curious."

"Curious about what?" I asked quickly.

"Whether Aarti used to be telling the truth about you..."

"What did she say?"

"She said y'all made a tape, but you kept it."

I chuckled. "You curious about the tape?"

"No, I'm curious about what she said you two did on the tape."

"So you gat some freak in you too," I shot, laughing.

"Every woman has some freak in them, it just takes the right man with the right tool and know how to bring it out. That's why my door is opened, as you put it."

"Well, talk to me, baby. Tell me what he don't do, so I can know exactly what to do."

"You want me to make it easy for you."

"You already did. You not to long ago told me that I had you curious. And, you said that Aarti bragged about me all the time: my reputation precedes me. You have a personal, reliable source as to what I'm capable of."

"You sound sure of yourself, eh?" she chuckled.

"Well, if you know Aarti as well as you say you do, you know she was a nympho."

"I know she used to talk a good game, but I never saw her in action."

"She ever seen you in action?"

"What?"

"I'm just asking. You might have let her watch or something."

"You just as crazy as she said you were."

"And, even better than she knew. I have more years of experience now."

"Just tell me where you live. Sherice and my brother are coming out of the store now," she giggled.

"You've got to promise me that you will bring your swimsuit."

"Just give me the directions," she giggled.

After I told her, she said, "If I do come to join you in the hot tub, a swimsuit will only get in the way," then ended the call.

CHAPTER 8

TV CRIBS

Sonia called from the gate shortly after 11 p.m. I gave her the final directions and buzzed them through. I was eager to see what this Sonia looked liked. If she looked half as good as she sounded, she was gonna get it. I knew from experience that women that sounded sweet and sexy on the phone could be a huge disappointment to the eyes, but Sonia had one thing going for her; she was Aarti's friend. Aarti didn't associate with eyesores. Eye candies; yes.

I opened the front door as they pulled into the driveway. Not bad: a new E Class Benz with nice rims and tinted windows. As expected, the engine was shut off. This wasn't going to be a quick pickup. Not with my nosey Bahamian people. Especially Sherice. She would definitely want to come in and see how I'm living so she can go back to work and talk. Well, she was sure going to get something to carry back to Nassau tomorrow. And I'm not talking about my mom's packages, either.

The Benz had stopped on the side of my Range, so when the doors started opening, the only person I could see was the driver. I knew I was in trouble. She hadn't lied. Even though she had that 'I'm tired of driving these people up and down' look on her face, she was fine as all outdoors. When she stepped out into the clear, her beauty captivated me: Picture Halle Berry's face and Sasha Fierce's Body. (Not the Beyoncé that looks like she's one meal from being fat...I'm talking Beyoncé's on tour body. Yeah.) "Gat's to be more careful," I mumbled to myself.

She stopped to wait for Sherice to get out, giving me a side profile. Then, I became enthralled by her booty. Wow, is all I could think as I tried not to salivate. I have to hit that.

Sherice joined her and they started up the walkway. Sherice still looked as good as I remembered, but even with her bowlegs and wicked-ass walk, she was running a distant third. Sonia had first and second place all by herself. Sherice shouldn't even walk near Sonia. Behind them was a familiar face. I knew dude's face from somewhere, but I couldn't place it. That's how it is when you're from an island that's 21 miles long and 7 miles wide with a little more than a quarter billion people.

"This is a nice house you have here, Khris," Sherice chimed.

"Thanks," I smiled.

"Nice community," Sonia added, looking around. "This is the first time I've been in the back here."

"Yeah, it's nice and peaceful."

"I see why Janet always hoppin' on the plane," Sherice chuckled as they came closer. "Khris, this is my boyfriend, Charles and his sister, Sonia."

"Nice to meet you, Charles," I said as I shook his outstretched hand. The more I looked at him, the more I thought I knew him.

"I know your face from somewhere, but I can't remember where," I finally said.

Charles laughed. "Jessica and Patricia," he said. "Back when you were in high school, you used to check Patricia and I was seeing her older sister, Jessica, at the time."

"Yeah, that's it." I laughed.

Sherice broke that little reverie up quickly. "Sonia told me that she knows you, too."

"Apparently so," I said, turning my attention to Sonia, "but I've never had the pleasure." As our hands touched, I felt electricity course through my body. She must have felt it too, because she blushed. Her hand was soft and warm: her eyes captivating. And she had the cutest dimples. Damn! "Nice to meet you, Sonia," I said. "I think I might have seen you before, too. Delray Beach: Boston's on Monday nights. Reggae nights."

She was nodding her head as I spoke.

"White dude with a 'Fuck the world' tattoo on his neck?"

She shook her head, frilled her lips and smiled. "My ex."

"He was one obnoxious dude. I would have beat my sister's ass if she was to bring home a dude like that."

"Shit! I wanted to beat his ass on numerous occasions," Charles chimed in, "but she was in love and couldn't see how bad he was treating her."

"Just talk all my business," Sonia shot, sounding a little offended. Then she punched Charles.

"I'm sorry," I said. "Y'all come on in."

"Well, you know I want the full tour so I could tell the girls at work how Janet does be living when she come over to see you and Yasmine."

"Oh, Lord," I mumbled, like I didn't know that was exactly what she was going to do. "Please don't have my business all up in the bank," I pleaded, knowing it was falling on deaf ears.

"You should have left her outside, then," Charles said snidely.

"She ga tell them what color sheets you have on your bed," Sonia jibed. "What brand of toilet paper you use."

"Damn, if I knew TV Cribs was coming through, I would have cleaned up a bit," I said sarcastically, and laughed.

After the full tour, we ended up in the kitchen. They sat at the island bar while I got them some drinks. The entire time Sherice had been "Oooooohing" and "Aaaaahing" and asking, "Where did you buy this?" but I knew she hadn't asked the one question that she was dying to ask. I knew it was killing her to ask me. Sonia lived nearby, so I'm sure Sherice already asked her how much the homes in this area costs.

At the same time I was wondering how she was going to fix her mouth to ask me, she took a sip of her juice, looked around, then said, "This is a really nice house, Khris. I don't believe you live in a big house like this all by yourself. How much you pay for this house?"

There it was. The one question I knew she was dying to ask.

I saw Charles cringe. Sonia almost spat out her juice. I pretended I didn't see their reactions, and answered Sherice's question. "I paid two seventy five..."

"This house worth more than that with all this marble and granite and crown moldings," Sherice said, cutting me off.

"Yes, it is worth more, but you asked how much I paid. I got a good deal from the bank. This was in foreclosure when I got it. It needed some serious work, but I took my time and spruced it up a bit."

"You must know someone in that bank," Sherice said, her eyes still scanning around in case she missed something.

"I do, but I had also flipped a couple of houses with them, so I had a good track record."

"You must have known about this area before you bought this house," Sonia said.

"Yeah, I bought my first house up in the front section: a little starter home. It was a 4/2, single car garage: about 2000 square feet. I paid one sixty for it back then. My mortgage was the same as I had been paying to rent my old apartment. I did a little work on it myself, and moved in. About a year later, my neighbor's son went to Atlanta to college, so she decided to move into a condo. I came up with the down payment and closing fees and bought her 3/2. I fixed it up and rented it for a year. The gates closed and the property values went up 20 G's. Then the housing boom came. I sold the 3/2 and cleared two fifty. I got offers for 475 for my 4/2, and after several sleepless nights, I sold that too. I cleared almost three hundred on that. I stayed in a townhouse I was fixing up for two years while I waited for the market to return to normal. A lot of people started finding themselves upside down and couldn't keep up with their payments. Bush fucked shit up: people started losing their jobs in record numbers, and the foreclosures started rolling in. I had the cash, so I had my people call me when the good deals started rolling in. I picked up this, and a few other places. The other places are all rented and taking care of themselves and this place. I'm living free right now. I work to pay utility bills, buy groceries and gas."

"Sounds like you made some good investments," Charles said. "I'm into real estate, too. I sell mostly land on the family islands, though."

"I may need to holla at you soon. I'm tryin' to find a nice piece of beachfront property to build my summer home."

Sherice chuckled. "Listen to you, 'bout summer home."

"My mother isn't gonna be working forever, you know. She's gonna need different places to bounce around so she don't get bored." Yeah, go back to Nassau and talk that, I thought to myself. I definitely have to call my mother and tell her what I did. She's going to get a kick out of this.

Charles gave me one of his cards as we headed to the door.

I got my mother's packages and carried them out to the car. Sonia popped the locks from her key fob and met me at the trunk. She held the trunk as I put the packages inside. She winked and whispered, "I'll give you a call as soon as I get rid of them."

"Cool," I replied, smiling as I closed the trunk.

I walked her to her door, opened it for her to get in, and smiled as I closed it.

I waved to them as I watched the car back out of the driveway. I couldn't help but smile. I'm going to hit that for sure. Sherice's bowlegged-ass, too.

CHAPTER 9

RESCUE ME

When Sonia called, it wasn't for her to come on over and join me in the hot tub: it was for me to come out and play Captain-Save-A-Ho. Let me stop. No, seriously, she was stuck. Something in the street sliced her tire as she was coming back up University Drive after having dropped off Sherice and Charles at their hotel.

It was well after midnight when she called, so I asked her if she was in a well-lit area. Fortunately, she had been able to pull into a well-lit parking lot of a strip mall at a busy intersection.

I told her to stay in the car with the doors locked until I got there. Those sexy shorts and midriff top that she had on would definitely attract the wrong type of attention at this hour of the morning: at any hour. An attractive young lady like her stranded on the side of the street in a tricked out Benz would definitely attract attention; and not the wanted kind either.

I kept her on the phone as I rushed upstairs and threw on some sweat pants and matching Jordan's. I opened my gun safe and took out my Taurus and my concealed weapon permit. I checked to make sure a round was chambered, and clicked the safety back on. I slid on my shoulder holster and snatched the Windbreaker as I ran from my room. The entire time I was driving down there, I kept her on the phone. When I pulled next to her car, I knew instantly that this was not going to be a quick tire change.

Sonia jumped out of her car as soon as I turned off my engine. "Thank you for coming."

"No problem, babe."

"I didn't know who else to call. I called my boyfriend, but he said he was busy. He had the nerve to tell me that he would come as soon as he was done handlin' his business."

"Don't let it stress you, I'm here now. But, you've got two flats, not one," I said, going in for a better look. "Could you get me that mag light out of the glove box, please?"

Sonia retrieved the flashlight and handed it to me. She leaned over my shoulder to get a look at what I was looking at.

"I have a couple can's of fix a flat. I can put the donut on the front and fix...shit! This is sliced bad. Fix a flat isn't going to help this one. The front one's probably sliced through, too," I said, getting up and moving to the front tire. I shined the light, and took a look. Of course, the front tire was worst. "You're going to need new tires, baby."

"I had a feeling I was going to have to get a new tire."

"Not a new tire: four new tires. If you change these two, you might as well change all four. How long these tires been on here?"

"From I got the car a little over a year ago."

"You're overdue for some new ones, anyhow. You're going to need a tow. You have AAA or any roadside assistance?"

"No," she said, looking down at her feet.

"Don't worry, I gat you covered," I said, pulling out my wallet to get my AAA card. "I'll take care of it. You might as well get your stuff and put them in my truck. I'll let them tow it over to my house. I have some jack stands, so I'll be able to take off the four rims and carry them to get the tires mounted and balanced, then after I put them on, we can take it back and have the wheels aligned."

Sonia got her purse and several bags out of her car as I called AAA. I gave them the necessary information, then hung up. "They say a tow truck should be here in fifteen to twenty minutes," I informed her. "We can wait in the truck. I brought bottled water and juice in case you're thirsty."

"Cool. Thanks," she cooed, throwing her stuff on the back seat.

Just as she closed the rear door and moved to the opened front passenger seat, a Cadillac Escalade turned into the lot and headed over in our direction. I casually eased the zipper down on my windbreaker: just enough to have access to my Taurus. These are dangerous times we're living in. Better to be prepared.

When I glanced at Sonia, I saw a frown crease her lips. She looked down and shook her head. Instantly I knew it was her boyfriend. Then she confirmed it.

"My busy boyfriend decided to show up after all."

"I figured that from the disappointed look on your face. And to think you were soooo looking forward to spending time with me...and now he came and ruined it."

That got a little blush from her.

The Escalade stopped on the other side of the Benz. I could hear the bass before he opened the door. I eased down into the opened passenger door and watched as Sonia walked over. When the door opened, a cloud of smoke spewed out and the music shattered the silent night air. Her boyfriend was a couple inches shorter than her—probably wanted a woman he could look up to. Lil light skinned, curly hair, pretty boy. Yeah, I was sizing up the competition. It wasn't much of a competition.

Oh, hell no! I thought as she moved more to the side and I got a better look at this cat. Dude had the nerve to be wearing skinny jeans. All white, at that. This dude straight trippin. I see why she said her door was opened. This dude didn't look like he could bring the freak out of Pinky the porn star. Pinky would probably strap up and fuck him.

While Sonia was busy—probably explaining who I was—the passenger door of the Escalade opened. A Lil Wayne wannabe stepped out and walked toward the Benz. Now he was a sight to behold. This fool had his dreads pulled up to the center of his head with a rubber band, then cascading down like a coconut tree. Then he had the nerve to mean mug me, showing a mouth full of Flea Market gold teeth. I watched as he examined the tires. At the same time, Sonia and her man, if he can be called that, made their way toward me. The closer he got, the more I saw the wear and tear on his face. He had that alcoholic look. Maybe because he was high, I thought, giving him the benefit of the doubt.

"Wat up, yo. Shorty gonna grab her bag outta your ride and you can bounce. We gat dis from here."

I know this lil joker een tryin to dismiss me like that.

"I already called Triple A, so I have to stay until they get here to give them my card," I said as pleasantly as I could.

Sonia turned to him. "I told you he took care of it already. I'm good, so you can go back to whatever it was you was doin when I called you."

"Who dis nigga supposed to be, Captain Save-A-Ho?"

"I een nobody's nigga, yo." I couldn't help myself. As much as I wanted to stay out of this domestic dispute, I had to say more. I chuckled and shook my head. Staring him dead in the eyes, I said, "You sure rackin up the brownie points tonight. First, you tell your woman that you was busy, then you show up here and call her a ho. You sure don't know how to treat a woman, do you? You were state raised, eh?"

"I ain't called my shorty no ho," he mumbled, sounding like a little scolded child.

"You referred to me as Captain Save-A-Ho, and it's Sonia that I came to save, so what does that imply that she is?" I asked, staring him down. I was intentionally being a smartass.

He mean-mugged me.

His homeboy started toward us. "Yo, my nigga..."

"I dun told this clown, now I'm going to tell you, I een nobody's nigga...and you need to pull up your muthafuckin pants before you talk to me, you lil broke, Lil Wayne wannabe-ass," I snarled.

Her boyfriend and his friend took offense, as I knew they would, and took a step forward. I had a smug, cocky look on my face as I stood up and stepped toward him. "What, lil nigga? Who da fuck you tink you talkin too? I'm a grown ass man, boy," I said, putting menacing emphasis on the 'boy'.

"Stop!" Sonia shouted, putting herself between the lil joker and me. "I told you to leave," she said to him.

He cut his eyes between her and me. "Get your shit..."

The flashing lights of the AAA tow truck cut off his speech.

"Good, they're here," Sonia, said to her boyfriend. "You can leave now."

"I'm not going anywhere. They can tow your shit, but yo ass is ridin with me."

"You've been smoking. I een goin anywhere with you," Sonia hissed.

That's one thing with us Bahamians, the angrier we got, the thicker our accents get. This turned to dis; that turn to dat; not turn to een...etc."

"Get your shit out dis nigga ride or get your wig split."

"Not on my muddafuckin watch," I stated, having already planned my assault on him and his friend. "If you two wanna walk away from here, I suggest leaving right now," I warned calmly, "because if you touch her, you and ya lil homeboy ga get carry from dis parking lot tonight."

"Nigga, you don't know who you talking to."

"I know who I talkin to: You her boyfriend. And right now, that's the only reason you still standing."

"I should split your shit!" he barked, but made no attempt to move toward me.

In my mind, I had already hit him and he was on the ground. I stopped talking to this fool. I didn't come out for this shit.

I took a deep breath and said to Sonia. "If you don't want to go with him, go and sit in my truck. I'm going to give the driver directions to my house."

"Why is her car going to your house?" her boyfriend asked.

"So I can take off the four wheels and get her four new tires in the morning."

"Why his place?" he said, turning to Sonia.

"You have a way to take off the four wheels and take them to get tires put on?" Sonia asked.

"I could get the tires," he said.

"You aren't reliable enough. I have money to go and collect tomorrow and your ass doesn't get up before two o'clock. I can't rely on you for shit!"

"Well, fuck it! If you want to go with this nigga, then go. I could go back to the strip club," he said, turning to leave. "Let's go, Jay. This bitch trippin," he said to his boy.

He stopped, turned around and smirked at us. He looked directly at Sonia and said; "I know you better have my pussy home when I get there. You know how I get down after the strip club."

"I know that's right," Lil Wayne wannabe said, laughing.

Sonia was fuming as he grabbed his dick and laughed. "Nigga, you better not bring your ass by my place. I'll call the fuckin police for your ass. You know they dun warned you."

"Just have my pussy nice and wet when I get there."

I knew she was going to try to go after him, so when she jumped, I was right in front of her. She was fuming mad. She tried to brush me aside, but that wasn't happening. There was no way her lil 5'8", 135 pound body—no matter how solid it was—could move my 6' 1", 180 pound frame unless I wanted her to.

As she tussled to get around me, her hand brushed against the Taurus under my windbreaker. She froze; her mouth went silent.

"Don't let this escalate, 'cause I won't hesitate. Get in my truck and close the door. Don't lower yourself to his standards."

Sonia got in the truck and closed the door without looking back at him or uttering a single word.

I walked over to the tow truck driver and gave him my address and directions. He said he preferred to follow me, if it was okay with me. I nodded, then hopped in my ride as the Escalade pulled out of the lot, tires screeching as it turned and headed in the opposite direction from we were going.

As I pulled out of the lot, I glanced over at Sonia. She was still upset as expected, but something about her look made me smile. Beautiful and feisty. She had one major flaw: she didn't know how to pick men. She always seems to pick the wrong dudes.

I smiled.

That works in my favor. I was definitely going to knock her off. She owed me now.

That's fucked up, I thought to myself. But, I was just being honest: just keeping it real.

Sonia glanced over and saw me staring at her with a wicked smile plastered on my face. "What? Why are you looking at me like that?"

I shook my head. "You sure know how to pick 'em. You ain't my sister, but right now I feel like taking off my belt and giving you a good old-fashioned cut-ass."

"Instead of a cut-ass, why don't you rescue my ass?" she sassed while twisting sideways in her seat to give me a full frontal stare down.

I had to admit, I liked this one. "I already rescued you," I retorted.

"I wasn't talking about the flat tire."

"I know," I said, grinning like the devil.

That made her blush. Again.

CHAPTER 10

WHO'S GOT GAME

While we were standing in my driveway watching Sonia's Benz being lowered, my phone vibrated with an incoming text message.

"Booty call?" Sonia teased, bumping me with her hips.

"Let me check," I said, pulling out my phone and checking the text. I smiled and turned it to her so she could read the text.

"Did San Antonio win?" Sonia read. "One of you boys texting you at this hour of the morning to find out about the Spurs. He don't have TV, eh?"

She thought it was one of my boys, but little did she know, it was indeed a booty call. It was Yvette. That was our little code. She would check the sports channel to see who was playing in one of the late games, then text me and ask if one of the teams won. If I text her back yes, that meant it was safe for her to come over. If I text her back no, that meant check me back in an hour. If I didn't respond, that meant I was on lockdown. Someone else was getting the dick: wifey as far as she was concerned.

I remembered that my boy, S, like San Antonio since he and Tim Duncan went to school together, so it would be S that I lied on tonight. "That's my boy, S. He was in the hole for fifty, so he bet me fifty that the Spurs would beat the Heat. He's pretending that he doesn't know the Spurs won. That's his way of rubbing it in my face. The Heat had a chance to win, but miss the shot at the buzzer."

"I like games that come down to the wire. Ain't nothing better than a buzzer beater," Sonia chimed.

I turned and stared at her. "What you know about basketball?"

"I have NBA League Pass! NFL, too."

"Stop lyin'!"

"And I gat mad handles on the court. They call me 'Shake, Rattle, and Roll': I will shake you out of your shoes, rattle your brain as you try to figure out which way I'm going, then cause you to roll both your ankles trying to guard me."

"Listen to you. You could talk shit, eh!"

"I was starting point guard on both the junior girls basketball, and senior girls team at SAC. And I started for two years on the National Team."

I was impressed. I was liking Sonia more and more as I got to know her.

"How much do I have to pay the driver?" she asked, breaking me out of the trance she had put me in.

"The tow is covered. If it isn't, they'll bill me."

"I'll reimburse you if they do," she said quickly. "What about a tip?"

"I'll slide him a slow twenty."

"I gat it," she said, pulling out some cash from her pocket.

We walked over together and thanked the driver. Sonia gave him a tip, and he thanked us and left.

As we watched him drive away, I felt a change come over her.

Before I could ask her what was wrong, she turned and stared at me. "Do you mind if I spend the night here?"

She was making this too easy. I pretended to think about it for a moment. Then I gave her a good, exaggerated once over. I chuckled. "Ah, I think it'll be all right."

As if she had to explain herself, she said, "I don't want to deal with that idiot again tonight. He started smoking dirty, and now he's losing his mind."

"Smoking dirty?" I asked, giving her a sideways glance.

"It's when they sprinkle cocaine on the weed, but in his case, he sprinkles crushed rocks, I heard: Geek joints."

"He's a fuckin crack head! Please tell me he doesn't have a key to your place."

She shook her head. "No! I changed the locks after I had to call the police for him two months ago."

"Why you still with this dude?"

"He's sweet when he's not high, and-and I get lonely," she said, looking down as if she was seriously embarrassed.

"Come on," I said, rubbing her back gently. "Let's get your stuff and head in."

"Can you run me by my place first, please. I've been like this all day."

"I've got lots of T-shirts and shorts for you to sleep in. My sisters (referring to Yasmine and Nishka) have all kinds of female bath gels and stuff in there, so why don't you just relax tonight and I'll take you home in the morning."

"That'll work," she said as we got her bags, locked up both vehicles, and headed inside.

I led the way upstairs and showed her to the yellow guest room that she had said she loved. I saw that she was a little shocked that I showed her to a guest room, but I pretended not to notice.

I opened the walk in closet. "You have towels here," then moved to the bathroom which was right next to it, "and new toothbrushes, toothpaste, and mouthwash here," I said opening the medicine cabinet. There's Herbal Essence Body wash..."

"You think of everything, don't you?"

I looked back into the room in time to see her fall back onto the bed. "This bed feels heavenly. It feels like I'm on a cloud," Sonia said, with her arms opened.

"Come on before you get too comfortable," I said, offering her a hand.

She took my hand and let me pull her to her feet. "If you insist," she said, rolling her eyes playfully.

"You can raid the female stuff from Yasmine's cabinet."

"I don't want to raid your sister's stuff."

"Don't worry, there's plenty, so she won't miss any. Trust me."

Sonia followed me to Yasmine's bathroom. I opened the cabinet and she gasped. "Bath and Body Works, Victoria Secret.... I like your sister already, and I haven't even met her. She even has my brand of antiperspirant. She has this cabinet stocked. Let me get what I need and get out of here," she said, grabbing a bottle of body wash, lotion, body spray and antiperspirant. "I'll stay up here smelling stuff all night. This is it. I'm good."

"Okay. Come with me for something to sleep in," I said, leading the way to my master suite. As we walked into my suite, she looked at my bed and asked, "Why can't I sleep in this big bed?"

"Because I don't allow clothes to touch my sheets."

"Is that so?" Sonia said, watching me as I headed toward my walk in closet.

"No woman allowed in my bed with anything on. Lingerie, negligee, underwear, bra," I said, giving her a soft cotton T-shirt and a pair of silk boxers, "they all get shed before she gets near the bed."

"I only need the T-shirt. It's long enough. I normally sleep naked, but since I'm a guest in your house, I'll make an exception and cover up a little," she said provocatively.

"You don't have to do that on my account. You can sleep butt--booty-naked if you'd like. However you feel comfortable. I know I'm sleeping naked. I can't sleep with clothes on," I said, taking off my sweat suit jacket, then my holster. I went back into my closet and put the gun in the safe, then pulled off my T-shirt as I stepped back into the room. I knew exactly what I was doing. I felt her eyes searing my body as I pulled the T-shirt over my head. I'm not big, but a brother is cut-the-fuck-up: arms, chest, and abs. I caught her biting on her bottom lip, but I didn't stare or lock eyes with her.

"Well, I'll let you shower. I'm going to do the same right now to make sure you don't use up all the hot water," she said, turning on her heels. When she got to the door, she spun around and opened her mouth to say something, but stopped.

I looked up to see if she had forgotten something.

She smiled rascally, shook her head, and said, "Never mind. Bye," and walked away, blushing.

I laughed. She just had to take another look. That was a snapshot. She's going to take that snapshot with her in the shower, then into her dreams.

After undressing, I took a long, relaxing, hot shower.

When I was done, I rubbed down with a little coconut oil and slipped on a pair of house shorts. I went downstairs, started the dishwasher, turn off the lights and set the alarm before heading back upstairs. On the way to my room, I stopped by to check up on my houseguest. Her door was slightly ajar and a bedside lamp was on, so I knew she was still awake. I knocked lightly on the doorjamb.

"Come in," she said, in a singsong voice.

I entered and saw that she had folded down the comforter and was tucked between the sheets. Her smile and the sweet botanicals wafting from her body pulled me toward her like a magnet. I noticed the T-shirt strewn across the reading chair next to the bed. That meant one thing: she was lying there in all her naked splendor.

"I was just checking to make sure you were all right before I go to sleep."

"Oh! You came to tuck me in?" she asked mischievously as she rose up on one elbow. She had that confident look on her face as if she had known I was coming to her. Even the way she held the sheet with her other arm resting right below her nipples was pre-planned. She held it just enough for me to see her cleavage and the swell of her breasts.

I smiled. Touché. She got me back for taking off my shirt earlier. She had game. I was beginning to enjoy this little sparring match. I was beginning to enjoy Sonia.

That confident 'yeah, I know I got you back' look on her face said it all. She was enjoying it also. Then she upped the ante. Sonia reached over to the other side of the bed, letting the sheet fall just enough to give me a glimpse of one of her honey- bronze colored areolas, then said, "You're welcomed to sleep right in here with me, if you can control yourself."

I didn't expect that. The look on her face told me that she knew I didn't expect that. She was trying to punk me: punk me in my own house. I was laughing my ass off on the inside. Clearly she didn't know whom she was fucking with. I turn down pussy on a regular basis, so controlling myself would definitely not be a problem. "I can control myself. It's you who I hope can control yourself," I said, pointing to her exposed flesh. "I'll be right back," I said, heading down to my suite. I knew she was in there probably thinking that I was going to get condoms, but I just went to turn off my lights.

When I returned, she had switched on the stereo—each room had its own independent audio and video system with full surround sound. She had the radio tuned to a Lite Jazz station. The light on the nightstand was still on. She smiled at me as I walked in and went directly to the other side of the bed.

"You sleep with music?" she asked, her eyes tracking me.

"That's my station right there. I tried sleeping with R & B, but it's hard to sleep with baby making music playing."

"Hard, I bet," she laughed, watching me as I slid off my house shorts, pulled up the corner of the sheet and slipped in next to her.

I shuffled a bit, fluffed my pillow until it was the way I liked, rolled onto my side and faced her. There was a glint in her eyes as she anticipated my kiss. I leaned in to kiss her. Her lips quivered expectantly, but instead of kissing her lips, I kissed her on her cheek. "Good night," I whispered, brushing my lips on her earlobe. Then I rolled the other way, turning my back to her.

She wasn't expecting that.

She chuckled and whispered, "Good night to you too" as she rolled and turned off the night lamp.

I smiled, as I got comfortable. I could hear her rustling to find a comfortable spot as I closed my eyes. I had her right where I wanted her. I would fuck her when I'm ready, not when she wants to give it to me.

I said a quick prayer, and an instant later fell fast asleep.

CHAPTER 11

FORMIDABLE CONTENDER

My internal alarm clock woke me up at seven a.m. I opened my eyes and saw Sonia's face. This is how a man's supposed to wake up every morning: staring into the face of a beautiful woman sleeping with a contented look on her face. Even though nothing happened during the night, she looked happy and contented, and she was still sleeping peacefully. My mind was all over the place, then Nancy's gorgeous face popped in my head. Shake it off, I told myself. Okay, time to get up.

I eased myself out of the bed as gently as I could muster. I didn't want to wake Sonia. She looked so peaceful. Besides, I had work to do. I went down to my room, threw on a pair of shorts and a wife beater, grabbed my cell phone and headed down stairs.

I grabbed the cordless from the kitchen along with both our keys and headed into the garage. I slipped on my work boots as I called my mother and gathered up the things I needed. I know my mother was up and getting ready for work. I told her about Sherice's visit and subsequent tour as I opened the garage and went out to take care of business.

At seven thirty, Nancy called. She was on her way to work. "Good morning," I said.

"Good morning to you," she sang cheerily. "I'm on my way to work. Just calling to say hi."

"You should have been on your way to school," I mumbled.

"Sweetie, don't start," she begged.

I was sort of pissed at her for stopping school, again. She didn't need to work. She lived at home with her mother and father, and didn't have any bills to pay. She's an only child, and yes, her parents spoil her. She's a smart girl, but she just didn't know what she wanted to do with herself. She's doing Pre-Law at Nova Southeastern and decided to take another semester off. I thought I had gotten her back on track after her old boyfriend talked her out of going to classes so they could spend time together. Now here she was taking time off again. No, she's not seeing dude again, he moved to Atlanta with a stripper that he met during Memorial Day weekend a couple years back. Nancy's excuse was that she was tired of school. She just wasn't driven, if you asked me.

My silence must have been too long for her. She must have felt guilty, because she said, "At least I'm working at a Law Firm. That should count for something. This is work experience," she added, trying to appease me.

At least she doesn't have a problem working, I thought. Normally, that would have made me feel better, but this morning, it just wasn't working. "You must know what you're doing," I said, then changed the subject. "How's your aunt?"

While she told me about her aunt, and all the rest of her family dirt, I was jacking up Sonia's car and taking off the wheels. We talked until she was pulling in the garage at work. By that time, I had all four wheels off.

I got a cardboard box and a drop cloth and spread it over the seats and the floor of the rear cargo hatch of the Range. I put the four wheels in and closed it up. I put up the tools in the garage, took off my work boots, then washed my hands and face.

When I went inside, the scent of breakfast being cooked drew me into the kitchen. Sonia was standing in front of the stove wearing only the t-shirt I had given her to sleep in. And, the t-shirt barely covered her cheeks. The display was sensational. It stirred my soul— among other things.

Hearing me come in, she glanced back smiling. "Good morning. Sleep well?" she asked with an arched brow.

"Sure did," I replied. "I felt energetic this morning. How 'bout you?"

"Best night's sleep I had for this week," she snickered.

"Last night was the first night of this week," I shot back.

She laughed. "Wow, you're brilliant, too," she said sarcastically. "I hope you like omelets," she said, glancing back at me.

"Sure, as long as it doesn't have any extra ingredients like a piece of your underwear or anything in it," I shot back, walking over to her.

"You got jokes early in the morning, too," she laughed. "I een trying to 'fix' you. I figured the least I could do is make you breakfast. I figured you'd be hungry after taking off all four wheels."

"How do you know it's food I'm hungry for," I said, walking up behind her and wrapping my arms around her waist.

She leaned her head back against my chest and shoulder like it was the most natural thing to do. It felt so easy: like we had been doing this for years. Her body felt so good against mine.

Her body fit like a ball in a well-oiled leather glove. I felt her melt into me as I bent forward and kissed her exposed neck.

She moaned ever so softly and rolled her hips back against my stiffening wood. As if sensing danger, she suddenly said, "Okay. Scoot. Get out of my kitchen before you make me burn up the first meal I'm cooking you."

I watched her handling herself in my kitchen. She seemed right at home. Diced up turkey sausage, onions, bell peppers, and tomatoes were on the cutting board. The eggs were already whipped and seasoned in one bowl; shredded cheese in yet another. I had to give her credit; she looked like she knew what she was doing.

"You want me to set two places?" I asked, pointing at the island bar.

"No. You can go and shower, let me handle this here. This is my domain. This is where woman reign supreme!"

"I thought it was the bedroom," I shot, laughing.

"Real women don't do it in the bedroom. We do it anywhere and everywhere except the bedroom," she said saucily. "Now get!" she ordered, pouring the eggs onto the griddle.

"I'll go shower and get out of your way," I said, liking how she took it upon herself to make me breakfast without first finding out what I liked. Then she had the audacity to run me out of 'her kitchen' as she so brazenly called it.

Nancy didn't do shit like that. Nancy very rarely cooked.

"Sonia, Sonia, Sonia," I sang softly as I headed upstairs. I shaved and showered, then threw on some fresh True Religion gear, and matched it all up with a pair of retro Jordan's.

When I returned downstairs, Sonia was pouring two glasses of orange juice. I shook my head. This girl is definitely trying to fuck up my happy home. She's trying to take me from my woman. Shit, and my sweethearts. I've known her for less than twenty-four hours and she's already proving to be a formidable contender.

Nancy had better watch out. For real.

Breakfast was laid out on the island bar. Sonia had already cleaned up behind herself. There was no sight of the griddle or any of the bowls she had used. Taking her in, she was a sight to behold: hair pulled back into a ponytail; freshly cleaned face, sparkling eyes; dazzling smile; cute-ass dimples. Just how I like my women: naturally beautiful; barefooted; wearing only a heart-warming smile and the white T-shirt that I had given her to sleep in with nothing on underneath. Beautiful.

I let her catch me ogling her.

"What? What are you looking at?" she asked in a sassy tone. She had that 'I know what you're thinking' look on her face, again.

I smirked and licked my lips. I was about to tell her exactly what I had just been thinking, but thought better at the last second. That would only swell her head.

I moved to the back of one of the high back chairs and held it for her. "Come and have a seat. You'll show me just what I was looking at in a minute," I grinned devilishly.

She blushed as she came around the island to be seated. "Such a gentleman," she sang. "Your mother trained you well," she added, giving me the googgly eyes.

As she took her seat, a napkin suddenly appeared in her hand and covered her lap. So much for her showing me what I was looking at. I didn't even manage to get a sneak peek.

Sonia stuck out her tongue and crossed her eyes like a silly child.

I couldn't help but laugh. She had been ready for me.

"Thank you," she said as I took the chair next to her.

"Don't thank me," I said, rolling my eyes and pretending to be hurt, "flash me."

"If you wanted to see, you would have looked last night, but nooooo, you turned your back to me and went to sleep," she teased.

"Now come on, eat!" she commanded.

That statement made me realize that she was disappointed that I hadn't tried her last night. She had probably wanted me to make a move so she could brush me off like so many women do at the start of a relationship. Was that where this was headed?

Breakfast not only looked delicious, it tasted delicious. Presentation was everything. It made the simplest things look more appetizing. Sonia had the island laid out: omelets, grits, buttered toast with jelly, orange juice, and water. On top of that, she had taken the time to slice up two small bowls of cantaloupe, dew melon, and strawberries.

They say the way to a man's heart is through his stomach, and after I took the first bite of my omelet, my heart actually fluttered. What the hell was happening here?

Not only was the breakfast scrumptious, but my breakfast partner was also an excellent conversationalist. We talked about any and everything as we devoured breakfast. Sonia got up to clear the dishes, but I sent her upstairs to shower so that we can get our day started. She protested, but when I put my foot down, she gave me a kiss on the cheek, then ran away giggling as I attempted to corner her to take a peek under her T-shirt.

After she vacated my kitchen, I went to unload the dishwasher only to find it already done. The entire time I was stacking it with the dishes we ate out of, I couldn't help but be amazed at how she had come into my kitchen and dove in like it was her own. I liked that.

"Sonia, Sonia, Sonia," I sang with a smile.

After Sonia showered, we headed over to her apartment so that she could change before going to get her new tires.

On the way there, she checked her messages and made several phone calls.

As we pulled to the gate at the front of Sonia's apartment complex, I couldn't help but wonder why she was driving a fifty thousand dollar Benz and still living in an apartment: It was a nice complex, don't get me wrong, but it was a waste of money.

She could be paying a mortgage with what she was obviously paying here. I smiled when I remembered that I too had done the very same thing before I found out how easy it was to get a mortgage. I'll have to school her on that, but I'll wait for the right time. I just met her and I don't want her to think I'm prying about her finances. People are very finicky about their money.

Sonia gave me the code to punch into the box at her gate.

As I waited for the gate to slide open, I couldn't help but think how much fun it was having her around. I glanced over at her wearing my red, white, and black Jordan basketball shorts and the matching t-shirt.

"Just so you know, I'm keeping these!" she stated, and had the nerve to stare me down.

"And here I was thinking I'd be able to sniff those shorts while I sleep at night," I said snidely as I drove through the opened gate. "I know you een gat on no drawers under there," I said, reaching over and tugging up on the hem of the left pant leg.

"Not dese! Dese going to the root doctor," she shot back.

"If the panty boiled in the grits don't work, the root doctor will know what to do with dese shorts...and I gat the shirt, too. Oooooh. Oooooh! You good as cooo-cooo," she sang, laughing.

She was laughing, but I didn't think it was funny, especially when I thought back to how sweet her grits had tasted. And, I remembered how happy she looked when I asked for an extra helping.

CHAPTER 12

MAX PLEASURES

Inside Sonia's apartment was tastefully decorated. I hadn't expected anything less. I see why she had liked my yellow guest room: yellow was her accent color in her living room and kitchen. Bahamian artwork hung from her walls, and she used conch shells for her potted plants to give the place a touch of home. "Nice."

"Make yourself comfortable," she said, pointing to the fluffy looking white leather sectional. "I'll just be a minute."

"A woman's minute?" I inquired, picking up the remote control and plopping down in front of the 50-inch flat screen.

"You know it," she sang, sashaying down the hallway.

"That's more like an hour," I shouted behind her as I powered on the TV and surround sound.

"Beauty has its price," she shouted back.

"But it shouldn't take a natural an hour," I retorted.

"You're calling me naturally beautiful?" she cooed from down in her bedroom.

"You have your clothes off yet?" I asked, flipping through the channels.

"What does that have to do with me being beautiful?"

"I want to see you in your most natural form."

"You should have looked last night," she shot, laughing.

"Here we go again. Am I going to ever hear the end of that?"

"No!" she laughed.

I could hear her rustling through the closet. She did have NBA League Pass. They were replaying last night's games.

"Has that shit ever backfired on you?" she shouted after a couple minutes of silence.

"Has what ever backfired?"

"That weak game you ran last night."

"What weak game are you talking about?"

"Don't try and sound all proper now. You know exactly what I'm talking about. The whole show me to the guest room: the kiss on the cheek: turning your back to me and going to sleep. That weak game! What if that was your one chance to hit this?"

"It wasn't," I stated confidently.

"What if it was? Then your little game would have caused you to miss out on your opportunity," she said.

"You can't miss what you've never had," I replied.

"Ha! That's just words that come out of our mouths when we can't admit that we fucked up and missed out on a good thing."

"What if that was your one opportunity to get some of this and you missed out?" I asked back for want of nothing smart to reply.

"I know that wasn't going to be my last opportunity to sample that dick; that's why I let you sleep. If I had thought that was a one time opportunity, I would have taken the dick, and wouldn't have been shit you could have done besides tell me how sweet it was while you enjoyed the ride."

"You does carry on like that?" I asked, grinning.

"You'll find out soon enough. When I want something, I find all kinds of ways to go after it. And, I always get what I want."

"So you'll just take you some dick?" I chuckled, not believing what she was saying. Sonia talked a good game, but she couldn't back that shit up: she een takin shit but what I have to give her.

"Yes! You think I invited myself over for the fun of it. I was checking to see how you would respond. Most men would have been all over me. That's the ones that are cocky, but not confident. They have no self-control. That's the ones that like to hit and run. A confident man like yourself, knew from our conversation when I told you that you had me curious, that I had already made up my mind to give you some; it was just a matter of when." She took a breath before continuing. "You're a player, Khris. You have a girlfriend, and probably a bunch of friends with benefits. The text you let me read last night was probably a code for a booty call, an ingenious one, but one nonetheless. My thing is whether I can fit into your little schedule, and whether I can handle it or not. Also, which position I really want to play. You've already proven to me that you will treat me a hell of a lot better than that 'Geek Monster' that I used to call a boyfriend—notice that I said used to call boyfriend, and no, don't worry," she chuckled, "I'm not leaving him because of you. I had already made up my mind to leave him from I found out he was smokin dat shit! You might ask why I stayed with him or let him back in my life after that. I had needs. And it was easier to stick with someone familiar than to go out and give it up to a stranger," she said, sticking her head out the door and looking down the hall toward me.

It sort of made sense what she was saying, but Nishka's question popped into my head: "Why does the woman always have to be the one to compromise?" She shouldn't have to compromise, but hey, who was I to complain? I was going to be on the receiving end of her decision.

"I rather have a little bit of good love than a whole heap of bad love," she said.

Right then, I felt guilty, because she deserved better. Every woman deserved better. Hold up! What the fuck is happening to me?

"I have three brothers," she chuckled. "Charles is the oldest. The other two are playas. My dad is a playa. Thank God he never married my mother or I probably would have hated him. I know how the game is played, and I can spot game. My problem is once I'm in I lose myself to love. Love makes my ass deaf, dumb, blind and stupid." She shook her head. "But, no more. After two fucked up men, I'm determined to stand up in love, rather than fall into it. Ya feel me?"

"One problem: all relationships start off good—that's the interview stage. Everybody puts their best foot forward," I said.

"That's why I'm getting all the dirt out in the open now, rather than later. That's why I'm calling you on the playa that you are. That way, you can be honest with me and not have to lie. Now you have no reason to lie, right?"

"How do you know I won't turn out like 'Fuck The World' and 'Geek Monster' in the white skinny jeans?"

"I heard how you treat your mother and sister, and your sister's best friend. Sherice talked all your business on the ride up to your house...and after we left. What I didn't remember from Aarti, Sherice told me. I feel like I know you, Playa," she sang, trailing her fingers across my shoulders as she passed behind me.

"So you want to be a friend with benefits?" I asked, twisting so I could see her over the back of the sectional.

She stopped, turned around, and stared at me on the sectional. Our eyes locked for what felt like minutes. Slowly, a devious smile creased her lips. "I don't know which position I want yet, but when I decide, I'll be sure to let you know."

What the fuck? She may as well come out and tell me she's trying to take Nancy's position. This girl's serious. She actually thinks she can pull my Playa's Card. I have to watch her.

"I just need to check my site right quick, then we can leave," she said, going over to her computer station.

"You have a Website? What type of site?"

"Get your mind out of the gutter," she giggled. "Not because I let you sleep naked with me means that I would get naked and stream it across the net. I'm not that kind of girl."

I was staring at her as she leaned over to work her keyboard. The computer chair was right there. She wanted me to look at her ass. And a scrumptious ass it was, too. I took in the entire package.

She looked fabulous: skinny designer jeans, strappy camisole top, and strappy heels. She hadn't taken that long, I thought, glancing down at my watch. The conversation had distracted me. But, she was fast; faster than most women I knew. She styled her hair and got dressed in less than fifteen minutes. That must be a record everywhere. Well, she didn't have to do much: she had that natural beauty.

"You're mighty quiet. You must be staring at my voluptuous ass. Yoga baby! Keeps everything tight!" she bragged. "Yes! Yes! Yes!"

"What the hell! You having an orgasm without me?"

"Yeah. A moneygasm! I got 54 orders overnight!" she said, jumping up and down.

"What kind of orders?" I asked, turning off the television and going over to her.

"I have an online business, well, two actually. One sells human hair: that good weave. Weave sells better than weed, and I sell it by the ounce and by the pound. And, it's totally legal. I can't keep enough on hand. Then I started selling MAX PLUS, an all-natural, nonprescription pill that gives you guys a bigger, thicker, longer dick! You know every man wants a bigger dick. I also sell cologne that contains human sex pheromones that makes men irresistible. Women won't be able to keep their hands off of you," she sang, turning and rubbing her hands all over my chest and face.

"Does it work?" I asked.

"I gave the Geek Monster a free sample but..."

"Ah, hell no!"

"Don't laugh," she said, "I mean, I don't really care about size: I don't want to get torn up or stretched open. Once a man knows how to use what he's got to please me, I'm good. My dildo is only as thick and long as these two fingers," she said, showing me, "and that does do the trick every time."

"Can I watch you play with your dildo?" I asked, pulling her into me.

"We don't have enough time for you to be starting this right now," she said, turning back to her computer. "You had all night to do as you wish, but nooooo, you chose to sleep," she teased, again.

"Keep throwing it in my face, I'm not going to want it anymore."

She laughed like it was the funniest thing she ever heard. I though it was funny, too. There's no way I'm giving up without hitting that ass.

"I hope your schedule is clear for today," she said, grinning.

"Why?"

"Because I need to go by my storage and pack these orders, and then mail them out by one. Can we do that and fix my tires later? It shouldn't take more than an hour to do; less than that if you help me."

"That's cool. Money first, baby!"

"Not always. Sometimes my man—when I get one—will come first. Money can't buy love or happiness."

"It could make a good down payment, though," I said, causing her to laugh. "So what do we have to do?"

"Well, first I have to print out the orders and postal labels. Then I'll print out the proper postage on my stamp machine."

As she spoke, I heard her laser jet printer whirring. Order forms were coming out of one machine, and mailing labels out the next. She took off the first sheet and handed it to me. "Check it out."

I read:

MAX PLUS billed as MAX PLUS VITAMINS.

Buy 7 get 5 free......................$419.93.......Save $299.95

Buy 3 get 2 free......................$179.97.......Save $119.98

Buy 2 get 1 free......................$119.88.......Free 30 Day Supply

Buy 1-month supply...............$59.99.........Save $20.00

MAX PLEASURE COLOGNE.......$29.99

"And they pay their own shipping and handling too?"

"Yep. We bill it as vitamins to avoid the embarrassment on their credit card statement. Pay Pal takes out their share and sends the rest to my account. The markups on those are incredible. Which deal do you think is my best seller?"

"How soon do you see results?"

"Smart," she laughed. "The very first day, then increasing results over 60-90 days."

"At first, I would have said the Buy 2 get one free for $119.98, but then the buy three get two free for $60 dollars more is a more attractive deal. So, I'm saying the $179.97 package plus the rush delivery of $19.99."

"Ding, ding, ding, ding," she chimed. "We have a winner. I have 11 of the 419, 37 of the 179, and 6 of the 119 for a total of $11,991.40. That's 335 bottles at 12 dollars a bottle. $4020. Subtract that, and the ten percent for Pay Pall, and I just made $6,777.66 profit, not to mention the handling fees."

"That's a good lick," I chimed, happy for her. She's a hustler. She's all about her paper. I like that. I like that shit, a lot!

"You realize that no one jumped for the cologne?"

"That's not a real good seller."

"I know why," I stated with a grin.

"Tell me?"

"A little oversight on your part, but nothing that can't be fixed. Look here," I said, pointing to the billed as MAX PLUS VITAMINS."

"Okay."

"Now look here."

"MAX PLEASURE COLOGNE."

"Anyone seeing that on a credit card statement will suspect something funny with a name like MAX PLEASURE. It sounds like a sex lubricant. Bill it as MAX PLUS ENERGY DRINK."

"I missed that. Damn! I could just kiss you."

"Not now, I'll collect later. I'm one hell of a kisser, and once you start, you won't want to stop," I teased.

"I'll change it now," she said, stroking the keyboard. "With your body and my brains, me and you can go far, Khris!"

"With my body, and you giving me brain, we can go even farther...and, I'll even cum."

"I'll make you cum right now," she said, picking up a phone book and chasing me.

CHAPTER 13

TAKING CARE OF BUSINESS

The storage facility wasn't too far from Sonia's apartment. She gave me the code to get through the gate, followed by turn for turn directions me to her outdoor units. She had me stop right in front of her unit, which was about the size of a single car garage. As we got out, I took a look around. There were security cameras, and a high wall with razor wire running across the top. It seemed safe enough.

After opening the lock, I helped her roll up the bay door. She flicked on the lights, and I wasn't the least bit surprised to see that inside was just as neat as her apartment. To one side was a desk for her computer, and a short packing table. Against the rear wall were cases of her products stacked to the ceiling. On the other wall, was a longer packing table over which a peg board held her tools: scissors, box cutters, tape...I couldn't help but think that if she had a house, all this could have been set up right in her garage.

There were three sizes of unassembled boxes stacked neatly against the wall between the computer desk and the small packing table, but we didn't have to use those: some were already assembled.

"Okay," she said, getting ready to put me to work, "I need you to put a dozen bottles in 11 of the large boxes. While you do that, I'll pack the 6 boxes of 3. Once we get them out the way, we'll work on the 37 boxes of 5 together.

We worked well together.

We packed the pills, filled the remaining space with packing peanuts, folded the order form and put it on top, closed the box and put the corresponding mailing label and postage on the box. Before taping the boxes shut, we made sure that the name on the order form corresponded with the mailing label and proper postage.

Next we attacked the 37 boxes. We developed a good rhythm, and had it all done in about forty-five minutes.

After placing the boxes into three big mailbags and throwing them onto the rear seat of the Range, Sonia opened the bay of the unit right next door. "This is the real moneymaker right here," she bragged.

When she flipped on the light, I saw stacks of dishwasher-sized boxes of human hair weave stacked up to the ceiling. There were different colors, textures, and lengths. She had the clear plastic packages and labels, and she had a digital scale that was so sensitive that it weighed a single strand of hair.

"This stuff," she said, pointing to all the hair, "I only mail out on Tuesdays and Thursdays, because it takes longer to package. The local beauty salons and supply stores normally orders once a week or every two weeks. But, if they get in a bind, I take care of them right away."

"So this is what you do." I was impressed. "Why don't you open up a store?"

"Too much overhead. These aren't items that people walk in to a store and buy everyday. I mean the weave, they would, but to drive to a particular location to my shop, they'd have to pass several other shops. Being able to buy it online and get it delivered to your door is much easier."

"You're right. I didn't think about it that way. And, you have more free time," I said, making googgly eyes at her and thinking about her spending some—the majority—of that free time with me. There I go again. What's up with me today? Did she really boil her panty in the grits? I wondered. I shook it off.

"That's it, thanks to you. All is done here, so we can lock up and head out," she said, pulling the roller door down.

"Can I ask you a question, it might be a little personal so if you don't want to answer, you can just tell me to mind my own business."

"Ask anything you want," she said, snapping the lock, then moving over to get the other one.

I smiled as I pulled down the other door for her.

"Not that," she laughed, obviously remembering what I had asked her the last time she told me I could ask her anything.

"How much does these storage units cost you per month?"

"Well, they give me a discount since I rent two. I get them for two hundred each."

"So that's four hundred a month. How much do you spend on

rent for your apartment?"

"Eleven hundred plus utilities."

"Fifteen hundred a month on rentals. You know you can get a house with dual car garage for the same money?"

"I know," she said, locking the final bay door as I opened the passenger door for her. "Thank you," she said as she got in.

As I walked around the front of the Range, she leaned across and opened my door for me. Considerate, too, I thought. "Thanks," I said as I got in and fastened my seat belt.

"You're probably wondering why I'm driving a Benz and paying rent and shit, so let me explain. When I graduated from Florida Atlantic, me and my cousin got the apartment together. So we were splitting the rent. I was working for this Web Design Company and they went under. Jobs were hard to find, and I started looking for other options. I found a place in China where I could get the human hair—the Beyoncé weave as they called it—and when I saw how much money there was to be made, I made the investment, designed my website, and took samples around to local beauty salons and supply stores. In six months, I was making the same money working less hours as I was making slaving 40 hours a week. My cousin got pregnant, got engaged, and then moved in with her man. I was comfortable and could afford the place by myself, so I kept it. I could always use the extra room for when my mother or brothers come over. Sherice makes too much noise, that's why Charles got a hotel room," she laughed.

Sherice makes noise. I like me some noise. I was liking this girl more and more. I was impressed at how she hadn't let losing her job beat her down.

"As far as the Benz, 'Fuck the World' used my Social Security number and bought it without my knowledge. He traded in his Honda Accord, put down another twenty grand, and financed the remaining twenty grand. I found out about the Benz after the bank repossessed it. A lady at the bank figured it out and called me. I pleaded my case to them and the credit reporting agencies, and the bank gave me first option on buying the car. They even helped me to get the repo off my credit, but this fool had gotten several department store credit cards as well, so I had to repair and rebuild my credit. I don't owe anybody, and I have excellent credit now. I even paid for that Privacy Guard that notifies me immediately if someone so much as runs my credit."

"That's good. I have that, too. So, dude didn't trip after you got the Benz from the bank?"

"Remember, he was an arrogant prick. He was too embarrassed to even talk to me. We had already been broken up for more than a year when he bought the car."

"That's fucked up. Soooo, how long have you and the skinny-jeans-wearin 'Geek Monster' been together?"

"All of seven months. The last two to three was off and on."

"Mmmmm-hmmmm," I mumbled as she rolled her eyes.

"What you were saying about a house makes sense. I could be building equity instead of pouring my money down the drain."

"And you can save on taxes, because you can claim the interest from the mortgage," I stated. "It would also be easier on you, and you'd be safer working from home. You wouldn't have to leave home to fill orders; you could work whenever you feel like."

"With the apartment, I don't have to worry about cutting grass and painting and when shit breaks, I call the office. It's just me. A house might feel too lonely."

"You could find you a modest 3/2 with dual car garage. You can get a lawn service, and you will still have neighbors. You don't have to get a house out in the woods."

"A nice little 3/2 might not be too bad."

"I could call my connect and find out if there are any good properties listed. Even with all the restructuring of mortgages going on, unfortunately there will still be some people that are going to lose their homes. Who knows, there may be something right in my community."

"Me and you living in the same community, psssss, that may be too close for you, playa. I might see your late night booty calls driving by. That'll make it too easy to catch you."

"Like you said earlier, everything is out in the open, so I wouldn't have to sneak: you wouldn't be concerned about who I'm with, you'll know."

"What if I get the number one position? What if I become the queen?" she asked, with a wry smile.

Without thinking, I said what I felt. "Then we'll put your place on rent and move you into the castle," I retorted, glancing over at her.

Her bright white smile almost blinded me. She liked that answer.

Realizing what I had just said, I had to rein her in a little. "All of my cheating will have to be done elsewhere. Those who don't have their own place—a safe place—will either have to rent a hotel room, or be replaced."

Sonia's smile turned to a frown. That bought out the raw Bahamian in her. "And you dead ass serious bout dat, eh?"

She looked offended for real, so I decided to lighten things back up. I decided to come clean. We were both laying our cards on the table, so I told her exactly how I felt. "As of right now; yes. Later today; next week; next month, if you're still around, or become queen, I might feel differently."

She shook her head. Her high wattage smile didn't come back, but there was a smile.

She twisted toward me and frilled her lip.

I knew she was up to something. I didn't have to wait long to find out what it was.

"So you think I can be the one, the one that you turn in your Playa Card for?"

"No! That's not what I meant. I meant that I'll probably start bringing them home for us to share," I said while leaning as far away as possible to get away from her little fists.

She had a little violent streak in her. She probably liked to wrestle in bed. She probably wants to get thrown in the headlock while getting fucked. Images flooded my mind as she continued to punch me lightly on my right am and leg. This was going to be sooooo much fun. I'm going to make her beg me to stop torturing her with the good loving I'm gonna put on her feisty ass.

The sound of my phone vibrating made her stop hitting me. I

looked at the caller ID: Yasmine. "This is my sister," I said to Sonia as I was putting my Bluetooth in my ear.

"I can do some work while you talk, then," Sonia said, grabbing her laptop from her bag.

I answered my call. "Hey, Sis, what's up?"

"You busy?"

"No, what's up?"

"Your girl, Ashley, brought a bag over here for you."

"A bag? Over there? Why?"

"She said that she thinks her husband is having her followed."

"Did she say why she thought so?"

"She said that she noticed a man when she was in Freeport and then she saw the same man on her flight coming back."

"So! Freeport is a popular tourist destination. That could just be a coincidence."

"True, but then she saw the same man while she was out shopping last night in Palm Beach, then again this morning at Boca Mall."

"No. Unh-unh. That's definitely too much of a coincidence. Did she say how she was going to handle it?"

"She said to tell you not to call her. She'll have me call or text you if she needs to see you. She left a letter in the bag. Want me to open it and read it to you?"

"Hell no. You too nosey."

"How about the present, want me to open it and tell you what it is? Looks like a watch box to me."

"No, don't open my shit."

"Well, you need to come and get it out of this dorm room as soon as you can, because I don't want to be held responsible if it goes missing."

"All right. I'll be up there in about two hours or so."

"You taking us for lunch when you come?"

"I have someone rolling with me."

"I have a name," I heard Sonia mumble.

"Stop eavesdropping," I shot at Sonia. "I'll let you know before I come. If this nosey-ass woman behave, then I'll take y'all to lunch."

"Is this a new one or someone we know?"

I laughed. "Come on, you know your brother."

"That means she's new. Nishka ga be pissed."

"What?"

"Nothing. Call before you come so we can be ready. Luv ya."

"Luv ya, too," I said, laughing, and ending the call.

"Oooooh, that's so sweet," Sonia crooned.

"You need to stop eavesdropping," I said, turning into the post office's parking lot. "Come on, put that computer up. Time to lift these bags. You get the two big ones; I'll bring the other one. You have my arm sore from punching me, so now I can't lift a thing," I said, parking.

"I can carry my own bags, thank you," she pouted.

"You look so cute when you pout."

She couldn't hold it: she started laughing. "I don't know what I'm going to do with you."

"Love me or leave me," I shot.

"Both seem so damn easy to do," she shot back, pulling the smallest bag from the backseat and sticking out her tongue at me.

"I can think of many more pleasurable things you can do with that sassy mouth and long tongue of yours," I shot, grabbing both bags and closing the door.

"You could have felt all the pleasurable and wonderful things that this hot, sweet mouth and skilled tongue could do last night, but nooooo, you wanted to kiss me on the cheek, turn your back to me, then go to sleep."

"Here we go with this shit, again."

CHAPTER 14

AH FAVA FO AH FAVA

"Yo, Khris, bwoy, you ga live a long time, meh son," S said as I hopped out of the Range in front of Supreme Wheels.

"Yeah, we even now, but you didn't have to text me about the game last night," I said, winking to him as Sonia walked around to join us.

"Yo, I told yo ass never bet gainst ah V.I. man," S shot, picking right up on the game I was running. "Waaaaaah! Dis meh prize?" S asked, turning his attention to Sonia.

"Me an you cool, but we een dat muthafuckin cool," I stated as a blushing Sonia sauntered over. I placed my hand in the small of her back. S knew what that meant: she was mine, but he could run game about a friend. "Sonia, this meh boy, S, from St. Croix: S, dis beauty right here is meh home girl, Sonia."

"Nice to meet you, Sonia," S said, giving her his full hundred watt smile. "Tell me you have a female friend. Dese days yo gah be specific when asking for ah hookup," S grinned.

"I don't do the friend ting," Sonia said, shaking her head, "because they always tryin to fuck ya man behind ya back—men and women," Sonia shot, "but erry now and den one a meh cousins does pop over for the weekend. If you like em lil tick, I have one cousin who like man wit long dreads...and you gat dat accent too. Yeah, she ga like you."

This girl can run game, I thought to myself. I got to keep an eye on her.

"Dats how I like em: Tick, baby!" S laughed, nodding his head. "Yeah, I like she, meh son. I like dis one here."

"Me, too," I shot, laughing.

"You better," Sonia shot, poking me in my side.

"When yo flyin again, meh bwoy? Meh daughter birthday on the weekend and we havin a lil ting by deh house, so you know I need a couple cases of dah Goombay Punch meh daughter like, and couple bottles of dah Nassau Royal and white Henny, meh son."

"I flyin Wednesday."

"Dat'll work, meh son. I wan fuck up some head when dey taste dis desert I gon mek with dah Nassau Royal. You two co come if yo not flyin out. Bring lil sis dem, too."

"Thanks," I replied, turning to Sonia, I said, "Da boy can cook."

"Now dat I gah wha I need, wha ya sayin?"

"Her tires got sliced up last night."

"Nah, mey son. A who do dat?" he asked, eyes darting from me to Sonia. "You need me to brush a bwoy?" he asked, staring directly at Sonia.

Sonia was shaking her head. "Noooo."

"Nah! Nah! Nah! Calm down, Rude Boy. Nuttin like dat. She was drivin and sometin in the road sliced her tires."

"Okay. Wha size wheels?" he asked as we started back to the Range.

"Twenties," I replied, opening the back hatch.

"Wha kind ah car?"

"Benz. E 350."

"Yo can drive round in no Benz on dese rims. Check dis out. I had to go collect ah set ah rims over from impound: the same size...some Lexani's with Michelin tires. Dude get touch, but he still owes me $1800 on da rims and tires. They confiscate his shit, but I couldn't let dem tek meh rims. Partner miss two payments and when I call he house, he mudda tell me he lock up and da Fed's tek he car.

I call de judge and carry all my papers down dere and deh let me geh all my shit, so I left he Benz sittin on four blocks. But anyhow, Partna only ride on dem for bout tree weeks, so deh still bran new.

Only cause you is meh bwoy, I gon give you dis deal. The Michelins on dat running $350 apiece and da rims, I een gon tell you how much deh cost. Gimme fifteen and go wit dem: you basically gettin the Lexani's for free, meh bwoy."

It was a good deal. I knew it, but it was Sonia's decision. "You want to take a look?" I asked her.

"Sure. Dis ya boy. If you say it's a good buy, I'm spending."

"Weh you find dis gal from, meh bwoy."

"Right on ma doorstep," I chimed.

We followed S over to his F-250. He hopped up on the back and turned the wheels so that we could see them. "Check dese out. Dese Lexani Obsessions; dey even have Swarovski Crystals on dem."

"Dey nice, fa real," Sonia beamed, her accent—like mine—getting stronger because of S's thick accent.

"What color da Benz be?" S asked.

"Black."

"Tell you wha, only cause you look so sweet, I gon do dis for you. See dese right yah," he said, pointing to the chrome inserts, "I gon put da black insert so the crystals co show up more."

Sonia turned to me, smiling.

The rims and tires looked brand new. And I knew S was giving her a sweet deal. I nodded.

"I'll take dem," she said, "You take Visa Check Card?"

"Same as cash," S chimed. "Where the Benz deh?"

"My house," I chuckled, "in the driveway on the tire stands."

"Tell you wha, leh we go inside and ring up da sale. I gon change deh insert, then I gon carry one of meh bwoy over and mount da tires dem. You co bring da car by later and we co do da alignment, or, if ah yo have tings to do, I can drive it back and do da alignment and call ah yo when it done."

Sonia looked to me. I guess this was my boy, so I'd make the decision and be held responsible. Or, it could be that she just likes her man to make decisions pertaining to these kinds of matters. There I go with that shit again. I'm not her man. Not yet. Shake it off, I warned myself.

"You remember the code to da gate?" I asked S.

"I was coming round deh last night to wake yo ass up bout dah game," he said, adding more to substantiate my earlier lie.

This boy's good. I gat to make sure I bring his shit for him.

We went inside and paid the bill. Sonia gave S the keys to her Benz, and I gave him the code to the garage so he could put up my stands and the drop cloth that he took out of the back of the Range along with the wheels. I knew S was going to make at least four hundred dollars off of Sonia's old rims, he's a natural born hustler, but it was a win-win situation for them both. He still gave Sonia the better of the deal, because Lexani's were much better rims, and the Michelin tires would definitely give her a smoother ride than she was getting with those other tires. Low profile Michelins were known for their smooth rides. They were just expensive as fuck.

When we left Supreme Wheels, Sonia was excited. "Meeting you has changed my luck," she sang. "You may be good for me, Khris," she gushed.

"You haven't even had none yet and you done falling for me," I teased. "Imagine how you ga act when I put dis good wood on you."

"I hope we both be feeling the same way when you do," she said softly.

There was a hidden meaning behind what she just said. She deserved better than me, or would I adjust my lifestyle to give her just the kind of man she deserved? Hmmmm.

"So, what now?" Sonia asked.

"Time for you to pay the piper. We go back to my place and make love for the rest of the day."

"Make love? People still does say that? You showing your age, now?"

"Oh, you gat jokes."

"We young folks say 'have sex', 'get lil bit', 'and get freaky'"

"That's why your lil young ass haven't found the right man to bring the freak out of your sexy ass yet."

"I thought I met him yesterday," she shot, eyes wide and bright.

"Yeah. You did, didn't you?" I smiled arrogantly.

"Yep. Met him while I was in the Louis Vuitton Store in Bal Harbour. Mmmmm! That reminds me; I need to call him."

"Yeah, call him so he could pick your ass up off the next stoplight," I hissed.

She was laughing her ass off now.

"You think that's funny, eh? Let's see if your ass ga be laughing at the next light that catches me," I said.

She was still laughing. "So now it's the next red light that catches us? There aren't any red lights on 95."

"Shit! It's your lucky day, then."

"You so full of shit!" she laughed.

"You feel like doing lunch with my sister and her best friend?"

"You want me to meet your sisters?" she asked, batting her eyes.

"I'm really only going to pick up my package, but you know college girls are always hungry. I remember back in the day a brother could have driven by the dorms with a Happy Meal and he damn sure was leaving with something to hit."

"That's back in the day, playa. It's steak and lobster and a bottle of champagne or red wine, depending on the type of girl: the price ah pussy gone up in case you didn't know."

"So I need to find you some surf and turf, then. That's what you telling me?"

"I don't eat meat."

"What? I know it had to be something wrong with your fine ass. You too good to be true."

She was laughing again. "I just playin. I eat meat."

"From your background check, it look like it was only white meat," I quipped.

"Oh, you want to go there? Well since we on the subject of background check, tell me about your girlfriend."

"Why should I do that?"

"I told you about mine."

"Yours are both ex-boyfriends."

"So!"

"Sew your pants with needle and thread!"

"You are so damn silly. You gone back grade school on me, eh?" she giggled. "For real. Tell me about your girlfriend."

"Hold on. Let me call my sister and tell her I'm on my way." Right after I hung up, she was back on me. She must have thought that I was going to try and dodge the question; she didn't even give me a chance to put my phone down.

"So tell me," she said, badgering me.

"No. If I tell you about her, you'll try to find all her weaknesses...things I don't necessarily like about her, or things I'm not too fond of her doing. Then you'll know what to do to try and steal me away from her. I'm not going to make it easy for you."

"If that's what I was up to—not saying that it is—what's wrong with that. I'll be doing the things you like, won't I?"

"Yeah, but you won't be doing them for the right reason. Well, yes, it would be the right reason, cause you'll get me, but you won't be being yourself, you'll be who I want you to be. And that won't last. As soon as you have me, then the real you will pop out. And I'll be like, "Who the fuck are you? Where's the Sonia that I fell in love with?"

"She done tricked your ass, and now you stuck with me."

"Exactly!"

"That sounds like your M.0," she jibed.

"The Joe Grind, or Jodie—as the Americans call him—role works. Right now, you're tryin to be Joann Grind. That's why I'm not letting you know shit. Just be you. If I like what I see, and I'm available, you get me fair and square. If you be you and I don't like what I see, then see ya."

"Een no see ya. Don't lie, you ga hit first."

"Of course, I can't let your fine ass get away without getting some. Are you crazy?"

"See. Men, y'all gat to hit first: if y'all don't like the sex, then y'all don't stick around long enough to fall in love. With women, decent women like myself, who don't give it up to every and anybody, we fall in love before we give it up."

"How so? You said that you already made up your mind to give me some from when you figured out who I was, so how would that have been true if I had laid this wood on you last night?" Gat her, I thought to myself.

"Who said I was going to let you lay any wood last night? I was calling your bluff. You would have gone to bed with blue balls fuckin wit me last night. I knew if I told you no, you would take that as no. I know you wouldn't have taken it," she said, staring at me.

"I een takin no pussy."

"I told you, not because we slept together in the same bed naked meant that we were going to make love."

"It's too much pussy out there for me to go to bed with blue balls. Me, all you had to do was tell me no one time, maybe twice, and I would have left your ass right there in that bed by yourself."

"You still wouldn't have gotten any."

"Shiiiiit! Not from you, but I would have jumped my hard-dick-havin-ass on the phone and call up one of the nosiest freaks I know to come over. You wouldn't have slept a wink last night. I could tell you that much! All you would have been thinking was, 'God, that could have been me screaming out his name like that.' I might have had to lock my door to keep you out. You probably woulda try to break my shit down to get you some."

Sonia screwed up her face and looked at me in disbelief. "You would have done that? You would have actually called a girl to come over while I was there in your guest room?"

"Me and you een gat nuttin!" I said to bring her confident-ass back down to earth. "We just met a few hours ago."

"That's cold," she mumbled, shaking her head.

Now it's time to reel her ass in. "Look, Sonia," I said, reaching over and gently stroking her cheek with my thumb. "We're just getting to know each other. I mean, I feeling you, and I like what I see so far. The reason I didn't try you last night." I let my voice trail off for dramatic effect and to heighten her expectations. I waited until I had her teetering on the edge to ask me to continue, then I continued. "The fact is, I didn't try you last night because I knew if I waited until I get to know you, whatever we eventually share will be a hundred times better than just one night of wild, freaky sex." I had one eye on the road ahead, and the other locked with hers. I had her.

The intensity of her stare told me that she was trying to read me. She was searching for a sign to help her determine whether this was game I was spitting or not. I didn't crack. I knew what I was sending out: nothing but the honest truth. If she were Dr. Lightman from "Lie to Me," she wouldn't have been able to read me. I got all the seasons on DVD. I learned some good shit from watching that.

Sonia smiled ever so sweetly. "What if you don't like me after you get to know me?" she asked with a raised brow.

She was trying to corner me. That raised brow was her tell, though. Nice try.

I smiled. "Then, neither of us will have any regrets."

She laughed. "That was the 'boost her ego' part of your game, right?"

"Here I am pouring my heart out like this and check how you carryin on."

"I told you, I could spot game. Now, you and I both know that even if at some point in this getting to know you process, you find out something that you don't like about me, you're going to get you some, maybe hit a few times to see if the sex is good enough to make you overlook whatever it is you don't like."

"Sounds like that's what you'll do."

"If the sex is all that, and I'm not being abused physically or mentally, I might overlook a lot of things. Like you having a girlfriend, for instance."

"Sweethearts too?"

She glanced over at me. Her lips were slightly parted as she ran the tip of her tongue over her teeth.

Damn that shit looked sexy.

She licked her lips just enough to rattle me. Her eyes lit up even before the smile reached her lips. I knew something witty was coming. "You must be ga make me believe 'you invented sex,'" she laughed, singing the last part right along with Trey Songz as she turned up the volume on the radio.

"Yeah!" I laughed and started singing, too. "Girl ya ga think, girl you ga think I invented sex."

It was only then that I realized that the radio had been on. That was the first time that I had heard it all day. Wow! This was a first. We'd been so wrapped up in conversation I hadn't missed my music. I loved my music when I'm riding. Me not missing it: that was a good sign. It could be a bad sign, too. We were doing way too much talking. It's like we had already decided what we were going to do—where this relationship was headed—and now we were putting together a contract and ironing out the final details.

This isn't supposed to happen until after I hit and figure out if the pussy—no, not the pussy, the sex—is good enough for me to stick around. I've had quite a few girls with some good-ass pussy, but they didn't know how to work that shit.

I sure as hell hope Sonia wasn't one of them.

CHAPTER 15

THE INTERROGATION

The rest of the drive up 95 was done to the pounding bass of the two Solo-Baric 10 inch subwoofers hidden in custom boxes in the rear compartment. It was Sonia's idea to let down the windows and let the woofers do what they do. Instead of turning down the music when we turned onto FAU's campus, we let up the windows and turned the AC back on. As luck would have it, Ludacris's song "How low can you go" came on as we drove toward the dorms. I couldn't help but remember how Nishka felt rubbing against my body.

As we got closer, I noticed Yasmine and Nishka standing at the top of the stairs waiting near the doors. They weren't the only ones. Several of the girls that happened by when I was hanging out up in their room last night were sitting out on the steps as well.

"I'm in trouble," I said to Sonia as I turned down the music and pulled behind two other vehicles that had stopped directly in front of the dorms.

"What's the matter? Is one of your lil girlfriends sitting up there? You want me to duck, or crawl over the seats and hide in the back?" Sonia asked, pretending to be frightened.

"Now, who's being silly? No! None of them is my lil anything.

You see those two," I said, pointing at Yasmine and Nishka. "They're not dressed for McDonald's drive through," I explained as they both started walking down the steps.

"You told them you had company, so they wanted to make a good first impression," she stated like it should have been obvious. "Is my hair fixed?" she asked, concerned.

"You look good enough to eat, but I don't know how you ga look after the interrogation. They're real protective," I warned.

"They are! Which one is your sister? No. The one with the Louis duffle bag has to be your sister," she stated. "She's pretty. You two look alike."

"So you think I'm pretty? What kind of shit is that?" I asked, waving at the girls sitting on the stairs as I pulled up to where

Yasmine and Nishka stood waiting.

"They," she said, motioning with her head, "obviously think you're something," she shot back right before both rear doors opened. "You're extremely handsome for an ugly guy," she laughed just as Yasmine and Nishka jumped in.

"Share the joke," Yasmine chirped as both doors closed.

"No hello. Nothing. You just wan jump in people business," I said.

Yasmine rolled her eyes as she leaned between the seats. "Hi, I'm Yasmine, his favorite sister. And this is Nishka, my best friend."

"I'm Sonia. Nice to meet you both," she said, shaking both their hands. "I remember you two from SAC. I think I was a senior when y'all were starting the seventh grade."

"Yeah! I think so. Everybody knew you in school," Nishka said as they shook hands. "You were on every team we had."

"Even chess!" Yasmine added.

"Alright. Tell me all the dirt," I said. "All the rumors and everything. She's been interrogating me all day."

"That's not true," Sonia said, punching me.

"And she lil violent too," I snarled.

"Before we tell you anything, may I inquire as to where you are taking us to lunch?" Yasmine asked, sounding all hoity-toity.

"He was planning on McDonald's," Sonia informed her.

"We're dressed to be seen," Yasmine snarled.

"Humph! McDonald's!" Nishka shot. "Happy Meal days were over from kindergarten."

"I feel like some surf and turf: someplace scenic," Yasmine stated.

Sonia started laughing first. Then I started laughing. Then she had to tell Nishka and Yasmine what the joke was. Then I got gang banged about modern women and where they shopped and ate. Nishka wasn't into it as much; she was sort of reserved, I noticed. She was feeling Sonia out. That's what she was doing.

We, they, decided on riding up to Palm Beach: Worth Avenue. 200 Block: Ta-Boo to be exact. I was just their driver.

While they caught Sonia up on what was going on in Nassau, I got a call from my mother. I really couldn't talk, so I just listened and "Mmmm-hmmmed" at the appropriate times while she filled me in on Sherice's report. Sherice couldn't stop talking about my house. She described every room to the rest of the girls. Obviously, my mother enjoyed every minute of it. The other girls started asking her about me, that's when Sherice switched to the topic of Charles's sister, Sonia, and how the two of us would make such a good couple. Mom informed me that Sherice had even brought a picture of Sonia so that she could see whom I might possibly hook up with.

Now what kind of shit was that?

When I didn't comment on Sonia, my mother laughed. She had seen the picture. She knew. "Khris, I know I hear my child in the background. I recognize Nishka's voice, but there is a third voice in there with y'all. Nancy ass at work, so who is the third female's voice I hearing?"

This woman was talking to me and listening to the background conversation at the same time. Now I knew where Yasmine got it. I laughed.

My mother knew me well enough that when I laughed like that, I couldn't call any names. So, she started guessing. She hit the nail on the head on the first try. "I know you. That's Sonia wit y'all," she stated. "I know that's who it is."

Mom's good, but not that good. She had already spoken to Yasmine. She had to get back to work, but she told me to call her home later.

It was as if they were just shooting the bo-bo with Sonia until I got off the phone. "So," Yasmine said, patting Sonia on the shoulder, "You want to get the '20 Questions' out of the way before we shop and eat?"

"20 Questions?" Sonia asked, stressing the '20' and twisting so she could look at Yasmine.

"Might be more, depending on your answers," Nishka shot.

Sonia looked to me for help.

"Don't look this way." I chuckled. "I want to hear the answers to what they have to ask too," I said frankly.

"You sure you don't want to record this?" she asked

sarcastically, folding one leg beneath her thigh so that she was facing me with her back against the door.

"Don't worry," Nishka shot, "we'll remember everything you say."

Sonia chuckled. "Okay, ask away."

This was going to be fun, I thought and smiled.

Yasmine went first. "Do you have a boyfriend, girlfriend, fiancé, or husband?"

"She's covering all the bases, isn't she," Sonia chimed, grinning across at me. Then she turned to her examiner. "No husband; no fiancé; definitely no girlfriend. But, a very recent ex that he," she proclaimed, pointing to me, "knows all about."

I nodded so that they could move on. No sense telling them that the body wasn't even cold yet. Besides, they didn't need to know all the details.

Nishka was ready. "Are you gainfully employed?"

"I'm self employed as of two years ago. I majored in Management Information Systems, specializing in Web Designs. I worked for a Web Design Company from my junior year and then another two years after graduation. It went under. Jobs were hard to find, so while I was looking, I decided to try something to make some cash. I found a place in China that sells human hair weave wholesale. I bought a batch, took them around to local salons and beauty supply stores, and they couldn't get enough."

"Tell them what else you sell," I said sweetly.

"A penis enlarging pill: that's what he wants me to tell you two about."

"Men actually buy penis enlarging pills?" Nishka asked, sitting forward.

"Spend some real good money on it," Sonia chimed.

"Does it work?" Yasmine asked.

"The makers say it does. I gave some to my old boyfriend, but he became my ex before I could find out."

"Don't look over here," I interjected. "I'm completely satisfied with what God gave me."

"It's not a matter of you being satisfied; it's a matter of your partner being satisfied," Nishka shot.

"Satisfaction guaranteed every time, baby!"

"Anyhow," Yasmine said, silencing Nishka and me. "Next question," she said, turning the attention back to Sonia.

"Where do you live?"

"Coral Springs: an apartment, not a house. But Khris has already lectured me about throwing away my money on rent instead of building equity by purchasing a house," Sonia explained, smiling at me.

"You just recently broke up with your boyfriend! So are you looking for a rebound affair, a Mr. Right Now, or a Mr. Right?"

"Actually, I wasn't looking for anything. I wanted to take some time and chill: get to know me, and get the last two bad decisions out of my life. But, as fate would have it, I met Khris yesterday," she said, and shrugged, "and who knows."

The entire time she had been explaining her situation, she had been keeping eye contact with them. As soon as she got to the last part about meeting me, she reached over and rubbed my leg ever so slightly so that I could turn and meet her eyes. Sonia's got game. She's good. I really have to watch her ass.

"All-righty-then," Nishka said with just a hint of sarcasm. "You like to cook?"

Sonia didn't hesitate. "I do."

"Your food taste good?" Yasmine asked.

Sonia giggled. "Ask him. I made him breakfast this morning."

"Damn! You does move fast, eh. You just met him last night and done cook him breakfast this morning," Nishka shot. "You een wastin no time at all."

"It wasn't planned. Circumstances just allowed it. I got two flat tires last night and he came to my rescue, so this morning while he was taking off my tires, I decided the least I could do was fix him breakfast as a way of saying thanks."

"Girl, I thought you was going to tell us that the way to a man's heart is through his stomach," Nishka chuckled, "cause I was going to tell you, you might only be giving energy to the hunter to go on the prowl: seek other prey."

"Nishka!" Yasmine shot.

Sonia laughed. "That's a good one. Don't worry, I know about his girlfriend and his little prowling. Back in the day, Khris used to check my friend, Aarti."

"Which Aarti?" Nishka asked.

"Psycho?" Yasmine asked. "Aarti from Trinidad?"

Sonia was laughing and nodding her head. "Yep, that would be her."

"Oh, so you're not new," Yasmine shot.

"Aarti bragged, talked, about Khris all the time, but we never met. I only ran into him because my brother's girlfriend, Sherice, had to pick up some stuff to take back to your mother."

"So since you know about him, how do you feel about infidelity?" Nishka asked.

Sonia laughed. Belly aching laughter.

"Next question," I shouted. "You don't have to answer that."

"Why not. I told them ask away, so I'm going to answer them."

Sonia looked at Nishka and said, "My first boyfriend was an asshole, but I was too much in love to see it. The second one wasn't as possessive, but he was an asshole also. I could admit that now. He started frequenting strip clubs and started smoking dirty. Along with the drugs came the infidelity and disrespect. I'm not going to be ignorant as to what men can do, but I rather know upfront and make up my own mind if I want to be in that type of situation. Feel me?"

"We feel you," Nishka said, warming up a bit more.

"With that said," Yasmine, drawled, "Are you insecure or jealous?"

"I'm not insecure about myself. I know I'm not perfect, but I know I damn near close. I know I look damn good."

"Spoken like a true Bahamian," Yasmine laughed.

"As far as being jealous, everyone has a little jealousy in them. Would I make a scene or act the fool in public? No, I wouldn't lower myself to those standards. But, een no woman other dan my ma ga put her hands on me and live to talk about it."

"Yeah, she still gat da real island blood in her," Nishka laughed.

"How do you feel about marriage?" Yasmine asked.

"I would like to get married and have a few children."

"Hold that thought," Yasmine said, getting her bearings. "We're here. Bro, park up on the 200 Block: there's a valet by the Via Encantada."

"Tiffany's, Hermes, and Bvlgari," Sonia said, fixing herself.

"And Gucci right across the street," Nishka beamed.

"Bro," Yasmine called. "Since Sonia know all your business, can I open your present now? You might not want to leave it in the car."

"You just wan open my shit. Go ahead and open it."

Open it she did. Just as she had guessed earlier, it was a watch. A Hublot Big Bang: 18K red gold, tsavorite stones and rubber accents with a pretty matching green alligator band. It was indeed a beautiful piece.

"I can't compete with the woman that bought that," Sonia shot. "How am I supposed to stand a chance?"

"I told you, you don't compete..." I started, but got cut off by my sister.

"Just be you," Yasmine advised. "She bought a watch, matching alligator loafers, custom Air Force One's, and a bag full of other matching clothing to go with it...but, first of all, she een from the islands, she wasn't even raised by islanders; second, and most importantly, she een here with him now. You are."

"She wasn't there to cook his hungry ass breakfast either," Nishka added to my surprise. "I'll tell you like a wise man told me: "Just know what you want and need to satisfy your relationship needs. Then you decide if you can live with the compromises."

Those words weren't exactly mine, but the way she prettied it up sure sounded good to me, I thought as I pulled up to the valet stand.

CHAPTER 16

ARDENT PLEA

Sonia smiled as I jumped back into the driver's seat after walking Yasmine and Nishka into the dorm. I went in under the guise of taking their bags. It was really to get their take on Sonia so far.

"Well, that was fun!"

"What? The interrogation; the shopping; or the food?" I asked as I pulled from the front of the dorms.

"Bonding with your sisters. I'm in with them," she stated confidently.

She was right, they did approve of her.

"Who do I meet next, Mom?"

"Wow! Slow down there. We haven't even consummated this-this..."

"This what? What is this?" she asked.

"I don't know," I mumbled, shrugging my shoulders.

"I don't know, either," she admitted. "All I know is that it feels good. I like the way it's starting."

"Remember, even bad relationships start out good."

"This doesn't feel like one of those."

I laughed. "You didn't feel it the other two times either, did you?"

"No, I didn't. But, I didn't feel like how you're making me feel either."

I should have been flattered, but for some reason I felt-I felt guilty. I felt the need to caution her. Don't get me wrong, I like her: like her in a good way. However, I do have a girlfriend. I had to slow her roll. I knew I was better than most, but damn!

At the rate she was falling, she would probably tell me she love me before the day is over. I couldn't let that happen.

"Sonia, don't forget that I have a girlfriend," I warned.

"I know. You don't have to keep reminding me."

"Yes, I do."

"No, you do not. I know you have a girlfriend, but from what I know about you, I know you won't do anything to hurt me. I can deal with you having a girlfriend, Khris. As long as you don't disrespect me, I'll be fine. I don't want to hear about the others, though."

"Listen, Sonia, I have to explain something to you. After I do, you'll have a better understanding of how I operate. I'll tell you about Aarti and me. When we met, Aarti knew I had a girlfriend. She didn't care. A little bit of me was worth more than a lot from some of the bums that were trying to get with her. It was good. I treated her like she was my woman when we were together. I never disrespected her. No woman ever got in her face when we were together— nothing. Then when my girlfriend and me broke up, Aarti got the idea that she was the main woman even though I specifically told her otherwise. That became a problem. She started making scenes and getting in females faces in the club. I'm talking about any girl I danced with or stopped to talk to. She started violating the same rules that once insured that she wouldn't be accosted when we were out together. One time she laid down on the pavement in front of my car..."

Sonia nodded her head and cut me off. "That dick had her gone. I knew that."

"Look, this is how it is: once a sweetheart, always a sweetheart. There is no promotion from within. If you start out as a sweetheart, that's what you're going to stay."

"That sounds cold," Sonia said flatly.

"Most men lie about it, I'm just keeping it real. How many married men actually divorce their wives and marry their sweethearts?" I asked to hammer home my point.

"Not many, that's for sure. But back to us—to me. So, what you're telling me is if I want to be your woman, I better not agree to take the lovin you offerin right now, because if the queen spot opens up, I won't be able to get promoted?"

"You got it."

"But, on the other hand, if I don't take the position that you have available at this time, then I might miss out on getting any love at all."

"Yeah, that's true too."

"So, you're telling me not to take the dick now? You're telling me that I should hold out until you get rid of your woman? What if I hold out and you don't get rid of her?"

"I can't answer that for you," I replied frankly.

"Why would you even tell me this? Why not just let it play out? A playa wouldn't do this."

"Because..."

"Because what? Because you fallin for me?" she asked provocatively.

"Yeah, didn't you see me looking at rings while we were in Tiffany's?" I asked sarcastically, and laughed. "Seriously, it's because I think you deserve better...no, you deserve more. You can't find a better man," I said playfully to lighten the mood.

"I deserve more than you can give, or more than you're willing to give me at this time?"

"More than I can give you at this time."

We drove in silence for a few minutes after my response.

"I have a suggestion," Sonia said, "sort of a compromise..."

"I'm all ears."

"How about I not apply for any of your two options, girlfriend nor sweetheart. We can continue to get to know each other the way we're doing now. We can hang out..."

"Nah! I een trying to enter the friend zone," I said, cutting her off. "Me and you can't be platonic friends. That can't work."

She giggled. "That's not where I was heading, but it's good to know that. What I was going to say before I was so rudely interrupted," she teased, "was that we could let nature take its course. We are both consenting adults. Whatever happens happens. If the feeling is there, we let it run its course. No strings attached. No promises. No commitments. No expectations. It will be like a one night stand," she said with a convincing smile.

"Then what happens when you want some more, because you are going to want more?"

She smiled deviously. "I'll pull out my toys and reminisce while I satisfy my own desires. Put out my own fire."

I shook my head. "Toys can't replace me."

"I didn't say they could. I would be imagining it was you: probably call you on the phone to hear your voice while I'm doing it," she said, sticking out her tongue.

"Stick it out again, I'm going to bite it," I threatened, leaning over and snapping my teeth together.

She stuck it out again and I snapped closer and harder. She squealed as she backed away, pressing herself against the door.

"Okay, so what happens if the sex is all that and I want some more?" I asked.

"Oh, it will be all that, so I know you'll want some more. When that happens, I'll tell you no. Simple."

"You won't do that to me."

"Yes, I will. You have an advantage, you can call your girlfriend or any of your little sweethearts who will gladly give you some."

"So let me ask you this: If you know I'm cheating on my girlfriend, how would you be able to trust me if you were to become my girlfriend?"

"That's a good question," she said, nodding. "Let me ask you a question before I answer you. How does your girlfriend trust you?"

"That's simple, I'm faithful."

Sonia erupted in a fit of laughter. She was rolling. Tears were coming from her eyes.

"Hold up! Why are you laughing? That shit isn't funny. I'm dead ass serious, she doesn't know that I cheat."

It took her about five minutes to stop laughing, then another minute to get a Kleenex and dry her face.

"She doesn't know? Does she spend time with you like I did today?"

"Yes."

"I saw how women look at you while we walked through the stores today. If it wasn't three of us with you, a few would have stepped to you."

"So. Just because women are attracted to me doesn't mean that I would cheat. I can be faithful if I wanted."

"That's exactly what I wanted to hear you say. You can be faithful if you wanted."

She paused like a lawyer who just got the witness to say exactly what she wanted. That's how I felt. I had been led into a trap: Sonia's trap.

"Soooo, if you find a woman that satisfies 'the majority' of your needs, because let's be honest, no one can completely satisfy all of anyone's needs, then you'll stop. I'm confident enough with myself to know that I can satisfy most of your needs. Let me break it down for you. See, if I'm your woman, I'll be willing to learn to satisfy all your needs. That's why I paid attention to your likes and dislikes as you interacted with your sisters and me today. That interrogation was also very informative for me as well. I listened to the questions they asked. Those were the important issues. But, I'm getting off track," she said more to herself than to me. "Back to learning to satisfy your needs. I'm not just referring to your sexual needs: I'm talking about everything. Most men go around other women because the other woman does something that the main woman don't or won't do. There's nothing I won't do for my man, and there's no place I won't go with him. I'm a girly girl, but I can hang like one of the boys. You can take me anywhere and I'll fit in. You won't want to leave me home. I'm too easy to be around. I get along with anyone. You can feel comfortable around me. You can be yourself. I am secured enough to see a big booty girl and point her out to you. I'm with you: she's not. But," she grinned, taking a breath, "I'm not applying for a position at this time, so enough about that. Now to answer your question: I will be able to trust you, because you said, just a few minutes ago, that I deserve more. If you commit to me, you would give me more. With that, I rest my case!"

"Bravo! Bravo! I'm sold!" I shouted. I whistled, clapped and laughed. I stared over at her. She was proud of herself. I shook my head. "I find it hard to believe, with a gifted mouth and the skill you have with words like you have, you couldn't find a job! That's hard to believe."

"I went on five interviews and I was overqualified for all five positions."

"I always found that strange that someone could be overqualified for a position."

Sonia screwed up her face. "What?" I asked.

"I didn't mind being overqualified in my professional life, but I just realized that you're basically telling me that I'm overqualified even in my personal life."

"That's not what..." I started to deny it, but then stopped myself. "I guess when you look at it, that's the way it seems. But I didn't mean it in a negative way. You have to realize that all I'm saying to you is that you're too good of a person to settle for playing number two. A good woman like you deserves to have a much better man than I am. That's what I'm saying. I'm not good enough for you. You should look at it as if you're the boss and I'm under-qualified for the job."

"I like your lil spin," she blushed, "but if I look at it that way, even though you may think you are under-qualified, I see that you have the potential to be just what I'm looking for. With a little on the job training and some workshops, you'll be everything I need and more."

I laughed. "I can't beat you talkin."

Sonia laughed and started bobbing her head and clipping her fingers. She's been doing this shit all day. The right song just happened to be playing for her again.

She reached forward and turned up the radio, then started dancing and belting away with Mary J. "Ain't nobody gonna love you better: Ain't nobody gonna treat you better..."

When we pulled into Supreme Wheels, she screamed. "Oh my God! Look at my baby. He cleaned it too."

"That shit sittin pretty, now. Dem rims set that baby off."

Sonia grinned. "Oh my God. That looks like a totally different car. I ga be stuntin hard," she sang excitedly.

"You ga be turning all kinds a heads on da road now."

"So, am I following you home, or you had enough of me for one day?" she asked as I stopped next to her car.

I looked over at her. I couldn't believe my luck. To have her just drop in my lap like she did. I just met her yesterday, but it felt like I knew her for years. It took Yas and Nishka a couple months to warm up to Nancy, but then again, Nancy's first impression comes off as spoil and pretentious. Damn! Why am I doing this? I realized that while I was lost in thought, I was still staring at Sonia, and she was staring back waiting for an answer.

"Earth to Khris? Earth to Khris? Where are you? Come on back."

I guess I took too long to respond, because she looked away and said, "It's okay, I'll head home. You probably need your space."

To be honest, I wasn't ready for her to leave me yet. I was really enjoying her company. She was right; it was easy to be around her. So, I told her the truth.

"Sonia, you're not overcrowding me. I was just trying to figure out why you would want to follow me home; you know where I live. You can lead and I can follow." I smiled deviously. "That way you'll get there first and I'll know that there's a sweet treat home waiting for me to arrive."

"And you say you can't beat me talking. Hah." Sonia laughed and opened the door. She paused halfway out. She turned back to me with a mischievous glint in her eyes. "I hate to admit this to you, but my Grammy was right."

"Right about what?" I asked, but shouldn't have.

"Boiling the panty in the grits works every time.

CHAPTER 17

DOWN, BUT NOT OUT

It was short1y after six by the time I turned through my corner. I knew something was wrong when I saw Sonia drive right by my house. I slowed down and picked up my phone to call her. She beat me to it.

As I answered, I saw the rear of Nancy's silver Lexus GS 300 in my driveway. "Hello?"

"I see you have company, so I just kept going. Call me when you can."

"Sonia, I'm sorry about this."

"I figured it's your woman, so I thought it best to keep going. Wouldn't want you to get busted," she laughed.

It was a forced laugh, but she was trying to be a good sport. "She doesn't do this: just pop up like this. We had a little..."

"You don't have to explain, Khris. Call me later. If not tonight, tomorrow. Bye."

I said bye and ended the call. Tomorrow seemed so far away. No, I would call her tonight. The puzzling question is why was Nancy here unannounced? She has a key, but she never just pop up. She always calls and let me know when she's coming. That's why I gave her a key. She thought it was a sign of a serious commitment; a sign that I was faithful. But truthfully, I only gave it to her because I knew she wouldn't abuse it. She wasn't the type to come and snoop. She had no clue. Did I fuck up in some way? This wasn't like her. And, she's here and didn't even call to see if I was home or when I was planning on coming home. What is she up to? I wondered as I grabbed my bag from the back seat and locked up the Range.

I walked to the front door to find Nancy standing in the opened doorway looking tantalizing: she looked absolutely yummy. She was still dressed in her work attire: a navy blue designer skirt suit with a sheer silk camisole beneath her jacket. Her stocking covered legs looked fantastic in the three-inch stilettos. As bad as I had felt for Sonia having to drive on by, I forgot all about her as soon as Nancy smiled and opened her arms to me.

"Surprise!" she sang. "You miss me?"

The throbbing in my pants didn't allow me to tell her a lie. "I sure am glad you're here," I said, walking into her arms as she backed inside. I dropped the Louis duffel as I crossed the threshold, and closed the door. Our lips met and we kissed like seasoned lovers do. Her lips parted and I wasted no time plunging my tongue into her mouth. Our tongues danced to their own secret melody.

Both our hands went to work. Her hands ran across my back before eagerly racing to the front of my pants. My hands caressed and fondled her firm body as she shucked down my pants. The wisps of pleasurable moans that escaped her lips had me harder than Chinese arithmetic in the dark.

Our groans got louder and started coming from deeper. They were guttural in nature. I had to do all I could not to tear her clothes from her body. I wasn't going to take them off of her. No, I was going to fuck her in all her clothes, stilettos and all. My hand shot under her skirt, going straight to her pleasure chest. I felt the heat and moistness through her stockings and underwear.

She was hot.

I was hotter.

I stroked her lips until they were plumped and juicy. My skilled strumming had her bucking wildly. I groped until I found the seam in the crotch of her stockings. I got a good grip on either side of the seam, making sure that the balls of my fingers made contact with her lips and clit, then I pulled, ripping a good sized hole. My fingers wiggled through the hole, found the outer fringes of her silky underwear, and pulled it to the side. I thought she was going to have an orgasm just from that. My fingers slid between her lips, then into her hot, wet sheath, massaging and stimulating every nerve ending they came in contact with.

Nancy ran her opened palm up and down my shaft while her thumb glided across my bulging head. When she wrapped her soft hand around my dick and started stroking, I closed my eyes and took a long, ragged breath. Her hand was amazingly soft. It felt sooo fucking amazin. But, a hand job wasn't what I wanted right then.

"Pull up your skirt," I ordered, my voice husky with sexual desire.

As Nancy peppered kisses all over my neck and cheeks, she did as I asked. She reached down and grabbed the hem of her skirt on either side of her thighs. While she gathered it up, I bent down just low enough to get my dick under the hem of her rising skirt and followed it all the way up.

When I pushed up between her lips and entered her, Nancy's body started to tremble.

"Fuck! I'm coming," she screamed, grinding faster against me. "I'm coming, baby. Fuck me, baby!"

I loved the cute way she said coming. I continued stroking her as she came all over my dick. The soft, silky feel of her panties and stocking gave an extra sensation as I continued to beat into her sweet pussy. But I was nowhere near ready to cum yet.

After her orgasm simmered, she fought frantically to take off her jacket. I helped her get it off, then lifted her and shuffled both of us to the dinning room off to the right of the foyer.

I pulled out one of the chairs and sat so that she had one leg on either side of the chair, straddling me.

Nancy loved to ride. She placed both hands over my shoulders, gripped the back of the chair and started using some of that belly dancing technique that she knew drove me insane. She pulled out a few tricks and rode me like I was a champion racehorse in the Kentucky Derby. She kissed me hard, then latched on to my tongue and started sucking it to the same rhythm as her flexing muscles.

My hands went up and under her camisole and bra to get to her ripe nipples. I pinched and rolled them between my thumb and forefingers causing light tremors to ripple through her body.

"Baby," she whispered hotly in my ear.

"Mmmm-hmmmm," I moaned as I pumped up into her and caressed her gyrating ass.

"I know...you're upset...because...because...I took this semester off. I don't want to-to disappoint you. I talked to my boss...and she...she said that...that she would let me work around my classes...ssssss...next semester."

I was happy she was going back to school next semester, but I didn't want to talk about that right then. My nut was rising. "That's good, baby," I growled, gripping her ass cheeks with both hands and humping up into her. "Don't disappoint me, then. Ride this dick like only you know how!" I demanded, spanking her ass.

She picked it up a notch. "Come for me, baby!" she begged. "Yes! Yes!" she screamed. "Fuck your pussy, baby!" she growled. "Yesss! That's it, baby. Ssssss."

"You. Like. This. Dick?" I asked, deep-stroking her.

"Yes, Khris. This...is...my...dick!" she growled, her gyrations deliberate with each word. "I...love...this...dick, baby!"

We fucked and sucked each other to toe curling oblivion.

I shot load after load deep into her. She rode my wave and I rode hers until all we had the energy to do was hold onto each other and try to catch our breaths.

"Are you proud of me?" Nancy asked.

"You ride like a champion," I panted.

"Not that," she giggled, and bit on my bottom lip.

"Of course, I'm proud of you. You're my baby and I love you," I said, kissing her gently. "But, Nancy, I don't want you to go to law school for me. I want you to do it if it makes you happy. Do it for you."

"I am doing it for me. I just needed a break," she explained. "Working is actually harder, so it's not that I'm lazy or ducking the work; I just needed a break from the classroom. I'll be back in class in a month, baby. And, I promise that I won't take another semester off."

"Okay now, don't make any promises that you can't keep," I warned.

"I have every intention of keeping every promise I make to you. I love you, Khris, and I'll do whatever you want to make sure that I don't ever let you down," Nancy said, then kissed me gently.

I swallowed hard. Right then, Sonia popped into my head. I thought about her hoping that Nancy would somehow fuckup so she could take her spot. Sonia had put in some good work in the short time that I've known her, but Nancy was still on the job. And Nancy didn't seem to be trying to fuckup at all. Not with the words that just came out of her mouth.

"Come on, let's go upstairs and take a nice, hot bubble bath. When we're done, I'll come downstairs and finish cooking dinner. I've got the steaks marinating; the salad is cut up. All I have to do is turn on the stove under the corn and pop the bake potatoes in the oven. While I do that, you can slap the steaks, and the shrimp shish kabobs on the grill. We can eat while we watch an old episode of 24."

I was impressed. It's not that Nancy can't cook. It's just that she doesn't do it enough. "What?" I asked, feeling her forehead. "Are you sick?"

"Yes. And the only thing that can make me feel better is more of your good loving."

"You keep talking like that, we'll not only miss Jack Bauer, but your mother will put your ass out when you don't come home tonight."

"I told her I was spending the night with you, so I won't be getting put out, we can start Jack Bauer whenever we like. We have all night to make sweet love, baby," she said, slowly gyrating and flexing her inner muscles around my semi-hard erection.

"Don't do that," I said, gritting my teeth.

"Why not?" she asked, squeezing her inner muscles so tightly that I could feel the blood pulsing through her inner folds.

"Oh shit!" I grumbled as the wonderful sensations caused me to start stiffening and grinding into her once again.

Nancy smiled seductively. "You like that, baby?"

"I thought we were going up to take a bubble bath?" I asked, gripping her waist and grinding deeper into her hot, wet sheath.

"Oh Yesss, baby! Oooooh that feels good. Just... Oh fuck, Khris! We...we're not going anywhere! Oooooh...ssssss. Right there, baby! This one is going to be quick," she said, rocking back and forth.

Quick it wasn't. We were butt naked; clothes littered the floor from the dinning room to the kitchen, then to the family room. We ate a hastily prepared dinner on the floor in front of the television. We didn't get that hot bath until almost midnight. By then, there was no need for any more lovemaking. We were both completely satisfied. By the time we went to bed, all we did was cuddle, kiss each other good night, and went to sleep.

The sound of my phone vibrating woke me up.

I didn't want to open my eyes, so I kept them closed and reached onto the nightstand where it was sitting on the charging mat. I felt my phone but it wasn't vibrating. But, I could still hear the vibrating.

I opened my eyes: it was almost three in the morning. And it obviously wasn't my phone. The sound was coming from Nancy's side of the bed. It was her phone. It stopped.

I closed my eyes to go back to sleep, happy that it wasn't Sonia blowing up my shit at this hour of the morning. Then the buzzing started again. Okay, time to wake her up. It has to be an emergency for someone to be blowing up her shit at this hour. I couldn't believe that she had lied to me. She hadn't told her mother that she was sleeping out. Now her mother was probably pissed at her for not coming home. That would give her mother another reason not to like me. What the hell was Nancy thinking? She hadn't even called—at least not since I got home. Her mother was probably worried to death. Who could blame the woman?

"Baby?" I said, shaking her gently. "Baby, wake up."

"Wha?" she said, groggily.

"Your phone. It's been blowing up. Did you tell your mother you were sleeping over?"

"Yes," she said, fumbling for her bag.

Her phone was vibrating again. She picked up her bag and pulled out her phone.

I dropped back onto my pillow and decided to check and see how many calls I had missed while she answered her phone.

To my astonishment, she didn't answer the call. She hit end, then turned the ringer to silent. She threw the phone back in her bag, then dropped it back on the floor.

"What? That wasn't your mother?" I asked, dropping my phone back on the charging mat.

"She knows where I am. If she were trying to reach me, she would have called on the house phone. She knows I turn my ringer off at night."

"So, why didn't you answer it? Who was that? Whoever it was calling you at three o'clock in the morning might be in some sort of trouble. It has to be an emergency for someone to call you at this kind of time."

She smiled and pecked me on the cheek. "That was Angie. Her and her man probably get into some shit. I'm not trying to ruin my night with you by listening to her problems. Don't worry your sweet little head about it, sweetie. Now, can we please go back to sleep? One of us has to go to work in a few hours."

"Yeah, but I don't know what kind of friend you are not answering to make sure she een in the hospital or something. I hope nothing ever happens to me late in the night and I have to call you," I said as she wiggled her warm butt, just right, against me.

"Mmmmm," she moaned as she felt my warm dick press between her butt cheeks. She reached back and stroked that bad boy to life in a second. "Now I'm going to need another dose of this to go back to sleep," she said, wiggling and positioning her ass so I could get it where she wanted it. She guided me until my bulging head was right at her entrance, then she rubbed my head up and down between her lips as blood began to fill them and her juices began lathering them up.

When she had my head lathered properly with her sweet juices, she unleashed the beast giving me total control. I reached up and over her with one hand, moistening my fingers in her wetness. I strummed her clit and spread her lips as I guided my swollen head to her entrance. She squirmed and tried to back up on it, but I didn't let her. I teased her for a little while, and then when she least expected it, I rammed everything I had up in her.

Five minutes and a multiple orgasm later, she was snoring softly. Again.

I was up now, so I grabbed my phone and as I headed downstairs to get something to drink, I checked my missed calls and messages:

5 missed calls and 2 voice messages: none of them from Sonia.

The first was from Paola, a little Brazilian flight attendant from Varig.

"Hi, Khris, I have a 24 hour layover in Miami. If you're free tomorrow, give me a call."

The second message was from Ashley.

"I'm just calling to see if you like your watch. Don't worry; I'm not using my phone. I'll be okay, so don't stress. I'll find a way to call you tomorrow. Love ya!"

I checked the missed call log. The three calls that hadn't left any voice mails were from the same number. It was a Miami number— one that I wasn't familiar with. I was tempted to call the number back, but I decided if it was that important, the person would have left a message.

I got a bottle of water from the fridge then went back upstairs. I made a pit stop in the bathroom, then eased my way back into bed, snuggling up nicely behind Nancy's soft, warm body.

CHAPTER 18

TOUCHING BASIS

I woke up early enough to make breakfast for Nancy. She showed her appreciation as we showered. After she left for work, I went back to bed. Today is supposed to be my rest day. I have to fly tomorrow.

I slept without interruption until almost eleven. It was my mother wondering why I hadn't called her back like she had told me to. After spending almost half an hour on the phone with her, I was wide-awake. I thought about calling Paola, but decided to call Sonia first. I had to check on her. I was curious to see how she would act after what happened yesterday and me not calling last night. I searched through my call log and called her.

She answered on the first ring. "I was waiting for you to call me," she said, sounding all chipper.

"You sound very excited. Is it me, or something else that have you in such a good mood today?"

"Both. I'm happy to hear from you, aaaand, guess what?"

"What?"

"You were right."

"Right about what?"

"The name of the cologne. I got eight orders yesterday, and six of the eight ordered the cologne."

"That's great," I said, happy to have helped.

"Am I going to see you today, or do you have plans?"

"I have a friend in town on a 24 hour layover. She called last night and left a message, but I haven't returned her call as yet. I wanted to touch base with you first."

"See how quickly I'm moving up the ladder," she chimed.

Moving up the ladder? I'm actually putting you on hold to see what the other woman wants to do and you think you're moving up? I thought, but dared not say.

"Okay, check your girl and hit me back. I still have about another hour or two here packing this hair."

"She's not my girl."

"Figure of speech." Sonia chuckled. "Relax, Khris, I told you I can handle it. Go handle your business."

"I'll call you back. Let me see if she wants to do lunch or something. Maybe we can all do something."

"I don't do girls, Khris. Bye," she said, laughing.

I laughed, said bye, and ended the call.

I called Paola.

"Ola, meu amor," she sang as soon as she answered. "Como vai?" she cooed excitedly in that sweet Brazilian accent of hers.

I'm good, I thought, then replied. "Eu sou bom."

"O que voce esta fazendo hoje?"

What am I doing today? Whatever you want to do. "O quer fazer."

"Eu quero foder," she said provocatively.

I want to fuck. Oh, she wants to fuck. There's nothing like a woman that straight up asks for what she wants. I grinned. Shit, I want to fuck, too. "Eu quero foder muito!"

"Gracas a deus!" she replied, laughing.

When she said thank God, we both enjoyed a good laugh. Then she told me that she and two of her girlfriends wanted to get some sun. These were Brazilian flight attendants. The hotel didn't allow the kind of no-line tan that they wanted to achieve, so she wanted to know if they could impose on me. I had no problem with it. I told them I would be down to get them, but she told me that their hotel was right next to a Tri-Rail station so they would catch the train up, and I could pick them up from the Sample Road station. It was just east of where I lived on Sample and Andrews. That was cool with me.

Nancy called as I was ending the call. She was just calling to tell me how much she loved me and to thank me for being me.

Wasn't that sweet!

My phone became a hotline from that point on. Monique called me from Freeport. She wanted me to pick up a part from Honda for her. That was good. In exchange I asked her to do me a small favor. I asked her to purchase me two cases of Goombay Punch, a half case of Nassau Royal, and six bottles of white Henny and bring them to the airport. She agreed. She wanted to see me too: "I'm long overdue for some good lovin, Khris," she said.

I wasn't going to the hotel tomorrow, Thursday, or Friday.

I would only be passing through Freeport. After those three days, I was off for the rest of the month. I suggested she hop over for a weekend. She said that was a wonderful idea. She had a bit of shopping she wanted to do before the month ended.

The good thing about my job as a Flight Attendant is that I work twelve to sixteen days a month; sometimes less if I had a project—a fixer upper—I was working on. Manipulating my flying schedule to fit around what I had to do was easy. I could fly my required hours in the first two weeks, then have the last two weeks of the month off. Then I could schedule my next month's schedule so that I fly the last two weeks, thus giving me a full month off in between.

The pay wasn't all that, but the hours, the insurance and the perks made up for it. It's not like I depended on that income to pay a hefty mortgage and car note. Those two things right there have most of the world living from paycheck to paycheck.

Best of all is the traveling privileges: and not only on the airline that I work for. We get traveling privileges on other airlines; discounts at major resorts, theme parks, rental car companies, even some restaurants. The discounts make traveling fun and luxury accommodations extremely affordable. I had met Paola on one such trip. Last year, some friends and I flew down to Brazil for carnival and she had served us up in First Class cabin. We had hit it off from on the flight. She volunteered to show us around, and even hooked up my boys with several of her friends and coworkers.

I got up and stripped off my sheets...and the sheets in the yellow guest room. I got a load started, then went back upstairs and made the beds. The entire time, I was wondering what I would tell Sonia. Should I invite her over and see if she could hang? Paola did say that she and two of her girlfriends were coming. That could mean that this was going to be a platonic visit. But then again, they are flight attendants. And if they were coming to sunbathe nude, then she might just get hers and not worry about them. Paola's a grown ass woman. She would fuck with them right there sunning their buns. Who knows, they might be down for whatever. Maybe I might get lucky and fuck all three of them. Hmmmm.

With that thought, it was time to call Sonia back. I'd have to get with her later.

I called Sonia.

"What's the word?" she asked.

"She wants to bring a few of her girls up so they can chill by the pool and catch a no-line tan."

Sonia laughed. "You can't possibly always be this honest."

"It must be the truth serum you fed me in the omelet," I said, wondering why I had told her about the no-line tan. I didn't seem to be able to run game on Sonia. I always felt like I had to be truthful with her, no matter if it set me back from getting some. What type of shit is that for a playa? This isn't good.

"So since you're being honest," she drawled sexily, "have you thought about my suggestion...or were you too busy to think about me?"

"You're special, Sonia."

"I don't want to be special. I don't want to be placed in a display case, Khris. I don't want to just be looked at and showed off to your friends."

"It's not like that, Sonia...I don't know what time I'm going to get rid of my guests, but I'll call you later and we'll get together and talk, if you're not busy."

"All right. I'm going to finish handling my business."

"Make that money, baby!" I shot.

"Oh, before you go, don't forget to call your connect at the bank to see if any good foreclosures came in. You had me up all night thinking about getting a house."

"And here I was thinking you spent the entire night thinking about me."

"You may have popped into my mind one or two times, but I can't say that I thought about you all night. I won't lie to you like that."

"Thanks for being brutally honest," I retorted.

She laughed. "I was too busy checking my credit score, personal account balances, and balancing my check book."

"So you're ready?"

"Yeah. I'm sort of organized, so I have all my tax returns, credit card statements, bank account statements, and my investment account statement."

"Cool. What's your credit score?" I asked so that I could pass that information on to my connect.

"780."

"That's good. You'll be able to get about as close to a 3 percent interest rate as possible with that. I can teach you a few tricks that will get you into the exclusive eight hundreds within three months," I added. My score is 820, but I didn't tell her that. I didn't want to seem to be gloating, so I kept it to myself. If she asked, I would tell her. "I'll tell my connect to stick to houses in Coral Springs, and to make sure the price range doesn't carry your monthly payments any higher than fifteen hundred dollars a month including insurance and association fees."

"I can go over that, but that sounds great. Anyhow, I have to get back to packing so I can make this paper. I have to get this stuff to the post before one. I'll call you...no, my bad, you can call me after one, if you can."

"You don't have to be like that. You can call me anytime you want."

"Just don't blow up your shit if you don't answer, right?" She laughed.

I was thinking the same thing. "You crazy! You know that, right?"

"Maybe! Look how quickly I'm getting attached to you. Byyyyye," she sang, and ended the call before I could respond.

My next call was to the bank. I listened to the automated greeting, waited for the appropriate time, then punched in the extension I wanted.

The extension was answered right away. "Destiny Richards."

I started singing Buju Banton's song. "I wanna rule my Destiny..."

"That's why the Fed's got his ass locked up now: he was trying to rule me. You know I can't be ruled," she laughed. "You gon live long. I was just thinking about you."

"You shouldn't be having sexual thoughts at work."

"I didn't start having those thoughts until I saw the foreclosure files in my in box. Some good stuff."

"In the files or in your mind?"

"Both. And you know what that means: You're going to have to satisfy the ones in my mind if you want first crack at what's in these files."

"I'm flying turns for the next three days, but I have the rest of the month off."

"So I can pick my date?"

"Just make sure it's not the date you ovulate. The last thing I want to do is get you pregnant," I ribbed.

"You know we'll have a pretty baby," she laughed, then continued, "nice complexion..."

"That's the problem. Your man would definitely know it wasn't his..."

"My baby could take my color..."

"It's not the color, I was talking about the baby's looks," I shot.

"My man may not be as easy on the eyes to look at as you, but he has nice ways...and he worships the ground I walk on."

"That's what counts right there," I admitted. "I'm just messin with you."

"I'm going to make you pay for that," she shot.

"I'm sure you're concocting something freaky right now," I retorted.

"Anyhow, as much as I'd like to sit and chat, I have work to do. I'll e-mail you the stuff in a bit. They're mostly single family and townhouses. There are two condos that come together as a package deal, also. That may be good for rental. I'll send you the ones from Plantation all the way north to Delray. That'll cover your favorite areas."

"Thanks. I have a friend from back home that's interested in a single family with a dual car garage in the Coral Springs area. Her credit score is 780 and she wants to stick around fifteen a month."

"I don't believe this shit! You want me to help you get one of my competitors into a nice house. Are you insane?"

"Divorce him and marry me," I shot, trying to catch her off guard, "Then you won't have to worry about any competition."

She didn't miss a beat. "Give me until I see you to decide."

"Can't do that. I need to know now. You have thirty-seconds to decide. If it takes you longer than that, then you must love him more than you love me. I can't marry a woman that loves another man more than she loves me. I won't be able to handle the cheating; if she loves another more than me, she will cheat."

"Okay! Okay!" she said, sounding disappointed. "We'll just have to continue living in sin like we've been doing. I'll help you get your girl in a decent house. I'm just happy to see that you're moving on from that spoil-ass young girl you were messing with. What was her name again?"

"Nancy," I stated, knowing that she remembered here name very well: she had a sister by the same name. "And we're..."

"Yeah, that's her name. Same as my sister's," she chuckled, cutting me off. "She's a gorgeous girl, but she sure as hell lowered her standards. That guy she's with now couldn't clean your shoes."

"What guy?" I asked, confused.

"Her new man!" she shot, and rambled on. "I saw them on Sunday when we were at City Place. You should have seen them walking hand in hand like little lovebirds. Psssss You should have seen them in Blue Martini."

Destiny had rattled on so fast that she didn't even hear me trying to protest; trying to get her to slow down; trying to get her to make some sense about what she was saying.

It felt like I had been kicked in the stomach.

It felt like my heart had been clamped in a vice. It felt like I was suffocating.

Nancy? My Nancy? My Nancy walking hand in hand with another man? Destiny must have been mistaken. She must have seen someone that looked like Nancy. It couldn't have been my Nancy. Nancy was with her mom and sick aunt on Sunday...in Palm muthafuckin Beach. Dat lyin, stinkin ass ho! She fucking lied to me. That muthafuckin bitch...

"Hello? Khris?"

I took a deep breath to reel in my anger. I had to calm down. Play it cool. "Yeah, I'm here. Sorry about that, I was just checking an email that came in. I thought it may have been you trying to impress me with your multitasking skills," I chuckled.

"I'm good, but I'm not that good. I'll have it done and to you in five minutes. Be good. And if you can't be good, be careful."

"I will," I replied, ending the call.

I sat there staring at the phone. All kinds of shit were going through my mind. There had to be some mistake on Destiny's part. Couldn't have been Nancy who she saw. Not my Nancy who just called to tell me how much she loved me. Not my Nancy that came and cooked me dinner, then made love to me all nightlong. Not my Nancy who told me that she would do whatever I want to make sure she didn't ever let me down. No! Not my muthafuckin Nancy.

As soon as I had decided to give Nancy the benefit of the doubt, the devil came stirring shit up in my head. The little demon whispered. 'What about those early morning phone calls. Who was blowing up her shit? Wasn't your ass, you was with her? And why didn't she answer the phone when you woke her up? What kind of man wouldn't want to see who the fuck was blowing up his woman shit at three o'clock in the morning on a gat damn week night?

A fuckin weeknight! I bet you if it was your shit getting blown up at that hour of the morning and she had heard it, you woulda had some muthafuckin 'splainin' to do...or you and your phone would have gotten fucked up!'

As quick as that, I wanted to call her ass and confront her. Fuck it! That's exactly what I was going to do. I was going to call her ass right now. I hit speed dial 2, thinking what the hell was I going to ask her. I couldn't just accuse her and cuss her ass out. Would Destiny lie about seeing Nancy in Palm Beach? Why? What would she have to gain from it? Nothing. But Nancy was in Palm Beach on Sunday. Coincidence? Could be. Okay, what if Destiny had seen someone that looked like Nancy? That's possible too.

No, I couldn't call and cuss her ass out yet. There were too many uncertainties: too many other possibilities.

Hell no, it wasn't my Nancy.

I quickly stabbed the 'END' icon right before the call connected. "Fuck it! I'll do some investigating of my own first.

Chapter 19

FLIP MODE

To say my mood was fucked up after that was an understatement. I wanted to hit someone or something, but that wouldn't solve my problem. Instead, I went downstairs, transferred my first load from the washer to the dryer, and set another load to wash. I needed to work off a little of my frustration, so I did a hundred push-ups. It worked up a nice sweat, but it wasn't enough. I did a hundred pull-ups and combination leg raises. That really got the sweat pouring. I did a hundred squats, checked the time, then did a hundred crunches. I felt a little better. Still in a funk, but a little better.

My arms, chest, legs and abs felt like they had been worked. I mixed a protein shake, and drank it as I went upstairs to get ready for my guests.

I was in a funk, but I wasn't going to dress the part. I pulled out a pair of knee length, white linen drawstring shorts, then I dug into Ashley's bag of goodies and pulled out a green Hermes wife-beater that matched my new Hublot Big Bang, then I grabbed the white Nike Air Force 1's with the green alligator Nike logo. There was even a pair Persol sunglasses that had green and Rose gold accents. This girl goes all out when she shops.

I turned on some 'getting ready' music to try and pull me out of the funk as I ran the steamer over my shorts and shirt, but it did little to keep the vile thoughts out of my mind. I shaved, showered and got dressed on autopilot. I saw the alert that I had received the e-mail from Destiny, but I didn't bother to open it.

I had too much other shit on my mind.

I made sure the house was in order, then went out to the summer kitchen and got a bottle of Kalik—our Bahamian brewed beer—from the beverage cooler by the wet bar. I was in a fucked up mode, so I needed an attitude adjustment. I took a healthy swig of the beer, grabbed a bottle of Bacardi Limon and poured a shot into the beer bottle. Holding my thumb over the open mouth, slowly turning the bottle over to mix the contents.

My phone buzzed: Paola. She had texted that they were coming up on the Sunrise station. Good timing, I thought. It was time to leave. Like I said, I was in a fucked up mode, so I took my attitude adjuster with me.

If Paola and her girls weren't already on their way up, I would have cancelled. But it was too late for that now. I wasn't in the entertaining mood. I wasn't even in the mood for sex anymore.

Suddenly I hoped that her girls were stuffy and in a cock-blocking mood. I didn't feel like sucking and fucking anyone's pussy today. "Fuck a piece a pussy today!" I shouted to the passing cars, even though they couldn't hear me.

As I drove east on Sample Road, I thought about pretending to feel sick once I got them settled by the pool. I could leave them down there to work on their no-line tans and I could sequester myself up to my room and figure out what the hell was going on.

That thought got better and better as I turned into the parking lot at the station.

The train wasn't there yet, so I pulled into a spot to wait. I rolled down the windows, navigated the touchscreen and scrolled down the genres until I got to Reggaeton. Daddy Yankee started things off. I cranked up the volume to try to change my mood before the train pulled in. I turned it up some more...not enough to disturb the peace, but enough so that I could feel the rhythm.

I sat there, feeling the music but not hearing it. My mind was elsewhere. I was trying to keep my mind off of what Destiny had told me, but I was failing badly. My mind was replaying every conversation, every memory, every action that I had with Nancy.

I was sifting through every detail looking for some sign...any sign that would make some sense of what was going on. I was searching for signs of deception. Something that I may have missed...

"Fuck!" I yelled, pounding the steering wheel. I shook my head. I didn't need to be here with all this shit on my mind. I opened the door, and sat sideways. I scanned around for a police officer. Didn't see any, so I took a good long swig. Then I heard the train. I wasn't in the mood for this. I needed to be alone with my thoughts. "I een fa dis shit today. Fuck Paola and her friends!" I cursed as the train stopped and the doors opened.

"Damn!" I cursed as Paola and two Brazilian beauties stepped from the train. I took off my sunglasses to get a better look. "Fuck me!" I said, almost dropping the bottle of beer that I had forgotten was in my hands. Exotic. Breathtaking. Paola was fine—a younger, shapelier Eva Mendes, if you can imagine that. But gaaaaaad damn! The other two girls were even finer than she was. Instead of her being a ten, they made her look like a nine at best. They had her in height, looks, and build. Even with that being the case, the three of them were fucking gorgeous. Abso-fuckin-lutely stunning!

Paola spotted me and pointed me out to her friends. They all waved and started walking over. They exuded femininity. They exuded sex appeal. Words couldn't describe how they looked. I always bullshit about some women being so damn fine that they could raise the dead, but I'd bet money that these three could do it: fitted shorts, sexy tops, high sandals, big designer handbags, and designer sunglasses—all tasteful, not trashy or slutty.

I noticed the three of them had Starbucks coffee containers in their hands. I sure as hell knew better than that. These young ladies were Flight Attendants. They were not drinking coffee. Something else was in those containers.

When they were near enough to hear the Reggaeton, they started winding and dancing as they came toward me. Whistles, cheers, catcalls, and applause came from every direction. They were indeed head turners. And they weren't stuffy. They waved and blew kisses to the guys. They were in the mood to party. Suddenly, so was I.

I stood up and walked around to the other side of the Range. I forgot all about Destiny and Nancy. I forgot all about my plan to go upstairs and ignore them. I changed my mind about not wanting to suck or fuck anything. I wanted to suck and fuck all three of them. I was ready to call in sick tomorrow.

Suddenly, questions just started running through my mind.

Not those questions. Other questions. Questions like: If two girls were considered doubling your pleasure and having twice as much fun, did three girls mean that it would be thrice as nice...and would I have to use my dick, fingers, toes and tongue? How many times do I think I'll be able to get them all to cum before we're all satisfied and done?

I had my irresistible thousand watts smile on my face by the time Paola walked into my arms. She French kissed me like I was her long lost husband. Her girls, who were flanking her on either side, hooted and cheered us on. The three of them smelled delightful.

If I could bottle that scent and sell it, no woman would ever complain about not being able to get her husband hot and bothered. I was right about the coffee. Paola's tongue was cold and sweet. It wasn't coffee in those containers. No Starbucks product at all. It was more of the sweet, fruity, alcoholic variety.

After she set my tongue free, she finally spoke. "Wow! I needed that," she cooed. "Khris, I would like you to meet Daniela and Tara. Girls, meet Khris. Don't be shy. He won't bite unless you tell him to," she giggled, stepping aside.

"Hello," they both chimed, eying me from head to toe.

"Hello, Daniela," I said, hugging her as she stepped into me.

"Hi, Khrrrris," she sang, rolling the 'R' in a sweet, sultry tone. She held me, pressed her DD's against my chest as she kissed me full on the lips, sliding the tip of her tongue over my lips.

Talk about not being shy. My God! They were setting the tone. They weren't stuffy. And, they damn sure weren't going to be cock-blockers.

"Can I have one of those, supersized, like Paola's, extra frisky tongue, please?" Tara said, winking.

"With pleasure, Tara," I said, embracing her and giving her exactly what she asked for.

No bullshitting. They were quite a team. Paola's kiss had stirred me and left me in a sort of semi hard state. Daniela stiffened me up. Tara had me throbbing. Today was going to be a great day.

Nah. Fuck dat! Today was going to be a 'Sexsational' day!

By the time we loaded ourselves into the Range, they had already made it clear that it was going to be a three on one date. They were frisky, and the conversation was raunchy. By then, I was down for whatever.

As much as I wanted to rush them back to my place to get this party jumpin, I had to make one little stop at the Honda dealership. They didn't mind. They had drinks and music, so they were good.

I turned into the dealership's lot and parked directly in front of the building. "I'll be right back. This shouldn't take but a minute."

Tara, who was sitting directly behind me, asked, "Are you ashamed of being seen with us?"

I turned around to see if she was serious. She had a lewd look on her face. "Ashamed to be seen with y'all? Are you crazy?" I asked, shaking my head. "Please tell me you're joking?"

"Well, why are you trying to leave us sitting behind these tinted windows out here in the parking lot?" Daniela piped up, using the tip of her tongue to play with the straw sticking from her drink container.

In a rebellious tone, Paola said, "We're coming in with you!" She reached over, turned off the engine, then pulled the keys out and dropped them in my lap, intentionally on my dick.

"I have no problem being the envy of every man in the building or out in the parking lot," I said, opening my door. "Let's go, ladies."

It's amazing how beautiful women can disrupt even the simplest of acts. People—men and women—lost their focus and forgot what they were saying or doing. They forgot to take a breath. They stopped walking. Some openly gawked.

The bad thing about this dealership was that we had to traverse through the showroom, past the service center, the cashiers, even the bathrooms, to get to the parts department.

All work ceased.

People stopped what they were doing to marvel at the exotic specimens as we gracefully passed by. It must have looked like we were models there for a photo shoot. I saw women staring, but I got the feeling that they weren't eyeballing me. I mean I wasn't chopped liver, but hey, women check out other women more than we men do. Very rarely it's sexual, though. Women are always sizing each other up or looking for ways to improve their own image and style.

They had the parts clerk so flustered that he brought me back a box of brake pads instead of the master cylinder that he had went for. When he did bring out the right part, he called his manager over and asked if he could give us a discount. We got a ten percent discount just because Daniela leaned over the counter, lightly stroked the manager's forearm, and said please. You had to hear the way she said it; see the way she stroked him ever so gently. The man actually closed his eyes and moaned. He might have bust a nut in his pants. It was crazy.

Sonia called as we wove our way back through the showroom.

She was on her way to make a rush delivery to a salon down in Southwest Miami. I was happy. Things like that always happened to playas: shit just works itself out in our favor. Now she wouldn't be able to join us even if I wanted her to. So of course, I pretended to be disappointed that she couldn't come. She laughed, so I don't know if she fell for my game. I told her about speaking to my connect and receiving the files, even though I hadn't had a chance to go over them yet. That got her excited. She told me she would call me later, and was off to make her paper.

I liked that shit. She was all about her business. With Nancy fucking around, Sonia was gaining ground. I smiled and put away my phone.

I glanced ahead of me and saw the sweet, rhythmic switching of three juicy looking asses. My dick stirred and my mouth watered: I wanted to taste them. I wanted to see if they tasted as sweet as they looked. Can I ever give up all this for one woman? I started laughing out loud. The three of them looked back to see what I was laughing at. All I did was lick my lips and they started laughing too. Hmmph, if they only knew what I was thinking.

Apparently, they were thinking one step ahead of me. I had barely pulled out of the dealership's lot when they started conversing among themselves in their native tongue. I was proficient, not fluent. I barely understood what they were saying, but it was sufficient for me to know everything was all-good. That shit sounded sexy as fuck. My dick got hard just from listening to them.

Tara's hands came around my seat and started caressing my chest and washboard abs. Daniela scooted forward, reached between the seats and started caressing my right thigh. Paola was giggling.

I was turned the fuck on.

Paola unfastened her seat belt, as Daniela's hand tugged at my drawstring. Paola leaned toward me and took over from Daniela. She got her hands down into my pants and freed me from the confines of my underwear.

I heard approving moans as Tara and Daniela got a good look at my dick. I couldn't help but admire how tall and firm my dick stood in Paola's soft hands. It was impressive by nature. They all thought so, too.

I glanced over at Paola, and she smiled and wet her lips. "Go for it, or let me get up there," Tara cheered from the backseat.

"No, you're going last," Paola, said, lowering her sweet mouth over my bulging head. Her agile tongue licked and flicked skillfully over my sensitive head. I wanted to close my eyes, but I dared not. I felt the trickle of saliva drip onto my head. I felt giddy as she took me into her cool, sweet mouth. She had pieces of crushed ice in her mouth and it felt spectacular. I was floating. Not only because of the incredible head I was receiving, but also from the sprightly cheers that she was receiving from her girls. Paola was putting on a show for them. I wanted to get that first nut out the way, but then again, I wasn't ready to come. I wanted them to know they would have to work hard to get me to come. Three of them! There was damn sure plenty work to be done.

They didn't want me to come yet, either. Paola did her thing for several minutes, then Daniela, said, "Slide in the back and give someone else a chance. Come on!"

Paola raised her head and smiled at me. Tara reached her left hand along my door and stroked me as Paola climbed between the seats and jumped in the back. Daniela somehow managed squeeze her way into the front and took over. Her mouth was warm and deep like a pussy. She took me all in. And she was a noisemaker. She made those guttural sounds as she sucked and puckered her cheeks to add that suction. I started humping up into her mouth. I was ready to knock out a molar. I was in the zone now. There would be no coming anytime soon. Daniela did her thing, and then it was Tara's turn. Thank God for all the red lights because I damn sure would have crashed if it weren't for the constant stopping and going. I was almost home, thank God. All I had to do was hold out for about three more minutes. This shit was sweet, but I wasn't for all this suckin, I was ready for some fuckin.

I should have known from the way Tara rolled her tongue when she said Khris that she was going to be the most talented of the bunch. They probably knew too. That's why they made her go last. Tara's tongue was something special. She did some things with her tongue that made me want to call every one of my boys and have him experience her head. She was the best. No matter how I tried to hold on, Tara would drive my nut to the base of my shaft, let it recede, then build it up again. It was as if she was telling me that she had control over when I came, not me. She kept me teetering until I stopped in my driveway.

Paola jumped out and came around to my door. She opened the door and got there right in time. Tara took the tongue tactics to another level.

I gripped her head and humped up into her descending lips as her tongue continued to work its incredible magic. The pressure in my balls built up. My stomach muscles tightened. I squeezed my perineum muscles to try to prolong my ejaculation.

Tara felt me do it. She knew what I was doing. But she had a trick for my ass. A countermeasure. A delightful trick too. My nut rose. It rose with more intensity in response to what she was doing. There was no stopping this nut. She sucked and deep throated me until the first load shot down the back of her throat. She got the second shot on her tongue. She moved her head, and Paola was there to get the next two shots and everything that spilled out after. Paola slurped and suctioned out every last drop.

I had my eyes opened, hands fondling breasts and legs in front and back. I fought to keep my eyes opened so that I could watch as Tara share the last shot that she had collected in her mouth with Daniela. Then, they kissed. That shit was spectacular. I couldn't wait to get them inside...

Fuck! My neighbors, I thought, looking around frantically.

None of the houses were as far back as mine, so no one could see from indoors unless they were specifically being nosey, but, someone could have been out or passing by.

The sound of a car made me look toward the street. I looked up in time to see a car pass the entrance of my driveway. My heart stopped. It was a silver Lexus, I was sure of it. But it drove by so quickly that I wasn't able to tell if it was an IS or a GS.

Was it Nancy? Did she get off early and came to surprise me again? Did I just get caught with my dick in two mouths?

My phone rang: Nancy.

CHAPTER 20

A SEXSATIONAL DAY

If my dick wasn't already getting soft, it would have definitely went lip when I saw Nancy's face flash across my phone's screen.

Paola signaled for Tara and Daniela to keep quiet and get their stuff. I hit the button on the rear view mirror and the garage door began rolling up. I pressed the button on my key fob and heard the house alarm disarm.

I answered as Paola led them inside. "Talk to me, I'll talk back," I said as soon as I answered.

"You miss me?" she asked.

I couldn't detect what kind of mood she was in. I couldn't hear if she was driving or sitting at her desk. I had to play it safe. "Is that a trick question?"

"You might have been too busy to miss me."

"Too busy doing what?" I asked, trying to bait her.

"Whatever it is you do when I'm not around."

What the fuck did she mean by that. I decided to try another route. "Why don't you come and do what you do when you're here with me?"

"I don't want to interrupt what you have planned for today. I know you're flying for the next three days."

Interrupt what I have planned for today? That was her! She saw me with Paola's head in my lap. No. She's too calm to have seen that. "You could help me do it, if you were here," I said, fishing again.

"You won't be able to do it if I were there."

"What do you mean? What can't I do with you here?"

"Why are you messing with my head, Khris? I called you because I need to talk to you about something."

"Something like what?"

"I can't talk about it on the phone..."

So that was her dropping by to talk to me. I was caught for sure.

"...We have to talk face to face. I-I..."

"What?"

"I'll talk to you later. I really can't talk now. I have to hurry back. I'll call you tonight."

"Okay."

"Bye," she said, interrupting me, then ending the call.

Damn. She didn't tell me she love me. Yep! She caught my ass. First time I've been caught. I never would have expected her to be this calm if she caught me. I at least expected her to go off. By her not going off, that meant that the bitch don't love me. How could she? She was so cool: it was like she didn't care if I cheated. What woman doesn't care if their man cheated? A bitch that's cheating too, that's who. A bitch that cares more about the new man, than the old man. Fuck Nancy! Da ho can kiss my ass. I don't give a fuck bout her cheating ass, either. There's plenty more women out there. In fact, there are three in my house right now.

I got out the Range and headed inside, closing the garage door behind me. I could hear the girls out by the pool pulling the loungers into the sun. They didn't waste any time. The three of them were already butt-booty naked.

Even while I stood inside the family room admiring them, I thought about Nancy catching me. Was she going to come back?

I walked back to the garage and hit the lock button for the garage door opener. That would block her from using her remote to open the garage door. Next, I went to the front door and put on the night latch. Now she couldn't come through there, either. I walked around to the east side of the yard and made sure the side gate of the privacy fence was locked. There would be no more surprises from Nancy. That shit was over.

Paola had seen to turning on the music, and Tara was mixing the drinks. Daniela danced over to me, cutting off my route. She grabbed my hands and started dancing provocatively. Remember, she was naked as the day she was born. Those DD's were money well spent.

"Come over here, let me help you relax and get out of these clothes," she sang with her sweet accent.

As much as I was upset and confused about Nancy's cheating and my getting caught, a waist winding, hip-shaking, breast-swinging Brazilian beauty was enough to get my dick hard again.

I let her lead me over to a lounger. I sat where she instructed, and she gave me a lap dance while taking off my wife beater.

Paola danced over and held a glass to my lips. I took a drink.

It was sweet and fruity. She removed the glass from my lips, dipped her finger into the drink, and seductively smeared it on her caramel areolas and perky nipples. Then she breast-fed me.

My right hand caressed her ass, then slid between her legs, parting her blossoming petals. She placed one leg on the edge of the lounger, giving me more of herself. My fingers massaged her petals, then dipped into her. I fingered her good, paying extra attention to her G spot and stroking her clit with my thumb, all while biting gently on her hardened, teardrop nipples the way I remembered she liked.

Daniela raised her heat up off of me enough to work my pants down below my knees. Tara took off my sneakers and socks, and finished removing my pants. I was naked before I knew it. I couldn't see what was going on below my waist: Paola's breasts were getting the full attention of my eyes, mouth, and nose, but I felt something warm and tingly squirt onto my dick and balls. Four hands massaged and stroked my erection and balls. I felt Daniela's weight shift. Then I felt two ripe nipples on my dick. She was teasing me. Daniela wrapped those two full DD's around my dick and started stroking up and down. Each time my head popped up through the top of her cleavage, her tongue met it.

I heard my phone vibrate. I ignored it.

Daniela stopped breast fucking me. I was fingering Paola toward ecstasy as I sucked and nibbled on her breasts. I felt the condom roll down my shaft. As soon as it hit the base, Daniela straddled me, gently slid down my pole, and started riding me real good. Where was Tara?

Ah! My toes answered that question for me. The cool liquid that was on my dick and balls was now being squirted onto my toes. I thought I was going to get a foot massage. Surprise, surprise! Tara mounted my toes. She was fucking my toes. I did what I could to assist her. I wiggled my toes and her body responded pleasurably.

We licked and sucked, stroked and poked, spanked and bit,

teased and pleased until euphoria was our regular playground. I flipped; twisted, lifted, spun around, and spun over...any and all positions I could think of, I tried putting their asses in. They took it every which way I gave it. All those questions I had earlier got answered. I used my mouth, tongue, fingers and toes to assist their orgasms.

They swapped places and positions numerous times until each had been sucked and fucked in their favorite positions.

The good wood didn't let me down. It took them where they wanted to go every time: the land of milk and honey. Yes, they did taste as sweet as they looked. And, they felt even better.

It took almost an hour for everyone to be satisfied. Daniela was the first to take a cold shower and jump into the hot tub.

She came faster and had more orgasms out of the three. Tara stayed with Paola and me a little longer. She loved the reverse cowgirl. She rode herself weak, and literally fell off my dick after she came. Paola and I got our last orgasm together, after which we took a shower and relaxed in the Jacuzzi.

After getting out the Jacuzzi, they plied on the sun tan lotion and laid out in the sun to work on their no-line tan. I didn't need any sun, so I went inside. I folded up the linen that I had washed earlier, put them in their respective closets, then got my laptop and took it out to the patio: the covered patio.

I fired up my laptop, but before checking my e-mails, I listened to my messages. The first was from Nancy:

"Hey baby, I had to rush off the phone because my boss was coming out of her office. I guess you're getting your rest, but I just wanted to say I love you. I didn't get a chance before I hung up. I'll call you later. Love you."

So I hadn't been caught. It hadn't been her Lexus. And here I was cussing her ass out. Fuck dat! She still deserved to get cussed out because she cheated. Well, I wasn't too sure about that either, was I?

The next message was from Keisha:

"Hey! Mi dehya. Call me. Mek we link up. Mi need mi ting. Lickle more."

I smiled, a ghetto girl with the wickedest slam. Keisha's

hardcore Jamaican, not uptown Jamaican. She's straight ghetto. She's cute and has a slammin-ass body, but she's not the kind of girl you take out. She opens her mouth one time, and she'll embarrass your ass. But—and this is a big but—she can fuck with the best of them. I've had better pussy, but Keisha knew how to work that pussy. She has the windin skill, and she could take a dick. You push it; she takes it and threw the pussy back harder. She's the kind of girl you call when you want to punish some pussy. You don't call her if you want to make love. She'll fight if you go around her with that soft shit. I'll call her on the weekend or something. She's been gone for damn near a month.

The last message was from Sonia. "Khris, I was calling to find out if you would like to be my escort on Friday night. It's an all white party, cruise slash fashion show slash hair show. One of my customers is having it. The huge order of hair that I was delivering is for the show. It's on a private yacht, so it should be nice. Call me back and let me know. Thanks."

All white party on a private yacht. That sounds like my kind of party. I didn't call Sonia right back because I didn't want her to ask me what I was doing or anything like that. I wanted to go through the properties that Destiny had sent me first. I opened the e-mail and skimmed through the properties.

Some time while I was reviewing the properties, I dozed off.

An ice-cold tongue teasing my lips awakened me. My eyes shot open. It was Tara.

She smiled. "I was sent to wake you," she said, kissing me again.

This time I kissed her back. Her lips parted and I gave her my tongue. Our tongues danced together like the devil. It was a hot kiss. She pulled away. "You keep kissing me like that, I'm going to want some more of this," she said, grabbing my dick.

"You're welcomed to some more."

"I thought we wore you out," she smiled, going down on me.

I closed my eyes as she took me into her mouth. She was blessed with a gifted tongue. She had me floating toward the heavens.

"I should have known," Paola said, causing my eyes to pop open about a minute later.

Tara didn't stop. I gazed over at Paola standing in the opened French doors. She was wearing a big T-shirt. What time was it, I wondered. Then I realized that the sun was already behind the trees that lined the western side of my property. I must have been asleep for three or four hours.

"Hurry up, the pasta is going on the stove soon," Paola shouted as she disappeared back inside.

Tara held up a hand in acknowledgement.

Tara was good, but I had enough suckin for one day. If I were going to get another nut, I would get it my way. I slid my hand along her cheek and raised her head, making her look at me. "Let me take care of you. I'm not going to come that way."

She smiled. She wanted some more dick. I stood up as she raced over to where they had the condoms and the lubricant. She ripped it open and unrolled it on my dick. She squirted some of the lubricant on the condom, then she climbed on the lounger and got on all fours. She wanted it doggy style.

As I got behind her, she reached back with the bottle of lubricant and squirted some in the cleft between her ass cheeks. She used her fingers to spread it around and press at her tight opening. She pressed against it, eventually letting her finger slide in. She gasped loudly. In and out, her finger slid as she squirted more lubrication until she was well lubed. Then she slid in another finger, stretching herself for what was to come.

She wanted me to fuck her in the ass. I've never had anal sex before. I liked pussy and mouth...never really penetrated any ass except with my fingers, but this seems to be what women were craving nowadays. The way she dipped her finger in and out of her puckered asshole made up my mind for me. Gotta start some time. What I once considered taboo—forbidden—suddenly seemed right. If I didn't like it, this would be the first and last time.

Tara stroked my dick, teased her wet lips, plunged me into her pussy a couple of times, then brought me up to her slick opening. She squeezed my head between her tight cheeks until it was ready to stretch her open. I let her control the entrance: I thought I might rip something if I did it. It was still too tight for me to get in. I kept still;

let her ease back onto it. When my head breached her entrance, her legs spasmed. I was barely in her, but it felt like I was forcing myself into her. She sucked in air noisily and her body trembled as she eased back further onto my dick.

I watched her asshole stretch to accommodate my girth. It was amazingly tight. It felt painfully tight. It was indeed a forbidden pleasure. My eyes shut tightly as the dark pleasure overwhelmed me.

Her tightness engulfed me. When she had me all in, she started grinding her hips, switching to an easy back and forth rhythm while making the tiniest of circles with her waist.

I started assisting; giving her a nice, slow grind. I had to get use to the feeling. It was different. Definitely different.

Her pace increased with her moans, and before I knew it, she was fucking the hell out of my dick and screaming, "Spank me!"

I spanked her and started pounding her harder and faster. Long, punishing strokes. I was plunging deep into her bowels.

"Faster! Harder!" she yelled between each stroke and spank.

I was spanking her so hard, her ass turned beet red. I wrapped her straight black hair around my fist and pulled back as I rammed in and out of her. I spanked her ass while she fingered her pussy and strummed her clit. Her body belonged to me. I could feel every quake, every quiver, as I stroked harder and deeper into her tightness.

She started screaming so loud; she brought Daniela and Paola out to see what was going in.

"Fuck her, Khris," Daniela shouted, goading me on.

"Fuck her ass real good," Paola said. "I sent her out here to wake you, but no, she wanted to get fucked. Fuck her harder! Beat her ass like she stole something!"

With Paola and Daniela chanting and cheering me on, I rode Tara's ass until she exploded. Her knees buckled and she fell onto her stomach. I held on, straddled her ass and the lounger and continued to pump my dick in and out of her tight ass. I pumped through her orgasm, but I still wasn't ready to cum. I might have been all cummed out.

Tara was, but Daniela wanted a stroke more, too. She came over with a warm towel and a fresh condom. Tara squirted Daniela's asshole as Daniela cleaned me and unrolled a fresh condom onto my dick. Daniela didn't want it doggy style. She wanted me on top.

She laid on her back, raised her legs up and let Tara tease, then guide my dick into her asshole. Daniela's ass was just as tight. I pounded into her as Tara sucked her breast, fingered her pussy, and strummed her clit. It didn't take her long before she was screaming in ecstasy.

I still wasn't ready to come.

Paola came over with her own rubber. She cleaned me off and put on the condom. "I'll make him come," she said to a panting Daniela. Come and sit over here, Khris."

I followed her and sat. Paola straddled me in the chair. She kissed me hard as she let me slide into her hot, wet pussy. With one hand on the back of the chair, she raised her right leg and placed it over my shoulder without either of us missing a stroke.

The angle and penetration depth changed giving me a different sensation. It felt like a different pussy. She stroked me like that for a minute before she brought her left leg up and over shoulder, crossing her ankles in the air behind my head.

My arms were on either side supporting her writhing ass while the back of her thighs flapped against my midsection and chest.

I cupped her ass and used my fingers to open and close her cheeks in rhythm to our stroking. As she started getting closer to ecstasy, I started lifting her up and down as she grind me in small circular strokes. Then she let go of the back of the chair and leaned back. I felt the top front portion of her pussy rub against my head. Every stroke had me rubbing against her soft spot. She was bucking and stroking me with all that she had. She was dying many little deaths with each stroke to her g-spot. My pace quickened: the downward pressure on my dick felt weird but absolutely fucking fantastic at the same time.

My toes started curling as my pressure built. My pace grew to match hers. I started giving her the jackhammer and mixed in the random stutter stroke that never failed to drive women over the edge.

She started begging me to come with her, first in English, then in Spanish.

The Spanish got me.

Her legs locked around my neck as her body seized up on her. She couldn't move. She couldn't stop the violent quakes that wracked her body. I did nothing to help her stop them. In fact, I was thrusting harder and faster.

It felt too fucking good.

My head swelled.

It felt fucking wonderful. I savored every gasp. Every sigh. I wanted to go deeper into her. I closed my eyes and turned my face to the heavens. My balls felt like they were going to explode. I strained and grunted with each and every stroke. I fought to maintain control. My dick pulsed. The pressure built up exponentially with each stroke. A few deep strokes later, I exploded into her. I shot load after load into her. Paola's body tensed with each shot. I continued stroking her until the two of us slowed to a snail's pace, eventually stopping as we became too exhausted to move anymore.

Daniela and Tara had to come and help Paola up and off of my dick. Juices spilled and drained everywhere. We were both soaked in sexual fluids.

"God, that felt fucking fantastic," I whispered out of breath as she slid off my dick. I looked down to make sure grab the base of the condom and saw why it had felt so fucking fantastic: the entire top portion of the condom was torn and hanging to one side. Fuck!

"Paola," I managed to get out. I got her attention. "Look," I said, pointing to the torn rubber.

I saw a fleeting look of panic in her eyes. Just as quickly as it had appeared, it disappeared.

Fuck! I hope she's on the pill, I thought, removing the remnants of what was supposed to be my protection. The last thing I need is for her to get pregnant.

CHAPTER 21

<u>WOMEN</u>

The next two days of flying went by in a blur. I had agreed to be Sonia's escort to the all white party—which was tomorrow night—and we had agreed to go and check out some of the foreclosed properties that were on the list on Saturday and Sunday.

Nancy and I had been playing telephone love all week. She had been putting in some late nights helping her boss with a big case that she had coming up. Nancy still hadn't gotten around to telling me whatever it was that she wanted to talk to me about, and I still hadn't figured out how to find out if it was her holding hands like teenage lovebirds up in Palm Beach last Sunday.

I had gotten S's stuff yesterday. They were in the back of the Range. On my way home yesterday, he wasn't in place, so he told me not to take them by his shop: he didn't want to have to kill any of his employees.

He was at his shop now, so that was exactly where I was heading. My phone rang as I drove out of the employee lot: Yasmine.

"Talk to me and I'll talk back," I answered.

"You back in town?"

"I sure am. How can I be of service?"

"Your mother is coming over tomorrow."

"My mother? She's your mother too. What time tomorrow she supposed to be coming, because I have an early morning turn. I won't be back in until two."

"I think her flight gets here at eleven."

"I'll have to leave the Range with you. You can pick her up, then get me at two."

"No can do. I have a test tomorrow morning and I don't get out until noon."

"What about Nishka?"

"That's the one class that we have together this semester, and she has a lunch date after we get out."

"Damn! Why mommy een try to get on a later flight?"

"She said that's the only flight that still had a seat available."

"Damn! Who Nishka have a date with?" I asked, just realizing what Yasmine had said.

"Dis cute guy from our class."

"How come I haven't heard about him or met him?"

"Stay out of it. Just leave my friend alone."

"Whatever," I snapped. "I'll call you back."

"Mommy wants you to call her. I'm going back to study, so call me back later and let me know what y'all ga do."

"Cool."

"Luv ya."

"Luv ya, too."

I could drop the trip in the morning and pick her up myself, or I could park at the terminal and tell her where I hide the keys. She don't like to drive over here, but...

My phone rang. I was pulled out of my thoughts. I glanced at the caller ID: Sonia.

"Talk to me and I'll talk back."

"You so damn crazy," she laughed.

"What's up? You back in one piece?"

"Mmmm-hmmm. Just got in. I'm heading to drop off S's liquor and get my ride cleaned."

"Tell him I said wass up."

"I will."

"What are you doing after that?"

"Heading to the crib. I've got to call my mom. Apparently she's coming over in the morning."

"Aren't you flying?"

"Suppose to be. Yasmine and Nishka both have tests in the morning, so they can't get her. I may call and have them replace me on the trip."

"You want me to get her for you? What time is she getting in?"

"Are you serious?"

"Yeah. I'll pick her up if you need me to."

"She's getting in around eleven."

"What time does your sisters get out of their exam?"

"Noon."

"That'll work. You can drive my car to work. I'll keep the Range. I get my mani and pedi done at nine, so I'll be done in time to pick up your mom. I can pick up Yasmine and Nishka after their exam and they can drop me to get my hair done. You can pick me up from the salon when you come in. I should be done by two or two thirty."

"That might work. Let me hit up my old girl and I'll call you back." I ended the call, and called my mother at work. I punched in her personal extension.

"Janet Harrison?" she chimed in her smooth, executive voice.

"Hello, Mother Dearest," I chimed right back at her.

"Are you flying tomorrow?" she asked without even a hello, and dropping the executive voice.

"Fine time for you to ask now that you already purchased your ticket," I said back, being a smart aleck.

"It was the only flight I could get on, and I want to catch Macy's One Day Sale on Saturday."

"That's what you coming for?"

"No," she laughed. "I'm coming to see y'all. What, you don't want to see your mother?"

"Of course I do. But, you know you should have said that before the 'catching the Macy's One Day Sale,' right?"

We both laughed.

"My flight's getting in at eleven oh five. You gonna pick me up?"

"I'm flying at five a.m. I don't get back until two."

"So who's going to pick me up? You know Yasmine and Nishka have tests tomorrow?"

"I've heard. I can park over at the terminal and tell you where I hide the key."

"I'll sit in the airport and wait until you get in. That's only a few hours."

"No," I laughed. "I'll have someone pick you up."

"Not your stuck up lil girlfriend, eh?"

"Nah. She's working," I chuckled. This should be fun. "I'm going to send Sonia."

"Who Sonia? You mean Stephanie's boyfriend lil sister?"

"Yes. That would be her."

"What does your little girlfriend have to say about that?"

"She doesn't know about that."

"Does Sonia know about her'!"

"Yes."

"And she's alright with that?"

"She's trying to take her place. To be honest, she isn't stressing."

"And?"

"And, what?"

"What are you going to do?"

"We're taking it easy for now. We're just friends," I chuckled, then don't know why I said, "Sonia's too nice of a woman for me to take advantage of like I do Nancy."

"What? Are you okay? Is this my son that I'm talking to? How many hours did I spend in labor with you? What time were you born?"

"Stop playing, Mother. This is me."

"This sounds serious."

I ignored that. "Oh, just so you don't be surprised, she's spending the weekend over," I said, playing the role of devil's advocate. I just wanted to see what she would say.

"Spending the weekend? Doesn't Nancy have a key to your house?"

"Yes."

"This is serious. I guess I have to be on my best behavior, then. At least she's not like Nancy. That lil girl rarely shows her face when I'm there."

"That's what I'm relying on. But take it easy on Nancy, Mom. She's a sweet girl."

"The only reason why I put up with her is because I know you cheatin left, right, and center on her. So what my future daughter in law drivin, so I can know what to look for?"

"She's not your future anything," I said.

"I'm not getting any younger, you know."

"She'll be in the Range, so you'll be able to spot her easily. Once she picks you up, she'll go and pick up Yas—Nishka has a lunch date—then y'all can drop her off at the hairdresser. I'll pick her up when I get in."

"So what you gonna be drivin if we have your truck."

"Her Benz."

"Benz? What does she do for a living?"

"You can ask her tomorrow," I said. "Write down her cell number so you can call her when you land."

I gave mother Sonia's cell number. She seemed to like the idea of me finding someone to replace Nancy. Nancy was just misunderstood. Honestly, it didn't matter if they liked her: I liked her. I liked Nancy. No one else needed to. It might make life a little bit easier if my mother and sister got along with my wife and children...What the hell? Where did that come from? That's just like my mother to be planting some shit in people's head.

I called Yasmine and told her the plan. She was cool with it, too."

I called Sonia back. "She's good with you picking her up. I gave her your cell number, so she'll call when she get in and you can tell her where to meet you. I might as well warn you now, she's going to question you to death: be all up in your business."

"I'll be fine," Sonia said nonchalantly.

"You can't help but be fine," I retorted.

"Ain't like you trying to do anything with all this fineness."

"There you go again."

She laughed. "You want me to cook you dinner?"

"Your place or mine?"

"Your place," she said quickly.

From her tone, I knew what it was. "Still afraid he's going to pop up?"

"He's been blowing up my phone and leaving all kinds of crazy messages. I don't even leave my car outside the garage anymore. I don't trust him."

"You may as well pack for the weekend and come and crash with us. I already told my mother that you were spending the weekend."

"And why did you tell her that?"

"Just to pull her leg and see what she would say."

"Oh, you was testing the waters," she giggled wickedly.

I knew her mind was reeling.

"What about your woman. She's not coming over?"

"Not when she finds out my mom's there."

"Your woman doesn't like your mother?"

"She likes my mother, but, my mother can be all up in your business sometimes. And, she's not used to that. Nancy's..."

"So, Nancy's her name," Sonia chuckled.

"Yes. Nancy is sort of a private person."

"Private? She has secrets," Sonia shot.

"We all have secrets," I said, in Nancy's defense.

"I don't. You can answer my phone. You can check my call logs, my e-mail..."

"Yeah, you would like that, wouldn't you? That would give you the right to do the same thing to me."

"Only those with something to hide don't let their woman or man answer their phone, or be afraid to answer their phone when they're with their woman or man. That's one good thing I like about you, you always answer your phone, even if you talk in codes." She laughed.

Was she talking about Nancy? No, she didn't know anything about Nancy. We never discussed Nancy. After the first time I told her I wasn't going to help her by giving her any information about the woman she wanted to replace, she never asked anything more.

I guess she was just generalizing about people that liked their privacy. I don't allow anyone besides Yasmine and Nishka to answer my phone, and they rarely do that. I can't allow anyone else to answer my phone because they might say the wrong thing...and, I do have something to hide: numerous things to hide.

"Back to the subject at hand. Mom is going to be all up in your business, so be careful what you tell her."

"You aren't worried about what she might tell me?"

"You already know the truth from me."

"No, I don't!"

"What haven't I been truthful to you about?"

"Me! You haven't been truthful about how you feel about me."

"I've told you that you're special."

"That's not good enough. I want you to tell me more."

"I'll tell you more when we're basking in the afterglow," I teased.

"I don see I ga have to take what I want...with your mama and your sisters in the house so you can't run or scream," she stated.

"I honestly believe you'll do some shit like that," I laughed.

"I'll pack and meet you home in an hour or so."

Home, she says. "An hour?"

"See, an hour seems too long, huh? You want to meet me home when you get there, huh, baby? You want to know that there's a sweet treat home waiting for you to arrive, huh?" She laughed deviously.

She used home again. Then she had the nerve to use my own words against me. This girl is too much. "Okay, smart ass. Remember the last time those words were spoken, you had to drive on by."

"That's why you're going to call and tell your lil woman that you're flying early in the mornin and that your mother is comin over for the weekend. That aught to keep her away."

"You got it all figured out, huh'?"

"I sure do," she sang confidently. "Oh, by the way, I'll bring you a free bottle of cologne. They're selling like hot cakes."

"You sure you want to bring me a cologne that makes me irresistible to women to wear on the cruise tomorrow night."

"You'll be going there with me, and you'll be returning home with me, so I don't mind being the bitch that all the women love to hate."

"Confidence or cockiness'?" I asked.

"I am whatever you need at any particular time. Taking you around a bunch of horny, money-hungry women, I think I need to be a little more on the cocky side. They'll know not to fuck with you unless a bitch knows how to swim."

"I don't believe you'll fight for me," I said, boosting her on. Hearing her talk like that was turning me on. She's just too damn fine to sound so vicious.

"No, Khris, I won't be fighting for you: I'll be fighting because a bitch had the nerve to disrespect me. If you want to leave all that I have to offer for someone that only looks good at the moment, then that would be your loss."

"You can't lose what you never had," I replied, trying to stir her up some more.

"Well, you better do something about that soon. Real soon."

"Or what?"

"I'll take it! Somehow, I get the feeling that you think I wouldn't take it. Keep playin with me: you'll see."

"Just for your mouth being so damn hard, you're gonna have to take this, because I een offerin it."

"Oh! Hold on. Let me get this straight. If I want it, I'ma have to take it?"

"That's what I said. I didn't stutter."

Sonia sounded excited. "Okay. Now if I take it, that doesn't count, right?"

"Doesn't count? What do you mean by that?"

"If I take it, then it doesn't mean that I am going to be on your sweetheart team. It can't count against me being your woman one day if that's what I decide I want to be."

"If you decide?"

"I didn't stutter. If the sex isn't all that I need it to be, then why would I want to have a relationship with a man that can't satisfy me sexually? It'll cause me to cheat, and at this point in my life, I have no intentions on cheating. So?"

"So, what?"

"Tell me if I take it, it won't count."

"How can I tell you that when you're going to take it from me, then judge my skills to determine if we have a future together?"

"I know how to handle a good tool."

"Yeah, but a good tool in your hands is not the same as a good tool in my hands."

"You're right! My hands are softer, so I'll get you to cum quicker," she chimed.

"You're full of jokes, aren't you?"

"That was a good one! You have to admit it."

"It was cute...in a corny sort of way."

"Anyhow, since you want to meet me home when you get there, I'm going to finish packing.... By the way, what's your favorite color?"

"Skin tone."

"Bye," she said, kissing her teeth, and laughing.

I laughed. "Just bye? What, no I love you?" I asked, teasing her. I knew that would catch her off guard.

"I know you do," she shot, then ended the call immediately.

That girl...what the hell am I going to do with her? "Just what she wants you to do, fool," I said, answering my own question.

As I pulled into S's yard, my phone went off again. "Regular hotline I have today," I mumbled as I checked the caller ID: Nancy. "Hey, baby."

"Hey, I know I might not get to see you tonight, but I wanted to ask if you would mind me going to a party tomorrow night. My boss invited me..."

"You know I don't mind you going out, besides, my mother is coming over in the morning, and a friend asked me to escort her to a fashion show tomorrow night, so I'll be out too."

"Baby, my boss asked me to be her brother's date."

"Her brother's date? Why you?"

"Well, that's what I wanted to talk to you about, but I didn't want to talk about it over the phone. But since we're not going to be able to have a face to face, I guess I have to tell you over the phone. I have a confession to make. Last Sunday, I wasn't with my mother in Palm Beach." She paused, probably waiting for me to say something.

I kept quiet, so she continued. "My boss invited me up to her house for lunch. After lunch, her brother invited the younger crowd to catch a movie at City Place, then we all went to..."

"Blue Martini," I finished for her.

"How'd you know that?" she asked, surprised.

I forced a laugh. Inside I was on fire. Shouldn't she get some brownie points for confessing? She didn't have to tell me the truth. Did she spot Destiny and decide to tell me before Destiny told me? No. That couldn't be it. She doesn't know Destiny. So, why the fuck is she telling me this now?

"This has been bothering me all week. I felt so guilty about lying to you, baby. It was a spur of the moment decision on my part, and since I didn't get your permission first, I got scared and lied."

You felt guilty about lying to me, but not about how you were all over that dude, I thought, but did not say. I was pissed, but I wouldn't give her the satisfaction of knowing that. She wants to fuck with her boss's brother. So be it. "I don't know why you would think that I would be upset...and about Blue Martini, that was easy. You say City Place and everyone knows you can't leave there without going to Blue Martini," I lied smoothly. I wouldn't let her know that she had been spotted holding hands and shit.

She laughed, but it was a nervous laugh. I could hear the relief in her voice when she spoke. "So you don't mind if I be his date?"

"You ain't fuckin him, are you?" I asked to fuck her up a bit. "This is just a friendly date, right?"

"Of course not, baby. The only person I'm fucking is you. I would never cheat on you," she said in as sincere a voice as I've ever heard. "So, can I go?"

I was silent for a moment. I wanted to see if she would say if I didn't want her to go, she wouldn't go. After a long pause, she won. She didn't say shit, so I was obligated to say something.

I had my own plans, but I had better warn her. Make sure she understood.

"Okay. As long as you don't cross that line, then I'm fine with you going. You cross that line, I'm talking put your toe on it...we're done."

"Thank you, sweetie," she sang, then asked, "You're not mad at me for lying to you, are you?"

"Just don't let that shit happen again. That's not going to become a habit, is it?"

"No, baby. I won't lie to you ever again."

That's a fuckin lie right there. You better quit while you're ahead, bitch. You diggin yourself into a deeper hole, and Sonia's steady shoveling dirt on top of your ass.

"I was feeling so guilty for lying to you on Sunday. You don't know how relieved I am to get that burden off of my chest. Thanks, baby."

Lyin fuckin ho! That's why you came over there unannounced, fucked me the way you did and cooked me dinner. And then spent the night and suck a nigga dry before you went to work. That conniving bitch! All that to try and fuck off your guilt. Hell yeah, I mad at your ass, bitch. But you can thank your lucky stars for Sonia's sweet ass. That's the only fuckin reason why I'm not going off. You will get yours in due course. Lyin Ass ho!

"So who are you escorting to this fashion show?"

Now you want to fuckin know who I'm going with? You don't fuckin care. You're just happy that I'm lettin your ass go. "One of my mother's co-worker's boyfriend sister who live round the corner." Damn that was a mouthful. That should be enough to confuse the bitch.

She laughed. "Well, you have fun, and be nice to her. Love you."

Sure you fuckin do. "I love you, too." Bitch! I thought, ending the call.

"Fuck da ho! I need a beer," I snarled, jumping from the Range. As soon as I closed the door, my fucking phone rang again. "What the fuck did Nancy want to tell me now; oh by the way, I fucked him," I mumbled, looking at the caller ID. It wasn't Nancy. My heart lifted and a smile crept on my face.

CHAPTER 22

URGE TO MERGE

It took Sonia about an hour to get to S's. We had decided that she might as well bring the Benz to get cleaned while I was there; we may not have enough time to get it done tomorrow. When she pulled up, we were drinking beers and playing dominoes under the tree.

Sonia gave one of the guys her keys, pointed to me, and strolled over. It was a rowdy game of dominoes, but everyone paused and watched as she made her way over. I hadn't seen her for a couple of days, and I don't know if that was what caused me to get all warm and tingly as I watched her walk toward me. She's so damn beautiful. And, sexy as hell! I gats to stop playin with her before someone else swoops in and take her.

"Which one a unna she belong to?" Flaco, my Jamaican partner asked, glancing around the table.

I had that shit eating grin on my face as I leaned the chair back onto its two back legs and took a healthy swig of my Heineken.

"Das meh bwoy, Khris, ting deh, meh son," S said.

"Gaaaad damn! You gat a nice fiiiiiine honey," S's partner, Champ stated.

Sonia did look nice. She had on a yellow Nike shorts that fell mid thigh; a white Nike polo with yellow collar and yellow trim on the half sleeves; white Nike sneakers with yellow Nike swoosh and matching anklet socks. That color looked beautiful against her smooth caramel skin. She looked like walking sunshine after a storm. It was a welcoming sight.

"Hello," Sonia gushed with a dazzling smile and small wave to the guys. She surprised me by leaning down, hugging me around my neck, and giving me a soft smack full on the lips.

Her lips felt soft and sweet. The kiss was so tender, and delivered so innocently. It was our first kiss and she made it seem so natural; like it was our regular greeting. She fucked up my head with that move there. I guess she really was tired of me playin. She damn sure seemed like she would take it if I weren't willing to give it. I felt myself blushing at the thought.

"Hey, baby," I said, then gave her another kiss. This kiss was a little longer and caused her to blush. "Guys, this is Sonia. Sonia, this is Flaco, Champ, and you already know S."

They all grinned, said some type of greeting, and nodded. Sonia took up my bottle of Heineken and took a swig. "What y'all playin, hold ya man, or partners?"

"Wha ya know bout dis?" S asked as she took another sip.

She swallowed, then stated. "I know whatever one y'all playin, I gat next. That's what I know," she sassed.

"We playin partners. Come sit here and play with ya man. See if you can win with him. We een been drawin nuttin but bad cards. See if you can change him luck," Flaco said, getting up.

Sonia took the seat opposite me. "I haven't played in a while, but let's handle dis lil bit right here," she smirked, nodding at S and Champ.

"Can I have some of my beer, baby?" I asked, licking my lips to try and taste her kiss again.

"Sure. I was just sweetenin it up for you," she said, and then took a healthy swig before handing it over.

The guys just shook their heads and laughed.

"All right now, don't think cause you fine we going to take it easy on you," Champ said to Sonia. "I pushin hard card down ya throat."

Sonia laughed. "Hard card down my throat. Ha ha. You look like one dem nice, sweet, take-home-to-mama dudes. You look like you like to take care ah woman. You probably ga spoon feed me every card I need," she said as S shuffled the cards, laughing.

"I like her, Khris," Champ said. "She drinkin beer from the bottle, and talkin shit, too. We ga see if she can play. She sitting under me, so you know she in the hot seat."

"Hot seat? Right." Sonia chuckled. "Flaco, can you please get me a Heineken so I can wash down all this shit Champ sitting down here talkin?" she asked, smiling up at him. "I can't whoop ass and talk shit if my throat is dry."

Everyone laughed as we drew our cards. Flaco went inside to

get a round for everyone.

Sonia drew the double six and came out. The game didn't change from the shit talkin that was going on before Sonia came. In fact, it got rowdier. It turned into smash-mouth dominoes. Men could still be men with her around.

Flaco arrived with the drinks just as Champ fucked around and played a three-five.

Sonia smiled. "I took one look at you and knew you would be sweet. Thanks," she said, laying down the double five, then dusting off the top.

S shook his head as he played. "Come on, Champ," S said, looking at him and shaking his head. "You supposed to let her carry that home in her purse, then see if she could spend it in the mall tomorrow."

I played on S's card. Bam! "Knock ya hand, son. You can't play!"

"Shit!" Champ said, knocking on the table.

"Nobody's home," Sonia laughed. "You ga hurt ya knuckles fuckin round with my man. Telling me bout you ga push hard card down my throat," she sang as she leaned forward and read the board. After a couple of seconds, she said, "I gat something fa you right here, S." Bam! Sonia slapped down her card and pointed down to the other end of the board. "Go down there. That's the only place you can play at."

The game was getting so sweet that we had drawn a couple of onlookers. Even Flaco was talking shit from the sidelines.

S studied the board. Then he studied Sonia.

I smiled as I gazed across the table at my partner. This girl is something else. Sonia could actually play. She was reading the board correctly, and she had already figured out what everyone had in their hands. She's absolutely amazing. She was right, too. I can take her anywhere. I could see myself getting use to having her around. And to think I was just getting to know her.

S played. Bam! "Knock ya hand, mey son."

"I can't fuck up my hands knocking on this hard ass board, meh bwoy," I said, imitating S. Bam! "Meh woman like soft hands on her silky soft skin."

Bam! "That's what I was looking for right there," Champ yelled at me, slamming down his card.

"Champ, I gat to be honest with you. You are one sweet mutha..." Bam! "If my man wasn't so good, mmmm-mmmm, I would marry you," Sonia said, rattling the table with her double four.

"Damn!" Champ mumbled.

"Me know, meh bwoy. You distracted by her beauty," S laughed, and played. Bam!

We went around two more times with Champ vowing to pass Sonia each time. Sonia had one more card to drop. Everybody was studying the board.

Bam! S dropped a five-one, acing up the board. "Ya pass, meh son"

"Yeah right," I smirked. "Baby, you ready to drop. He can't stop you."

"Watch me pass her ass," Champ stated. "Play, and watch me make your woman cry," he said, staring at me.

"Shiiiitt" Sonia laughed and took a swig of her beer. "You can't stop this card here, Champ. You done been sweet to me this whole game. You fed me so sweet I dropped the double five and four and gonna win as soon as you play."

"Here, Champ." Bam! "Now try to stop my baby from dropping."

Sonia laughed. "You see why he's my man," Sonia chimed, looking up at Flaco. Sonia rest her card on the table. "When he play, turn the card over for him. He comin right to mama. Any place he plays."

I knew what she had. He couldn't stop her, but I was setting him up for something sweeter.

Flaco reached down and peeped the card. Flaco laughed.

Champ was studying the board hard. I had dropped the ace deuce on the board. So there was an ace at top end of the board, and a deuce on the bottom end. Champ smiled like he had seen something.

I knew he had read her for the wrong card, because if he had read her correctly, her wouldn't have been smiling.

Champ played on the ace at the top of the board. Bam "You

pass!" he yelled, slamming down the ace-six.

Flaco laughed and turned over the card. "Deuce-six. She won on both ends. She told you you couldn't stop her."

The little crowd roared and high-fived Sonia.

We played several more games and won three out of the next five. By then, both vehicles were showroom clean. Sonia insisted on paying for both vehicles, so I left the tip.

"Yo. Y'all comin thru on Sunday?" S asked, as we got ready to leave.

"Mom's comin in town for the weekend, but we'll try to swing thru."

"I'll try to stay away from the domino table," Sonia chimed.

"We let you win today because it was your first time. Next time we won't be so easy on you," S said to Sonia as I opened the door for her.

"Thanks," she said sarcastically, laughing and shaking her head as she got into her car.

"I'll be right behind you," I said, closing her door.

"Dat's wifee right dere, meh son. Don't fuck dat up."

"Good advice," I said, giving him pound, and jumping into the Range. "I'll see you on Sunday, even if it's only for a minute."

"Come tru, meh son."

"I'll be there," I said, hopping into the Range.

I drove behind Sonia thinking back to our first kiss. It wasn't how I had expected our first kiss to be, but it stirred me deep. Her lips were so soft and so sweet. I had watched her lips the entire time that we had been playing dominoes. I couldn't wait to kiss those lips again. I felt myself getting aroused at the way she teased me during the game. She had been subtle with her gestures so that no one else noticed, but they had done the trick. The way her lips kissed the mouth of that Heineken bottle made me envious. I should have kissed her days ago. Now I was regretting my decision to keep her at a safe distance. All the rules that I had didn't seem to make any sense when it came to Sonia. Sonia transcended all rules.

What was happening to me?

Had I met my soul mate? Was Sonia the one true love that the magazines and books talk about?

Was I falling in love with Sonia?

CHAPTER 23

HOME AT LAST

All sorts of questions flooded my mind as we drove into my community. Why had I told my mother that Sonia was spending the weekend? Why did I even let Sonia volunteer to pick up my mother? My early morning turn would have been easy to drop in the morning. In fact, I could still drop it. Then the two of us can go and pick up my mother. That might not be a bad idea, I thought as I hit the garage door opener right before turning into my driveway.

Sonia had stopped. I blew and waved for her to pull inside. We just got both vehicles cleaned, and I wasn't planning on going back out anymore for the evening, so we may as well park inside.

Sonia drove in and I parked on the side of her and closed the garage doors.

"Next time we come home, you park on this side, closer to the door," I said as we both got out. Now she had me saying home. What was up with me? I stared at her. I didn't grab my phone. I didn't grab my bag. I headed straight toward Sonia.

She knew what I wanted. She smiled, knowingly. "Something sweet?" she asked, arching her brow.

I wrapped her in my arms and kissed her lips. Her arms twined around my neck as I pulled her body into mine. Sonia sighed as she parted her lips. My tongue invaded her mouth. Shards of electricity raced through my body. Fire coursed through my veins as our tongues intertwined. Her body fused with mine as I pulled her even closer: held her a little tighter. Like a tailor made suit, she fit my body perfectly. Even though our kiss was hot and filled with passion, it was not hurried. It was menacingly slow. Tender. Spicy hot. Sweet. It was slow and deliberate. It felt like home. Safe. Comforting.

Our kiss was more than a kiss. It had meaning. It was the beginning of something wonderful. Something everlasting.

We were both gasping, but neither of us wanted to pull away. We didn't want to break our connection, but we had to eventually. Our lips finally separated to let each other catch the breath that we both so desperately needed.

"I knew if I hadn't stopped, you would have let yourself die," Sonia panted, as I peppered her lips and chin with soft little kisses.

I couldn't keep my lips off of her. "I was thinking the same thing," I managed to say as I kissed her cheeks and moved around to suck on her earlobes and neck.

She closed her eyes and let the sweetest little wisps of moans escape her lips as she leaned her head back to let me kiss all over her precious neck. "I love the way you kiss," she whimpered, caressing my neck and back. "I can kiss you forever."

"Forever's not long enough," I said, nibbling gently on her chin. "Can I kiss you again, Sonia?"

Her body shivered. "Kiss me, Khris," she whispered, her voice sweet and husky. I traced my tongue teasingly around her lips, then sucked on her bottom lip. Her eyes closed and her body trembled against mine. She sucked on my top lip, then slid her tongue playfully into my mouth. Our kiss was hot, playful, and lustful. Her leg raised and wrapped around mine as her hands roamed and explored my back, hips, and arms. With her pelvis grinding against my erection, she moaned ever so sweetly into my mouth.

My hands fondled and caressed her ass as we dry hunched each other like two horny teenagers. Our kiss became more fervent and impassioned.

Sonia's hunger grew. Her hands became frolicsome. They shot to my belt and worked on my pants. We never stopped kissing. Our fire raged higher. It burned hotter. My pants and boxer briefs were down around my ankles in no time. I kicked them loose to free my feet. Her shorts and lacy boy-shorts went shortly thereafter.

She kicked one leg free, but the bundle somehow got entangled around her left foot. It didn't stop anything, so she ignored it.

Sonia massaged my dick. Her soft hands and exquisite fingers working their mojo on my hard, hot flesh. I was burning up. She had me hot. Pre-cum oozed onto her skilled fingers. That made her hotter. With one leg already up and locked around the back of my knee, she put both hands around my neck and jumped into my arms. She moaned pleasurably. She felt my throbbing hot flesh between her thighs pressing and sliding against her wet, pulsing lips.

She locked her athletic legs around my waist. I had no choice but to cup her voluptuous buttocks to support her. I was pulsing. Her flesh against my flesh. Her heat against my heat. I wanted to be inside her. She wanted me inside her. I was dying to feel her. And, she was dying to feel me.

Sonia shot one hand down between us as my fingers slid between her cheeks caressing and fondling every erogenous spot until they fond her soft, wet lips. She was so fucking hot. So fucking wet.

My slick fingers danced easily through her fleshy folds making her moan: making her anxious: making her needy.

Sonia's entire body seized up. Her pussy clenched, then pulsed.

She kissed me harder, grasped my dick, and raised herself so that she was able to rub my head between her fleshy folds. Her body trembled with each stroke. She was torturing herself. Stroking her own fire. She rubbed my head against her swollen clit and bit down on my tongue as the sensations overwhelmed her. I felt her juices oozing out of her and soaking my fingers.

I slipped a finger into her and felt her muscles grip it. Sonia couldn't wait. Neither could I.

She wanted me in her. And I wanted to be in her.

She used my head to nudge my finger out of the way. She had my head at her entrance before I was able to get my finger completely out.

She couldn't wait. I couldn't wait.

She pushed me into her tight, wet sheath as she lowered her body. At the same time, I gave one firm upward thrust. I went impossibly deep. She gasped loudly as the initial shock of my possessing her threatened to bring her to orgasm. It threatened to bring me to orgasm. It felt wonderful being in so deep: filling her so completely. I groaned and held her savoring the initial consummation of our relationship. It was a perfect fit.

Her mouth shot open and she gasped loudly.

Her moist center pulsed on my girth, then she started winding in small tight circles.

I started grinding slowly along with her. Her pussy was soooo-fucking wet. So fucking sweet. She fit me perfectly. She started grinding on my dick. Our bodies were in perfect rhythm. We synced immediately. Her mouth again found mine. She kissed me slowly, like the first time our tongues had met. I had fire raging in my balls. I wanted to drown her with my love. I wanted to stain her insides with my seed. I wanted to mark her, make her mine.

My fingers danced around her entrance as I slid in and out of her. My lathered thumb circled and pressed her tight little chocolate star making her desire rage higher. We were grinding each other slowly, passionately, and purposefully.

Sonia struggled to get her polo off. She used one hand, and I used one to assist her. We succeeded in getting it off and freeing her firm, succulent breasts from the confines of her lacy bra.

Her chocolate kisses shaped nipples were perky and ripe. My mouth watered as it descended onto her breast. My mouth, lips and tongue worshiped and adored her two precious mounds. Her dark areolas were a pleasure to tease, but it was with her nipples that my tongue fell in love. The way they responded to my tongue incited me to do even more. Sonia started grinding faster. Her gasping, panting and moaning grew louder and harder as I continued to map and explore every inch of her body—inside and out. Sonia's body was incredible: totally delicious and fully responsive. It responded to my every touch. Every kiss. Every nibble. Every suck.

She loved being loved. The quakes and pleasurable moans told me so. She was on the brink of euphoria. I would take her over.

I, too, was on the brink. Her pussy felt-felt...

"Cum with me, Khris," she sang softly in my ear. "Pleeeeeease?" she begged.

How could I say no to her? How could I say no to her body for it, too, was calling me? Her muscles trembled against my dick as she rose up and down, swishing her fantastic hips around and around.

She lost control.

I didn't feel the usual build up like I normally did. Suddenly, I was just overwhelmed by a deluge of sensations. My mouth formed an orgasmic "0" like I had seen so many women do before. Not a sound came out. My knees trembled. I fought to maintain our balance as I continued to pump furiously into Sonia's sweet pussy. My strokes became unorthodox and unrelenting.

Sonia was pushing her pussy back down to meet my every stroke: I was convinced that she was determined to get every bit of pleasure she could out of every stroke we made. How else could I explain her trying to get every millimeter of me into her with every stroke?

Her mouth covered my own. She sucked my lips, then her breath caught. Her body told the story even if she couldn't voice it. She held her breath as her orgasm descended on her. She had no control over her body. It shook her to her core. Even with her contorted orgasmic face, she was beautiful. Her mouth devoured mine as she peaked and crested. About a minute later, I felt her body building up for another one. A couple strokes later, she told me.

"Oh God, Khris. I'm cumming again," she mumbled into my mouth.

She fucked me harder. Faster. Wilder.

I felt her body shivering from the inside out this time. This was going to be the big one. This would be the orgasmic wave that I would ride with her.

Sonia was determined to take me with her this time. "Cum-cum with me this time!" she managed to demand forcefully.

My body was hers to command. My stomach muscles tensed. My nuts felt like they were on fire. I had to get that nut out. I pumped harder. I could feel my head hitting her back walls. I could feel my balls slapping the entrance to her pussy. I felt like I was straining to get my nut up and out of me. The pressure rose quickly. I couldn't talk. I couldn't warn her if I wanted to. My impending orgasm felt so powerful; it was borderline painful. It felt like liquid fire shooting up my shaft as my seed blasted up into her hot quivering pussy.

Her body writhed, and convulsed violently as each shot of my seed blasted into her orgasm. She screamed one long agonizing scream as my seed continued to spew up into her.

We continued riding each other until our pace slowed and we were to tired to stay up. We ended up in a panting, sweaty heap on the cold garage floor. Even though we were both out of breath, we couldn't stop kissing each another.

Sonia had that sweet, satisfied afterglow. She looked extra beautiful. Her eyes smiled at me longingly. I caressed her cheeks and stared into her eyes. Now, I would tell her how I feel about her, just like I had promised.

"What?" she cooed, blushing in the afterglow. "Do you have something to tell me, Khris?" she asked as if she knew exactly what I was thinking and feeling.

"I'm just admiring you," I said, brushing her hair behind her ear, and kissing her again.

She didn't wait on me. She said it first. "I love you, Khris," she whispered.

"I love you, more, Sonia," I whispered, back.

CHAPTER 24

NEWFOUND LOVE

I never knew love like this before. I knew all relationships started off great. I knew that the getting to know you phase was exactly like a job interview: you put your best qualities forward to secure the job. I knew all this. But still, I never experienced a feeling quite like this before. It was scary and exciting at the same time. I've never, ever been a man that used the love word with a woman and didn't mean it. I didn't use the love word just to get some pussy. Never did. Never will.

Last night and this morning has been absolutely terrific. No. Every minute from we arrived home, has been fantastic. Sonia and I went at it again on the garage floor to get rid of all the built up lust from the past week. We weren't as gentle the second time. We fucked like animals, then laughed about it as I carried her upstairs and relaxed in my whirlpool bath. After that—actually we started in the whirlpool—we kissed and nibbled and sucked and licked each other from head to toe and back again. We made sweet tender love and fell asleep in each other's arms. We both woke up shortly after midnight hungry as hell, so we decided to raid the kitchen. We heated up a Digiorno's supreme pizza and some microwave Buffalo wings, grabbed a couple bottles of Kaliks and had a picnic on the family room floor. We fed each other, ate and drank off of each other. It got a little wild and freaky in front of the TV: wilder and freakier in the shower. By the time we got in bed, the two of us were too weak to move.

Of course, I called in to be replaced for my trip. No, I wasn't whooped. Sonia made it to my advantage to call in: she asked me one simple question, "How much is tomorrow's trip worth?"

I pulled it up on the computer and showed her. "Two fifty with per diem."

"I'll pay you to stay home. Two fifty, tax free, dollars."

I picked up the phone and started dialing. Not that I needed her money. It was just sweet of her to make the offer. Most females weren't trying to dish out any cash to a man. They were trying to collect. I have a few that do, but they're rare. Very rare.

Sonia had raped me this morning, but I decided not to call and report it to the police. She'd proven that she could, and would, take the dick from me. I laughed as I thought back to her strong-arming the dick from me this morning. Now, she was trailing me to drop off the Range to Yasmine so that they could have transportation for later. We would pick up my mother after Sonia's nail appointment.

My phone buzzed: Sonia.

"Tell me you love me; I'll tell you back," I answered, laughing.

"So, you got one taste a dis and you done change your greeting," Sonia sassed, and giggled. "Tsk-tsk-tsk."

"It was good enough to change for," I retorted.

"You were a'ight. It wasn't all that, but you good enough for me to keep," she laughed. "With a lil more practice, I could see me keeping you around."

"So now you gat jokes."

"You know I'm just teasing. You all that, some pizza, and some buffalo wings," she laughed, referring to that freaky shit we did last night.

"You are a straight up freak."

"You brought it out of me, so now you're going to love every second of it. We better stop talkin like this, you getting me wet and I'm planning on getting a bikini wax when I get my hair done later."

"You're the one called and brought it up," I shot; fixing my dick at it grew in my pants.

"I had called to tell you that your mother called and said that she was at the airport checking in for her flight. Everything was on time so far. She would call me back when she's boarding. I didn't tell her that you weren't flying. I figured it would be a nice surprise for her."

"Cool," I said, turning into the dorm's parking lot. I found a vacant spot, and parked. I pulled out the parking decal from the glove box, put it in the front windshield, then locked up. Yasmine had a set of keys.

"You're driving," Sonia said, already in the passenger seat when

I got to her car.

"Why can't you drive?"

"I drove this morning." She giggled, and stuck out her tongue. It was like that, back and forth, as we drove to the nail salon. The place was packed for so early in the morning. I went in with her to chill, but when I saw the empty station next to where she was being pampered—one lady doing her feet, another doing her hands I decided to get a manicure myself. I got my cuticles pushed back and cut, nails filed and buffed, but none of that gloss shit.

The other ladies in the shop were all telling Sonia how they wished their men would come with them to get their nails done, so me being a true playa, I had to defend us men.

"Y'all know y'all don't want y'all man up in here. Y'all won't be able to brag to everyone else how y'all put it on him good in order to get that cash to come and get y'all nails done."

One lil fast sister, hollered. "Well, how come you came with your woman?"

I was ready for that one. "Shit, she put it on me so good I didn't want to let her out of my sight."

The nail salon wasn't good after that, as my Jamaican colleagues would say. Sonia was blushing her ass off. And she had a nice ass, so I tried to get her to stop blushing.

"Girl, your man is crazy. He fine, too. But he crazy," another lady chirped. An older lady.

"Shit, I don't care what your reason is. The fact that you came inside with her and didn't drop her off and go around the corner to the strip club until she's finished, makes you a good man in my books."

"I came in on a fact finding mission. I came in here to listen."

"Listen to what?" the lady filing my nails asked.

"I want to hear what women complain about their men not doing, so I can make sure I don't slip up."

"Girl, I don't know where you find him from, or what you put on him, but you better hold onto him and keep doing what you doing," Sonia's manicurist said.

"They look so cute together," chimed the lady doing Sonia's feet.

"Y'all are going to have some beautiful children. If y'all don't already have some," a pregnant lady shot.

Pregnant women always wanted other people to get pregnant, I thought. "We don't have any...yet," I said, winking at the pregnant lady, then Sonia. That's when it hit me that we hadn't discussed any contraceptives and I hadn't used any protection at all. Didn't even pull out. I tried to remember how many times I came in her last night and this morning. I gave up. What was done was done.

Sonia laughed. "No. No children, yet. We're going to enjoy each other for a while, first," Sonia chimed, winking right back at my ass.

She didn't seem concerned now, nor back when she was begging me to cum with, and in her. But, that was in the heat of passion.

People say all kinds of shit in the heat of the moment and be damned with the consequences later. I stared at her and she was still smiling. She didn't seem worried.

"Don't worry, ladies, I'm going to play his game too. I'm going in the barbershop with his ass when he goes: hear what they gat to say." Sonia sassed.

A ghetto fabulous girl that was getting her toes done, smirked. "Girl, them mens ain't gonna talk with you up in there. Only thing they ga be doin is sweatin you and tryin to slip you they phone number when your man head turn."

The ladies took over from there. The conversation ranged from what men do, to what they wanted their men to do. It didn't sound all that hard, but as I knew, we men get complacent after a while. Women do, too, but they always find a way to blame everything on us. So ultimately, it's our fault.

Sonia stepped up to pay for both our manicures and her pedicure, so I tipped the three ladies that worked on us. One fast mouth heifer asked, "How come she paying the bill? You the man."

"I gave her the money to pay for everything so when other women see her paying for her man, they would think that a brother has been puttin it on her real good for her to be paying the bills."

The same fast mouth heifer, said, "She probably is using her money to pay the bill."

Ms. Ghetto Fabulous looked me over from head to toe, and said, "And you probably is putting it on her real good."

Sonia smiled. "I don't have a problem paying. He pays. I pay. Left Pocket. Right pocket. It's the same thing. But, just so y'all know, he put it on me so good last night and this morning, I paid his ass to take the day off."

"Daaaamn!" the pregnant lady shot.

"You go, girl. I'm not mad at you. I woulda paid his fine ass too," another lady shouted, causing everyone to laugh.

"You ladies enjoy you day," I said, holding the door for my queen as she waved bye.

She kicked it with my boys; I kicked it with her girls. Well, not really, but it was just as good, for now. At least I made the effort.

I was closing Sonia's door when her phone rang. By the time I got behind the wheel, she said, "Mom's plane just landed. She called from on the plane: say they're taxing. She's coming out upstairs."

"Less traffic up at departures than down at arrivals. And she don't travel with checked baggage when she's coming."

"Only when she's going back," Sonia finished for me, laughing.

We cracked about the girls in the nail salon until we arrived at the airport. We got there just as my mother walked out the terminal door.

"There she is," I said, pointing to my mother as we pulled to a stop.

"Your mother looks young."

"Don't tell her that."

I saw my mother looking around, so I let down Sonia's window. "Looking for someone, Mrs. Harrison?" I shouted.

My mother's smile brightened as she saw Sonia, then me. "I thought you were working. Hello?" she chimed at Sonia as she walked toward the car.

"Hello, Mrs. Harrison," Sonia replied, opening the door and getting out. "Come, sit in the front. I'll get in the back."

"No, no, baby," my mother chimed, stopping in front of Sonia, smiling. "Nice to meet you, Sonia. I've heard so much about you. I feel like I already know you. Come give me a hug."

Sonia blushed and gave my mom a big hug.

"You stay in front, I'll ride in the back," my mother said as she let Sonia go. "It ain't often I get chauffeured in a Benz. This is nice," my mother said, sliding into the backseat.

Sonia closed her door and jumped back in front.

"I mean, you wouldn't even let me do the introductions," I said to my mother as I pulled back into traffic just as I saw a policeman walking in our direction.

"If you had gone to work like you told me you were going to do, you wouldn't have been here, and we would have had to introduce ourselves, right, Sonia?"

"Yes, ma'am. You're right," Sonia agreed with a smile.

"Hold on, baby. Let you and Mom get something clear, don't call me Mrs. Harrison or ma'am: Janet or Mom."

Sonia laughed. "Okay, Mom," Sonia said, catching on to the "You and Mom" hint.

"Good! You picked the right one. Now I know you have good intentions on sticking around for a long time. Me and you are going to get along real fine," my mother said, patting Sonia on her shoulder. "So, since Mr. Man done changed the plans, what's the new agenda?"

"I'll pretend I'm not here," I said to both of them.

"Yasmine has his truck; she's going to call when she gets out of her test. Meanwhile, you two are going to drop me to my hair appointment. We just got our nails done."

"Let me see them," mom said, leaning between the seats. Sonia twisted and showed mom her left hand.

"That's pretty," mom chimed. "What do you call this?"

"It's a regular French manicure, but I asked her to use a gloss white and put the stripes and diamonds on one finger on each hand to spice it up a bit."

"Oh, that's nice. You have some pretty fingers, too. All you need is a real nice rock and you'll be complete. Hint, hint."

Sonia giggled. "Thank you, Mom. You listening, Khris?" Sonia asked, poking me on the thigh.

"I'm not here, remember?"

"He heard me, and he heard you," mom said, getting in on the poking, too, and laughing.

They were getting along too good, too fast. Believe it or not, I kinda liked that. "You don't even know her and you done trying to marry me off. What's up with that?" I asked.

"I thought you wasn't here?" mom shot, sitting back. "You ain't even interrogated her yet."

Sonia was laughing. This was all funny to her. She knew she already had my mother on her side.

"I don't interrogate anyone," mom interjected.

"You just be all up in their business," I shot. "I've already warned Sonia about you."

"I don't believe this son of mine," Mom turned her attention to Sonia. "Sonia, when your mother or father meet my son, aren't they going to ask a few things to see if they can spot something that you might have missed. You know how we get blinded by love."

Sonia nodded her head. "Well, Charles already knows him. And, I don't have to tell you about Sherice. You work with her."

"Girl, she brought pictures of you to work to show me. She just knew you two would hook up. Of course, she told me all your business, too."

"Oh my God!" Sonia shrieked. "What did she tell you?"

"Nothing bad." Mom chuckled. "She did tell me about Mr. Tattoo on his neck and the other…"

"Oh my God! She can talk," Sonia said, shaking her head.

"That she can do," mom agreed, laughing. "They must have wiped her mouth with dishcloth when she was a baby."

We all laughed. It went on like that until we dropped Sonia off. Mom wasn't in the front seat good before she started. "I like her, Khris."

She had already put Nancy out of my life, and I haven't even told her about Nancy dating her boss's brother. That didn't even bother me anymore. I guess it's true what they say: the easiest way to get one woman off your mind is to get another one on it.

"She's a beautiful young lady, and I heard she's doing good selling that human hair. Now that I've met her, I'm going to talk to my hairdresser and find out where they buy their human hair. I could probably get her some business in Nassau. Remind me to talk to her about that before I leave. Now, back to you. You ain't gonna mess around on her like you did Nancy, are you?"

"I-I..."

"I, I, shit! Boy, you gettin too old for all this runnin around. You don't think it's time for you to settle down? You don't think you have enough notches on your belt?"

"I just met Sonia. She knows I have a girlfriend, and..."

"Listen to me, Khris, that lil girl, Nancy; ain't no future there for you. Her parents don't think you good enough for her, and I don't like her...let me not say I don't like her: we just don't get along. She too hoity-toity for me. Sonia, on the other hand, is down to earth; she's smart; much prettier than Nancy: has a better shape, too. I hear she can cook, and she has her own business. I don't know how she is in the sex department, but even if she isn't as good as your lil Nancy in bed, you can always teach her to please you, just how she can teach you to please her. Sex is a big factor, but it isn't everything. If sex is all you have in a relationship, it's not going to work. You need other things like communication—and you know Nancy is a private girl."

I wasn't going to discuss the sex department with my mother, but I felt inclined to defend Nancy's privacy issues. "That's not fair, Mom. I'm private, too."

"That's because your ass is cheating left, right, and center. Too much things out there for you to be fooling around like that. How long you plan on running the streets? Ain't nothing out in them streets but disease and problems. Find you a good woman who you can grow old with, give me some grandchildren with, someone to make some memories with. Lasting memories. All the places you've travelled, all them lil girls you done been with, you probably had fun, but I bet you forgot all about what you saw and whom you went with."

Mom did have a point. Several points. But, I had some things I had to deal with. Sonia's nice. Yes, she has Nancy whooped in every department so far, but is that the real Sonia? Will she change? Will I like the real Sonia? Could I be happy with her? Would she make a good mother to my children? Would she make a good wife? Most importantly, could I give up all my other women for her?

CHAPTER 25

THREE QUEENS

"When you see Sonia, you're not going to feel overdressed," Nishka said, sitting on my bed, watching me get dressed.

I had chosen a white Z Zenga 3-button, linen and silk blend summer suit to wear after Sonia had laid out her strappy, curve-hugging Chanel dress; matching open-toe, high heel sandals; purse; white Chanel ceramic watch.

"The trick to wearing an all white suit is to dress it down," I said, slipping my feet into my white Silvano Latanzi crocodile loafers with the soft soles.

"How is that dressing down when those shoes cost…"

"It doesn't matter how much they cost, Nishka. It's how I'm wearing them: no socks. And this silk blend T-shirt under my jacket will also help tone things down a bit."

"I think you need to put something around your neck. Sonia's wearing a nice diamond necklace with a heart shaped diamond pendant to go with her drop earrings. You need to tighten up, homeboy, your girl in there looking good. You don't want to go out behind her looking like the help, rather than her date. Someone might swoop in and snatch her right out of your hands."

"I don't want to outshine her with my jewelry."

"Even on your best day, you can't steal her spotlight," Nishka stated.

That was high praise coming from Nishka. She might have said something nice like that about Nancy a couple of times, but it took her months—if not at least a year—to do so.

"You know you could put your shit together, but…humph! Wait until you see her. Your mother's down there looking like she about to cry like mothers do on their daughter's wedding day."

"Not you, too! Just throw the white croc band on the Daytona," I ordered as I put on my white crocodile belt.

My mother burst into my room. "You ain't ready yet? Sonia's ready. You better hold on to something," she said as Sonia walked in with Yasmine trailing behind her.

Damn! Sonia took my breath away. My speech, too. I couldn't tear my eyes away from her. She looked like an angel. She wore her hair pinned up with a few loose curls dangling. Her makeup, the little that she wore, was impeccable. She was perfect from head to toe. I don't think I've ever laid eyes on one woman so well put together. Flawless.

"Yeah, you speechless now, eh?" Nishka ribbed. "You gat to step it up a notch."

I was nodding to Nishka, but I couldn't tear my eyes off of Sonia. I am definitely making her mine. Knowing her as I did, and seeing her like this in my room with my mother and sisters all smiling, I knew I had to make her mine. On top of that, I didn't even want to begin to think about another man possessing her. I would do what it takes to make sure that doesn't happen. Does that mean that I would stop trickin? The jury's still out on that one.

Sonia stood posing and giving me a captivating smile. "Well, do you like?" she asked seductively.

"Wow!" I nodded, trying not to salivate on myself. "I like."

I realized that my mother and Yasmine and Nishka were all waiting, watching and listening. I didn't care. "I can't take my eyes off of you. Sonia, you look stunning; opulent; nubile; irresistible; alluring."

Sonia blushed. "Why thank you, kind sir. Khris, you look kingly; handsome; resplendent; intoxicating; suave." Sonia grinned and winked.

"Touché!" I laughed, shaking my head.

"Y'all just pulled out all the adjectives y'all know, eh?" Yasmine shot. "Y'all just too romantic for me."

"No, ditzy. They just spelled out each other's names with adjectives," Nishka said, handing me my iced out Daytona.

"I didn't even catch that," Mom gushed. She turned to me with a proud look on her face. "That was so sweet."

"I must say, that was a first for me," Sonia admitted.

"You were quick enough to not only catch on, but to get his smart, charming-ass back," Mom said, admiringly.

"Come, mister, you need to finish getting dressed. You still think you're overdressed without the accessories?" Nishka asked.

"What accessories?" Sonia asked.

"He doesn't want to wear any of his diamond necklaces, bracelets, or rings," Nishka informed her.

"You need to break out with the bling so you don't look like you just tagging along," Mom said.

"The watch makes a statement, but you need to add a little more to let the other guys know that you can afford to keep yourself looking good enough to be with Sonia," Yasmine chimed, walking over to my jewelry safe.

Thanks to Ashley's unlimited spending and numerous shopping sprees, I had more than a million dollars worth of watches and diamond jewelry. The Daytona I was wearing, she picked up for seventy five g's when she met me in Vegas on an overnight layover. She spots something she likes; she buys one for me and one for her husband, unless it's something that only young people wear.

"Pull out my short platinum and diamond necklace: put the small cross pendant on it. And grab one of those plati and diamond bracelet sets. Y'all can choose which one."

"I see I have a lot of catching up to do in the jewelry department," Sonia said, sounding astonished as she peaked into my safe. "And they say diamonds are a girl's best friend?"

"He has more diamonds than me and I been on this earth longer than him," mom added.

We took our first sets of pictures together before we left the house. We did look good together. I won't even pretend, with Sonia dressed in all white, my mind wondered how she would look on our wedding day. They say that a woman is more beautiful on her wedding day than any other day in her life. I suddenly got the urge to see if it was possible for Sonia to look more beautiful than she looked tonight.

The Yacht was leaving from a private Yacht Club in North Fort Lauderdale; so it didn't take us long to get there. We valet parked the Benz and was instructed to follow the signs after we came out the back of the yacht club. The red carpet and bright lights would lead us to the mega-yacht at the end of the pier.

Sonia draped her arm in mine as we made our way to the yacht.

I was happy that I had indeed spruced up my outfit with my diamond accessories. Everyone that we had seen so far was blinging. And, they were taking second and third looks at Sonia, too. That made me feel good. I had something others wanted. This night was going to be great!

As we got closer to the yacht, I realized that the yacht looked familiar, but it wasn't until I read the name, that I was sure: The Lady Ashley. I smiled.

"This is some yacht," Sonia chimed. "I wonder how much money you need to own one this size."

"Forty two point five million to buy it. That's not including maintenance, upkeep, or crew salary, not to mention fuel," I stated remembering exactly what Ashley and Bobby had told me the yacht cost them.

"I'd have to be a billionaire to own one of these."

"Trust me, the owner is."

"Good evening," the hostess chimed as we approached a security stand where they were checking names on the guest list. "May I have your names, please?"

"Sonia Symonette and Khristin Harrison," Sonia replied.

The hostess scanned the first page. Turned and scanned the second page. Her smile vanished. She looked up at us, then she looked back down and opened a royal blue portfolio with The Lady Ashley printed in gold lettering. She looked up and her smile was brighter than ever. "I'm sorry for the little delay. Your names are among the owner's special VIP guest list. They just had it delivered to me, and I forgot all about it for a minute. Please forgive me?"

"Not a problem," Sonia said.

"Thank you. Now, you can walk to the front of the yacht, and a hostess there will announce your arrival. Enjoy your evening."

"Thank you," we both said, and started toward the SVIP entrance.

"Well, I wonder who did that?" Sonia asked.

"I'm a close and personal friend of the owners of this yacht."

"Stop playing," Sonia said, bumping her swaying hip into me as we walked.

"You don't believe me? Wait and see. They probably recognized my name and moved us up to the top tier of the food chain.

"If that is so, I promise you one night of being your sex slave. If it isn't so, you have two nights of being my sex slave."

"That's not a fair, but we have a deal. Kiss on it"

"I've been dying for a kiss," she chimed, turning her head and stretching up for a kiss as we walked.

It was short and sweet: just a hint of tongue to get the juices flowing.

"Khris, there you are!" I heard a familiar voice sing as we approached the front of the 280' luxury yacht. It was Ashley.

Ashley was dressed similarly to Sonia in a strappy, designer dress and sling-backs. Her dress wasn't bought off a rack, though. I know Ashley. That dress was designed just for her and just for this cruise. The way it fit her body, it was worth every penny. She was adorned in diamonds. I'm sure she had on several million dollars worth of jewelry, and I'm not counting her six million dollar wedding ring. She was queen of her floating palace.

"Hello, Ashley," I called back, elbowing Sonia ever so gently. "Sex slave!" I whispered.

"He's always armed, but they're with me," Ashley said, winking at the security guard and waving us through the checkpoint and onto the yacht. "Khris. I told Bobby that had to have been you. You look very stylish, as always," Ashley said, hugging and kissing me on the corner of my mouth. "And who is this beautiful young lady on your arms, Khris?" she asked all bubbly.

"This lovely young lady gracing my arm is Sonia Symonette. Sonia, this is my longtime, greatest female a man could ever have as a friend: the beautiful woman after which this yacht was crafted and christened, Ashley Chase. Sonia, Ashley: Ashley, Sonia."

"It's a pleasure to meet you, Sonia," Ashley said, hugging her and kissing her on both cheeks. "Any friend of Khris is a friend of mine. I'm sure we're going to be seeing lots of each other."

"It's a pleasure to meet you, too. And, thank you," Sonia replied with an ingratiating smile.

"You're just so darn beautiful! Do you model?" Ashley asked, stepping back and checking Sonia out.

"Noooo," Sonia blushed. "If I looked like you and had your eyes, I would, though. They're beautiful."

Compliment for compliment. Sonia's good.

"Baby, I would die to have your body and youthful beauty," Ashley admitted. "Not boasting, I look excellent for a white woman, but look closely," she said softly. "Don't look at the color of my eyes: look at the crows feet sneaking in," Ashley whispered as she leaned closer to Sonia.

"You've been drinking," Sonia, whispered right back. "You don't have any crows feet." Then she laughed.

Ashley snorted. "I like you, Sonia. Come, let's get some champagne so we can drink and get this party started. You do drink and party, right?" Ashley asked, giving Sonia a sideways glance.

Sonia smiled. "I do indulge every now and again."

"Well, you and me are going to indulge now, probably regret it in the morning, then go back out and do it all over again tomorrow night," Ashley said, laughing.

Sonia laughed as well. "I've got to use that one."

We all laughed as Ashley steered us to where photos were being taken. Ocean Drive, Boca magazine, and a few others were there taking names and pictures. Crystal flutes of champagne were delivered on a silver tray and passed to us with white-gloved hands.

"Krug Rose," Ashley stated.

Then I was planted in the middle of two queens: Sonia, Queen of Hearts, on the left close to my heart, Ashley, Queen of Diamonds, on my right. We posed and hugged for several shots. I felt on top of the world. I was in the middle of my two most precious possessions, and, they were getting along. Sonia's quick, she'll probably figure out my connection to Ashley, if she hadn't already done so.

"Come on, let's go up to the top deck. All the celebrities are up there kissing up to Bobby. Bobby's my husband," she said to Sonia as we trailed her up the circular glass stairs. "Khris played a very important role in my getting married to Bobby. He helped me to see the error in my way of thinking. I was young and dumb—and broke," she leaned close to Sonia's ear and whispered. "And Khris was wise beyond his years. I have him to thank for everything I have today. A loving and reciprocal marriage, a sweet, loving husband that worships and adores me...and all of this," she sang, opening her arms. "That's why Khris is so dear to me. I don't know what I would do without him. So, don't you dare try to take him away for yourself." She turned, smiled, then said playfully, "Please, Sonia."

I knew there was some seriousness in that statement.

"Sonia, me and you are going to have to be friends if you're going to be Mrs. Harrison one day," she added, smiling sincerely.

Did we have "Stupid In Love" written on our foreheads? Could people see how we felt about each other? Why was everyone trying to marry us off? It hasn't even been a week, yet, for Christ's sake!

Sonia must have felt the same way. "Well, we just met, so you don't have to worry about that right now," Sonia chimed.

"I know Khris," Ashley shot, "And I know that look. I can see what you can't." Ashley took Sonia's hand. "Come on, Bobby will be so delighted to meet you. He loves beautiful women, doesn't he, Khris?"

I grinned and nodded. "He fell for you the first time he laid eyes on you. I don't think I want him to meet Sonia. I can't compete with all this," I teased.

"Don't worry, baby," Sonia said, smiling sincerely at me, "Ashley is his queen. A man can only serve one queen at a time."

"I like that," Ashley gushed. "Are you Khris's queen?"

"Like I said, a man can only serve one queen at a time," Sonia said sweetly. "I am hopeful that one day—sooner rather than later, I might add—I may become Khris's queen."

"I like her, Khris! Sonia, you have my vote. And trust me, my vote counts right up there with Mom's. I think Mom's going to like you, too," Ashley beamed.

Ashley's making sure Sonia knows what time it is. Sonia's no slouch. She caught on to the fact that Ashley knows my mother. This was a dangerous game Ashley was playing. But, I guess she feels a little threatened on her home court: I had never brought a woman other than Yasmine, Nishka and my mother to any of their functions before. I normally travel solo and entertain myself with the single women. Tonight wasn't my fault, though. I was invited by Sonia and didn't know where I was coming until I got here.

Ashley said to Sonia conspiratorially, "Just stick with me, girlfriend. I'll get you on the throne in no time."

Sonia knew. I could see it in the way she turned and smiled at me. So far, she was playing it cool. I sure hope she wasn't playing. I hope she really is cool. Sonia had delivered some messages of her own to Ashley, as well. She basically said that I couldn't have Ashley as my queen, because she's Bobby's queen. Sonia also told Ashley that she knew Nancy is my queen. Powerful, brilliant, and delivered with class, even though the part about Nancy being my queen was now questionable.

Bobby was being entertained by a group of three people—two women and a man—as we made our way through the crowd toward where he was parked. He was facing us; his guests forming a semicircle with their backs turned to us. Bobby spotted us over their shoulders and his smile brightened as it always does when he looks at Ashley.

I never understood how he fell so deeply in love with Ashley so quickly, but with what I was feeling for Sonia, I sort of began understanding that it was possible.

"Darling, look who's here," Ashley sang when we were within earshot of Bobby.

Bobby's guests turned to see who had approached. There was an elegant older lady around Bobby's age, a somewhat ordinary looking young man, probably a few years my junior with a dark-skin young lady draped on his arm. Our eyes met. Those eyes: so familiar, but somehow different. I guess it was the surprise and apprehension in them that made them look different.

Nancy.

Busted!

"Darling, this is Khris' date, Sonia. Isn't she just the most gorgeous woman here tonight?"

"I beg to differ, dear. You are the most gorgeous woman on the yacht tonight, and every night," he said, kissing his wife. His gaze landed on Sonia. "No offense, Sonia. You are indeed very beautiful...A very, very close second."

"No offense taken, and thank you," Sonia blushed.

"Honey," he said, gazing lovingly at Ashley, "she can share first place with you, if you are so inclined, but you can never be second to any woman, baby."

Gat's to be more fucking careful. Bobby is one smart, smooth-talking man. He's the best. If he only had the stamina like I did, he would be a perfect man.

The look on Nancy's face when she heard that Sonia was my date was priceless and unforgettable. My father told me something back when I found my first girlfriend, that I never forgot: If you're going to cheat and take a woman out in public where you risk getting caught, make sure the woman you are out cheating with is finer than your woman. Your woman will be upset, but she's going to forgive you—she may even pretend she didn't catch you. She'll think you cheated because she's not pretty enough: that you're upgrading. She may even step up her game to try and keep the other woman from taking you away completely. But, if you cheat with an ugly woman and get caught, your woman will drag your ass through the mud and never take you back. She won't respect you ever again because you downgraded. You would never again be worthy of her.

Nancy sure as hell won't be able to drag me through the mud. And, the dude she was with? Destiny was right, Nancy damn sure downgraded.

"It's a pleasure to meet you, Sonia."

"The pleasure is all mine," Sonia smiled, shaking his hand.

"Khris, my dear friend. Once again, you've touched me deeply. Another beautiful woman."

"I'll keep this one, if it's alright with you, Bobby."

"Not to worry, my friend. I've got more than I can handle with Ashley," he joked. "Well, it's about time you find you a good woman—a good, beautiful woman—to make you as happy as my Ashley makes me. I am happy for you. Oh!" he said, as if he just remembered there were others standing there. "Let me introduce you. We were just tossing out some business ideas when you all walked up," he chuckled.

I remembered Bobby telling me that he doesn't enjoy talking business when he's supposed to be enjoying himself or spending quality time with his wife.

"This is an old college friend, Corporate Attorney, Susan Holtz; her younger brother Michael, a young and upcoming Investment Banker. You might want to get his business card; send some business his way. And this lovely young lady is his girlfriend..."

His girlfriend? Not his date, his girlfriend!

"...Nancy Jackson, she's Pre-Law and working at Holtz's firm."

Nancy hadn't said one word. She didn't even interrupt and say that we knew each other. That's my Queen of Spades: she just keeps digging herself into a deeper hole.

"Hello," I said, shaking everyone's hand. "Nice to meet you all." I even shook Nancy's hand, but I didn't let her get off that easy, though. I didn't want to cause a scene, but I did want to rattle her cage a bit. "Nancy and I are actually very well acquainted," I said with a smile, looking her dead in the eyes. I released her hand, turned and motioned Sonia closer. With my palm resting right at the small of her back and the rise of her hips, I eased her closer, still. "I would like to introduce you all to my date, Sonia Symonette. Both of us recently found ourselves single, so perhaps on this star-filled night among so many loving couples, I may be able to persuade her into becoming my girlfriend."

Sonia smiled invitingly, and nodded. "Hello," Sonia sang, turning her attention back to the others, and started shaking their hands.

"We're going to help you persuade her," Bobby chimed. "Don't you worry, Khris, I've got your back."

Sonia and Ashley had caught on that this was my Nancy. Neither had ever seen Nancy or met her, but they now knew who she was.

They were both happy for different reasons, and it showed.

When Sonia got to Nancy, she said, "It's especially nice to meet you, Nancy." With her back slightly turned to the others, she silently mouthed, "Thank you."

The entire time that Sonia was shaking their hands, Susan was sizing me up? Did she know who I was? Did she catch on? Did she see or feel something?

Once Sonia and Nancy's little exchange was over, Susan took a sip of her champagne, then smirked. "Khris, what exactly is it that you do?"

This is where the conversation normally gets interesting at these high society parties. Everyone starts throwing around his or her job and position: their status in society. They want to establish the pecking order: the food chain. I didn't mind. Didn't mind at all. I know who I am and what I'm worth. I took a sip of my champagne, smiled, and said, "I'm a flight attendant."

"A flight attendant?" Michael shot, looking at the others. "What type of business can you send my way? Oh wait, you can probably pass out my business cards in First, and Business Class cabins."

Michael and Susan laughed. No one else did. Nancy held her head down.

Bobby turned and stared at Michael, but before he could say anything, Ashley draped her arm through mine. "Michael, you know that building that your sister has been kind enough to lease you a unit until you get yourself together?"

"Yes."

"Well, you know what those units go for, don't you?"

"Yes, he knows. They," she said, pointing to Michael and Nancy, "want to purchase one in a year or two. But, why are you asking Michael such irrelevant questions," Susan asked, coming to her brother's defense.

I saw the look on Bobby's face. It was clear that he didn't take too kindly to Susan talking to his wife in that manner. In a stern but calm tone, he jumped in. "Well Susan it is relevant because while he is a flight attendant, Khris here happens to own not one, but two, ocean view units on the floor directly beneath the penthouse level in that building. One of my management companies gets paid to run his rental properties not just in that building. So, don't any of you dare take that condescending tone with him? He does what he does because he wants to, not because he has to."

Bobby was right. I did own two units in the luxury condo towers in Palm Beach. What he didn't tell them was that he gave me the two units for hooking him up with the deal. Destiny had given me the foreclosure list and it had the almost completed building listed. The builders ran out of money and the bank was letting it go for thirty cents on the dollar. I did a little research and number crunching, and took the deal to Bobby. He was impressed with my presentation and jumped on it. Destiny got her a nice chunk of cash, and I got two units. All the remaining units sold out completely before the building was completed. Bobby tripled his investment in a year.

Bobby's face softened as he turned to me. "Khris, I apologize for asking you to send any business his way. Please forgive me. Why don't you and Sonia, join my wife and me in our private quarters so we can get to know Sonia before we push off and the partying starts. The air out here is a bit too stuffy for me tonight."

I smiled at the jab. "No apology necessary, Bobby, and it would be our pleasure," I answered for Sonia and me.

"If you would indulge an old man, my dear?" Bobby asked, bowing slightly with his hand extended to Sonia.

"Yes, you may, kind sir." Sonia smiled, gave a little curtsey before taking his hand.

Bobby nestled her hand in the crock of his arm and led us away without another word to Susan, Michael, or Nancy.

I smiled at Nancy as me and Ashley followed behind her king and my queen.

"She's great!" Ashley said softly. "Forget about Nancy. If she's with that crew, then she doesn't deserve you. I never did like Susan's pretentious ass. Her brother seems to be the same way, too. It's in their blood. So, tell me about Sonia."

"I'm not telling you about her, that'll give you an unfair advantage."

"I'll always have an unfair advantage when it comes to you. But, from the looks of things, I may only have a few good years left. Maybe less."

I didn't respond.

"I know we can't keep this up forever, Khris. But, I'm not giving up. You're going to have to stop me," she teased, kissing me on the cheek with a loud smack.

Yes, all this will have to come to an end one day. Yes, Sonia may just be the one.

Sonia: My Queen of Hearts.

CHAPTER 26

NIGHT MOVES

The night was a complete success. Sonia and I drank champagne and danced the night away with Ashley and Bobby. I tried not to look, but I couldn't help but notice that Nancy was having a miserable night. She drank, but she hadn't danced.

The fashion slash hair show was also a huge success. At the end of the show, Sonia was called up to the stage and was given special thanks for being the supplier of all the human hair that was used in the show. After a rousing round of applause, Sonia was overwhelmed with people wanting to know how they can purchase her hair products. She hadn't come prepared. She hadn't brought any business cards, but Ashley quickly remedied that. Ashley gave Sonia the use of the computer and laser printer in the suite's office. Sonia quickly designed and printed out one hundred business cards which Ashley had two of the hostesses pass out to those that requested information on purchasing Sonia's human hair.

Ashley even brought over her own stylist. He was also very much interested in purchasing human hair for his chain of a dozen upscale salons in Florida, Georgia, and the Carolinas.

Like I said, Bobby didn't like discussing business while he was supposed to be partying, so we went out on the private rear deck and did what guys did when their women were away: we drank Louis XIII, smoked Cuban Cigars, and admired all the exposed flesh that was on display down below.

The Lady Ashley docked at two a.m. back at the Yacht Club. Sonia and I walked out with Bobby and Ashley. I was happy to see that their chauffeur driven Rolls Royce Phantom was there to whisk them to their Palm Beach Estate, because they were wasted.

Bobby waved, said, "Good night," then fell into the backseat. Ashley gave Sonia a kiss on the lips, then fell into my arms.

She gave me a quick smack on the lips and laughed. "I'm going to put it on him real good on the drive home. You two should try it in the car. It's sooooo goooood," she sang as I helped her into the back of the Phantom.

"You have a chauffeur: one of us has to drive," I replied. "Have fun."

Ashley laughed. "Drive safely and you two be good." The driver nodded to us and closed the door.

We waved bye as they pulled off. The Benz was brought around and Sonia said, "I can't drive. Too much excitement. Too much..."

"Alcohol," I finished for her.

I opened the passenger door and helped her inside. I tipped the valet and got behind the wheel. I wasn't drunk. I was feeling good, but I wasn't drunk.

"Are you okay?" Sonia asked as I pulled out of the Yacht Club's parking lot.

"I'm better than ever," I replied, "Why?"

"I was just wondering. We hadn't had a moment of privacy to talk about you seeing Nancy there like that."

"I knew she was going out as Michael's date, but I would have never expected for us to end up at the same function."

"And you were okay with her going on a date with her boss's brother?" she squeaked.

"Yes. I didn't have a problem with it," I said, glancing over at her. "I had my own date that I was concerned with."

"So, now that you know those two are an item, are you and me...are we a couple. Boyfriend and girlfriend?"

"Do you want to be my girlfriend?" I asked, running my fingers across her sweet lips.

"I would love to be your girlfriend."

"Do you want to be my boyfriend?" she asked seductively.

"I would love to be your everything, Sonia Symonette."

"Ooooooh!" she shivered. "You just made my kitty purr!" Sonia said. "She's getting wet."

I shook my head and laughed. When I glanced over, Sonia had her hands under her dress and was wiggling out of her underwear. "What are you doing?"

"What are you doing?" she giggled, imitating me, then hung her lacy black thong on the rear view mirror.

"You drunk?"

"What difference does it make? I'm your girlfriend and you're my boyfriend. So hush and push the seat as far back as it can go. Lay the seatback down," she ordered, reaching over, loosening my belt.

"Someone's feeling freaky tonight," I said with growing excitement. I set the cruise control while raising my hips so she could slide my pants down.

"Oh yeah, baby!" she said, grabbing and stroking me lovingly. She leaned her head down and took me into her hot mouth. No licking: no kissing: no teasing. She took me all in. I felt my bulging head rub against the soft spot all the way in the back of her mouth.

She went down too fast, causing herself to gag.

"Take it easy before you hurt yourself," I teased, running my fingers on the back of her neck.

She eased up, sucked, stroked, and licked me proper for a little while, then she rose up. "Back up a bit. I'ma climb over and straddle you. I'm gonna ride you while you drive," she giggled. "I hope my ass doesn't bump the steering wheel," she said, climbing over.

My dick was throbbing now. I kept one hand on the steering wheel, scooting up onto the back of the seat.

Sonia climbed over and somehow managed to lower her hot wet pussy onto my dick without using her hands.

Both of us sighed and moaned loudly, savoring the satisfying feel of each other.

"I know you couldn't wait to get up in this sweet pussy."

"Mmmm-hmmm!" I mumbled as I rotated my hips, pushing deep into her.

"I felt your dick rubbing up on me as we danced. I wanted to feel you in me all night. I couldn't wait to leave."

Sonia's shoulders were slouched; her neck bent low, so that her head wouldn't hit the roof or block my view of the road ahead. I couldn't stroke her too hard, and she couldn't ride me as hard as she wanted. The limited movement made it all the sweeter. Her swollen clit was making direct contact onto me, and my dick was pounding against her back walls. I felt her orgasm coming.

"Khris! I'm coming," she gasped, biting on my earlobe.

"Mmmmm Come... Ssssss. Come with me, baby," she whispered hotly next to my ear.

"You come, baby. I can't come yet. I want you to come for me. I'll get mine later." I kept looking over her left shoulder to watch the road ahead, but I used one hand and got it up under her. I lathered up my middle finger real good as I rocked into her and caressed her ass, waiting for just the right moment.

Sonia sang sweetly in my ear. "I love you, Khris." She sounded as if she was getting ready to cry.

"Show me how much you love me," I said, getting rougher with my strokes.

Her breathing and her strokes got erratic. She was at the brink. I slid the tip of my finger into her ass. Her body clenched. Her pussy and ass tightened. I got wicked with my strokes as I slid the tip of my lathered finger in and out of her ass. Then went deeper as both sets of muscles spasmed.

Sonia let out one long curse. "Fuuuuuuuuuuuuck!" Her orgasm came crashing down. She started grinding down on my dick like a wild woman. Back, forth; left, right; clockwise, counterclockwise. Ambitious. Seeking.

Sonia rode my finger and my dick to two more orgasms before I pulled into the garage. That's what I loved about sex with Sonia. She didn't hold back. Once she started coming, she just couldn't stop.

The garage door rolled back down as I shut down the engine.

I made her climb out, then followed her. I was ready to get my first nut and I couldn't wait to go inside.

I braced her up against the Range, hiked up the back of her dress and rammed my dick deep into her pulsing pussy. My strokes came from my knees and went all the way up until I was almost lifting her up from the ground.

"Fuck me hard, Khris!" she growled like she was possessed.

I grunted and fucked her hard: like I was possessed. I reached in front of her and squeezed her breast, pinching and plumping her nipples through her clothes. I was fucking her with animalistic need. I was fucking her with reckless abandon. I felt my orgasm coming. It was way out, but I was thrusting harder and faster: fighting to bring it in closer. I wanted this nut. I needed this nut. It felt like it was coming up, then backing down. I was straining—fighting—to get this nut.

The automatic light clicked off. Sonia started coming again.

I wanted to come with her. I was pounding harder. Faster. I was panting and grunting, sweating and cursing.

She exploded. My nut was getting closer. I heard a car turn in my driveway.

My nut was coming closer. My balls churned and tightened.

I heard the motor to the garage door whirring.

The door started up. The automatic light clicked on.

I had to beat the door. I pumped harder. Faster. It was right there, but being difficult.

Everything seemed to be happening in slow motion.

Sonia turned her head toward the opening garage door. Light spilled under the door lighting our feet.

Sonia was still coming. My nut was right there. It was rising. The door was rising. The light was up to my knee and getting higher.

My nut was halfway up my shaft. I was going to beat the door. I pumped faster, going as deep as I could. I gripped Sonia's ass cheeks, spreading them all the way open. I had to come.

The car's headlights switched to high beam. It was lighting the way.

I stroked harder.

The car horn blew long and hard, shattering the silent night.

My nut blew powerful and strong.

Sonia screamed and reached back to try and pull down her dress. I kept stroking as my first load of liquid love shot into her.

Sonia tried to wriggle free. By then, I had two handfuls of her firm ass cheeks. I gripped tighter, rammed harder, and sprayed my liquid love deep into her.

We were bathed in light. I couldn't stop until every ounce of my liquid love was in her. I had to give Sonia all of my love.

A car door opened. The garage door motor stopped whirring. I heard the sound of running feet.

A shadow crossed in front of the light.

I heard a piercing scream.

I heard a barbaric cry. Then Sonia was free.

The cool night air replaced Sonia's warmth. The last of my liquid love spilled onto the cold concrete. I looked down at my wasted love.

I looked up. Nancy and Sonia were fighting.

My big head took back control of my body. "Oh! Hell fucking no," I yelled, hopping toward the fight with my pants still down around my ankles. I knew better than to grab Sonia; that would be an easy way for Nancy to get free blows in. Instead of grabbing any of them, I ducked and put myself between them, then rose up.

I was trying to keep them from hitting and kicking each other while trying to pull up my pants. I should have pulled up my pants first, but hindsight is 20/20. It was hard as hell to separate them while trying to pull up my pants. I was bent over with my ass poking out to try and bump Sonia back, while I used my free hand to push Nancy back toward her car.

The noise must have woken up my mother, sister, and Nishka, because the next thing I knew they were in the garage.

"What the hell is going on out here?" my mother asked as Yasmine and Nishka ran and pulled a kicking and screaming Sonia back toward the garage.

There I stood, my mother, woken up out of her peaceful sleep, staring at me in my driveway with my pants down around my ankles and my wet dick still standing tall in the night air. How fucking embarrassing.

"Boy, pull up your pants!" my mother said in disgust. "And what the hell's going on out here."

"Your no good son! That's what's going on out here," Nancy screamed back at my mother.

"You need to go the fuck home or back to Michael," I shouted, pulling up my pants.

Nancy pointed at Sonia. "He parading this bitch around all night, and then had the nerve to bring her back here to our house and fuck her."

"Our house?" I snarled.

Sonia was still trying to break free. "Come here! I'll show you who is a bitch. Y'all let me go!" Sonia yelled. "I promise I een ga kill da ho: I just ga beat her muthafuckin ass."

"Our house?" I snarled. "You and Michael saving to buy y'all one in a year or two, right?"

"That man and Michael's sister don't know what they're talking about," Nancy snarled, but made no attempt to get to Sonia.

Sonia was still ranting and raving and trying to break free from Yasmine and Nishka. I know if my mother weren't here, they would have let Sonia go.

"Ho, you don't know me. I will beat your ass. I don't know who you callin a bitch," Sonia ranted.

"Who you callin a ho, bitch?" Nancy shouted back. "You the ho. You the one getting fucked against a car in the garage."

"Why don't you bring your ass in the garage, let me show you what else I could do up in dis bitch! Een nobody holdin you back. Come on, ho! All this talkin een even necessary."

"Sonia!" I yelled, pointing at her. "That's enough!"

"Yeah! You need to put a muzzle on that bitch," Nancy yelled.

"Nancy, give me my fucking house keys, my transponder and my muthafuckin garage door opener," I snarled, then hit myself in the forehead with my opened palm. "I don't believe y'all gat me out here cussin in front of my mother."

"Yeah! Free up, ho!" Sonia chimed victoriously. She stopped fighting to get loose from Yasmine and Nishka.

I saw the hurt in Nancy's eyes as the waterworks started. "Just because this bitch fuck you in the garage and sucked your dick in the driveway on Tuesday...Oh! My bad," Nancy said, forcing a laugh through her tears, and staring over at Sonia, "that wasn't you sucking his dick, was it? I forgot it was the little Brazilian fight attendant. All y'all hos look alike with his dick down y'all throat."

Fuck! Nancy had seen me. That was her ass. Fuck! Fuck! Fuck!

"And while you was there laughing up and talking to that green-eyed bitch, you never even realized that her pussy juice was probably all over his mouth and dick that you was sucking and fucking. I wonder how Bobby's going to feel about his dear friend when the private detective that Susan put on Ashley's ass gets the proof. I'm sure he's not going to be happy to find out it's his dear friend, Khris, that's fucking his beautiful queen."

I was stunned. "Nancy! Get the fuck off my property. You round here spreadin rumors. I. Am. Not. Fucking. Ashley!"

"Tell her. Tell her who bought you all those fucking diamonds and watches. You can't afford them on your salary."

"I have other assets and income that you have no clue about."

"So I learned tonight...probably the money that green-eyed bitch paying you to fuck her. I wonder if she knows that the same dick she's spending all that money to get, you out here giving it to every bitch willing to drop her drawers?"

Sonia was quiet.

My mother was quiet.

Yasmine was quiet.

Nishka was quiet.

"Yeah, you thought Nancy was plain old stupid and didn't know what the fuck you was doing, huh? I know all about your tricking. My mother and aunt saw you out tricking, Khris. That's why their attitude changed toward you. I loved your ass so bad, I lied and told them that was one of your co-workers you were out with, and that you had told me where you was going and who you was with. I even made up a bitch's name. I lied to cover your shit. And, the worst part is that they knew I was lying. I never cheated on you, Khris. Never. I went up to Susan's place for lunch on Sunday and she tried to hook me up with her brother because she thinks I deserve better. She doesn't like you because she found out how close you are to Ashley. She hates Ashley. I didn't want you to get angry, so I lied. And I felt guilty for lying about where I was and who I was with, so I had to tell you. I asked you if I could go out tonight. Susan introduced me as Michael's girlfriend. I never even kissed Michael. All I did was let him hold my hand when we walked through City Place. And I only let him get away with it because I didn't want to embarrass him in front of his friends. I felt fucking guilty the entire time. I thought if I loved you with all I had, you would love me and eventually stop sleeping around, but you can't stop, can you? You're not gonna stop until someone kills you for fucking their woman, or till you catch something you can't get rid of."

The only sound I could hear was Nancy's car idling. And that's a brand new Lexus. They don't even sound like they're on at idle.

"All of you standing there like y'all pitying me," she paused, looking at each of them. "That's why I don't come around when y'all here. Y'all know he sleeps around, and when I'm around, even if y'all are being nice to me, I feel as though y'all are laughing at me and calling me a naive little ass. Yes, I love him," she shouted, focusing her attention on Sonia. "But I want you to remember, bitch, the same thing he's doing to me, he's going to do to your ass. And," she paused, turning her gaze on me, "the same thing some man is going to do to the two of them," she said, pointing at Yasmine and Nishka.

Sonia, Yasmine, nor Nishka said a word. I was speechless. She had me fucked up.

My mother spoke up. "Boy, you need to settle this. I'm going back inside. Sonia, come inside and let them sort this shit out."

"She needs to go the fuck home!" Nancy stated.

"I was invited to be here. You wasn't," Sonia retorted.

"Bitch, I have a key. I don't need a fucking invitation. I can come and go as I fucking please."

"Sonia," I said softly, "go inside, please."

"No! She's right. I'm going home," she said, turning and heading for her car. She jumped in, started her engine and started backing up. I couldn't let her go. I ran to the car and knocked on the window for her to stop. I tried to open her door, but she hit the power locks on my ass. She didn't stop. I banged on the hood and begged for her to stop.

Sonia maneuvered around Nancy's car, down the driveway, and then sped off.

Nancy stood in the driveway with a shit-eating grin on her face and waved bye to Sonia.

I wanted to slap the shit out of her, but I don't believe in hitting women. There's no excuse anyone can give me for hitting my sister or my mother, so I could not, would not hit someone else's sister or mother...any woman. My father once told me 'If a woman makes you angry to the point where you want to hit her, it's time to let her go.

This time you can stop yourself from hitting her; next time, you might not be so strong.'

I reached into Nancy's car, switched off the engine, and removed the key from the ignition. I snatched the transponder off the top of her windshield, and grabbed the garage door opener off the visor at the same time.

"What are you doing?" Nancy yelled. "She's gone. I'm angry with you, Khris, but I still love you. Why are you taking those?"

She started trying to grab the stuff out of my hand, but I kept turning so that she was always trying to reach over my back. I found my house keys and removed them from her key ring. I gave her back her keys. "You have two minutes to be off my property or I'm calling the police.

"But, Khris, I love you."

"Love died when Jesus died."

"Khris, you don't mean that..."

"Nancy, you and your boss and Michael are all alike: y'all a bunch of pretentious muthafu...wannabes. Y'all trying to ruin something good for y'all own personal agenda. Don't you realize that Susan is jealous of Ashley? She wants Ashley's man. Bobby doesn't want Susan." I was pissed at Nancy for causing Sonia to leave; I wanted to hurt her. I snickered and shook my head. "You and me, we could never be, Nancy. It's because of you that I still cheated with all those other women. You're just not woman enough to make me give up that life. The woman that I just let drive away, I may not have known her that long, but at least she had me thinking about giving all that shit up. That's more than I could say for you. What we had was fun while it lasted. It's over, so close the book on this chapter of your life and try to make the next chapter better. Good night."

I signaled for my mother, Yasmine and Nishka to go inside. I could see my mother wasn't pleased at what I had just said: not pleased with this whole shit. I knew I would get a good tongue lashing for this. But, I would cross that bridge when I get there.

I walked inside the garage and pressed the button to lower the garage door. I watched it roll down, closing out that chapter of my own life. "Good bye, Nancy," I whispered, then waited for the light to shut off.

Before it shut off. I heard Nancy's car start. Her door slammed close about the same time. Then the car backed out of my driveway.

The light clicked off.

The car drove off. Then there was silence to go with the darkness.

Darkness in front of my eyes.

Darkness in my heart.

CHAPTER 27

WIPING THE SLATE CLEAN

I closed the door to the garage and turned. Bap! My mother slapped the taste out of my mouth.

"Don't you ever disrespect a woman like that ever again, you hear me?" she snarled. "You know I raise you better than that."

I was stunned. I hadn't gotten a cut-ass since I was about fourteen. I just proved you're never too old to get a cut-ass.

"I guess I deserved that," I said, rubbing my face and flexing my jaw.

"You damn sure did. Did you hear yourself out there?"

She must have arthritis in those hands. I swore I tasted blood in my mouth. I was embarrassed for what I had done; what I had said. I couldn't look my mother in her eyes. "I'm sorry," I said, turning and heading into the kitchen. "I messed up."

"You damn sure did," Yasmine said, following us in the kitchen.

"You watch your mouth before you get slap, too," my mother said, wheeling around.

"I'm just sayin. I don't really like Nancy, but he messed up with Sonia."

"Yeah," Nishka said. "God knows I wanted to let Sonia go."

"I have to call her. She was drunk. I don't know if she could make it home." I reached for my phone, then I remembered it was in her car. "Shit!"

"What?" my mother asked.

"My phone is in Sonia's car." I walked over to the phone on the wall and dialed Sonia's cell phone number.

My doorbell chimed as the phone rang in my ears.

"That's probably the police: all that racket y'all was kickin up out there," my mother chimed, heading toward the front door with Yasmine and Nishka right along with her.

Sonia's phone kept ringing, but she didn't answer. It went to the voice mail. I tried my cell. That rang and rang. I hung up and dialed Sonia's number again. Voice mail again.

I was hitting the redial button when my mother walked back into the kitchen followed by Sonia, Yasmine and Nishka. I let out a sigh of relief. "I was just calling you. I didn't hear you pull up. I was worried about you driving in your condition," I riddled as she walked up to the island bar and took a seat.

"First of all, Mom, if I can still call you Mom?"

My mother nodded.

"I want to apologize to you and Yasmine and Nishka for the language and the way I acted earlier. I'm sorry."

"Your apology is accepted, baby. Just so you know, back in my day, I had to put a few heifers face down in the dirt for my man, too. I would lay hands on a heifer like a Baptist Minister. These hands of mine were quick," Mom bragged.

"Still quick," Yasmine giggled, bumping Nishka. "Khris still een know what hand he get slapped with."

"Shut up before you see if you can take one and remain standing," mom shot,   staring Yasmine down.

"I didn't want to fight Nancy. I just didn't want her to scratch me. That wouldn't have been fair for me to fight her. I just wanted to stop her from hitting me. I wanted to get Nancy angry. People say exactly how they feel when they're angry."

"She said too much, if you ask me," Nishka shot.

"So why did you leave when I specifically told you to come inside?" I asked.

"If I had came inside, Khris would have felt obligated to turn Nancy away. He wouldn't have had a choice. With me storming off like I did, and him thinking I was gone for good, he was free to choose how he wanted to deal with Nancy."

"You're too levelheaded and in control for me," Yasmine shot.

"How did you know I would tell her to leave?" I asked, sitting down at the island bar.

"You asked me to be your girlfriend earlier tonight. I accepted. I trusted you to do the right thing. A man can only serve one queen, remember?" she said, staring into my eyes.

"Humph!" Mom snipped.

"What?" I asked, not believing my own mother found that hard to believe that Sonia trusted me.

"I know, Mom. I know everything that Nancy said tonight was true. Khris is what he is. I know he was intentionally trying to hurt her when he said what he said, but," she paused, looking my mother in her eyes, "I am not Nancy. He told me about Ashley. Ashley basically told me tonight. And I knew about the three Brazilian flight attendants. He didn't tell me what he was going to do with them, but we're all adults. I knew what he would be doing. I would have thought he would have been more discrete than in the driveway."

Nishka snorted. "Like in the garage."

"You're right. Heat of the moment." Sonia smiled sheepishly. "The point is that I came in knowing what he is. Khris," she said, looking at me, "I know you're a good person. What we share is...I can't even find the right words."

"Y'all used up all the adjectives earlier," Yasmine joked.

"It's amazing," she chimed. She glanced at her hands for a second. "I want to be with you, Khris. But..."

"Why does there always have to be a but?" I mumbled.

"I was standing there listening to Nancy. I believed her. That could be me in a few months or a year. Like I said, I know who and what you are up front. You never told Nancy. She found out on her own. You hurt her, Khris. You hurt and embarrassed her with her family. I could see me doing the same thing; defending my love for you against all others, but I can't see me letting you make a fool out of me. I can't let you disrespect me."

My brows furrowed. "So what are you saying?"

Mom signaled Yasmine and Nishka. "Maybe we should leave."

Yasmine and Nishka pouted and folded their arms across their chests defiantly. Of course, Mom didn't see them.

"No, y'all stay," Sonia, said, signaling for them to sit.

"I want you all to hear what I have to say. I love Khris. I didn't intend to fall in love with him, at least not this quickly, but it happened. Khris, you have issues. Issues you need to work out. You want to be a good man, but for some reason, you don't seem to be able to be the man you want to be. You're fighting with yourself."

I could only stare. What could I say? She was right.

"Khris, you asked me to be your girlfriend. I accepted. I asked you to be my boyfriend. You said you wanted to be my everything, right?"

I nodded. "That's what I said, and I meant it."

"Well, prove that you want to be my everything. Prove that you can be the man you want to be. Stop cheating. And don't do it for me. Do it because you want to do it. You can think about it over the weekend. I'm not going anywhere. If I need to help you: If you need me to handcuff you to the bed...maybe that's the wrong thing to suggest. If you need me to lock you in the house and watch you in case you start having physical withdrawal symptoms, I'll do that. I'll be here for whatever you need."

I looked at her. I couldn't believe what she was telling me. I looked at my mother and I could tell she agreed with Sonia. I didn't bother looking at either Yasmine or Nishka.

"Mom, she asked you to stay, so..." I let my voice trail off, then I turned to Sonia. "What if my problem is that I'm addicted to sex?"

She chuckled. "Addicted to sex with different partners, or just addicted to the act itself?"

"The act itself."

"If that's the case, and you are indeed trying to be the man you want to be, then I'll make it available anytime and anyhow you want it."

"She already prove that in the garage," Yasmine joked, drawing light chuckles from everyone.

"This is serious business going on in here, Yasmine," my mother scolded, while chuckling herself.

"She's right, though. I thought I proved it, too," Sonia smirked, eying me.

I smiled and shook my head.

"Are you willing to try?"

"Of course," I replied. I really didn't want to lose Sonia, but I really would have to think about what she was really asking me to do. This was the answer to make everyone happy so I could go upstairs and take a shower, and hopefully get into Sonia again.

"Okay," Sonia said. "We can hang out for the rest of the

weekend, but we'll have to tune it down several notches until you make a firm decision and show that you really are serious."

"How am I supposed to show that I'm serious if you holding out on me? That's going to push me the other way?"

"Curb your gat-damn appetite for a while." Mom let out an exasperated breath. "Stop thinking about sex as just a physical act. Start thinking about it emotionally. Sex is exponentially better the stronger the emotional connection is. Now, I'm going upstairs to sleep. Macy's sale is in the morning and I don't plan on missing it. Sonia, you coming?"

"Wouldn't miss it. Make sure I'm up. I'll drive. We can leave him my car."

"Good night," Sonia said to me, wiggling her fingers as she waved. "Sleep tight."

"Aren't you coming..."

"Nope. The yellow guest room where my clothes are," Sonia said, cutting me off.

"Go take a cold shower and go to bed," Mom said as they walked out of the kitchen.

Sonia stopped and turned to face me. "Before you do that, you can go and get my car from around the corner," she said, pointing to her keys on the island.

Damn! I had to sleep by myself tonight.

I went and got Sonia's car and parked it in the garage. I took down her thong from the rear view mirror and twirled it around my finger as I went upstairs. On my way to my room, I stopped and tapped on her door.

She opened the door with a towel draped around her. "I was just going in the shower. Want to join me?" she asked in a sultry tone.

"Don't be playing with me. You know I want to."

"Come on," she said, pulling me in. "Shower. No sex, okay?"

"I better shower in my room, then. I can't promise you that. You and me naked together."

"Control, Khris. You have to learn to practice control. If you start with me, you'll be able to resist others."

"No. I don't want to resist the woman I want to spend the rest of my life with."

"You proposing?"

"No. I don't have a ring. Yet."

"You had control when you slept naked in the bed with me the first night I stayed here."

"That was different. I hadn't had a taste of that sweetness, yet."

"You are so full off shit. Come on. Take off those clothes and get your ass in the shower. I done see how I ga have to handle you."

"How?"

"Don't ask you to do anything."

"What? Isn't that a little extreme?"

"No. I'll simply tell you what to do," she stated and dropped the towel.

"What makes you think I'm going to do what you tell me to do?"

"If you love me, you will. If you don't love me, you won't. It's that simple."

I nodded and started taking off my clothes. "You make it sound so simple."

"You love me?"

"Yes. As long as you do right by me."

Sonia rolled her eyes. "A simple yes or no would suffice."

"Yes."

"Okay. Kiss me and get in here so you can wash my back."

"Yes, dear."

I woke up to an empty house and a note. Yes, we had slept in the same bed, and no we didn't have sex. We cuddled.

I took a deep breath and thought about my life. Sonia was all that I was looking for. She's a go-getter; she has a good head on her shoulders; she's fun to be around; she's fun to have around; she's sexy; thoughtful; considerate; kind; loving; my mother and sisters love her; my friends love her; I love her...

I needed to start cleaning house. I have to let some of these women go. I did say some, because Ashley wasn't going anywhere: not yet, anyway. That reminded me: I needed to call Ashley and tell her about Susan putting that private dick on her. I looked at the time and decided it would be better to call later. It wasn't noon yet. And as wasted as Ashley and Bobby were last night, I knew they were still asleep.

I slipped on a pair of shorts that Sonia had so kindly placed on her pillow, and went downstairs to the kitchen. There was a place setting at the bar with a post it notes on an empty glass. Breakfast is in the microwave. You can pour your own juice. Sonia.

"What the hell?" I opened the microwave. "Boil Fish! I could get used to this. I gat to start calling and canceling some of these bitches."

My phone rang: the house phone. The caller ID read: Nancy.

"Already cancelled." I didn't bother to answer.

I didn't know where to start or how to start, so I decided to wait until they call me. What the hell would I say: 'Hey, we can't do what we used to do anymore; I have a girlfriend.' Fool, you always had a girlfriend. 'I decided I'm going to be faithful.' Ha ha haha ha haaaa. I could hear them laughing at me.

I heated up my food and tried to decide what I would do with my life. Could I stop? I could if I wanted to. I know what I'll do: I'll see how long I can go without sex. And, I'm going to do this for me. I'll start off slow. I'll start off with one day. Then I'll try for two. Then I'll try for a week. "I wonder if I could make a month?"

I finished off my breakfast, which was delicious, by the way. The girl can really cook.

I called Ashley, and to my surprise, she and Bobby were out shopping. "We were just talking about you," she said. "What are you and Sonia doing today? Why don't you two join us for lunch?"

"Sonia's at the Macy's One Day Sale with my mother and sisters."

"Oh! You did tell me Mom was here. Right. So what's up?"

"I found out who put the PI on you."

"Who?"

"Susan."

"That bitch! How did you find out?"

"Got caught with my pants down by Nancy last night, and she said she knew about me and everything I do. She accused me of sleeping with you."

"Duh! I practically told Sonia that last night."

"Sonia, but not Nancy. Bobby must be out of earshot."

"Yes. He's shopping, not me. I'm just here for support." Ashley laughed. "So, Nancy accused you, and you say you got caught with your pants down."

"Literally. Following your instructions, Sonia started in the car. We ended up in the garage, then Nancy showed up and caught us in the act right when I was getting mine."

"I hope Sonia got hers." Ashley laughed. "And Sonia didn't leave you? You say she's with your mother, right?"

"Yes. You know she got hers, she was on the good end of this dick," I bragged. "Of course she stayed."

"Smart girl. She's a keeper! You have to keep her, Khris. That's real love right there. And, I want to apologize for coming on so strong last night. I felt threatened by her. I could tell that she came to take you away: not emotionally, but sexually."

"She does want me to stop what I'm doing."

"What do you want?"

"I want to stop, but I don't know if I can."

"Are you willing to try?"

"Why?"

"Because if you're willing to try, then that means that you truly care for her. It means that she can be the one for you. I want you to be as happy as you've helped me to become."

"Are you saying that you're willing to stop?"

"Last night in the back of the Rolls, we got to talking, and we decided it's time we started working on a family."

"That's great!"

"I've never told you, Khris, but Bobby had a nip and snip before we met. He said he didn't want any woman to intentionally get pregnant to hit him up for child support. A couple weeks ago, he went to Switzerland on a business trip. Last night, he told me that he had actually gone to have his procedure reversed. He wants us to have children. When he told me that last night, it made me the happiest woman alive. I know he gave me all the material things I could ever want, but giving me children. That's the greatest gift I can get."

"Congratulations, Ashley. I'm-I'm..."

"And, guess what? His stamina has increased since the plumbing is connected again. It must have been a mind thing, but my baby slinging like an eighteen year old...well maybe a thirty five year old," she added, giggling.

"So, do we get one for the road?"

"We can, if you want to. When?" she whispered conspiratorially.

"Just checking to see if you still loved me," I chuckled, relieved that the pussy was still available if and when I wanted.

"Of course, I still love you. I will always love you. I am just so happy-happy for the both of us. We need to press pause for a while; get that Susan bitch off my case. Let that ho waste some money, then I'll find a way to get back at her ass."

"Cool. I'm going to try and be celibate for a while."

"What?" Ashley squeaked.

"You heard me," I retorted, laughing along with her. "For how long?"

"I'm going to start with a day and work myself up: see how long I can go."

"Whose idea is this?" Ashley asked skeptically.

"Mine. I want to give up the running around. Sonia deserves a good man, and I want to be that man."

"Well, good for you. Even better for Sonia. You know if you need anything: if you're suffering from withdrawal and need a fix, call me. I know I damn sure will be calling you."

"Bye, Ashley," I sang, laughing.

"Bye, and give everyone my love. You can go ahead and keep a little for yourself, too. Smooches."

"You're crazy." I laughed, and ended the call.

That went rather well, I thought. I looked at the phone and smiled.

"Wiping the slate clean might just be easier than I thought."

CHAPTER 28

YES, I CAN

Whatever my mind can conceive, I can achieve. Sounds great, doesn't it? I made it through the weekend without sex. Hurray.

We dropped my mother to the airport, then went and took S's daughter her birthday gift. We ate, drank and hung out for a few hours before dropping Yasmine and Nishka back on campus.

Sonia was skeptical, but supportive in my effort to see how long I could go without sex. We're still affectionate and everything, but I knew I would have to alter my no sex rules soon.

Sunday night, I got a text: Did the Heat win? I responded: Sorry, I can't get the scores anymore. You'll have to get the scores elsewhere.

A reply came back a few minutes later: I figured something was up. I probably need to stop gambling on the games, anyhow. Gambling is getting too dangerous.

Another one down.

Lisa was a problem. She wasn't going away nicely. She kept blowing up my shit. I blocked her number. Well, I let Sonia block that bitch. The number, not Lisa. Lisa was a good person, but she was busting our massage groove, and Sonia was closer to the phone.

I packed Sonia in her car on Monday morning so that she could go to the storage facility and handle her business. After that, she was going over to her apartment to do laundry and straighten up a bit.

I had a full day all to myself, and for the first time, I really didn't know what to do with myself. I really didn't have anything to do: I was almost afraid to stay home by myself for fear of falling weak and finding some pussy to run up in. I decided to check out the foreclosure list and see if anything looked worth checking out. I went out to the patio and did just that. I checked the listings, then used Google earth to get a shot of the house or complex. That didn't do much, so I got dressed and decided to hit the road. I carried my laptop and my digital camera, just in case I saw something worthwhile.

I had just entered the second of the two Boca condos when Sonia called me crying. "I just got home. You should see my apartment. My apartment has been broken into."

I stopped instantly, locked up the unit, placed the key back in the lock box, and headed out of the building. "Have you called the police?"

"Not yet. You should see the place."

"I'm on my way," I said. "Don't touch anything. Go back outside and call the cops."

It took me twenty minutes to get to Sonia's complex. When I got there, the police were already there. I rushed to Sonia's side. Her eyes were red from crying, but other than that, she looked fine.

The police asked the usual questions: "Do you have anyone that's capable of doing this? A jealous boyfriend, perhaps? An angry co-worker?"

Blah, blah, blah.

Sonia gave a curt reply. "No."

I said nothing.

It didn't take them long to do their dusting and come back out to tell us their usual scripted speech: "Chances of finding the perpetrators are slim, if any."

Shortly after, we were allowed to walk through to see if we could spot anything missing—anything that may have been taken. On the way in, the officer pointed out the entry point. It was easy to see. It was right there: the front door. It was plain to see that a crowbar had been used on the doorjamb to pop the locks.

The place was totally trashed. The vandals destroyed everything: electronics and clothes especially. I say the word vandals, not thieves, because the things that are normally taken to be sold, were destroyed. The big screen was smashed, her computer busted, speakers punctured: her clothes—what hadn't been shredded—had been tossed into the bath tubs, basins, and toilets, then soaked in bleach and whatever other household cleaning products she had around. Paint had been poured on her leather furniture; glasses and dishes had been smashed.

With a shine of tears in her eyes, Sonia said, "Everything I have is gone except for the stuff that I took to your place."

"We can go on a shopping spree," I said, hugging her. "My treat," I said, trying to cheer her up.

"I can't let you do that."

"Shush! If you love me you will do as I say. Now, let's go through and see if there is anything here that you can salvage. Then I'll take you home."

"I can't..."

"This place isn't safe. You can't stay here. You can move into the guest room that you so like, since you don't want to shack up with me. If you keep protesting, I'm going take away the room and board that I was going to have you pay," I said, kissing her on her forehead.

"I don't want to impose."

I ignored her. "You can transfer all your calls to your cell phone if you don't want to forward them to my land line. We can forward your mail to my address, or we can get you a private box. Your choice, but you are not staying here. What type of man would your parents think I am? And, I'm not trying to get slapped from my mother again. Now, let's go and see if there is anything valuable that we can salvage."

"I don't think there is anything left here to salvage. It's a good thing I had my jewelry case and laptop at your place. I'll look for a cleaning crew..."

"I'll take care of that. There's a company that I use that can come in, clear this place out, clean it up, and take away the trash when they're done."

"I'll go by the leasing office and see if I can get out of the last two months of my lease. So I hope you found a house for me to buy."

"No house, but the condos I was looking at looks like a good investment."

"Investment?"

"What, you scared of making money? You only have to come up with three to five percent down, and the money to spruce it up a bit."

"You can break it down to me later. Let me go and see if I can save two months rent so I can have money to pay you room and board."

"We can always swap the room and board for sexual favors," I said, blowing her a kiss.

"That's exactly what you're going to do, anyway."

"You know me so well." I laughed as she spun around and walked away. "I'll call and set up the cleaning crew."

I watched her sexy ass as she walked away. She just had a naturally sexy walk. I had to shake it off. I started wondering what would have happened if she had been home. This had to be the work of her junkie ex-boyfriend. But why hadn't she told the police?

It's a good thing I don't know where to find his ass, because I would have called S, Flaco, and Velt and go snatch his lil ass and take him on a nice ride. But that's all right, if I ever see his ass, I'm going to beat him to within an inch of death.

CHAPTER 29

SUCCESS
THREE MONTHS LATER...

My idea of a shopping spree was to go out and buy everything you need one time. Mall hop. Sonia's idea was to buy everything piece by piece, as she needed. Three months later, and she still hadn't filled the walk-in closet in her room.

The good news: I hadn't cheated in three months. I hadn't cheated because I revised my 'no sex' to 'no sex with anyone besides Sonia.' And Sonia not only appreciated that, but she was true to her word. She gave it up anytime I wanted, how I wanted. She also amended the contract. She added in 'whenever and however she wanted it' clause. That protected her from me being able to tell her no.

Everything was going great. We were in love and couldn't be happier. We purchased the two condo's in the Boca complex—I purchased one, and since we didn't find a house that we liked, I decided to let Sonia get her feet wet by flipping a condo. She only ended up having to put three percent down. We decided to redo the kitchen and bathrooms in each of the units: those we contracted out. Sonia and I did the painting, changed the ceiling fans and light fixtures ourselves. The AC unit was serviced, the ducts cleaned, then finally, the new carpet was installed.

My property sold first. It was the cheaper of the two. I closed two weeks ago. After paying off the mortgage and deducting what I spent, my account balance increased by one hundred fifteen thousand dollars and some change.

Sonia, who just closed, made a little over one hundred twenty seven thousand dollars. Her unit was two levels above mine and overlooked the lake.

"I can't believe how easy this was. We have to do it again!" she bubbled excitedly as we drove from the real estate office.

"We have to celebrate," I said, glancing over at her. I was happy that she was so excited. We had done some pretty good work together. Sonia wasn't afraid to get dirty or get a little paint on herself.

"I think I'm going to pay myself about five grand for all the hard work I did," she chimed.

"I say you deserve ten. Splurge. Take yourself on a shopping spree."

My phone rang interrupting us. I checked the caller ID: Ashley. Today was the day she and Bobby were going to the doctor to find out if she really was pregnant. She had already taken six home pregnancy tests.

"Tell us the good news, or don't tell us anything at all," I answered.

"Am I on speaker? Can Sonia hear, too?"

"Hold on," I said, connecting the phone to the Bluetooth connection. "Speak. You are now in full surround sound."

"Tell us the good news," Sonia chimed.

"It's confirmed. We're nine weeks pregnant!" Ashley and Bobby shouted excitedly.

"Congratulations!" Sonia and I shouted.

"You two decided who's going to carry the baby for the next seven months?" Sonia joked.

Ashley smirked. "I wish Bobby could."

"And take away all your glory. No way," Bobby interjected. "You carry the baby, I'll carry you!"

We heard him kiss her and we all laughed.

"We need to celebrate. How did the closing go?" Ashley asked.

"I'm still staring at this fat check. We were just on our way to my bank to make this deposit."

"What are you two doing after that?" Bobby asked.

"We're planning on celebrating. Sonia's treating today since she has that fat check. We're going to do lunch and a little shopping."

"We're planning on doing the same thing. Call us when you guys are finished down at the bank and we'll meet up for lunch," Bobby said. "And, Sonia..."

"Yes."

"Congratulations on your first taste of real estate investing."

"Thank you," Sonia chimed.

"And don't listen to Khris. Deposit that check. I'm going to let you and Ashley take her new Black Card for a drive."

"Yeah, girl!" Ashley yelled. "We're going to be the first to ever max out a Black Card!"

"You're silly," I chuckled. "You can't max out a Black Card."

"I'm making money faster than she can spend it, so I'm not worried," Bobby chimed.

That had to be every married man's dream: make more money than his wife can spend. "Must be nice!" I chuckled.

"Your money's making money for you right now, too, so if you had a wife, you'd know exactly how I feel. Hint. Hint," Bobby said, laughing. "You keep up what you're doing, you'll be able to say the same thing when you two get married."

Sonia and I stared at one another and smiled. That is exactly the direction that our relationship was heading.

"That is my goal," I said.

"Stick with me, Khris. You'll achieve that goal."

"Thanks for your confidence," I said sincerely.

"You deserve it, my friend. This baby has me getting all emotional." Bobby pretended to sniffle. "Call us soon."

"We will," Sonia chimed, and ended the call.

We laughed and talked all the way to the bank. I went in with Sonia while she handled her business. It was a delight just watching her. Her eyes sparkled when she saw how much her account balance increased by.

We met up with Ashley and Bobby. We hit Worth Avenue from A1A to Cocoanut Row, stopping to eat, of course. Sonia was a bit put off by the spending until Bobby told her, "Sonia, one hundred million dollars gives me thirteen five in interest a day. I am a billionaire. So you and my lovely wife aren't going to spend more than a days interest no matter what you two buy, so don't look at the prices. If you see something you like, just point and it's yours."

"Don't worry. Either she pick out what she likes, or I'm going to shop for her," Ashley assured her husband.

I can't begin to tell you how much money was spent. Bobby

insisted that I picked out a few swatches of material with him, then we both got measured for a few hand-tailored suits from Brioni at Maus and Hoffman. Every store he made a purchase, he made sure I made a purchase. I had bags from Giorgio Armani, Hermes, Hugo Boss, Neiman Marcus, Saks, Salvatore Ferragamo, and Cartier. And I was doing the least amount of shopping out of the four of us.

The Black Card was working, and didn't show any signs of slowing. Ashley had Sonia actually having fun, after a while. It was a joy to watch them laughing and trying on clothes.

At one point, Bobby and I found ourselves sitting side by side in Neiman Marcus watching them go through the maternity clothes. Bobby turned to me. "Khris, I don't have many people that I consider to be friends. I have a lot of associates, but they're only there because of what they can benefit while they're around me. Very few people did what you did for me, my friend. First you helped my wife to understand that it was okay to date a man a little more than a decade older than her. I knew you two were friends with benefits when I first laid eyes on her."

Oh shit, where is he going with this, I wondered.

"You could have done everything to ruin it for me, but you didn't. In fact, you did quite the opposite. You pushed her to me. I thought that strange at the time. I wondered to myself why would you give up that great piece of ass. Only one reason came to my mind: you were out to see what you can get."

Shit. He knows I've been fucking her.

"So, and I hope you don't be upset with me for what I'm about to tell you, I hired someone to do a background check and a little digging to find out about you. That's how I knew you were one of the good ones. You knew you and Ashley had no future together. You two weren't even in a relationship. You were doing you: having fun. She was searching for love and enjoying what you had to offer. You convinced her to look past my age and see that I really cared about her and wouldn't intentionally do anything to hurt her. You never mentioned anything about how well off she would be, or how much money I had. That's when I knew you weren't out to gain anything. I knew all about the late night phone calls Ashley made to you when she was confused and wanted to make sense out of what was going on. I knew you counseled her at night. After she told me she loved me, I stopped it all. I didn't need to find out anything else. You gave me what all my money couldn't help me get: a beautiful, wife that loves me with my money, not for my money. For that, I can never thank you enough."

Whew. I felt a weight come off of my shoulder right then.

"Thank you, Bobby. I'm glad it turned out this way. I'm happy to be a part of what you two have."

"I'm not finished, yet. I'm feeling emotional today; so let me get it all out. Like I said, I haven't had anyone do much for me without it somehow benefitting them, but you have."

"I've benefitted," I corrected, pointing to my bags.

"That's nothing, Khris."

"Psssss. This means the world to me. I know you don't look at prices, but..."

"Khris, my friend," he chuckled, patting me on the shoulder. "That one deal that you brought to me, how much money do you think I made?"

"A little over a hundred million," I remembered calculating back then.

"Your calculations on the building were a little conservative due to the values of the other older buildings on that stretch of beach. But with the luxuries that we added, the building made me two and a half times more. Two fifty."

"Wooo-weee! But I benefitted from that. You gave me two units."

"They were worth what...about six each back then. So I gave you twelve out of two fifty. A little less than five percent."

I nodded. "That was good for a couple hours of research work, a fifteen minute talk with you, and a five minute introduction to Destiny," I chimed.

He laughed and patted me on the shoulder. "That's what I like about you, Khris, you're not all about the money. We'll talk about that some more at a later time. Right now, I have something extremely important to ask you: it'll mean the world to me if you say you'll do it."

"I'll do it," I said sincerely.

"I haven't asked you, yet," he said, chuckling.

"Well, go ahead and ask me, then."

"I would be honored if you would be our baby's godfather."

"What kind of question is that? I thought that was a given. I figured if I wasn't going to be the godfather, the baby must not be having any godparents at all," I teased.

Bobby nodded, pleased with my answer. "I know I can count on you to step in if anything were to happen to me."

"I'm your man, but don't be talking like you gonna be dying or anything soon. You aren't that damn old. And, when I have kids, you have to be their godfather: with the price of Pampers these days, I don't know if I'll be able to afford them. I'll be sending my baby over to you bare bottom: 'Tell your godfather to buy you some Pampers; Daddy can't afford any.'"

We both laughed until tears were coming out of our eyes. Ashley and Sonia were watching us, so we quieted down a bit.

Bobby pointed to Sonia. "You need to hurry up and do something with that young lady, my friend. Don't make the mistake I made: waited until I'm an old man to have children. I'll be there telling my baby: 'Go to your godfather and tell him to teach you to ride a bicycle. Daddy's too old to run beside you.'"

We started laughing again.

"We're getting there," I mumbled, thinking about Sonia and marriage and children. It was still a bit too soon. We've only been together three months. It's going great so far, I admitted to myself. We'll see what the future holds. Yes indeed. We shall surely see.

With my Range stuffed with bags, we followed Bobby and Ashley back to their home where we were invited to join them for dinner. The dinner, the service, the company: it was all fantastic. It wasn't until after dinner that Bobby surprised me once again. He asked me to join him in his office for a cognac while the ladies were coming up with design ideas for a nursery.

Bobby opened a wall safe and pulled out a soft black pouch. "Khris, back to what we were talking about earlier. I want you to experience the happiness that I enjoy. I know it's a bit early, but you have to be prepared. I am telling you this because I think Sonia is the one for you. She could be the one that provides you with all the love and happiness that I have." He paused and poured out the contents of the pouch onto a handkerchief that he had pulled from his pocket and spread on his desk. "I know you probably have no idea what shape stone she likes yet, so pick one of each and hold onto them until you decide to pop the question."

My mouth fell as I watched him pour about fifty loose diamonds of all shapes and sizes onto the handkerchief. I was stunned speechless. I realized that I was doing that a lot lately. "I don't know what to say..."

"Don't say anything. Just pick a few stones for when you're ready to pop the question. These are all certified, D-flawless stones. You've got round, emerald, pear, heart...grab one of each.

"I've spoken to her parents, but we haven't officially met yet," I said as I started sifting and picking out four of the medium sized stones. "I'll give us a year..."

"Man, I see I'm going to have to pick the stones for you. You're picking the wrong sized stones. You can't go wrong with big stones. What you're picking is for earrings."

I watched him pick out four of the larger stones.

"These are all about eight to twelve carats. Women love these. It tells other men and women to back the fuck off; you can't afford me," he laughed.

I picked up the four stones as he went back into his safe and pulled out a soft pouch big enough to fit the four stones. "Thank you, Bobby. I guess this will make it much easier when the time comes."

"It should, and I hope you decide to do it sooner rather than later. Strike while the iron is hot, my friend."

"Good advice, Bobby. Good advice."

CHAPTER 30

DATE NIGHT

Sonia and I decided to set aside Friday nights as date night.

We normally go to the Premier Movie theatre off of Glades and Perimeter Road, because we can have dinner while watching a movie ensconced in a love-seat. After the movie, we would hit the club for a night of dancing, or at least a few hours.

It was on one of such Friday nights that both of us came face to face with our pasts. Thank God Yasmine and Nishka both had dates and weren't with us.

We were in VIP chilling. The music was nice, and the club was packed. We had a table for two in a dimly lit corner. Perfect for lovers. The slow songs were setting the tone for what was to come. So instead of sitting, Sonia was standing between my legs and dancing real close. I wasn't seated; I was more or less leaning on the edge of the high stool, perfect height and position so that all the right parts were lined up and rubbing pleasurably. Sonia never wore pants when we were out like this. She knew I liked to be able to touch her supple flesh at will. She enjoyed having me touch her soft, supple flesh at will. It turned her on.

Sonia, with her back turned to the crowd, had her arms around my neck and her lips against my earlobe, singing along with Alicia Keys. I had both my arms wrapped around her waist, holding her close as we danced breast to chest and pelvis to pelvis.

Sonia was feeling the music. She was feeling me. She whispered two words: "Touch me."

My right hand slid down her hips until it touched her warm thigh. I let my fingers graze against her flesh as my hand came around the front and up her inner thigh. I stopped.

"Don't stop there," she whimpered.

I kept dancing, but I said softly. "I've got a problem from my past heading over here. It's the number that I let you block that nigh you were giving me that sensual massage. Keep dancing and don't turn around. I'll handle it."

Behind her, heading toward us, was Lisa and her cousin Tamia. Tamia likes trouble, so I know she's the one that jinxed Lisa into coming over here. Hopefully, Lisa would use her better judgment and not make a scene.

"I knew this was your ass up in this corner!" Lisa shouted over the music. "You blocked my fuckin number and I haven't heard from you in months...now you up in the club with some bitch grindin up on your dick!" she snarled.

There goes not making a scene. "Lisa, chill out."

Sonia's body tensed just a little when Lisa called her a bitch. "I'm not going to be able to remain calm if she calls me a bitch again," Sonia said softly into my ear without turning, or missing a beat.

"This is not the time nor the place for this, Lisa. Can't you see I'm with my woman?"

"Your woman? Muthafucka, where was your woman last time you was in the club fucking me in the broom closet?"

Surprisingly, Tamia hadn't said one word.

"That's in the past. Now if you'd please leave, I sure would appreciate it."

"Bitch," Lisa yelled, reaching forward and yanking Sonia's shoulder. "Stop grinding on him and pretending like you don't know I'm here."

"Hey! Don't you touch her," I said, knocking away Lisa's hand from Sonia's shoulder.

Sonia stopped dancing and pressed her body into me to keep me from getting up. Sonia turned around, putting her ass on me and stared at the two of them. Sonia wasn't smiling. She was dead ass serious. "Look, I don't know you, and I don't care to know you. But, don't you ever put your hand on me or call me a bitch again."

"Or you gonna do what, bitch?" Tamia snarled, twisting her neck and stepping in closer.

Without another word, Sonia lunged forward and delivered a straight right to Tamia's chin. Tamia fell like a sack of potatoes.

While Tamia was falling, Sonia pivoted and delivered a devastating left to the side of Lisa's head that impacted directly on her temple.

Lisa was falling by the time I bounced to my feet. That's how quick it went down. Both of them were out cold. I was shocked and hyped. What the fuck was that? What just happened? I looked down at both girls; as did those close enough to have seen them drop. I looked at Sonia as she stepped over Lisa's legs and came back to the table. I was still staring at her when she stopped in front of me.

"I tried to stay out of it." She shrugged, not even breathing hard. Not even sounding upset. "Better I hit them than you," she smirked, and winked. "They'll be alright," she said, grabbing the bottle of Dom P. from the ice bucket. "They're just knocked the fuck out. They'll wake right up. Watch," she said, stepping back over to them and pouring the champagne on their faces.

Both girls coughed and came too with a start. By then, security was there.

Needless to say, the four of us were escorted from the club.

Neither Tamia nor Lisa said one word on the way out. They never even bothered to look in Sonia's direction.

When valet brought the Range around, I opened her door and let her in. I tipped the valet, walked around to the driver's side and got in. "What the hell was that?" I asked, staring over at Sonia as she inspected her knuckles.

She looked up and our eyes met. "Korean martial arts. Tae Kwan Do. Literally translated, it means foot-fist-way. I would have preferred to use my feet," she said, clenching and unclenching her knuckles, "but I didn't think you would want to flash the entire club."

"That's not what I meant. Why did you hit them? I don't like scenes..."

"Neither do I, Khris. Your little girlfriend touched me, then her bully stepped to me."

"You should have let me handle it."

"I know, and I'm sorry."

She sounded so sincere. "How sorry?" I asked, reaching over and trailing my fingers lightly up her inner thigh.

"Sorry enough to do whatever. You. Want. Me. To. Do," she said, one word at a time, as she leaned over and started kissing my cheeks and nibbling on my earlobe.

To be honest, the way she took out Tamia, the bully, and Lisa turned me the fuck on. That shit was sexy as hell. Then I realized she really hadn't wanted to hurt Nancy that night in my driveway. I twisted my head so that she could get to my lips. Her lips felt like fire against mine. Her kiss was hot and her tongue was extra frisky as it entered my mouth.

Bam!

What the hell! I almost bit Sonia's tongue when we got rammed from the back.

Sonia jumped and twisted so she could look behind us.

I sped up and glanced into the rear view mirror. At first I thought it was Lisa and Tamia, but neither drove an SUV.

"That's Mario!" Sonia shouted.

"Mario? Who the fuck is Mario?" Then it came to me: her junkie ass boyfriend. "Dis shit ends tonight," I snarled, reaching over to open the glove box. I took out my Taurus.

"What are you doing? You can't..."

"I can't! I can't what?" I snarled, looking around for a good place to stop.

"Don't! I don't want you to get in any trouble, Khris. Just keep driving."

"No. This shit isn't gonna happen no fuckin more. I can't afford to be worrying about this fool fuckin with you every time you go out. I can't be lookin over my shoulders every time we hit the streets."

I found my spot and stopped.

The fool behind me did exactly what I wanted him to do: he stopped.

I threw the Range in park, jumping out at the same time, raced toward his Escalade, my Taurus held low against the side of my leg. I didn't know what he had, so I went ready for whatever. I rather be judged by twelve, than carried by six.

Three doors opened, the driver's door, the rear passenger door behind him, and the front passenger door.

I checked their hands. Empty. Good. They didn't have any weapons: their mistake.

I didn't flip off the safety. In fact, I wanted it on. Mario was closest to me, so it was him that I went after. He was the one I wanted. I don't know if he even saw the gun in my hand, but he charged at me like a runaway bull. He probably was high. Didn't matter. I pivoted to the side as I raised the Taurus. When he was right there, I arched it into the side of his head. Blood sprayed as the butt of the Taurus sent him face first into the dirt. The other one was on me quickly. He caught me with a running punch to the head. He didn't get to throw another one. I brought the Taurus up and pointed in his face. He stopped instantly. He was raising his hand to surrender when I clocked him with a quick left, and then kicked him in the nuts. I gun-butted him in the back of his head as he fell. I heard shuffling behind me and spun around in time to see Mario trying to get to his feet. He was still doubled over, so I raced over and kicked him in the face, then the ribs once he was down.

Where was the other one? I wondered, looking around frantically. I didn't see him, but I heard blows coming from around the front of the Escalade. I looked in that direction and saw shadows from the light on the ground. Sonia.

I raced around the front of the Escalade, jamming the Taurus in my waistband. Sonia was punishing the little gold teeth coconut tree dread that was with Mario the night we first met. I didn't feel sorry for him, but I pulled her off of him, anyway. He was hurt bad. His face was bloodied and he was crying something awful.

Sonia spun out of my arms. This time she wasn't calm like she was in the club. She was angry. She was breathing hard, and her eyes seemed dark and cold.

She drew a bead on Mario and raced over. Forget what you heard about not kicking a man when he's down. Sonia kicked him in his ribs, face, ass...any and everywhere. "You destroyed my shit! You busted up my apartment, now I ga bust your ass up."

I let her get a few more kicks in for good measure, then pulled her away. He had to have some cracked ribs or something by now. Yes, I wanted him to feel some pain. "Sonia, that's enough," I said softly as I grabbed her around her waist from behind. I had to lift her away. "Calm down, baby. Go back in the truck so we can leave before the cops show up. I'll be there in a second."

She stopped fighting. I heard her sniffling. "Where are you going?" she asked.

"I just want to have a word with Mario right quick. I'll be right behind you."

I walked over to Mario. He was still squirming around on the ground. I kneeled down on the side of him and dug out his wallet from his back pocket. I opened it and took out his driver's license. "Mario Gifford," I read. "I'll hang on to this license. I've got your address, now. If you ever fuck with Sonia or me again in any way, send anyone to fuck with us, I'm going to have my cousins come over in a boat, and we're going to come to this address and we're going to take everyone we find there—even your dog if you have one—for the boat ride of their life. We ga feed some sharks. You understand me?"

He nodded.

"Say it, muthafucka!"

"I-I under...stand," he managed to say, spitting out blood.

"You need to get to a hospital. And if the police come and question us about you and your little friends, the same thing applies," I said, getting up and throwing his wallet in his face. "Get up and get in your shit," I ordered, then went and kicked the other two up. "Y'all get the fuck out of here before the police arrive. I know y'all gat some dope in that truck, I can smell it."

That got them hustling. They pulled off just as I jumped in the ride. "You okay, baby?"

She nodded. "You?"

"I've had enough war for one night."

"Me, too," she said somberly.

"Times like this makes me think back to all those old movies with those signs that read: 'Make love, not war'."

She nodded again. We drove in silence for a while. "You think your ex is going to try to get some get back?"

"Not if she values her life," I chuckled. "You are one bad..." I stopped. I couldn't call the woman I loved a bitch.

"I know I'm a bad bitch. But thanks for respecting me enough not to call me one."

"I not only respect you, Sonia, I looooove you," I sang, leaning over for a kiss.

She kissed me. "I loooooove you more," she sang, acting just as silly as I had.

"Well, we already waged war, let's go home and make love."

Sonia grinned naughtily. "How about we fight for it? I beat you, you give me some: You beat me, I give you some."

I licked my lips as I eyed her down. "How about we not fight and just give each other some," I suggested.

"Sounds good. We can start now. We don't have to wait until we get home," she said, fluttering her eyelashes. Her hands disappeared and I watched as she wiggled out of her underwear.

I shook my head and laughed. I created a monster.

She hung her lacy thong on my rear view mirror and started laughing. "Put the seat back. You know the drill!"

"You're fucking crazy, you know that, right?"

"You gat me this way. That shit was good last time...and, I have more room to operate with this time," she said, reaching for my pants. "I want you to fuck me like you did the last time when your crazy ass girlfriend caught us. That race you had going, trying to bust your nut before the garage door was all the way up, was alllllllll dat!" she sang.

"I could do without the garage door this time."

"I'll definitely put her ass face down in the dirt tonight for fucking with my man."

"Your man?"

"My man!" she said saucily, climbing over and onto my dick. "Mmmmmmm!" she moaned contentedly as she slid down my pole. "My dick!"

CHAPTER 31

TEMPTATION

It's been two months since the incident with Lisa and Mario. Neither Sonia nor I had heard a peep or had any trouble from them since. Sonia and I were spending more and more time together, and the more I got to know her, the more I fell in love with her. And, it was reciprocal. I even started cutting back on my layovers when I flew. I started flying turns—trips that originated and ended at my home base on the same day. No overnight hotel stays...unless it was a trip out to LA, San Francisco, or Vegas where I had thirty-six hours on the ground. On those trips, I would take Sonia along.

Sonia was extremely busy after the fashion slash hair show. She got the contract from Ashley's stylist, Jean Paul, to supply all twelve of his salons, and he turned her on to other salon owners that he knew that were scattered all over the United States. Needless to say, Sonia had to hire help to keep up with the increase in business. Not full time help, just a few hours: three days a week.

She was up to five full sized storage units in order to keep up with the increase in demand. But, the other three units weren't side by side, so it wasn't as convenient as before. She had to order a larger amount of hair, because she had crossed over from just black hair; she was also supplying white hair. I never realized that white folks spent almost as much money on weaves as blacks do. Yasmine and Nishka found a way to make some extra cash by working with Sonia when she was doing her heavy monthly orders. I helped out, too.

We were visiting with Ashley and Bobby one evening and we were discussing Sonia's business expansion and the trouble with the storage units. Bobby came to the rescue. He told us about a new office and warehouse complex that he owned. It consisted of ten buildings that housed three to five businesses in each. It was home to all sorts of businesses...including the US Postal Office and UPS. It was very safe, right off of University Drive; about ten minutes drive from the house. It was perfect. It had high-speed Internet connection, office, kitchen, bathroom, on the second level, warehouse space on the bottom with a huge garage bay that would allow a delivery truck to drive in. And, Bobby offered it to her at a good discount: free, for as long as he owned it.

Sonia shook her head. "That's bad business."

They went back and forth for a while, then Ashley waddled into the conversation. "What about when your godchild wants to drop by and see you. You don't want her coming to a storage closet, do you?"

"Storage unit," I corrected.

Bobby jumped on that like a shark smelling fresh blood in the water. "Here's the best deal I can give you. I will let you pay exactly what you were paying for the five units. But, there's a catch."

"What's the catch?" Sonia asked, watching as Ashley sat in his lap and he rubbed her little bump tenderly.

"Since my baby might be dropping by there to spend time with her godmother, I want to make sure that the place is suitably furnished. With that being the case, you will have to let Ashley see to furnishing the place. Our baby," he paused, pointing at each of us in turn, "is involved now, so there will be no debate," he said sternly, but laughing. "Just tell Ash what you need, and she'll do the rest. You can consult, but she controls the purse."

"I need the space, and it would make life easier...Okay. I'll take it."

"Honey! You are good," Ashley chimed, kissing Bobby. "You sure know how to work a deal."

"You like how I used our baby to back her into that?"

"I want you to back me into something," Ashley sang, kissing him hungrily.

"Thank goodness you're already pregnant," I said, laughing and shaking my head as they tongued each other down proper.

"Best sex is pregnant sex," Bobby stated. "It's always wet and juicy. You won't be able to get enough."

"He'll find out soon," Ashley chimed, smiling at me.

I could have taken that any way I liked. But, both Ashley and I were being good, so I pulled Sonia closer and kissed her.

"You're not going to find out until I get a ring on this finger," she said, pointing.

"Okay now, what if I was to pop out a ring right now?" I said, letting my mouth get me into trouble.

"Pop it out and find out," she retorted sassily.

I had to back peddle real fast. "Unh-unh! You're not going to embarrass me in front of my friends."

Ashley and Bobby, who were listening intently, laughed.

"Why do you think I'll embarrass you?" she asked, sounding a tinsy bit serious.

"Because, I haven't made my intentions known to your father yet," I said, quickly. "You know, I have to follow protocol. I have to do this thing right. Besides, you never told me what shape diamond you want."

"That's because we never discussed any of this."

"Well, how about we discuss it over a nice candle lit dinner with some nice, soft romantic music."

"That sounds nice," she cooed, and gave me a sweet, sensuous kiss.

"All that romantic talk has me horny. Come on, honey," Ashley said. "Let's go upstairs."

"But we have guests."

"They're not guests! They practically live here. And, they don't need us," she added, standing and pulling Bobby's hand.

"That's our cue," Sonia said, standing. "We'll see y'all."

"I would tell y'all to have fun, but y'all don't need me to. What I will say, though, is practice safe sex...don't be ruff and hurt our godchild."

Ashley made a silly face at me.

Bobby smiled and pointed to Sonia. "I'll email you the address and set up the details so you can go and take a look at the place at your convenience tomorrow."

"Thank you, once again," Sonia said as we hugged them bye.

Sonia and I came home last night, cooked dinner, discussed marriage, and made love. If someone had told me that at the age of twenty seven I, Khristin Harrison, would be talking about getting married and having children, I would have thought they were crazy. I wouldn't have believed that I could have been as faithful as I've been to Sonia. I haven't cheated, not once, since I made my commitment to her. Damn, I even added the word commitment to my vocabulary.

I found out a lot of things as we cooked and dined last night. I would have never believed it, but getting married and having children had me more excited and intrigued than all the trickin I had ever done.

My phone rang, disturbing me from my thoughts. I reached over and grabbed my phone from the nightstand. Chris.

"What's up, Chris?"

"You sound like you still in bed," he said. "I een disturbin nothin, eh?"

"Nah, man. Wifee's out makin her paper, so I'm just here relaxing. What's up?"

"Man, I coming over...and I was wondering if you could pick ya boy up."

"When you coming over?"

"I'll be in Fort Laudi-dadi at six."

"Six today?"

"Yeah. On Thursday nights, some of my boys over there does have a club on South Beach. Tonight, they have an old school party going on. I want to check that out."

"You talkin 'bout Club Liv in the Fontainebleau. I heard about that. They gat a bunch of guest DJ's coming for that. My boy S was telling me about it."

"So you wanna roll through?" Chris asked.

I thought about it for a second. "Yeah, we can do that."

"Cool. I'll call you when the flight's leaving Freeport."

"Alright. Later," I said, ending the call.

I called my baby.

"Hey, honey," she answered, her voice soft and sweet. "How's everything going?"

"Good. I'm about finished here. I just have to order some more Max Plus Vitamins," she chuckled, "then I'm off to meet Ashley and the interior decorator at the shop."

"The shop? That's what you're calling it?"

"Yep."

"You're still lying in bed naked, thinking about me?" she asked.

"Just got interrupted by Chris. He's coming over from the Ports today."

"You picking him up?"

"Yes. He's coming for that old school party that S had told us about."

"I told you, you could go. I'm going to stay home and chill. It's all boys going tonight. No one is taking their girl with them."

"That's because their girls aren't as cool as you."

"I know!" she laughed. "But, you go and have fun with the boys."

"If you insist," I said, sounding disappointed.

I picked up Chris and the three of us went out to have dinner, then we dropped Sonia home and headed down to South Beach. It wasn't time to go to the club yet, so we met S at the W Hotel. Some of his homeboys from the Virgin Islands were staying there for the weekend.

We laughed, joked around as we drank—some of them smoked---before it was time to go to the club.

When we got to the Club, the club was rammed pack. A sea of girls rushed us in the VIP section. They could spot the big money, out-of-town-men from a mile away. And I'm not talking about ugly girls, either. Remember, this is South Beach. South Beach, Miami, has the number one ranking in the entire country for beautiful people. I'm talking model quality girls showing lots of skin.

Flaco and Velt showed up with their own harem of exotic girls. The girls were gorgeous, and definitely not shy. They were fine, and they were aggressive. I knew right away that I would be tested tonight. Tonight would be the ultimate test. But, I would not fail. I will not fall weak to temptation. Try as the devil may, I will return home to my Sonia the same way I left her: a faithful man.

After a few hours of drinking and dancing, I had to admit that the devil was sure busy in there, and he had sent out all his best workers. Every shape, size, and color were winding and dancing provocatively: a sea of gyrating hot flesh. But, I held firm. Not to say that I wasn't tempted. I had two exotic goddesses grinding all up on me. But, I wouldn't let my little head control my big head. I was in a committed relationship.

I slid from between the two goddesses that had me sandwiched. I had to go to the bathroom. Everyone was engaged in some kind of pleasurable act, either kissing or fondling...the way the little Oriental was sitting and grinding on Velt, they may have been fucking. Flaco had his tongue so deep down one girl's throat; he probably never heard when I told him I was heading to the bathroom. S had three thick girls surrounding him. One in back, two in front tongue kissing him and each other at the same time. I knew where that was heading. Chris was nowhere to be seen. Too many women about, and he already had a hotel room.

I should have taken backup. I went into the bathroom and all the urinals were filled, so I went into one of the stalls.

Just as I started relieving myself, I got shoved in the back. I heard guys hollering "Hey!" and some other shit. Someone stepped in and the stall's door closed behind me. I was so busy trying not to pee on my feet; I never got a look at who was in the stall with me. I knew it was a female: I smelled her scent.

Her scent was intoxicating. She didn't speak. She drew in closer. I knew she shouldn't be there, but I paid her no attention.

I finished emptying my bladder. I felt her firm breasts press against my back as I shook my dick. Her hands snaked around my waist and grabbed my dick with familiarity. She moaned sweetly as she stroked my manhood.

I released my dick, turning it over to her. Everything told me to stop her, but my dick was in control. It grew rigid in her delicate hands.

She used my dick to control me. She turned me until I was sideways against one wall, then she squatted in front of me and took me into her deliciously hot mouth. Her mouth and tongue knew my dick intimately. She knew everything I liked.

My mind was telling me to stop her, but I couldn't bring myself to doing it. I fought and fought with the pleasurable sensations, but they were too much. Too good. Too strong.

I got up enough strength to get my hand up to her head. But

instead of grabbing her hair and pushing her away, I found myself gripping the back of her head as my hips thrust forward and back, pushing my dick deeper into the back of her mouth. It felt so fucking good. I felt my toes curl. My nut was rising. I felt like I was going to blow out the back of her throat, as I pumped harder into her mouth.

"Oh yeah!" I mumbled as my nut rose up. I was grunting and pumping. My eyes grew blurry, then closed down completely as my nut blew down the back of her throat. "Oh Fuck, Sonia! I love you, baby."

I felt her tap my thigh. I must have been holding her head too tight, or pushing too far down her throat, because she kept hitting me harder to let her up. I let her head go and she shot up, opened the stall door, and was gone before my eyes could adjust.

Some freaks were in there cheering and clapping. Some idiot even had his camera phone out. I slammed the door on his punk ass. I wiped myself off, then bought a wash towel from the bathroom attendant to clean myself up properly.

By the time I got back into the club, I knew I wouldn't find her with the club being as packed, and dark as it was. I went back up into the VIP lounge. I didn't feel like being bothered by the devil's workers anymore. I was ready to go home to my woman. So, that's exactly what I did.

CHAPTER 32

OUT OF THE OVEN
SEVEN MONTHS LATER...

Twenty-three days before Christmas, Bobby woke us up at five in the morning. "Ashley's water broke. Contractions are closer. We're on our way to the hospital. The baby's coming."

That was it. He didn't wait for a response. He hung up. Sonia and I jumped out of the bed and started putting on the clothes that we had set out for this exact moment. Sonia and I were Ashley and Bobby's coaches. Bobby would attempt to keep Ashley breathing properly. Sonia was Bobby's coach, and the backup breathing coach just in case he fainted. I was there to catch him if he did.

We got dressed, raced into the bathroom to brush our teeth and splash a little water on our faces, and then we hit the stairs.

We were out the house in five minutes and heading toward the hospital. Their driver, Josh, was awaiting our arrival and directed us where we needed to go. We got there as Ashley was getting wheeled into the delivery room. Her contractions were extremely close and she was dilating. The baby was almost ready to pop out.

This is what Ashley had prayed for: a quick and easy delivery. It was indeed quick as far as labor goes, but it wasn't easy.

All the breathing exercises went out the door when the labor pains intensified. Ashley screamed, cursed, and squeezed the shit out of anyone's hand she could get a hold of. I don't think that any woman—or man, for that matter—should ever go into a delivery room if they don't have children already and are thinking about having children: It will change your fucking mind.

I was absolutely sure that there was no pain worst than what a woman endures during childbirth. Not even a kick in the nuts.

A man suffers some excruciating pain as well. I witnessed that first hand. This was a very valuable lesson. I know one thing for sure: when I have my children, I am wearing a cup in the delivery room. Ashley got a grip on Bobby's package, and I'm sure he wouldn't be able to use his dick for the same six weeks that Ashley was going to be out of commission. Maybe that was Ashley's plan. Hmmmm?

The baby was playing hide and go seek for a few minutes, but twenty minutes of torture later, a beautiful bluish-green-eyed baby girl popped out. Even bloodied, she was beautiful.

When the doctor spanked her, she let us all hear her healthy lungs. Bobby looked like he wanted to hit the doctor for spanking his little baby girl so hard.

Bobby did the honors of cutting the baby's navel string,

I took the pictures. It was beautiful being there. It was a wonderful experience. An experience that I think men and women who don't have children, but are planning on having children, should have. It will confirm your decision to go through with it. To see the anxious faces of both mother and father as they wait and watch their baby being cleaned and swaddled is absolutely spectacular.

I felt myself tearing up and had to blink away the tears. Sonia had tears of joy streaming down her face as Ashley received her baby girl.

It was a beautiful sight to see.

Ashley was ragged, but glowing as her six pound, nine ounce baby girl was placed tenderly in her arms. Bobby looked as innocent as a baby himself. He was now a proud father. He was right there with Ashley, a protective arm draped over his wife's shoulder, as he gave his baby girl his pinky finger to grasp. And grasp it she did.

It was indeed a picture perfect moment and I captured it.

The nurse took a group picture with the baby and the four of us in the delivery room: the parents and godparents there from the absolute beginning.

Ashley and Sonia had gotten very close, and Ashley had asked Sonia to be the baby's godmother. Sonia and I took our pledge to be the baby's godparents seriously, that's why it was important for us to be there from the very first breath.

The baby's name: Lauren Brittany Chase.

CHAPTER 33

CAUGHT ON CAMERA

"Here's what I'm thinking: dinner, I pop the question, give her the loose heart shaped stone, she accepts, we come back home to a surprise party..."

"Why are you giving her the loose stone? Why not get the stone set?" Yasmine asked.

"I want her to pick her own setting," I said.

"I don't think you should propose on Valentine's Day. That's so cliché..."

"When do you think he should propose?" Yasmine asked, cutting Nishka off.

"Surprise her on a regular day."

"I wanted to propose for New Years, but I haven't spoken to her Dad about it yet."

"I say you should propose on a regular old day; just do it out of the blue. Catch her off guard."

"I was thinking about proposing to her on her birthday or something like that so it would be easier to remember," I joked.

"That's just like a man," Nishka mumbled.

"If that's the case, you should propose on her birthday this year, then get married on her birthday next year. You won't forget her birthday, the day you got engaged, or your wedding anniversary," Yasmine shot.

"It would be cheaper, too. I'd only have to buy her one present for both our anniversary and her birthday."

"I don't know about all that," Yasmine snarled under her breath.

"I know when I'm going to propose..."

"When?"

"February 21st."

"Why then?" Nishka asked.

"It was exactly one week after Valentine's Day when we met."

"Now I know you really in love!" Nishka laughed, twisting sideways to look at me. "You remember the day y'all met?"

"I remember the first time we kissed. The first time we..."

"You remember the day Nancy caught y'all in the garage?" Yasmine asked, laughing.

"Ha, ha, ha. Funny," I said, turning in the driveway. "Good, Sonia's home."

"I hope she cooked already: I'm starving," Yasmine said as I parked next to Sonia's Benz.

"I'm starving too," Nishka shot, hopping out the front.

"The only reason y'all was rushing me to come over here was so y'all could eat. Y'all should have eaten at the caf."

"We eat cafeteria food as little as possible," Yasmine chimed as they got their stuff out of the back.

When we went inside, I knew something was wrong: Sonia hadn't cooked. She wasn't anywhere downstairs, and when I called out to her, she didn't answer. That was so unlike her.

I helped Yasmine and Nishka take their stuff upstairs. The door to the yellow room—Sonia's room—was closed. Why was she in there with the door closed? She hadn't slept in there one single night since she moved in.

I dropped the girls' stuff in their rooms, then went back to Sonia's room and knocked. I thought I heard her sniffling as I stood there waiting for her to tell me to come in. After knocking again, and not getting an answer, I twisted the knob and went in. Sonia was on the bed, balled up in a fetal position, crying. I closed the door and rushed over.

She hadn't called and said that anything was wrong, so what could she be crying for? "What's the matter, baby?" I asked, sitting on the edge of her bed and reaching out to comfort her.

She squirmed to my touch, and scooted away from me. "Don't touch me?"

"What?" What the hell was wrong with her? I wondered, then asked. "What's the matter, Sonia?"

"Just leave me alone."

"I came home expecting to find my beautiful woman waiting excitedly for my arrival and instead, I find her lying in bed crying. Naturally, I am concerned. I reach out to comfort her and ask her what's wrong, she won't tell me, and I'm supposed to just accept that and leave her alone?" I said, more to myself, than to her.

Meanwhile, I was trying to make some sense out of what was going on. "Yes, Khris, please leave me alone. If you don't leave me alone, then I'll leave."

What the hell? Who is this woman?

"Is that what you want? You want me to leave?" she asked, turning onto her back, and looking up at me.

She had me dazed and confused. "What happened to you? Why would I want you to leave? Can you please tell me what's going on? You're scaring me, Sonia," I admitted, trying to remain calm. It took everything I had not to snap. I didn't do anything, so why was she treating me like this. I felt like a lil bitch. Is this how love makes you feel when things aren't right? Is this the flip side of all those warm, fuzzy feelings? Love had me fucked up.

I guess what I had said had somehow made some sort of sense to her: her eyes stared up at me as if she was contemplating something. Her eyes were red and angry. She folded her hands under her breasts. "Let me ask you this, Khris. That night you went to that old school party, what happened?"

Oh shit! How did she find out? 'Shit! Lie muthafucka. Lie,' I heard a little voice whisper inside my head.

'Nah, homeboy, tell her the truth. The truth shall set you free,' another voice whispered.

Shit! Shit! Shit!

"And don't lie to me, Khris. If you lie, what we have is over."

I wanted to tell her the truth, but the truth would literally set me free: Sonia would leave my ass for sure.

There are three truths: the truth truth, what actually happened; there's Nancy's truth, her version of what happened; my truth, what I want Sonia to believe happened.

I decided to tell my version of the truth. "There were some girls there...and I danced with a couple of them..."

"Dancing? Dancing with just some random girls?" she snarled.

"I mean we were dancing real close and shit, but nothing for you to get upset like this about. Remember I told you to come."

"So the only way I can trust your ass is to be foot and foot behind you?"

"That's not what I'm saying, but if you're going to cry damn near a year later about some shit you heard about me dancing in the club with some bitches whose names I didn't even get, then by all means come out with me. You are my woman and I plan on spending the rest of my life with you, so I don't care: in fact I want you to be foot and foot behind me."

"Don't count on that."

"What?"

"You heard me. If you out there doing shit like this, then gonna sit here and lie to me about it, then I will no longer be your girlfriend, your woman, your nothing."

I smirked and shook my head. I couldn't believe this shit was happening. "Do you hear yourself? You're talking about ending our relationship because I danced with some bitches."

"No, Khris, I'm talking about leaving your ass because you're sitting here in my face lying to me when you can simply tell me the truth. You started off telling me the truth! Why lie now? What, you can't keep it real with me anymore? Now that I'm your woman, you can't keep it one hundred with me no more?"

"I am keeping it one hundred."

"You say you love me, but you sit here and lie to me. You really want to do that, Khris?"

"I do love you. Haven't I proved it to you? Haven't I given up my old ways? I did that, not for you, but for us. I did it because you deserve it. You're special, Sonia, and I want to be the man that gives you...that loves you the way you deserve to be loved."

"That's definitely not going to happen now."

I lost it for a second. "What the fuck is that supposed to mean?"

"Khris, don't talk to me like that," she said softly.

I took a deep breath. I felt confused. Frustrated. Angry. And scared to death. I was afraid of losing the only woman I have. The only woman I have ever loved like this.

"Khris, I know you've tried to be faithful since becoming my boyfriend, and I'm proud of how committed you've been. I didn't expect you to do as well as you did. I love you with all my heart, but like I told you in front of your mother, I will not let you embarrass me...nor make a fool out of me. If you come clean, then we can work this out, put it behind us, and move on."

Tell the truth, fool.

No! I wasn't falling for that shit. That was a trap that women used to sucker their weak-ass men into confirming what they already believed to be true, but didn't have the evidence to convict his ass. I wasn't falling for the old okey-dokey. I will not condemn myself. "Work what out? I haven't done anything."

"You're lying to me, Khris."

I shook my head. "I told you I..."

"Fuck it! You want to do it that way." She sat up and reached under the pillow she was lying on. "Here, Khris," she said, stuffing the glossy 8 x 10 photo in my hand. "That doesn't look like dancing with two exotic bitches to me. That's not even dancing." She shot up from the bed and went into the closet.

I was stunned. I was caught on camera. Shit like this never happened to me when I was out there runnin hos.

"As soon as I find a place, I'll come back and get my clothes."

I looked down at the photo. It was a picture of Nancy walking out of the bathroom stall with tears running down her cheeks. She was crying because I had called her Sonia, as I was cumming down her throat. I was standing sideways with my dick up in the air.

I was furious now. I wanted—needed—to know who was to blame for this. "Who gave you this?"

"Why does it matter?" she shot as she snatched down a duffel bag and started tossing things into it.

"Who. Gave. You. This?" I asked between clenched teeth.

"I don't know who gave it to me. It was in the mailbox at the shop when I got there this morning."

I didn't know what to say to that.

"I know I should have kicked that bitch's ass that night. If I had fucked her up, she would have been to muthafuckin scared to have been in the same club as your ass, much less in the men's fucking rest room."

I didn't know what to do, or what to say at that point. I wanted to kill Nancy for ruining my fucking life. That stinkin fuckin bitch.

I was so lost in thought that I didn't even realize that Sonia had ran out the room until I heard Yasmine and Nishka asking her what happened and where she was going.

Her reply was short and simple. "Away from his lyin ass."

Then the door slammed shut.

Nishka and Yasmine raced upstairs. "What the fuck did you do?" Yasmine shouted.

"I don't know what you did, but you need to get up off your ass and go after her," Nishka said, yanking my hand for me to get up from the bed.

I felt like the weight of the world was on me. I couldn't get up. I was angry. I was hurting like I never hurt before. It felt like I couldn't breathe. "What the fuck am I supposed to say?" I asked, pushing the photo into Nishka's hand. "What can I say that will explain that?"

Nishka looked at the photo and shook her head. "You always get caught with your dick up in the air."

"At least your pants ain't around you ankles this time," Yasmine shot.

"Off all the times, you two choose to have fucking jokes now?"

"Sorry. I was trying to get you to cheer up so you can take your...." Yasmine paused. "Too late now: she just pulled off."

Nishka grabbed the cordless. "You need to call her!"

"Where did she get this picture?" Yasmine asked.

"She said it was in her mailbox at the shop."

"That means it could be anyone. She put the new address all over the Website and the receipts."

"This is Nancy's work. That fucking bitch set me up," I said, dialing Nancy's number. "Answer, bitch!" I said impatiently as the phone rang the second time.

She answered on the fourth ring. "What?"

"You fucking bitch! Why you gat to fuck up everything?"

"Nigga, who the fuck do you think you are, calling me cursing and shit. Muthafucka...seven months I haven't heard from your sorry-fucking-ass after you call me your bitch's name, and you have the fucking nerve to call me cursing. The only reason I answered my phone is 'cause I thought your sorry-ass called me to apologize."

"Apologize? Bitch, you the one run up in the rest room and grabbed my dick while I was pissin and shoved it in your mouth.

"You didn't stop me. You never said no."

"Why the fuck now, Nancy?"

"Why the fuck now, what, nigga?"

"You know what the fuck I'm talking about?"

"Nigga, what the fuck are you talking about?"

"The muthafuckin picture of you walkin out the gaddamn rest room stall."

"What fuckin picture, nigga? I don't know anything about no muthafuckin picture."

"Someone sent Sonia a picture taken from that night in the men's rest room."

"Nigga, you think I would have sent a picture of myself coming out the muthafuckin men's rest room stall to your bitch?"

"So if you een send it, who the fuck send it, then?"

"Nigga, I don't know, and I don't fucking care. Just make sure that picture doesn't end up on the muthafuckin Internet. If anyone tells me anything about a picture with you and me on it in a fucking rest room, I'ma burn your shit, and I will fuck you and your bitch up. And, nigga, don't call my muthafuckin number no more. Go back to your ho. Forget you ever knew me, you slimy-ass muthafucka"

Bam!!!!

Nancy slammed down the phone so hard, that bitch sounded like she smashed that shit to pieces.

The fucked up part about her cussing my ass out like that was that I actually believed her. I looked up at Yasmine and Nishka. "I don't think she sent the picture. Nancy might be fucked up, but look at that picture of her, she would never send out a picture of herself crying..."

"I would hope not," Nishka said, pointing to the side of her mouth, "especially not with cum draining out the side of mouth."

"It was taken in the men's bathroom, and Nancy obviously couldn't take it herself," Yasmine said.

"And even if she had one of her girls go in there with her, I'm sure she could have gotten a better picture than this."

"Besides, if it was a female that took the picture, that means that she would have had to be in there the entire time..."

"Wait a minute. I remember slammin the door cause a muthafucka was pointing a camera phone at my ass in the stall."

"But, how would that strange man know to send the picture to Sonia?" Nishka asked. "It's not like Sonia was there with you and he saw her and tracked her down."

"What if it wasn't some strange man? What if it's a man that knows me and knows that I'm Sonia's man?"

"Who? Her ex?" Yasmine asked.

"Wouldn't you have recognized him?" Nishka asked.

"Not really. I didn't look at anyone's faces. Sonia's daddy could have been there and I wouldn't have recognized him," I admitted.

"I think it's a little too coincidental for Sonia's ex to be there in the right place at the right time," Nishka said.

"Well, there's only one other option."

"What? Who?" Yasmine asked.

"The PI that was following Ashley."

"That was before Ashley got pregnant. And why would he want to follow you? You and Ashley ain't doing anything, anymore," Yasmine countered. "Right?"

"We aren't, but Nancy still works for Susan, and the PI still works for Susan."

"So it could have been a set up," Nishka said.

"There's one sure way to find out who dropped off the photos," I started to explain, but got cut off.

"How?" Nishka and Yasmine asked almost at the same time. "The security cameras. The cameras should have caught it."

CHAPTER 34

COMING CLEAN

I was about to call Bobby but I stopped. Did I really want to explain all this to him? Did I really want to get him and Ashley—with their newborn baby—all upset, and into me and Sonia's business? They would blame me anyhow. After all, it was my fault. And, does it really make a difference who sent Sonia the picture? I would like to find out who the hater is so I could put my foot in his or her ass, but would that change the fact that Sonia was gone, never to return? Or, could I win her back?

"You need to call Sonia," Nishka said with Yasmine nodding in agreement.

"She probably won't answer."

"You ain't gonna know until you try. Call," Yasmine said.

I hit speed dial 1. It rang once; twice; three times. "She's not answering," I said, looking up at the four eyes staring at me.

Then she answered.

"I'm fine. Now leave me..."

"Sonia, come back," I begged. "Please."

"You lied to me."

"Come back and let's talk about this. I'll explain everything to you."

"You had time to come up with a story, so you can explain now. When I asked you a few minutes ago, you couldn't answer. All of a sudden you can explain now."

She was angry. I couldn't really blame her. I had fucked up and she had given me the opportunity to come clean. "Sonia, listen to me..."

"No, Khris. I gave you all the opportunity in the world to talk and you didn't talk."

"Come home, baby. Please."

"No. I'm going to a hotel, and tomorrow I will start looking for a place. I can deal with you cheating, but I can't deal with you lying to me about it."

Fuck it. I tried. Wasn't shit else I could say to her. I was already out there. She knows how I feel about her. Fuck this shit! She gat me acting like she's the only woman on earth. Fuck this. Maybe this marriage shit isn't for me: too much women out there for me to be putting up with this bullshit.

I must have been quiet too long for her. "Do you have anything else to say to me?" Sonia asked. "I don't want to hang up on you."

"It sounds like you already made up your mind what you want to do, so, no I don't have anything else to say."

"Well, bye. I'll let you know when I'm coming to get the rest of my stuff. I'll leave your keys and stuff then."

"So kind of you. Thanks. Bye," I said without emotion, and ended the call.

"She coming back?" Yasmine asked.

"To pick up her shit and drop my keys when she finds a place."

"You can't let her go!"

"I can't stop her either. She already made up her mind." I was angry. Not at Nancy. Not at who had sent the picture. I was angry at myself for letting myself fall in love with one fucking woman. If I hadn't, I wouldn't be feeling as fucked up as I'm feeling right now.

"I'm going to call her," Yasmine said, turning to walk out.

"Do what you like. I'm going to get drunk and get back on my game. This one woman shit ain't worth all the bullshit."

"You don't mean that," Nishka said. "You were just all excited about getting married, now you ga let one lil bump in the road destroy it?"

"Me!" I shouted, getting up. "Look at all the changes I've made to prove to her ass that I loved her. I gave up all my hos for her ass. All the good I did. I did ninety-nine things right and the one thing I did wrong overshadowed it all. What kind of fucking sense does that make?"

"We're going to call her and see if we can help you out," Yasmine stated as they both headed out the door.

I went downstairs and took out a brand new bottle of White Hennessy and cracked the seal. I didn't need a glass. I was feeling fucked up, and I wanted to get fucked up. I took a healthy swig straight from the bottle. The alcohol burned its way down to my stomach. I took it as punishment for letting Nancy suck my damn dick. I should have stopped her. One muthafuckin blowjob changed my muthafuckin life.

I took another mouthful as I walked upstairs to my room and closed my door. I started stripping off my clothes as I entered the bathroom. I wanted to drown my sorrows, and wash off the bad fuckin luck.

As the whirlpool filled, I poured bath gel into the water; White Henny down my throat.

I sat in the tub and turned on the stereo. The first thing I heard was Usher singing, "Sign these papers."

"How fucking appropriate," I said, switching to the CDs. I tried every genre. Nothing sounded good. Nothing could change my mood. So, I gave up and switched that shit off.

After an hour or so, I was down to half a bottle. I was feeling good. The Henny was tasting even better, now. I was fucked up. Not drunk, fucked up: emotionally fucked up. Tears were running from my eyes and I couldn't stop them. "This fuckin woman gat me crying for her ass. How the fuck did I let myself get like this?" I asked out loud.

"Cause your stupid ass fell in love," I answered out loud. "I een never gonna let that shit happen again. Fuck love! Fuck marriage! Fuck all dat bullshit!"

My question and answer session was cut short when Nishka and her twin—or was it triplets—walked into my bathroom. "Damn, girls, y'all just what I need."

"It's only one of me," Nishka said. "I should drown your drunk ass right in that tub. What the hell you think you doing?"

"Drowning my sorrows and washing away my sins."

"Give me this damn bottle," she said, snatching the bottle from my hand.

I was too drunk to stop her. Actually, I grabbed at the wrong one. I damn sure was seeing two, sometimes three of them.

She placed the bottle on the vanity and came back over. "You got to get out of this tub," she said, turning off the jets.

"Why don't y'all come in," I said, my words slow and slurred.

"You don't think your dick already got you in enough trouble?" she asked, pressing the button to drain the tub, then reached for my towel. "You probably can't even get it up."

"Hell yeah, it could get up. See," I said, grabbing a handful of flaccid dick. Then I looked down. "Wait! Just give it a moment," I said, trying to stroke it to life.

"Boy, try stand up and leave your dick alone."

"It broke. It een workin no more," I said, staring down at my limp, shriveled up dick. Then I started crying again. "Sonia done turn me soft," I said, letting it go.

"It need to be broke," she retorted as she tried to help me up.

I tried three times to get my hand on the edge of the tub, so that I could brace myself to stand, but each time my hand slipped.

Nishka had to get behind me and put her two hands under my arms to pull me up.

The room was spinning. I had to brace myself against the wall as Nishka dried me off. When she was done, she walked me over to the vanity and made me lean over the basin. "You have to brush your teeth. Stand still," she ordered.

Next thing I knew, I was getting my teeth brushed.

Next, I was lying in bed. I don't know if I walked, crawled, or if Nishka carried me to the bed. I had no clue. It was as if pieces of time were vanishing.

My eyes popped open. I wanted to pee like a racehorse. My dick was working again. It was hard and pressing into my stomach. I rolled onto my back and looked over at the clock too quickly.

The numbers on the clock wouldn't keep still. I think it was three something. The room started spinning again, so I closed my eyes for a few seconds.

"What the fuck is wrong with you," I shouted as water splashed on my face, in my mouth and nose. I opened my eyes. No one was there. I had been dreaming. I had fallen asleep that quickly. I looked at the clock. The numbers weren't moving as much this time. It was five forty five. I wiped the water from my eyes and mouth. The room wasn't spinning as much. What the fuck? My face was wet, and so was my chest and stomach. Suddenly, I realized that I didn't need to pee anymore.

"Aww fuck! I done pissed on myself." I crawled out of the bed cussing like a sailor. I turned on the light, and sure enough, my drunken ass done pissed my bed. The last time I pissed the bed; I was probably three or four years old. I was disgusted with myself. Look what I let a woman drag me to do to myself.

After stumbling into the bathroom, I decided peeing on myself was the absolute bottom. I would not let myself sink any lower.

I kneeled over the throne, stuck my finger down my throat, and brought up everything that was in my stomach. The only thing in there was liquid, so it came up easily. I brushed my teeth, took a shower, changed the bed, then I took the dirty linen downstairs to the wash room and threw them in the washer.

All this shit was because of Sonia. Fuck Sonia! Fuck Nancy, too, while I was at it.

I was hungry as hell, so I went into the kitchen to fix something to eat. The sun was almost up, so it didn't make any sense to go back to bed; might as well fix some breakfast. I was up now.

I opened the fridge and saw Sonia. Not her body: everything in there to eat reminded me about her. Why had I let her ass into my life like I did?

I fucked it up....

No, my dick fucked it up.

No, I fucked it up. I wasn't strong enough to resist temptation.

Maybe I didn't deserve Sonia. Maybe it was better that this happened now, rather than after we got married. Could I have been faithful? Nah, I don't think so. Look how easy it was for Nancy to get my dick into her mouth. Maybe this is better for Sonia. She deserved better than me.

Suddenly, I wasn't hungry anymore. I closed the fridge. I needed to do something. I didn't want to be alone with my thoughts anymore. I was missing Sonia already. I felt empty. I felt like a piece of me was missing.

"I wonder where she is? Is she thinking about me? Where did she sleep last night? Was she able to sleep last night?"

Damn! There I go with the questions again.

I went into the family room, grabbed one of the cashmere blankets, and sprawled out on the couch. I flipped through the movie channels and came across a good action flick. I had seen it in the movie theatre when it first came out—Sonia and I did---but I could stand to watch it a few more times.

I found myself just staring blankly at the TV. Then I saw Sonia at the movie theatre that night. I closed my eyes to get rid of the image.

The phone startled me awake. I don't remember falling asleep. I looked around and the sun was fully up now. I looked at the time: nine twenty five. I checked the caller ID: Mom's work number. Yasmine probably called her and told her what had happened. It was really too early to deal with her right now, but, I had no choice. "Good morning, Mother," I said flatly.

"Don't good morning me. You need to get your ass to Nassau immediately. I don't care if you have to charter a damn flight. Get your ass here on the first thing smokin."

This couldn't be about Sonia and me. I panicked. "Did something happen to Daddy?"

"Boy, een nothin wrong with your damn daddy. Something might be wrong with your ass. You all about fucking with these fast ass lil gals."

"What are you going on about? What's so important that I need to be in Nassau?"

"Boy get your ass on a flight and get here," she snarled.

I had never heard my mother talk like this while at work.

"Look, I don't know what Yasmine told you, but Sonia doesn't want to talk to me."

"Sonia? Sonia don't want to talk to you? What the fuck does Sonia have to do with this?"

My mother cursing like this? This shit is serious.

"You know what, Sonia ga leave your ass for sure now. You...you... Boy..."

She couldn't even get out what she wanted to say. "Mommy..."

"Don't mommy damn me."

"What's wrong? You cursing and carrying on, but you aren't

telling me what gat you so riled up. Sonia did the same shit to me last night. This must be a woman thing." I mumbled that last part under my breath.

"Boy, you een never too old to get your ass kicked, so you better watch what the hell you say to me. I een in the mood. My gat damn blood pressure done through the roof as it is."

"I'm sorry, mother. Can you please just calm down and tell..."

"Don't tell me to calm down!"

"Well can you please just tell me what is going on?"

"Your lil fast-ass Brazilian girlfriend just walk up in here and drop a gaddamn baby on my desk and said that it's yours and she couldn't keep it because her boyfriend said he will kill the poor baby if he lay eyes on it," she replied in one breath.

Did I hear her right? Did my mother just say a baby? "A what?"

"A baby. I didn't stutter. I said a gaddamn baby! So you better get your ass down here now. I gat so much shit going on at work today I can't even take the day off. Thank God this baby sleepin. Get here now!"

I groaned inwardly, then let out a weighty sigh. "I'll call you as soon as I get to the airport and find a flight."

"And if I were you, I would tell Sonia before Sherice does...if she een call her yet." With that warning, she hung up.

What the fuck? Paola had a baby. No wonder I couldn't get in touch with her ass. But why would she hide from me if the baby were mine? Fuck! I have a baby. What the fuck am I going to do with a baby?

I was racing upstairs, deep in thought, when my phone rang again. I didn't even look at the caller ID. I figured my mother had to forgotten to tell me something. "Yes?" I answered tersely.

"What did I do?" Ashley asked in mock horror.

"My bad, I thought it was my mother calling back," I explained in a lower tone.

"I know you're upset, but don't take it out on everybody. You're the one that got caught with your dick out."

"Yeah, yeah, yeah. I take it Sonia called you."

"I'm her friend, who else would she call. I'm your friend too, so I sort of worked things out."

"Waste of time," I replied, running into my closet.

"I don't think so. She's agreed to have a sit down. Come up to the house at three."

"I can't."

"Why the hell not?" Ashley asked with attitude.

"I have to go to Nassau right away. That's why I thought this was my mother calling back. Apparently, a young lady just dropped off a baby at her job and told her it's mine.

"Oh my God! Is it yours?"

"It's possible, and the mother said so. She left the baby in my mother's office and my mother can't take the day off. Too much stuff going on at work, so I have to get down there immediately."

"Take the jet. I can call and have it ready to go by the time you get there."

"Thanks, but that's alright. It'll be cheaper for me..."

"I didn't ask you about cheaper, Khris. You have an emergency. Go to Boca Executive and the crew will be there waiting on you. I'm going to call them now, and I'll call you back in five minutes," she said and ended the call.

I wasn't planning on staying down there, but I tossed a few things into an overnight bag and pulled down a pair of slacks and a button down shirt. I changed quickly, then I remembered Yasmine and Nishka. I would have to wake one of them to run me to Boca Executive so that they could have transportation while I'm gone.

By the time I woke them, Ashley called and told me the crew would be at the hanger ready to go when I arrived.

We both agreed to keep this between us until we knew more. It would be my place to tell Sonia, not hers.

On the way to the airport, I filled Yasmine and Nishka in. Forty-five minutes later, I was racing down the runway in a Gulfstream 550. I was on my way to a destination from which I would never return.

The destination: fatherhood.

CHAPTER 35

A HARD PILL TO SWALLOW

My mother took an early lunch so that she could feed the baby and meet me at the Nassau International Airport's Jet Center. She was there waiting when the Gulfstream touched down. I wasn't staying. My mother had told me that Paola had seen to bringing all the necessary legal documents that I needed for the baby to travel. Ashley gave the pilots instructions to wait, however long was necessary, until I was ready to return. I had to return today. I had a flight tomorrow afternoon.

My passport was stamped and I made my way to the parking lot where my mother was waiting. I got to the car and saw that she was feeding a baby. This was no joke. She looked up as I opened the car door and got into the front seat. Tears were rolling down her cheek. "Jesus, Khris," she said, looking down at the baby in her arms. "She's so precious."

"She?"

"Yes, it's a little girl. She's so beautiful."

"I didn't know about this, Mom. Believe me, I had no idea. I don't even know if the baby is mine. I always used protection when I.... The last time I even heard from Paola was the same day that Nancy had referred to about me and Paola in my driveway."

"Well, she had the baby right in Miami at Jackson Memorial. Why didn't she call you?"

"We weren't in a relationship, Mom. Sometimes we went months without talking to each other. I don't know why she didn't tell me she was pregnant, though. I don't know why women do what they do."

"We can't worry about why she did what she did. She's gone now. What you have to think about now, Khris, is what are you going to do with this baby. I mean this is you all over," she stated with conviction. "Look how long she is. She has..."

"I can't believe I could possibly be a father.... I have a daughter. A daughter."

"Yeah, God sure knows how to run jokes, doesn't he? After all the hell you gave other people's daughters, you end up having a daughter."

"I have to get a DNA test to confirm that she is mine."

"Son, believe your mother when I tell you, this lil girl is my grandchild. She has your ears, your nose, and your hands: she has her mother's pretty eyes, lips, and hair. At least you won't have to learn to plait. This that good old wash, brush, and wear: no perm necessary. She's going to be a little darker than her mother. Look at her ears, that's her color right there."

"The daddy might be my color."

"Boy don't get me upset. This your baby! You the damn daddy," she whispered loudly as to not scare the baby.

"And if I'm not the father?"

"Well, Paola's gone. She said that her crazy man threatened to kill her and the baby if she came back with it. She didn't want to have an abortion, so she ran to Miami to get away from his family. She hid in Miami until she had the baby and the baby was old enough to travel. The doctor wouldn't clear her to fly until she went for her six-week checkup, which she did yesterday. I think she said her man got locked up a couple of months before she got pregnant and he's coming out next month. You were the only man she slept with since he's been locked up.

I couldn't understand this shit. "So why didn't she keep the baby and leave him? What kind of woman would give up her baby for a man?"

"One that's afraid. Her man threatened to kill the baby and her when he gets out."

"Same way she ran away to have the baby, she could have ran away, and stayed away from his ass."

"That's not the only reason, Khris."

"What's the other reason?" I asked with growing anger.

"She can't take care of the baby, and take care of herself."

"Money? Money couldn't have been an issue. She moved to Miami.

She hid and didn't call me for any assistance. Then she flew down here and dropped the baby off to you. Why do all that? Why not leave the baby and a note on my doorstep. She knows where I live...and I'm sure they still have phone books."

"I asked her the same thing."

"And what did she say?"

"She couldn't face you. She wouldn't have been able to tell you face to face."

"But she could tell you face to face," I snarled. I felt like crying, but I held back the tears.

"Listen, son, she figured you needed to hear what she had to say from someone that loves you. I don't know how she found me, but she flew in yesterday evening and she was in my office as soon as the doors opened at nine. I—I..."

"What? You may as well come out and tell me. What else did she tell you? What is it that she couldn't tell me face to face?"

"She can't take care of the baby, because she's-she's HIV positive and her health is rapidly declining. She's dying, Khris."

"What? No. Tell me this isn't happening. Tell me this is a joke." My bowels threatened to loose. My stomach churned. I had to swallow the bile as it threatened to come up. I couldn't even look at my mother. I stared out the window and up at the clouds. One cloud in particular looked like the Grim Reaper staring down at me grinning.

"She found out the same time that she found out she was pregnant. That's why she hadn't called you. She couldn't face you. She was trying to keep it together for her baby."

The world started spinning around me. This bitch done gave me the package! The modern day black fuckin plague. I'm a dead man walking.

"She said that she confronted her man about him infecting her, and yes, he confirmed that he was HIV positive. He found out he had it before they even met. He gave it to her. She was with him for a while, so like all couples eventually do, she got comfortable and started having unprotected sex with her man...after all, they were living together. It was the natural thing to do. This thing is so prevalent out here now...everyone needs to go and get tested. You meet a girl, you need to ask her name, phone number, and the date of the last time she took an HIV test."

"Fuck!" I cursed, punching the dashboard. I not only startled my mother, but the baby as well.

The baby started crying. Mom had jumped, causing the bottle to pop out of the baby's mouth. Mom put the nipple back to her lips and she stopped crying and continued feeding at once. Mom gave me a dark look. I knew better than to do that shit again.

"Sorry," I said softly.

"I know you're frustrated and scared, Khris. Christ, I cursed and carried on this morning, too. The good news is that the baby isn't infected. That's a miracle right there. Paola said the doctor told her there's a good chance you are not infected, but you need to get tested immediately. I want you to get tested today if possible, Khris."

I was crying. I just received a death sentence. I wondered how much time I have to live? No one knows how or when they're going to die, but to receive a death sentence like this was the scariest shit in the world. Why is all this bad shit suddenly happening to me? Is this payback for fucking other men's wives and girlfriends? Goose bumps popped up all over my arms. I had to get a hold of myself. If the baby isn't infected, then there is a good chance I'm not, either. Okay, calm down, I said to myself.

Mom checked to see how much formula was left in the baby's bottle, then looked over at me. "She said y'all always used protection, but the last time, the condom broke."

Damn! By the pool when she did that acrobatic shit. Fuck! I thought as I remembered. I glanced over to mom and nodded my head. It sure had been sweet. My gaze dropped to the little baby's face. Yes, she sure looked like she could be mine. A smile threatened to creep out from beneath my tears. That sweetness produced this beautiful little baby girl.

"She left you a letter. I didn't open it. She also said that there is a letter in there for the baby once she gets old enough and starts asking for her mother, that's if you decide to tell her about her real mother. She said it was all up to you how you handle it. She's not going to interfere, she may be-may be gone by then. That poor girl was so scared, Khris. I am upset about this, but this is God's work, so I can't question this. This is probably what you need to settle you down."

"Well, you can forget about me settling down with Sonia, now. And if I have HIV, then you'll just have to deal with me being by myself."

"Don't think like that, son. Think positive. Go and take the test. Keep a positive frame of mind. Talk to God about it. Only he can help you turn your life around. You have a daughter to raise, Khris..." She paused as my head shot up. "I know. You go back, and you get both tests done. See if you can do it today. In a few days, you'll know everything for certain."

I nodded. She's right. I don't think Paola would have gone through all of this if she weren't certain who the baby belonged to. I'm still going to make sure, but in my heart, I knew the baby was mine. She had too much of me not to be. "You're right, Mom. First thing's first. I'll get the tests done immediately."

"Khris, you have to figure out how you're going to raise a daughter with your job." My mother glanced down at the empty bottle. "Thank God money isn't an issue, because she sure has a healthy appetite," she said, smiling. She removed the empty bottle from the baby's mouth, handed it to me, then wiped up the little that was draining. She draped a cloth napkin over her shoulder, then held the baby upright against her shoulder, gently rubbing her back until she burped.

"That's a good girl. You want to go to your daddy?" she asked, easing her back from her shoulder, then passing her to me.

I took my precious little girl from my mother and held her up in front of me. I took a good look at her. She did resemble me a little, but she's as beautiful as her mother. "What's her name?" I asked mom, without taking my eyes off of her.

"Erica Christina Harrison."

Paola had named her after me, and listed me as the father on the birth certificate. In the Bahamas, the father had to sign the birth certificate in order for the baby to carry his last name. Not so in the U.S., apparently.

Erica's eyes opened at the sound of her name. She knew her name. She stared straight ahead and into my eyes. She had the most beautiful hazel eyes with little golden flecks splashed around her iris. Our eyes locked. Now I knew exactly how Bobby felt in the delivery room. It was love at first sight. I smiled at her and she smiled and dribbled back at me. My heart melted in that moment. "Am I your daddy, Erica?" I asked in that voice that grown ups use when speaking to babies.

Erica smiled and cooed. I guess that's a yes.

I remember thinking that I had never felt love like what I felt when I fell in love with Sonia. I know that's a different love all together, but damn: that feeling paled in comparison with what I was feeling now. This is real love: parent and child. True unconditional love.

"Jesus. She just answered you." Mom grinned and shook her head. "She knows her daddy. I changed her pampers and fed her, and she didn't smile for me not one time. But you come here and hold her for two seconds and she opens up those pretty eyes, and smile for you. If that isn't enough confirmation for you, then go take your DNA test. You don't even have to call me and tell me I was right. I haven't told you father about the other thing: I didn't want to worry him. But, he knows about the baby. You know how he is. He said he didn't want to see her until he was sure it's his granddaughter: he doesn't want his heart broken if she isn't yours." My mother smiled and placed her hand on top of my shoulder. "Everything's going to be okay. This is God's plan. We can't question it. Just believe in Him, and everything is going to be fine."

"Yes," I smiled, and kissed Erica. "We will be fine, right Erica?"

I have a daughter. I wasn't even thinking about what else I might have. I put that in a box and compartmentalized that shit. "Her birth certificate and a certified letter from Paola allowing you to travel with her is in there," she said, pointing to the baby bag. "Your on there as the father, and both of you are US citizens, so you shouldn't have a problem or need the letter. Go, do your test and whatnot. Christmas is in less than two weeks, and I want my grandchild home for Christmas."

"Yes, ma'am. I love you, Mom," I said, leaning over and kissing her. "I'll make this right. I promise."

"I know you will, Khris. And I love you, too...and you, too, Erica. Grandma loves you, too." Then she kissed both of us.

We had no trouble going through immigration and customs.

The flight attendant helped me get Erica's carrier strapped in safely, and we took off for home. Twenty minutes later, we touched down at Boca Executive with my brand new baby girl.

Yasmine and Nishka were waiting for us; I had called them from the plane. However, I was surprised to see Ashley waiting along with them. It had only been a week since she was released from the hospital.

The copilot helped me with the bags, and Ashley relieved me of my baby girl as soon as my foot hit the tarmac. "What are you doing here? And where is Lauren?"

"Spending some quality time with her father. She has to start learning how to use her power over him. And, I came to see my godchild," she smiled. "She's gorgeous, Khris. Isn't she girls?" she asked, holding the carrier, so Yasmine and Nishka could see.

"Thank God she looks like her mother," Yasmine said, snidely.

"Unnnn-uung. She has his nose, his ears, and look at her hands," Nishka said.

Ashley nodded. "What's her name, Khris?"

"Erica Christina."

Ashley looked up and smiled. "Erica Christina Harrison. That's a lovely name. Come, let's get her away from these jet fumes," she said, turning to walk toward the Range. "How old is she?"

"Six weeks."

"She's going to be tall. Her and Lauren are going to be god sisters and best friends."

"First thing's first."

"I made some calls while you were gone. I knew you would want to know for sure, so I checked to see where you can get a paternity test done."

"You did? That's great! Where?"

"There's a lab in Palm Beach. You can go today if you want. They give same day results."

"Let's go now," I said immediately. "The faster I get this out of the way, the better."

"Here's the address. You all go ahead. I just came to bring you the information and take a look at my godchild. Call me and confirm what I already know when you get the results," she chuckled, hopping back into the Rolls.

Josh, her driver, nodded, and they were off.

We arrived at the lab about twelve thirty. I paid the extra for top priority. I also got two other tests done while I was back in the examination room. I did a rapid HIV test and got the results fifteen minutes later. I breathed a little easier when I heard that it was negative. They also took blood to run the commonly used ELISA HIV tests which screens for antibodies. Those results would take about two to three days. Those were the results that I really wanted.

I didn't tell Yasmine or Nishka about the HIV situation.

I didn't need the extra stress. I will also wait on the results to see if it is necessary to contact any of the females that I had sexual relations with since Paola. Luckily I had eased up on my trickin: the list wasn't too long. Hopefully, I wouldn't have to call anyone to inform them that our sinful pleasures had condemned us all to death.

CHAPTER 36

THE AWAKENING

The paternity test proved exactly what everyone had already concluded: Erica was indeed 99.9 percent my daughter.

I got the call to return to the lab for the results while we were out buying some of Erica's necessities: formula, diapers, wipes. Paola had made a detailed list of all the brands and sizes that Erica used. Everything from her pediatrician's name, contact information, and next appointment, to Erica's feeding schedule had been left in her bag.

I called and informed my mother and father that they were 99.9 percent grandparents, and when it was just me and mom on the line, I told her about the rapid test results, and the other one—the ELISA—that I took.

Even though Yasmine and Nishka volunteered to baby-sit for me while I went to work tomorrow, I decided to call in sick. By the time the call was answered, I had already decided to take an extended leave. By the time I asked for the extended leave, I had already resigned in my mind. I decided to wait before telling them, though.

My next call went to Ashley: I just wanted to hear her say it.

"I told you so, Khris. I'm so happy for you."

"I wish I could say the same."

"What do you mean by that? Aren't you excited that you're a father?"

"Of course, I'm happy about that. It's just that this is all so sudden. Last night the woman I wanted to marry walked out on me, then today, I'm a father of a six week old daughter...not by the woman I was going to propose to."

Ashley's voice softened. "Have you spoken to her yet?"

"No, I wanted to get the results from the paternity test first. I don't know why: I don't think it's going to make a difference."

"Why do you think so?"

"She's not going to be too receptive to me having a daughter that she would have to help raise. The last thing I want is for someone to feel obligated to doing that. This is my responsibility."

"That's true, but don't you think you should let that be her choice whether she wants to do that or not? Men do it all the time: women, too. You can't get the yacht without the life raft, Khris."

"Yeah, but some of those people mistreat the children because they're not their own. I will not let that happen to Erica," I stated firmly. "I will call Sonia, but I won't feel right putting her in that position. Take me, you have to take my six week old baby, too."

"So, you're going to stay single until Erica's legal age and goes off to college?"

"If that's what I have to do, then I will."

"You and I both know that's not going to happen. And, we both know you can't be bringing a bunch of different women around her either, so don't even think about going back to your old lifestyle."

I laughed. I wasn't going back to that lifestyle regardless. Not with what I might have. "I know. Anyhow, let me call Sonia and break the bad news."

"Good news. My godchild is good news, Khris. And don't you forget it. Bye."

"Bye."

Sonia had wanted to talk to me today, so I really needed to call her and explain why I hadn't been able to meet with her earlier. I owed her that much. I really didn't know how to say what I had to say, but I knew I had to find a way. I was at fault for everything that happened between us, I was responsible for Erica, and for possibly exposing and infecting Sonia with HIV.

With my baby freshly bathed and fed, I laid on my back and placed her on my chest right over my heart. She twisted her little body until she was comfortable, then she settled. With one hand gently caressing her back, and the sound of my heart beating beneath her, she closed her eyes and went to sleep. It felt wonderful having her on my chest. Before I knew it, our breathing synchronized.

It was the most wonderful feeling in the world. I was already under her spell.

I kept Erica there. Having her there soothed me. She calmed me; got rid of my nervousness. A baby's fresh powder scent was enough to calm a savage beast, and I was no savage.

Using my free hand, I hit speed dial "1." I didn't know if Sonia would answer. I was almost one hundred percent certain that Sherice had already called and broken the news.

Sonia surprised me. She answered on the first ring. "Hey! Is everything all right?" she asked, sounding anxious and concerned.

"You heard?"

"Ashley told me you had an emergency in Nassau. She said you would call me when you got everything sorted out."

Was she playing a game? I knew Ashley would leave my secret for me to tell, but Sherice? That, I didn't believe for one-second.

"Khris? You're quiet. What's the matter?"

"Maybe you should come home...come over so we can talk face to face."

She was silent.

"You were willing to talk earlier. I'll be honest, Sonia, a lot has changed in the past twenty-one hours and thirty-two...thirty three minutes since you walked out on me."

That caused a little chuckle. "It's only been twenty-one hours and twenty-nine minutes."

"I'm counting from the time you walked out of the closet, not the front door."

She chuckled.

That was a good sign, even though it might not last long.

"I'm coming through the gate now."

"Oh, so you were already on your way home," I chuckled, liking the fact that she hadn't walked out on me for good.

"I found a place, Khris," she said softly.

That caused panic to set in again. Where the hell did all that cool I had a minute ago? My breath caught, throwing our synchronized breathing off. Her little body shifted. I quickly got back in rhythm and she relaxed again. Then I remembered where my priorities lied. I kissed the top of her head and smiled. Even if Sonia had planned on forgiving me for lying to her, she wouldn't forgive me for having a baby with another woman. Worst, she wouldn't forgive me for possibly infecting her with HIV.

"I'm sorry, Khris, but I..."

"It's probably for the best that you did, but let's talk when you get inside."

"I'm here. I'm coming in now."

"Alright," I said, ending the call.

Nishka and Yasmine had made a pallet with a couple of baby blankets on my bed, and surrounded it with four pillows in case Erica rolled. I placed Erica on her stomach and rubbed her back until she was comfortable again before easing off the bed. I stood and looked down at my little angel, nodded and smiled as I turned and left the room. I patted my pocket to make sure I had the tests results.

I heard Sonia talking to Yasmine and Nishka. She sounded chipper. Then she was on her way upstairs. I stood at the top of the stairs. All the love I felt for Sonia came crashing back down upon me. I wanted to get on my knees and beg her to stay. I-I.... No, I had to be strong. I had to be strong for Erica.

"Hey!" she said, smiling up at me as she came up the stairs.

I smiled back. I just couldn't help myself. I really loved this woman. "I missed you."

"I know," she said, blushing.

I opened my arms as she came up the last two steps. She walked into my arms. My arms closed around her as her hands snaked around my back. She felt sooooo wonderful. She smelled delicious. I wanted to kiss her. I felt myself getting aroused. I had to shake it off.

I held her for another second then let her go.

"Come," I said, turning toward her room. "We can talk in your room."

We started walking. She glanced sideways at me. I guess she was a little shocked that I hadn't kissed...hadn't tried to kiss her.

"I have so much that I have to tell you. But first, let me start by telling you that I love you. I'm madly in love with you, and I never, ever wanted to hurt you. I'm also sorry for lying to you last night...actually I'm sorry for not telling you that I had fallen weak the night that shit with Nancy happened. I wanted to tell you, but I was so used to covering my ass, that I just couldn't bring myself to telling you. Old habits. Last night, I had an internal battle going on. I wanted to, and I knew I should have come clean, but I was too afraid that I would lose you to tell you the truth. When I weighed the pros and cons of telling the truth, I was convinced that lying was the best way to go. It was the easier of the two. I figured the lie would save me from hurting you."

"Wow! And that's just the opening," she said, sitting on the bed. She patted the spot next to her.

I sat, then fell back and looked up at the ceiling.

Sonia followed suit. "Khris, I know you tried. And-and I owe you an apology, too. After all the good you did, I never should have walked out of here last night the way I did. You deserved better. I let my love for you, my emotions—my jealousy get the better of me. My emotions overruled my common sense: overruled my better judgment. Don't get me wrong, I am pissed that you had Nancy meet you at that club, but..."

"Wait a minute, you think I had Nancy meet me at the club? I never called Nancy. I had no idea that she was there. Let me explain to you what happened..."

When I finished telling her the story, right up to me leaving the club to come home to her, Sonia sat up. "So you called out my name. That's why the bitch was crying. Good for her ass. But, your assumption on who took the picture is incorrect."

"Huh?"

"Nancy didn't set you up. It was Jay, Mario's little gopher. The one with the coconut tree looking dreads and the skinny jeans."

"Lil Wayne wannabe? How do you know?"

"I went to security and we reviewed the recordings from the security cameras. It caught him dropping the picture in the mailbox."

"And I called Nancy and cussed her ass good."

"Shit! You een do nothing wrong. That bitch deserve more than a cussing. She better be glad you got a hold of her, rather than me. A nice hospital stay would have been in order for her ass."

We laughed for a minute. Sonia twisted to her side and propped her hand on her elbow. "So what was your emergency in Nassau?"

"You want the long or short of it first?"

"Give me the short of it, then you can go back and explain."

Sounds like she already knew. She probably did. "At nine thirty this morning, I found out that I'm the father of a six week old baby girl."

That took the wind out of her sails. There was real surprise on her face. She didn't know. She couldn't fake that. No way.

"What? How? With who? Who you was fuckin in Nassau?"

"I'll answer them in order. What: I have a six-week-old daughter. How: sexual intercourse by way of a busted condom. Who: the Brazilian flight attendant that Nancy saw me in the driveway with. Who I'm fucking in Nassau: no one. Paola—that's her name—Paola flew to Nassau to drop the bomb on my mother."

I could see her calculating, and then she looked me dead in my eyes as if she was a human lie detector.

"How long have you known about this, Khris?" she asked between clenched teeth.

I stared right back at her. I had no intentions on lying to her anymore. I had nothing to fear. She was going-gone already. "I hadn't spoken to Paola since the day she and her two coworkers spent up here. I had a woman, so I didn't try to call her, and she didn't call me. I found out when my mother called and woke my drunken ass up this morning."

I told her the entire story from start to finish. I even gave her the paternity test result, as well as the rapid test result. She read both without a word.

"Sonia, I'm sorry for possibly infecting you."

"I'm not infected, Khris. And, neither are you. If you were, I would be...the way we were going at it without protection."

"You have to go and get tested, Sonia."

"I've been getting tested every six months ever since I found out Mario was on that shit. I got tested at the end of January, again in July. You had to have made the baby in February...the week when we met. You say you haven't slept with her..."

"I haven't slept with anyone beside you except for that little stunt that Nancy pulled."

"So you should be relieved. Your test will come back negative. I hope this serves as a wake up call, Khris. I know I fucked up, and if I had contracted HIV, I would have nobody to blame but myself. I knew you were out there sleeping with multiple partners and I never once asked you if you had been tested or if you use protection."

"I do. I used to strap up back when I was out there like that. I never used to be running up in all dem hos raw dog."

"Yeah, that may be the case, but look at how much you put yourself at risk by having multiple partners. You're not just sleeping with the one woman. You're sleeping with everyone she is sleeping with; everyone that her partners and their partners are sleeping with. And me with my dumb ass, who knows better, let love cause me to jump on your dick every chance I got. Love and good dick made me stupid."

"I should have used protection with you."

"It's not just about protection, Khris. Look at what you made with protection; a baby girl. While your condom couldn't stop you from creating life, it could have caused you to catch something that could have taken away not just your life, but many other people's lives because of your lifestyle."

"That lifestyle is behind me now. This has been a rude awakening for me, but a valuable lesson has been learned. And, I'm not going to expose my daughter to a bunch of strange women, either. I'll be a non-dating, single father if I have to."

"I hope so, for Erica's sake. You don't want her growing up with any and everybody. You have to be careful who you expose her to. You have a responsibility to her until she's legal and beyond. If something happens to you, you won't be able to fulfill that responsibility."

"Well, rest assured, Erica is my number one priority from this day forward. Erica comes first. Any woman—if I get involved with anyone anytime soon—will have to understand that before I even let her meet my daughter. And I'm not letting any and everyone meet Erica, either. All females will first have to go through stringent screenings, background checks, and HIV tests. If a woman can't go through all of that, then she can't be with me and my daughter. You can't get the boat without the life raft. We come as a package deal. Today marks a new beginning for Erica and Khristin Harrison."

Sonia rolled onto her back and stared up at the ceiling for a minute. Both of us were silent. It was a companionable silence. Suddenly, she sprang up and stood at the foot of the bed. Her eyes were steady on me, but she had an apprehensive look on her face. "Well, can I meet Erica Christina Harrison now, or am I not allowed?

A.C. HUMES WRITING AS E.X. FELON
RISKS, REWARDS & CONSEQUENCES
CHAPTER ONE

"How do you think you did on that test?" Sophia asked as soon as the classroom door closed behind us.

"I think I did alright," I said, smiling as she strode alongside me. I couldn't help but let my eyes feast on her well-proportioned body: perfect sized breasts, and enough booty to cause a double take.

She smiled at me with those seductive, almond shaped blue-green eyes. "That means that you aced it. And thanks to our study sessions, I think I aced it also," she said as I opened and held the door for her.

"You didn't need my help for that. You just used that as an excuse to come over to my place and seduce me."

"Can't retain any knowledge if I'm stressed and backed up," she sassed, walking into the parking lot. "Want to go and celebrate?"

My dick stirred, but before I could respond, my phone started vibrating in my pocket. It wasn't my regular phone; it was my money phone. "Hold that thought," I said, pulling it from my pocket. The caller ID read what I knew it would: Unknown. "I have to take this," I said as she stopped beside her car. "I'll give you a call later."

Sophia pouted, tiptoed and gave me a kiss on the lips. "Don't forget about me," she chimed as she sashayed between the two cars and opened the door of her brand new E 550 Benz coupe.

Her parents have her spoiled rotten, I thought as I answered my phone. "Yo?"

"Where you at?" the caller asked as Sophia started the car, puckered her glossy heart shaped lips, and blew me a kiss.

I recognized Unc's Bahamian accent right away. "Just leaving school. What's up?" I asked, watching the black E 550 pull out of the parking spot and regretting it immediately.

"I sent you two hundred. Cuz should call you in a few minutes to deal with dat."

I watched Sophia go, but business before pleasure. I started toward my Lexus GS 350. "What bill you want me to pay with that?"

"Sears and Macy's. A hundred each."

"They due today, right? I have to work early in the morning."

"Yeah. I just send the numbers for you to play, too."

I opened the car, slid in and hit the start button to get the AC going. "Cool. I'll link you later," I said, ending the call. I cranked up the volume and pulled out of the parking spot.

My money phone rang as I was turning off campus. I checked the caller ID: Unknown. I answered it on the third ring. "Yo?"

"Wha ya say, Lil Cuz? Unc tell me to link you. Where you at?" The caller was another Bahamian, but his accent was thicker.

Raw. Probably from one of the Out-Islands: Andros, maybe. "Where you want me to be?" I asked.

"Well, I headin by Broward Mall to pick up some Jordans for me and my son, and I have to pay some bills for the wife while I there. From there, I goin to get me some shrimp scampi from Red Lobster."

"A' right. I should be there in about twenty minutes. I have the number, I'll link you when I get there."

"Yeah," he replied, ending the call.

I hit the turnpike, and twenty minutes later I parked by Macy's and entered the mall. As I walked through Macy's, I saw a fine ass salesclerk putting out some new T-shirts. One caught my eye, also, so I went over, asked for an XL and followed her to the cash register.

A few minutes later, I strolled toward Foot Locker with her phone number in my pocket, and a bag in my hand. I passed the store and went out the nearest exit. As soon as I got outside, I spotted the rental van. No, there wasn't anything obvious about it: it was the only white Dodge Caravan parked around there. To make sure, I walked down the isle in front of it. Sure enough, there were stuff on the front dash: coupons for Red Lobster on the driver's side; stuck hard on the passenger side was a torn off piece of a Jordans' box.

I kept walking, scanning the parking lot as I pretended to look for my vehicle. I stopped, pulled out my key fob, held it up and spun around like I was looking for some blinking lights. When nothing chirped or blinked, I walked back toward the door that I had come out off, stopped, scanned the parking lot one more time, then went back into the mall.

I pulled out my phone, hit dial—the storage spot for the 1-800 number and PIN for the prepaid calling card that I had bought for these types of calls. I listened, then entered Cuz's number that Unc had sent me when I was told to do so. When he answered, all I said was, "I'm here."

"Cool. I doin lil shoppin.... I see you," he lied, then ended the call.

I repeated the process with the calling card and called 'Sears.'

That was a code name for Osei; we call him 'S' for short. He's a Virgin Island brother that lives over in Tampa. Now, the Virgin Island accent is totally different from my Bahamian accent, so I had to listen carefully to make sure I understood him correctly.

"Yow, meh boy. Where yu deh?" he asked, knowing it was me calling. "Broward Mall checkin out dese new Jordans."

"Yeah! I up in da area. I ga swing thru in bout five minutes."

"Yeah," I said, ending the call as I walked into Foot Locker.

I scanned the new selections, tried on a couple pairs, then bought a pair of Jordans, two pairs of matching socks, and picked up a couple cans of sneaker cleaner at the register.

I took my time strolling through the mall, admiring some of the eye candy as I did, then decided to stop in Mayor's to get the scratches polished off my stainless and gold Rolex Yacht Master.

Thirty minutes after I placed the call to S, he called back using a calling card as I had; it was part of our safety net. He had picked up the van, driven where he needed to go, off loaded his hundred, and dropped the van off at the Red Lobster that's two minutes south of the mall.

I ended the call, hit speed dial 1, then entered the phone number for Macy's. Macy's was the code name for my boy, Dinker, from Houston, Texas. He doesn't work the same state he sleeps. He was expecting my call, so even though the calling card would cause the call to show up on his caller ID as unknown, he answered on the first ring. "What up, Kinfolk?" He calls everyone kinfolk.

"Just out paying some bills. I'm heading over to Red Lobster over on University to get a bite to eat."

"I'm about ten or fifteen minutes from there. I'll head that way and link up with you."

"Cool," I said, ending the call. I put the money phone back in my pocket, pulled out my iPhone and called Erica. Erica is a bad ass lil twenty two year old Indian I does knock off that goes to Nova Southeastern University, which is less than five miles south on University Drive from Red Lobster.

"I was just thinking about you," she chimed.

"I'm sure that's what you tell all the guys," I chuckled as I walked to my car.

"You know you're the only man for me," she laughed. "So, what's up?" she asked sensuously.

"I'm heading over to Red Lobster. Wanna meet me?"

"Just for lunch?" she asked, "or am I gonna have you for dessert too?"

"Come and find out." I paused and chuckled. "Unless you have someone...ummm, I mean, something else to do," I drawled.

"I'll be there in ten minutes," she replied quickly. "Five if I catch green lights." Erica laughed and ended the call.

It took me three minutes to get to Red Lobster. I drove around the parking lot, scanning for anything unusual, spotted the van—the Red Lobster coupons were gone from the left corner of the dash. I drove around to the front of the building and parked. I sat and watched the parking lot for a few minutes before getting out and going inside to get a booth: one with a window view on the side where the van was parked.

I was seated at a booth with a perfect view of the van. I ordered two stuffed mushrooms, cheese bread, along with a Heineken for me, a bottle of White Zinfandel for Erica.

By the time the drinks arrived, Erica breezed in. She was casually dressed in a pair of fitted designer jeans, breast-hugging camisole top and sandals. But there was nothing casual about her.

I smiled as her face lit up when she saw me. I was happy to see her, but I was smiling because of the reaction she gets when she enters a room: the busboys, servers, other diners, they all stopped and stared at her fine ass as she navigated her way toward me. I filled her glass, and stood up as she drew closer to the booth.

Without a word, Erica stepped into my arms and plastered her lips on my mouth. She darted her frisky tongue into my mouth, reuniting our tongues; stimulating our palates. It was a quick kiss, but it was filled with hunger and desire. She sighed breathlessly after pulling herself away, ending our kiss. "God, I needed that," she sang as she slid into the booth. "I'm starving," she said, taking a sip of her wine as I slid in next to her. "Mmmmm."

"I ordered stuffed mushrooms and cheese bread to start."

"You know how to make a woman happy," she beamed, reaching beneath the table. "But I wasn't talking about starving for food; I'm starving for this dick. You holding out on me," she said, caressing my length and licking her lips. "You think if I slide under the table anyone would notice?"

If I know one thing about Erica, it was that she is a freak: a bold freak. Not one to be dared. With that being the case, I knew I had to be careful what I said to her. "You slide under there, everyone will know. I'll be climbing the walls and moaning so fucking loud...dudes will come running out the kitchen to try to get some of what I'm getting. And you know I een trying to share. I don't want to have to fuck up no one up in here."

Erica was laughing and shaking her head. She was about to respond, but the waitress came with our appetizers. That put that conversation on hold for a bit. We both dug in.

By the time our salads arrived, I saw Dinker hop in the van and drive off. Everything was going as planned.

Lunch was filling and the conversation was quite stimulating.

By the time the check arrived, Dinker called and reported that he was at Foot Locker in the Broward Mall.

I reached for the check as I hit speed dial 1. Erica snatched it. "I gat this. If I pay for you to eat steak and lobster, you know you're gonna have to beat my back out." Erica grinned and reached into her Louis Vuitton bag for her purse.

"What kind of shit is that?" I asked, dialing Cuz's number. Erica grinned deviously. "If a man buys a woman steak and lobster, he expects to get some pussy, right? So I'm buying you steak and lobster...that means you have to give me some dick."

"This dick cost more than steak and lobster..."

Cuz answered as I was speaking. "Who's trying to buy some dick?" Cuz asked, laughing.

"Lil Indian gal trying to buy some dick for steak and lobster lunch." I laughed. "You still shopping?"

"Yeah. Tell her I'll give her some dick for free. I know she bad to death if you fucking with her."

"She done pay, Cuz, so I gatta take care of it."

Cuz laughed. "Gone handle your business then."

"Yeah. Holla at me before you go back. I might need to send some toiletries and shit back Nassau with you," I said, watching Erica give our waitress a twenty-dollar tip.

"Cool," he said, ending the call.

Erica nodded as the waitress thanked her profusely. "Your place or mine?" Erica asked as soon as I slid my money phone into my pocket.

"Mine. Een no man opening no door on me," I teased.

"Better don't have no woman opening no door on me," Erica sassed. "I'll beat the bitch and make her eat my pussy."

I laughed. "I believe you does swing both ways," I said as we stood to leave.

"I don't, but I know a bitch will never be able to talk shi.t to me if she already took a beat down and had to suck my pussy."

"A bitch will bite your clit if you try forcing her to suck your pussy. Unless she's bi."

"Ouch!" Erica winced, leaning into me as I hugged her. "I didn't think about that. Fuck my shit up. No. I'll make her suck your dick instead," she said as we strolled towards her hot red BMW M 3. Erica hit the button on her key fob and popped the locks. "You want to follow me to drop my car back on campus," she drawled sensuously, "or you want me to drive over to your place?"

"Drive. You know I won't have any strength left by the time you're finished with me. And I have to work early in the morning."

"You're right," she chuckled as I held the door open for her to get in. She kissed me, then slid into the buttery-soft tan leather seat. "Last one there gets tied up," she said, closing the door and starting the car. Nikki Minaj and Gyptian pumped out of her speakers. She threw the car in gear and pulled out.

I had to jump back so her chrome Lexani rims didn't run over my feet. "Fucking freak!" I yelled, not worried about her getting to my place before me: she couldn't get into my community if I wasn't at home when the security called. She damn sure didn't have a transponder. She would have to wait at the gate.

I jumped in my ride, pulled out my money phone and hit speed dial number 1. I entered Unc's number in Nassau and let him know that the bills were paid. As soon as I ended the call, I powered off the phone, popped the back, and took out the battery and the SIM card. I opened the armrest and pulled out a packet containing a Windex towelette and used it to wipe off all the pieces, then carefully placed each piece into a brown paper bag. I opened the car door, used my lighter and lit the SIM card. When it caught, I dropped it. While it burned, I took the brown bag over to the garbage container just outside the restaurant. I dumped the contents and made my way back to my car. By the time I slid into the driver's seat the SIM card was a chunk of melted plastic. I picked it up with the Windex cloth, then drove off. That I would flush when I get home.

I checked the time as I pulled out the lot. Two hours since I received the call from Unc. Two hours work; $400,000 earned.

Why do I even bother going to college? Why do I even bother working a regular, full-time job? Because what I just did was totally fucking illegal: thank God it went smooth as glass. One fuckup by either of us and I could have easily found myself standing in front of the federal magistrate judge at arraignment charged under Title 21 USC §§§846; 841(a)(1); 841(b)(1)(a) which is: Conspiracy to posses with intent to distribute 5 kilograms or more of cocaine, which carries a Mandatory Minimum of 10 years. However, under the Federal Sentencing Guidelines, with the aide of a Pre-Sentencing Investigation prepared by the US Probation Office, based on the 200 kilograms of cocaine, I would be assigned a Base Offense Level of 38. Although I am a first time offender with no criminal history, based on the significance of the large amount of cocaine, the judge would have no choice but to sentence me within the guideline range of 262

- 362 months, barring any mitigating factors like enhancements such as committing the crime in a school zone or leadership role.

All in all, I would have to hope and pray that the judge is lenient and sentence me to the low end of the guideline, 262 months. Just in case your mathematics isn't working, 262 months is 21 years and ten months. 21 years and 10 months! That's a lot of fucking time for $400,000. That $400,000 works out to $1526.72 for every month of my freedom that I would lose. Oh! I almost forgot, along with the 21 years and 10 month sentence, the judge—at his discretion---can order me to pay a fine of up to $4 million. So while I'm serving time, I'll have to pay a possible fine. Don't worry, if I don't have the cash, they will confiscate (order of forfeiture) all my assets to put toward it, and whatever I don't pay while incarcerated, they'll take out of my paycheck when I'm released from prison and start working a regular 9 to 5.

Is it really worth it? To me, it is. Why? Because I'm too sharp to get fucking caught. On top of that, I don't plan on making a career out of this shit. That's why I go to college. That is why I work a regular, full-time job. Besides, what I do is not a job; it's a fucking **adventure!**

A.C. Humes

Scandalous Tales

Volume 1

HIGHWAY TO HEAVEN

You sure you're not too drunk to drive?" Sheryl asked Toya.

"Girl, I'm not drunk. I'll be all right."

"Okay, drive slow...and watch out for the police."

"We're going to follow you. We've got to pass your place to get to my house anyhow," I yelled as I opened the car door.

"You don't think she's going to make it home in one piece?" Sheryl asked as she slid into the passenger seat and fastened her seat belt.

"We're going to follow her home to make sure. You, on the other hand, definitely ain't going to make it home in one piece?" I stated, running my hand up her bare thigh.

Sheryl had been grinding all over me in the club. We had been grinding up on each other all night. She even let me slip my hand beneath her little black mini to feel how wet she was. She had been soaking wet for me. It's been about three weeks, and I hadn't hit yet. I was tempted to try and get me some right there in the club. If her girl, Toya, hadn't been there cock blocking, I probably would have.

"I've got an early flight in the morning, so you know you can't keep me out all night. I can't even take the chance of coming inside when I stop at your house to pick up my car. You might not want to let me go home."

"Well, in that case, you need to go ahead and take that skirt and those drawers off now," I said, glancing over at her as I pulled out of the parking lot behind Toya.

"You're kidding, right?" she giggled.

"No, I'm not," I replied, stroking her love sponge through her wet undies. "You're so wet...been wet from in the club."

"Mmm, that feels good, baby."

"Take these drawers off and I'll really make it feel good," I said, tugging on the edges of her undies as I got onto the on ramp for the highway.

I slipped my index finger between her underwear while she unfastened her seat belt and wiggled out of her skirt and underwear.

I stroked her wet lips and her hips rose up from the seat to meet my fingers. I prepped two fingers in her juices, letting them dance across her outer folds before penetrating her. Her inner muscles snuggled my fingers as I let them dance around in her.

Sheryl dropped her seat back and kicked off her heels. She had this salacious glow that had me hard as steel. She swiveled until she was sideways in the seat facing me, giving me a better angle to work from. Our eyes locked, and then she tore off her top.

My eyes travelled down to her perky, cupcake-sized breasts. The way I had my hand positioned while fingering her became uncomfortable, so I had to rotate my hand. Now my palm was cupping her wet sponge and making contact with every part of her sex. I leaned over to suck her breast, trying to keep my eyes on the road at the same time. She squealed when I nibbled on her left nipple. That only encouraged me on. I let my thumb run circles around her swollen clit while my tongue worshipped her breasts.

Sheryl bucked and rolled her hips, fucking my fingers. She struggled to reach across me. Pressing her breast hard into my mouth, she unfastened my seatbelt, and then started unbuckling my pants.

I turned loose her breast and tried to focus on the road, all the while continuing to finger her.

I stroked her so good that she couldn't concentrate on what she was doing. She sprang up and tried to crawl away from my fingers. She was wide-eyed and panting. I brushed my fingers across her clit, causing her to scoot way back on the reclined seat back. She was damn near sitting in the backseat. "What are you running for? Come back here," I ordered, reaching my sticky fingers back for her.

"I'm not going to let you make me cum like that. If you want me to cum, you're going to have to fuck me!"

"Fuck you? But I want to make love to you."

She started laughing. "Make love to me? You order me naked in a moving vehicle and you want to make love...this isn't the place to make love," she chuckled. "As much as I would love for you to make love to me, right now, a simple fuck is all we have time for."

Shit! She just laughed at me. But on the real, what kind of weak shit was that? 'I want to make love to you!' Look how a player like me let this woman laugh at me. Fuck is what I had in mind all along. So what she said was actually music to my ears."

Must be the alcohol talking, 'cause I know that wasn't me just say that weak shit...not that I don't want to make love to you. It's just like you said, this isn't the time, or the place to make love," I said, trying to clean up that shit. I was fucking up my words left and right. It's a good thing she's already naked, if not, I might have talked myself out of the pussy for sure.

Sheryl grinned. She lunged forward and attacked me.

Remember, I'm driving on the highway...with my dick pounding against my stomach...with a half naked woman that I haven't fucked yet.

She pulled my face to the side and kissed me enthusiastically. Our tongues intertwined and a melodic moan escaped her lips. I felt her melt. I was floating. I was elated. This was paradise, heaven...or a foretaste of it. I had to strain to keep at least one eye on the road ahead. Her hands had my belt and pants unbuckled in no time. Chris—nickname for my dick, short for Christopher Columbus the explorer, discoverer of new worlds—was out and in her warm hands in no time. "Don't stroke him," I said as I slid the seat all the way back. "I can stroke him myself. Do something to him that I can't do."

Sheryl pulled off what was left of her torn top. She was completely naked now. "Raise up," she ordered, reaching over me to pull down my pants. After a bit of twisting and turning, she was able to get my pants down below my knees without me swerving from lane to lane. I got my left leg out and didn't worry about the right leg. "Lay the seat back so I can get my feet up and behind you."

I laid the seat back as flat as it would go, then I scooted up on it just a little bit so that Sheryl could squeeze her slender frame between the steering wheel and me. Sheryl hopped over and straddled me. It worked out perfectly. She was dripping wet again. I could feel the warmth coming from her love sponge. Her clit was short and perky like her nipples. Same size too. A nipple at the apex of her lithe thighs: a nipple that I wanted to put my lips and tongue on.

While she teased the opening of her love canal with Chris's head, I had to find a good angle that would allow me to suck on her delicious cupcakes and still be able to see the road ahead. Sheryl's breasts were just the right size to fit completely into my mouth. Her nipples were like ripened cherries on top: mouthwatering and delicious.

I plucked at her cherry, made circles around her sensitive, glazed areolas, then took the entire breast into my mouth when she slid Chris into her love canal. I wanted to sing out loud as I entered and discovered a whole new world. It was a perfect fit. Nice and snug. I wanted to stay in there forever. If she knew how to work her muscles, I would be in heaven.

"Fuck!" I yelled as my tire hit the warning grooves then the gravel on the side of the highway.

"If you're going to run off the road, as much as I would hate it, I'm going to get up off this sweet dick," Sheryl cooed, gyrating slowly on my dick.

"Chris wouldn't like that," I said as I got the car driving straight again. I really couldn't keep my focus on the road. It felt too damn good. The things that she was doing to me had my toes curling in my boots. I kept one hand on the steering wheel, the other I used to fondle her breasts. As much as I wanted to suck on her sweet little cupcakes, I dared not. I kept my gyrations and strokes short. I let her do most of the work. If I tried to give her the loving that I had for her, we might end up wrapped around a pole or something.

I steeled myself against the accentuated rise and fall of her spiraling hips. I wanted so badly to get into a groove with her, but I knew I wouldn't be able to hold on. This pussy was too good; I've been waiting too long for this pussy to fuck up and cum too quickly. As soon as I thought it I felt my nuts churning, I stopped moving.

Sheryl kissed my lips, moved to the tip of my nose, over to my cheek, and then finally, she nibbled on my ear. Her breath was hot and sweet against my flesh, "Cum!" she whispered, oscillating her hips more erotically, more energetically.

"No!" I mumbled, fighting to hold on.

"Why not? I. Want. You. To,"

"Unnn-unnn!" I said, shaking my head and trying to focus on Toya's car up ahead. "When I cum, I want you to cum with me," I said, gritting my teeth, and fighting with everything I had.

"That's so sweet...but...it's going to take your second round to make me cum. I don't cum easily. You've got to put in a lot of work..."

"I...Oh, yes! I want to put in a lot of work. I...I want to put in some overtime."

"Cum for me...and then you can put in some work. Don't you like how this pussy feels?" she asked seductively.

I started grinding deep into her as her muscles clamped gently around Chris. Her loving was so soft and tender: her canal narrow and so, so sweet. I wanted to profess my love for her right there and then. Pussy does that to a man. It makes us weak. This woman...Oh, God...this woman was going to make me cum.

AIN'T NO FUN...

"I'm just saying, he's too old for my baby," Cecile stated, staring at her best friend, Angela.

"Anastacia is not a baby. She's 21, for Christ's sake. And so what if he's a few years older than her? A mature man can help her..."

"Can take advantage of her.... All my baby knows is sports and her schoolwork. She's not into men like that. He's going to hurt my baby..."

"You don't even know the man..."

I know men!" Cecile stated firmly. "All of them are just alike. They all think with their dicks and not their hearts."

"That's not fair, besides, she just met him...what...three weeks ago when she was home. All they've been doing is talking on the phone."

"She chases me off the phone to answer his calls," Cecile said, exasperated. "He's the first person she talks to in the morning, and the last at night."

Angela chuckled. "You're going to have to let go...cut her navel string one day, Cecile. You should be happy that she's finally getting a taste of love."

"That's not love," Cecile snarled. "That man wants to fuck my baby and then he's going to leave her high and dry. He's going to hurt my baby's heart."

"How you know he's not Mr. Right?"

Mr. Right Now," Cecile scowled.

I think you are being too hard on the man. Besides, give him time to show who he really is. If he's a dog, in time, it'll come out. A dog can't hide forever."

"That's just it, Angela, we don't have any time. He wants to take her on a cruise when she comes home for summer break."

"That's so nice," Angela swooned.

She comes home in a week."

I know you're a concerned mother, but don't do anything that will cause Anastacia to be mad at you."

"I'm going to do what I have to do to make sure this dog doesn't hurt my baby."

Be careful, Cecile: very careful. This shit could backfire on your ass and ruin the relationship you two have."

"This is a grown ass man I'm trying to protect her from. He's nothing but an old dog trying to take advantage of my baby. And I'm not going to let that happen!"

* * *

"Coming out to the club ain't nothing like it used to be, bro," Jerome said to his younger brother, Mikey, as they waited for the parking valet to bring Jerome's Maxima. "I remember when I coulda come to the club and pick, choose and refuse hos."

"You ain't lying, bro. All I come out for now is to get my drink on and unwind after busting my ass all week," Mikey explained.

"I feel you," Jerome said as the valet stopped in front of him. He tipped the valet and jumped behind the wheel.

Mikey jumped in the passenger's seat. "That's why I always pick up one a my lil tricks, get her some weed, something to eat, and take her to a hotel til I come back from the club."

Jerome laughed as he pulled off. "And what do you do if you find something in the club?"

"Go fuck! Then go to the hotel and fuck again," Mikey stated like it should have been obvious.

Jerome started laughing. "You always fucking with hos that live with their man."

"Them the best ones. Let someone else deal with them hos problems. I fuck. That's what I do. Them some nice hos that I fuck, but hos have too much drama when involved in relationships."

"So, what you saying is that it's stress free and less drama when you the other man?"

"Hell yeah! See you wouldn't understand 'cause you have all them hos feeling like you're their man..."

"But I don't have no drama." Jerome laughed.

See, you be fucking with them good girls. The professional women. I ain't gonna lie, bro, you run your hos..."

The sound of Jerome's ringing phone stopped Mikey mid-speech. Jerome checked his caller ID. "Anastacia's mom! What the fuck?"

"Anastacia? That tall, fine ass chick that plays volleyball for UCON? The one you met in the club about three weeks ago?"

"Yeah. Wife to be." Jerome grinned.

What the hell you doing with her mother's cell phone number, bro? More importantly, what her mother doing calling you at three forty five in the morning? Booty call?"

"Shut up!" Jerome said, pressing the green icon. "Hello?"

Hello? Where are you?" a female voice asked.

It wasn't Anastacia for sure. The woman sounded a little older. "On my way home?" Jerome answered tentatively.

"I thought you were taking me to get something to eat?" she asked, sounding disappointed.

She sounded a little tipsy too.

Jerome stifled a laugh as he looked across to his brother who was making fuck faces and humping motions in the passenger seat. "May I ask who you want to speak to?"

"Who is this?" she asked, sounding alarmed. "Is this Jermaine?"

"No, I'm sorry you must have dialed the wrong number."

"Who is this? Your number is programmed into my phone," she demanded.

This is Jerome. I'm a friend of Anastacia's..."

"Anastacia's friend? What your number doing program in my phone?" she asked with a little attitude.

"Is this her mother?"

"Yes, it is!"

"I met her when she was home three weeks ago. She had your phone... I think her phone had gotten stolen..."

"Oh yeah, I remember now," she chuckled, sounding a bit at ease. "I'm sorry for calling you at this hour..."

"That's quite alright..."

"I was trying to call a friend of mine. He was supposed to take me for something to eat, but he disappeared on my as...listen to me, I'm telling you all my business. Alcohol just loosens my tongue. I'm sorry for calling you."

"That's okay. It was nice talking to you," Jerome said, chuckling.

"Please don't tell Anastacia...she hates when I go out for drinks."

"It'll be out little secret," Jerome said, chuckling.

"Promise?" she cooed.

"I promise."

"Thank you," she said. "Okay. Drive safely."

"You too," Jerome said. "Bye."

"Byyyyyye," she sang, ending the call.

Mikey laughed. "That was a booty call. Mama wants some."

"You crazy, bro. Besides, her mama doesn't know me."

"Mama fine?" Mikey asked with a raised brow.

"I don't know. I've never met the woman. She sounds sexy as hell, though."

"If her daughter takes after her, she probably is fine," Mikey said as he fired up a joint. He hit it and passed it over.

Jerome cranked up the volume as he got on I-95 North. He took a hit of the joint and passed it back. "You know what, I'm going home. I don't feel like being bothered with none of my hos tonight. She done have me thinking about Anastacia. And this weed only ga make me hungry. I'll drop myself off and you can take my ride."

"My car already by the hotel. Why can't you just drop me off?" Mikey asked as he took out a napkin from his wallet. He unrolled it and took out half a blue pill and threw it in his mouth. Then he chugged the remainder of the water that he had brought out of the club.

"Because I don't feel like passing home to drop you off. Just drop me and carry the car."

Five minutes later, Jerome pulled in front of their house, pressed the button for the garage door and hopped out. It wasn't until he was inside and upstairs getting undressed that he remembered his cell phone. He had left it in the Max.

Three minutes later, Mikey stared at his brother's ringing phone. *Anastacia's mom. What the fuck does she want now? I'm not answering that shit,* he thought as he headed on a collision course for the hotel. The phone stopped ringing, then started up again. Mikey ignored it again. The third time it rung he answered it. *It has to be an emergency.* "Hello?"

"Are you home already," the female asked.

"No."

"Well why weren't you answering the phone? You making a booty call or something?"

"No," Mikey said, then took a pull on the joint, laughing because she didn't know it wasn't Jerome she was talking to.

"Are you smoking?"

She sounded intrigued rather than repugnant, so he said, "Mmmm-hmmm."

Her voice became soft and sounded sexy. "I called to ask a favor..."

"What kind of favor?" Mikey asked.

"Well my friend had to run home to his nagging ass wife, and I'm hungry. But I don't want to sit in IHOP by myself, not at this hour. Why don't you join me? My treat."

"Which IHOP are you at?"

"I'm not there yet. I was calling to see if you'd meet me first."

"Which one are you going to?"

"I live in Sawgrass...there's one right off of University."

"I know where it is. I'm about five minutes away."

"Alright. I'll meet you there. What are you driving?" she asked.

"A black Nissan Maxima. You?"

"I'm in a burgundy Jaguar XK."

"Niiiice," Mikey sang. "I'll be in the parking lot when you get there."

"Don't smoke it all before I get there," she purred.

Mikey hung up the phone and laughed. *If mama fine, I'm damn sure gonna try and fuck, especially if she trying to get her smoke on.*

Seven minutes later, Mikey watched as the burgundy XK pulled in at the IHOP. She pulled right next to him, shut off the engine and got out. From what he could see over the roof of the car, Mama was pretty as fuck. And young looking. When she walked around the back of the car and he got a good look at her body, his dick started getting hard. "Damn, Mama fine as fuck!" *Voluptuous. Now I know why she didn't want to go into IHOP by herself. Anywhere she goes she'll get all kinds of unwanted attention. Especially in the skirt and top she's wearing.* Her outfit wasn't revealing or slutty or anything; it was classy and tasteful, but emphasized everything she had.

Mikey took a hit and leaned over and opened the passenger door for her. Her smile lit up the interior.

"Oh that smells wonderful," she said as she hopped in and closed the door behind her. "I haven't smoked since college," she said, taking the offered joint.

"I plan on stopping when I get my MBA." Mikey chuckled.

She took a long draw.

"You might want to take it easy with that," Mikey said a second too late.

She started coughing, but she refused to pass the joint. She held it as she eyed him over. She took another hit, pulling a little easier this time. She kicked off her sling backs and twisted sideways to face him. She caught his eyes locked onto her cleavage and smiled. She brought the joint up to her lips and took another pull. The weed had her feeling good. And the wine she had drunk earlier had made her extremely horny. She knew she could get any man she wanted, so this was going to be fun. *And easy. I'll expose the dog and save Anastacia from a broken heart.*

She ran her fingers playfully over her collarbone, then down between her breasts.

Mikey's dick stiffened. The blue pill was in full effect. Either he was going to fuck mama, or he had to get to the hotel to Shelley Ann. "So you gonna let me hit that?" Mikey asked.

"You're not shy at all, are you?" She blushed. "You sure you can handle me?" she asked, leaning forward and rubbing the inside of his thigh.

"I was referring to the joint, but since you brought it up," he said, making his dick jump in his pants, "I'm sure I can handle whatever challenges I'm presented with." Their eyes locked. "My question is, can you?"

Her hand slid from his thigh to his throbbing dick. "Mmmmm, this is nice," she swooned.

"You can take it out to get a better feel of it. Underneath all this cloth really doesn't do it any justice. It really is a work of art," Mikey boasted.

She accepted his challenge without a moment's hesitation. She unzipped his pants and took it out. *Ten inches of throbbing black meat.* "Oh, God. This is...we need to go someplace. Anyplace," she said as she skinned the foreskin back, leaned over and started kissing and licking his head.

"Ohhh shittttt!!! Where do you want to go?" Mikey barely got out as his eyes threatened to roll back into his head.

"Anywhere," she mumbled as she kissed and licked and flicked her tongue around his head greedily.

Mikey leaned the seat back until he was almost lying flat. He hit the joint one more time, as she got more enthusiastic with her tongue. He knew he wasn't going to come from a blowjob, but it felt too fucking good to stop her.

He reached over and started caressing her ass. *Damn!* Her ass was so soft it made him whimper. He wanted to get up in her, but he couldn't do that in the Maxima. And he definitely couldn't do it in

IHOP's parking lot. He couldn't take her to a hotel, because he didn't have enough cash for that. And he didn't want to go to her place, because he didn't know if he could do that, nor what her relationship status was. The only place he could take her is home. "What about your car?" Mikey asked.

She didn't stop to answer. She flailed her hand as if she didn't care about that.

Fuck it, he thought and fired up the Maxima. He positioned his hand so that he could steer over her as she continued to feverishly work his dick. She was sucking; he was caressing and fondling her breasts, and every part of her that he could touch.

Both of them were making all the appropriate noises as he raced home.

When he pulled into the garage and shut down the engine, she finally raised her head from his lap. She kissed him like a possessed woman. Hungrily. Greedily.

Mikey's dick ached to get up in her. "Let's go," he said as the garage door finished rolling down and the automatic light flicked off. They got out the Maxima, and as he stood at the front waiting for her to come around to him, he really got a good look at her. She didn't seem a day over thirty-five. As young as he was, he was confident that he was gonna kill her sexy old ass with dick.

Lust was oozing from her face. She grabbed his hand and pulled him tightly against her body. They were about the same height, so everything lined up. Their lips smashed against each other's. Wisps of pleasurable moans escaped her lips as their tongues darted back and forth in each other's mouth.

Mikey's hands fumbled with the zipper of her skirt. He got it unfastened, then got a firm grip on her cheeks. He picked her up as if she weighed nothing, spun her around and placed her on the top of the hot hood.

She swooned in surprise, wrapped her sculptured legs around his waist and pulled him right into her so that his dick was rubbing her the right way.

His hands fumbled with her skirt until he had it up and out of the way. Both of them fumbled with his belt and pants and underwear until nothing was between them except her sodden underwear that she savagely pulled to the side so that his raw head could glide up and down between her blood-engorged lips.

She was grinding desperately against his hot, throbbing head now. Her pussy was hot and wet and aching to feel that throbbing mass of meat. Gripping his hips, she pulled him forward, plunging his rock-hard ten inches into her. She shut her eyes and screamed as his dick stretched and filled her to the brim. She hadn't felt pain and pleasure like that since she lost her virginity. She was trying to get use to the feeling, but he didn't give her time. He started moving that big dick around inside of her. It was hot and hard. Fire coursed through her body. Then there was the additional heat beneath her ass. She found the more she gyrated her ass up and into his deep punishing strokes, the less she felt the heat beneath her ass.

This was the first woman over thirty that Mikey has ever had the pleasure of fucking, so he had something to prove. He was fucking her like he had all mankind riding on his performance. His strokes were bringing out all the appropriate noises and fuck-faces that he got out of younger women, so he knew he was beating that pussy up good. That was all the boost his ego needed.

He picked her completely up off the hood and slowed down to his wicked winding.

"Awwwwwww fuuuuuck, baby! Ssssssss!"

"You like that," he asked.

"Mmmm-hmmmm," she mumbled as he guided her hips into a slow rocking motion that made her clit rub against his muscular pelvis.

She started nibbling his lip. "Oh God, yeah. That feels good."

"I want you to cum for me before we go inside," he muttered against her sweet lips.

"You don't have to worry about...about..." Her whimpering got cut short as tiny jolts of lightning struck all through her causing her body to spasm involuntarily. "Oh God, I'm cumming." Her pace quickened and her entire body vibrated as her orgasm resonated through her.

Mikey felt good taking her inside. Now he was going to take her upstairs and put a proper fucking on her sexy old ass. He continued stroking her until her orgasm subsided, then he walked toward the door, stirring the pot as he went. He told her to reach behind her and turn the knob. She got the door opened without any problem.

The door opened directly into the kitchen, and as they were passing the refrigerator, she stopped him. "Grab something cold to drink."

Without losing rhythm, he stopped. She opened the fridge, leaned in a bit, and pulled out two bottles of water. He bumped the door closed and started for the stairs.

Going up the stairs was a bit more difficult. Unsteadily, they made their way up bumping into the wall and railing. She was giggling. They slipped and fell. She started laughing, and he covered her mouth quickly as he landed on top of her. Her legs found their way around his waist and she locked both arms around his neck. They kissed passionately as he stroked down into her. She started grunting and humping up to meet his strokes. He felt his head slamming against the gristle at the very back of her pussy. His head felt as if it was curving and going into another portion of her pussy. Each time his head bounced against the gristle, her body convulsed. She bit his tongue as he sped up his thrusts to see if he could get one long convulsion.

He got it as she came a second time right there on the stairway.

Her legs unfolded from around his waist as he withdrew about eight of the ten inches he had inside her, using only two inches to grind around the front portion of her sweet pussy.

She started humping on it and adjusting her hips so that she was angled properly. Then she asked for a little more.

He gave her about an inch more.

"Ah, fuck yeah! Right there!" she growled as she kept his mushroom head rocking against the spongy area at the top of her pussy. "Fuck!" she hissed. "What are you trying to do to me?"

"What every woman wants a man to do to them: satisfy them...and then some," Mikey replied, turning it up a notch.

"You...you sure are doing that," she whimpered. "Ohhh God! This dick too damn sweet...oooooooeeeeeee. I'm coming again, baby. Fuck meeeeeeee!"

Mikey readily complied. Fuck her and then some.

Once she caught her breath, Mikey decided it was best to take her into his room before they woke Jerome up.

RENT-A-DREAD

Eighty-six degrees, white sandy beaches, and crystal clear waters: all the sun and fun a white girl like me need. This is my dream vacation. Me and a few of my sorors planned this trip down to the Turks and Caicos Islands since Lisa Raye's divorce from the Premiere brought the islands to our attention. Drinks were flowing, guests were frolicking, and skin was showing. Lots of skin. Bikinis were extra skimpy here.

We were loud and boisterous, but so was everyone else on this stretch of beach.

"'ello, ladies, care to buy a few souvenirs?" a young, well- built islander with long dreads asked as he stopped in front of us.

"What are you selling?" Jenna asked mischievously.

"Wha'ever unna wan, mi can give unna fa da right price. I might even give unna a discount on account a unna look so sweet," he said, eyeing each one of us.

We couldn't really understand every word, but I'm sure we all understood what he was offering. And from the print in his tight, cutoff jeans, he had plenty for sale. I couldn't help myself. Maybe it was the alcohol mixed with all this sun, but I was feeling heathenish. I took a sip of my drink, then asked, "So what are you...like a Rent--A-Dread or something?"

"Wha you know 'bout dat?" he asked, showing his pearly whites.

"I only know what I've heard."

"And what have you 'eard?" he asked, taking off his bag and sitting on the edge of my lounge chair.

"Yes, do tell," Jenna chimed, twisting to face us.

"We definitely want to hear this," Susan chimed in.

"What am I missing," Becky asked as she sauntered over with four fresh glasses of alcohol laced tropical drinks.

Jenna looked up, accepted her refill, then said, "She was just going to tell us what she heard about the Rent-A-Dreads."

"What's a Rent-A-Dread?"

Susan twisted toward her. "As soon as you sit and sip, she's going to tell us," she snapped.

"Alright! Alright! I'm sitting. Tell us, please," Becky sang, taking the only available lounger.

"I've heard—now correct me if I'm wrong," she said, turning to the Rent-A-Dread. "What's your name, by the way?"

"My friends call me 'S'," he replied with a smile.

"What is the 'S' for?" Jenna asked.

"Super Sexy. Can't you see?" Becky blurted.

"That's S-S, smarty, not S." Susan laughed. "I still don't understand how you graduated."

"Does fucking the Dean of Students and giving head to all her teachers count?" Jenna asked with a raised brow.

"We're getting way off course here," Susan said, interrupting the laughter. "You're supposed to be telling us what you heard about the Rent-A-Dreads."

"Oh, right, right," I said. I took another sip, then decided to drain the glass. I burped. "Excuse me," I chuckled, covering my mouth with one hand. S was watching me with eyes of a predator.

"Here's what I've heard. I've been told that the Rent-A-Dreads are young island studs that roam the beaches and rent out there special services to lonely female tourist—like us—traveling without male companionship."

"Exactly what type of special services are we talking about here? Do you mean like a dinner companion, an arm candy, or someone to fulfill your sexual desires."

S smiled deviously and started his Rastaman chant:
/"She means a man that can set your soul on fire/
/Fulfill yo every need and desire/
/A man that will kiss from your head down to your toes/

/Make you feel so sexy, you'll never wan wear clothes/
/Kiss and nibble on your succulent breasts/
/Have you screamin 'yes! S yes'/
/Lick on your pussy...Ooooh so slow and sweet/
/Have you pullin out ya hair, and rippin up da sheets/
/Toss your salad so good and nice/
/To remember you own name, you'll have to think twice/
/By da time I put dis here island wood pon you/
/You'll know everything you heard 'bout a Rent-A-Dread is
true/
/Now the four of unna can sit here and drink all day/
/Or you can split the hundred dollar fee four way/
/I givin unna a special package deal/
/'Cause unna look sweet and me wan mek all a unna squeal/
/Now Stamina Daddy can please unna one after da next/
/But all four a unna one time would be best/
/More fun if four a unna a scream and cum togedder/
/Dat'll mek tree a unna no have to wait in line forever/
/So wha? Unna wan the package deal/
/Or fi make up unna mind, unna need a free feel?/"
S ended his song holding his snake.

I wanted a free feel. Furthermore I wanted to find out if what
he chanted was true. I knew exactly what I was going to do. Even if I
had to pay the entire hundred dollar fee all by myself, I was going to
find out if the Rent-A-Dread myth was true. Nothing in this life is free.
A shower and some condoms, and his fine, island ass might just be
paying me, I thought but did not say.

"I thought I read somewhere that Dreads don't eat?" Jenna
asked S with a raised brow.

"When I was a likkle yout growing up in the Virgin Islands, I
never use to eat, but den I went foreign and girls were so easy to get,
that I turned into a freak. Ever since I tried it, my life hasn't been the
same. Now I know how to drive all de women dem insane."

"How much you charge for a little treat?" Becky asked,
uncrossing her legs seductively.

"He said one hundred dollars," Susan answered.

"That's the package deal price," I said.

"Well, I don't want to get my treat with all of you watching."

"Well, you pay the hundred dollars and get your little treat. The three of us will follow to take care of all that delicious, island meat," Becky chimed, imitating S's Rasta chant.

S was laughing. Four pieces of juicy, sunbaked, saltwater-seasoned white meat.

"Okay, here's what me can do. If unna ashamed to show unna freaky side to each other, I can let unna go one at a time and charge unna by the hour."

"By the hour?" Jenna screamed. "My partners can't even go for half an hour, and you want to charge by the hour."

"Mi normally charge by da inch."

"Do I get a discount if I want more than one hour?" I asked before he could raise the price.

"Oh. My. God. You are such a freeeeeak!" Becky bellowed.

"I want to know how much it costs for one hour?" Susan asked, looking S directly in the eyes.

"For you? Stand up, let me see wha I ga be workin with," S ordered.

"So you charge according to what we working with," I asked, bouncing up with Susan. "Well, I must be free as fine as I am. This," I said, spanking my booty, "is not a white girl's booty."

"All a unna look good. Lotta cushion back dey fa pushin. I tell you wha. Fifty dolla an hour fa each a yunna."

"I'm first," Susan said, "I don't want no limp dick."

"Your bougie ass needs to go first. Maybe you will let loose a little after you let off some of that pent up shit you have in you," Jenna shot.

"Yeah, you can serve as a warm-up. After all, he has to warm up on someone," I joked.

"You 'ave someplace we can go?" S asked.

"Of course," Susan said. "We have a suite right here."

"Good," S said. "Give me unna suite number. Me go take a quick shower and get mi tool ready fi wok. Me meet you dey in forty-five minutes."

"Suite 6-1-3."

"Me'll be there," S said, smiling and getting up. As he walked away, I said to the girls, "Okay, I understood that he said he had to go and take a shower, but what did he mean about going to get his tool ready fi wok?"

"Whatever it is he's gone to do, I'll be sure to let you all know if it worked," Susan chimed as she bounced up.

"Where are you going? He said that he'll be up there in forty-five minutes," Becky chuckled.

"I'm going to get every crack and crevice ready for when he arrives. I want him working for the entire hour that he's on the clock."

"Slave driver," I snickered, then regretted saying it. It wasn't a nice thing to say. Even though I didn't mean it that way, it could be misinterpreted that way.

"Time is money, ladies. We, of all people, should know that," Susan said, then took the rest of her drink to the head.

"Leave some for the rest of us," Becky chimed as Susan sashayed away, fixing the string that had disappeared up her ass.

"That must hurt," Becky said, causing all of us to erupt in a fit of laughter.

****

S knocked on the door. Bam, bam, bam!

The door opened immediately. Susan reached out and grabbed him by his shirt collar and pulled him into the room. "You're five minutes late."

"Island man always cum late," S retorted.

"For that, you're going to be punished," Susan snarled, closing the door behind him. "Get on your knees," she ordered.

S was surprised by the change in her demeanor. She went from quiet and reserved, to demanding and dominating. S took one look at her and knew right away that he had misjudged her. She was an undercover freak.

She had her hair braided into two tight pigtails, and she wore a black, crutch-less teddy with heels. She must not have travelled with her leather get up and whip, he thought. She still looked too soft and tender to be into S & M, but fuck it, he would play along with her little game. "So wha da punishment for being late?"

Bap! Susan slapped the words right out of his mouth.

S glared at her in surprise. He hadn't been expecting that. He was angry. No woman slapped him. No one slapped him. He licked his lips, checking to see if there was any blood. His fist clenched reflexively.

She was smiling at him like she was demon possessed. Susan raised her hand to hit him again.

This time, S caught her hand by the wrist. His other hand shot to her throat. He closed his fingers around her throat and slammed her into the wall. He brought his face right up to hers. "Don't you ever slap me again," he snarled between clenched teeth.

Nice, big, white teeth, Susan thought, then laughed." So big and strong and terrifying," she teased. Her wet tongue shot between her lips and licked his chin first, then his mouth, up his nose, between his eyes, and up his forehead.

"Dis wha you like?" S snarled, releasing her wrist while keeping his fingers tight around her neck. He unbuttoned his pants, then slapped her hands away as both of her hands reached down to grab his dick.

Susan growled. Using her feet against the wall for leverage, she pushed him with all her might. S was surprised by her strength. His hand came loose from her throat as he slammed into the wall and bounced off. His pants fell around his thick thighs hampering his movements. Before he had a chance to respond or recover, Susan attacked him. She jumped up on him like a prizefighter. She wrapped both her legs around his waist and wrapped both her tiny hands around his throat. Her legs tightened around his waist, squeezing him. She shook him as she tried to choke him.

S ripped off her teddy, then his hands gripped her firmly around her waist to try to push her loose. Susan snarled like an animal, then bit his bottom lip.

S, with his hands on her waist, ran across the hall and slammed her into the opposite wall. Susan grunted as the air got knocked out of her. He pulled her off the wall, moved further down the hallway, and slammed her into the wall again. S, snarled, "You wan play rough? You wan me fi take dis pussy?"

Susan felt the air come out of her. This time her head bounced off the wall as well. She didn't answer. Instead, she licked her lips and smiled. Triple pleasure: the pain in her head; the pain as the air was forced out of the lungs: the feel of his monstrosity of a dick pressing hard against her opening. She wiggled and squirmed to aggravate him and his monster. Susan humped up and down until the monster slammed against her opening. She could feel the bigheaded monster forcing her lips apart. She laughed and licked his thick lips. He had come prepared. His tool was in complete working order. It was rock solid and condom covered. Studded condom: her favorite next to the French tickler.

Susan bounced up, and then slammed down forcefully. His monster ripped her wet lips apart, stretching her insides uncomfortably. She howled in pain. Even with the pained expression on her face, she was smiling. She lived for the pain. She enjoyed the pain.

S had no mercy. He forced the monster in and out of her: slowly at first. She gritted her teeth and pounded on his shoulders. She knew the harder she pound, the harder he would pound her back. She wasn't taking it lying down, it was hit for hit, plus she was moving her hips, ardently. Susan's insides were on fire. The harder he pounded, the hotter the fire burned. It didn't take long for the fire to reach her critical melting point. The temperature was so extreme that her body automatically released fluids to cool things down. It didn't work. It felt sweeter, but the fire burned hotter. The monster was so thick that not even her fluids could get around his shaft to get where it was needed. S continued to fill her up and stretch her beyond her limits. The heat rose up through her. Even though the air-conditioner was blowing, she was drenched in sweat.

Susan felt as if she was being pulled underwater. She was suffocating. It felt like his fingers were around her neck. She could barely breathe. She couldn't scream. She could barely grunt.

Taking devastating blows by such a monstrosity had her feeling...had her feeling confused. She felt like she was going to burst into flames as the heat continued to rise. She knew she needed to cum in order to combat the intense heat, but she was too afraid. She was afraid that the big monster would force her fluids back up in her. She was afraid that the monster, as it continued to pump in and out of her stretched-beyond-its-limits vagina, would force her release back up the wrong way. She pictured her head exploding. The more she thought about her head exploding from the built up pressure of the forced reversal of her release, the harder she fucked him. She knew pain, but she didn't know fear. Fear of the unknown had her where she hadn't been before.

S felt her trembling in his hands. He knew it was fear, not pleasure that had her shaking beneath his body. He knew that he was punishing her. He knew she enjoyed pain, but he began to worry.

He began to wonder if he was really hurting her. He couldn't be hurting her that bad if she was forcing herself down on his dick the way she was. Nah! She was a sucker for punishment. She was paying cold cash for this punishment. He had to give her her money's worth. He was a Rent-A-Dread, and this is what she was paying good money for him to do. Punish her little ass.

S tightened his grip on her waist and started assisting her with her strokes. Her eyes widened as he went deeper. Behind the pain, S now saw signs of her fear. Along with that fear, he also saw pleasure.

Oh...you...Mandingo Warrior! Susan wanted to say, but couldn't. She had to concentrate to do something as natural as breathing.

S's assistance brought the head of the monster all the way to her entrance, then plunged it deep into her womb. So deep, his nuts were slapping against her ass. Taking in the scent and sound of sex was her downfall. Susan succumbed to the most heart-wrenching orgasm she had had since her very first. And back then, she hadn't quite known what to expect. Her fingernails dug into his flesh. She was like a wild woman as she slammed and bumped and jumped, not only on his dick, but also the wall behind her. She died a sweet and painful death.

S continued to drill her until the last squirt of her juices flowed out of her.

He hadn't cum.

Good! Susan thought, wondering how much time she had used out of her hour.

"Get on the ground," she ordered, finding her breath and voice again.

S lowered them both onto the cold marble tiles without withdrawing from her. They were both skillful in their maneuvers: so skillful that they made it to the ground still attached.

"Take it out," she commanded him, even though she could have easily just raise up off of him. "Now I want you to lick my pussy and toss my salad the way you said you could."

S smiled. With his hands on her tiny waist, he raised her slender body up off his dick, and brought her up to his lips. For the next thirty-five minutes, he had table d'hôte—a complete meal served at a stated time and set price. Susan d'hôte, he thought as he licked her pussy and tossed her salad.

Susan pulled her own plaits, swore, kicked and squirmed as she came over and over again. At one point, she wondered what the hell was the woman's name that was sitting on this Rent-A-Dread's face.

When her hour was up, Susan paid S and gave him a hundred dollar tip.

S didn't get a chance to catch a break. We didn't let him. We were too horny after peeking and listening through the cracks in the door. Me, Becky, and Jenna had been on the way inside when we heard the commotion inside. So of course we stopped and listened through the cracks; and timed them. One hour was all she was going to get. We had plans for S's fine, Mandingo ass. We had dubbed it 'Operation Triple Threat'.

Scandalous Tales

Erotic Short Stories

vol. 2

By: A.C. Humes

SCANDALOUS BITCH

"Girl, my boo don't even hesitate to give me what I want. If I tell him I saw a new pair of shoes I want, Bam! I have that cash in my hands to go get it."

"If he payin' like that, he must be lackin' in other departments," Nakia shot under her breath.

"Not my man. Trust me, my man knows how to lay the pipe. He gat that hammer! He eat, beat, and treat the coochie right," Jennifer bragged.

"He doin all that and you ain't marched his ass down the isle yet?" Nakia asked.

"Girl, I don't want no man to think he can have me on lock down for life. One man can't handle all of this."

"Shit, girl. If he payin' the bills and giving you thrills, you better hang on to him. Men—real men—are hard to find," Ursula chimed.

"You live with him..." Nakia interjected, but got cut off.

"Sooo! Girl, he ain't the only man in my life," Jennifer said in exasperation. "I have other men that are just as good, some even treat me better. I just use what I have to get what I want," she said arrogantly, picking up her Apple Martini.

"Aren't you afraid you gonna get caught?" Ursula asked.

Jennifer laughed. "Caught? Rookies get caught. I have them so pussy whooped that even if they see me, they'll pretend they didn't, then convince themselves that it wasn't me. No man wants to lose out on all of this."

"Humph," Nakia smirked. "You better watch out you don't catch something that you can't wash off with soap."

"I don't mess with the type of men that you do," Jennifer frowned and snarled under her breath right before her lips touched the rim of her martini glass.

"You don't know what kind of men I mess with," Nakia responded indignantly.

"I haven't seen you with anything too impressive at any of the company functions," Jennifer snickered, staring directly at Nakia.

"Why you always gat to look down your nose at everybody. You think you all that, but you een none ah that," Nakia said, her voice dripping with anger.

"I must be all that. You see the men drooling and lined up to get some of this..."

"They only lined up because they all know that you're an easy fuck."

"I select...and screen...who I fuck. I can do that! If you had half of what I have, you'd be able to have it going on like I do. And, I get all my bills paid on time, too. Can you say the same?"

"I don't need no man to pay my bills," Nakia snarled.

"And you don't have what it takes to find one to give you no thrills either," Jennifer snapped back, laughing at her own wit.

"You two behave. This shit is getting too personal here. Y'all attracting attention," Ursula said, trying to keep things from blowing out of proportion.

"I'm going to leave..."

"Yeah, you do that," Nakia snarled, cutting Jennifer off.

"I've got things to do and people to see," Jennifer shot, digging into her Gucci bag and pulling out a crisp fifty-dollar bill. "Here the drinks are on me. I'm out," she said, flicking the fifty at Nakia, then sashaying away.

"More like things to see and people to do," Nakia shot back.

"But thanks for the drinks. I know you'll make it back on your knees out in the parking lot," Nakia shouted over the music.

Jennifer didn't even bother to turn around or glance back over her shoulder.

"Don' t mind her..."

"How you mean, 'don't mind her'? That's your girl and all, but every time we come out for drinks she acts like she's better than us. Like-like her shit don't stink or something. This is the last time I'm coming out if she's going to be there. I don't know who the fuck she think she is, but one of these days I'm going to take off my shoes and go right up side her muthafuckin weave-wearin--ass head. Let her keep letting my color fool her. She een ga keep dissin me like that and get away. I is a project bitch and I will beat her ass right-the-fuck-down. I ain't no regular white girl. Let her keep gettin fooled by that shit on TV..."

"Calm your Conch-Joe ass down." Ursula giggled. "What projects y'all have in the Bahamas?" Ursula asked, trying to lighten the mood.

"We gat ghettos like everywhere else. Don't think it's just a rich man's playground...crystal clear waters and white sandy beaches. It ain't all fun in the sun. My ancestors wasn't just the peaceful Arawak Indians that Christopher Columbus and his men found and gave syphilis to and killed off. My ancestors were also slaves that bucked and jumped off dem damn slave ships before they could reach to America, plus the warriors that got captured and brought to America then start acting the fuckin fool fuckin the Massa's wife and daughters before they escaped and ran off to the islands. Mix dem with the whites that wasn't high society, or rich enough to go all the way to America and you get us, the Conchy-muthafuckin-Joes—white Bahamians. I gat all kind of mix-up blood runnin through my veins. So just as nice as I am, that's as mean as I could be."

"Listen you with the history lesson. But you gat more passive white blood running through you than what African warrior blood."

"Dem wasn't no passive whites that risked their lives sailing on no wooden ships to some far away land. Dem was killers and robbers trying to escape like muthafuckers runnin to Mexico."

"Girl, you're too crazy. I was starting to believe your ass, too."

"These are facts that I'm telling you. Girl, you really don't want me to get started. Her stinkin' ass does piss me the fuck off...stir up the slave-warrior blood in me. She had it easy. She probably went to an all black school. Let her go to a school where she was outnumbered damn near fifty to one, and see if she don't have to fight."

"You went to a damn private school," Ursula hissed, "and all that money your people have, I know you didn't grow up in no damn ghetto."

Nakia laughed and shook her head. "I don't know why I does let that gold digging ass bitch get to me. She might as well be selling pussy the way she does do it. I don't understand why her man put up with her shit."

"He whooped just like she said."

"Can't be. Een no pussy dat damn good for a man to have a bitch living up in his place and she out trickin' like that."

"You'd be surprised. People do stupid things when they in love," Ursula said.

"Can't be that much love," Nakia snarled.

"They say love is blind."

"Yeah, but not deaf, dumb, and stupid."

Ursula laughed. "Don't let her fool you. Her ass is crazy jealous about Dante. She in love too. I was shocked when she moved in. Jealousy caused that though. She moved in so she could watch him."

"So he trickin too?"

"I don't think so. Dante is a good dude."

"How come a bitch like her gets the good dudes, and good girls like us get the fucked up ones?" Nakia asked the age-old question.

"Because opposite attracts. The only way for us to get us a good man is to turn into a bitch like her. Men are suckers for women like her."

"Turn into an evil bitch like her," Nakia repeated, smiling and nodding her head.

"What?" Ursula asked, taking note of the wicked grin plastered on Nakia's face.

"Oh nothing," Nakia lied. "Nothing at all."

ONE MONTH LATER

Nakia sat at the bar in the VIP lounge and watched Dante and his boys. She had found out all that she could about Mr. Dante Stuart. He worked as a Computer Analyst for Global Satellite Cable and Communications. From the little time that she had spent investigating him, she had concluded that Dante was indeed a good man, but like every man, he liked to flirt. So she would use that.

Nakia sat at the end of the bar sipping on a bottle of Dom P Rose. Contrary to what Jennifer thought, Nakia did have money...and she had the body of an islander: Lush cleavage, small waist and peas-n-rice bungy—that's what the Bahamians call ass, bungy. She had a perfect hourglass shape. Everything was just the way it was supposed to be: perfectly proportioned. Nakia just didn't flaunt it for the whole world to see. Not too often, that is. Tonight, she did. Nakia wore a short, curve-hugging, cleavage-revealing black dress that had heads turning and saliva dripping from the mouths of everyone that she had passed. Men and women. Her hair was pulled up, pear shaped diamond earrings, and that cute little diamond nose ring that was like an illusion beneath her beautiful grey eyes.

Men admired her from a distance, but they were afraid to approach because it was rare to see a beautiful woman sitting alone at the bar drinking a bottle of expensive champagne. She had to be waiting for someone. Not just a regular someone either, someone 'big', especially with her copping that expensive bottle of Dom P. If she had been drinking Moet White Star or Rose, that would have been okay. But Dom P.! Shit! Ain't too many ballers did shit like that. Not in there.

Nakia knew how she would get Dante. She timed it perfectly. She spun around and caught Dante and his friends all ogling her. She made eye contact, and smiled at Dante.

He smiled and nodded his head slightly in response.

Nakia motioned him over with her eyes.

His boys started looking back and forth between the two of them in disbelief. They were wondering how come he was the lucky one that had been selected.

Dante gave them a wink, received pats on his back and words of encouragements as he turned his swagger on and strutted over.

"Hi," Nakia said with a dazzling smile.

"Hello to you," Dante replied, locking eyes with her as he leaned against the bar.

"I was just wondering if you could do me a favor..."

"I'll do anything for you. Your wish is my command. I'll suck your toes...drink your bath water..."

"Hold up!" Nakia said, laughing. "You kind a frisky, aren't you? You don't even know me and you want to suck on my toes. Suppose I gat athletes foot or something?"

"I'll be brushing my teeth with Lamisil when I get home," Dante retorted, causing her to laugh. "Damn, your accent sexy. Where you from?"

"The Bahamas."

"What island? Nassau, Freeport, Bimini?"

"Abaco. But let's not get into all that right now. I called you over here to ask you for a favor?"

"You name it. I'll do anything for you..."

Nakia laughed and held up her hand to stop him from singing. "All I need for you to do is to hold my seat for me while I go to the ladies room. Can you do that for a sistah?"

"Damn, that's all you called me for...to Bo 'guard your seat?"

"I mean if it's too much to ask a man who was just willing to suck on my toes, I could call another one of these fine men and have them do it for me," Nakia said in a way that was supposed to make Dante feel like it was an honor to have been selected.

Dante chuckled and shook his head. "I can watch your seat for you. Go ahead."

"Order yourself another drink while I'm gone. Tell the bartender to put it on my tab."

"Thank you, but it's not necessary."

"Oh, you one of those brothers that's uncomfortable with a woman buying you a drink?"

"No, it's just that you don't have to pay me to watch your spot."

"Not with a drink you mean?" she said in a sultry tone as she carefully slid down from the barstool.

Nakia sauntered off toward the ladies room, leaving him with something to think about...after he finished watching her tight ass swish away. She could feel his eyes burning her ass as she walked.

Dante's eyes were riveted to her butt as it swished from side to side. It wasn't exaggerated. It wasn't put on. It was natural, graceful, surefooted and seductive.

Dante's boys were giving him hell via sign language from over in the corner where they stood. He knew he was going to get an earful if he went back over there without getting her phone number or some kind of contact info. Then, suddenly, she was back.

"Thank you," she chimed, smiling.

"Damn, I like your accent. I could listen to you talk all night."

"Just talk?" Nakia asked, sitting down and crossing her legs.

Dante's eyes couldn't be controlled. They automatically focused on the shapely, well-toned, perfectly tanned legs turned toward him. His eyes moved up her body slowly, as if mapping her curves, her flats, and her luscious mounds. His eyes travelled up to her sensuous mouth, her cute nose with that sexy ass diamond, those steamy bedroom eyes.... Those eyes: they had been watching him the entire time.

He was caught. He blushed.

"Did you get it all, or did you miss something?" she asked in a sultry tone as she picked up her champagne flute.

"Well since you asked, I would love to do a much closer inspection."

"I bet you would," she purred. "I'm Nikki, by the way."

"Dante. It's a pleasure to meet you, Nikki."

"So, Dante, are you going to let me buy you that drink?"

"No, I would prefer what's behind door number two."

She appraised him over her glass. "And that would be?"

"I don't know," Dante admitted, "but I hope to find out."

"You always this straight forward, Dante?"

"Always."

She smirked. "With a strange woman you just met?"

"We're only strangers until we get to know each other. And I definitely want to get to know you."

She stared directly in his eyes. "You have a woman, Dante?"

He hesitated.

She smiled. "I thought you were straight forward."

"You didn't give me a chance to respond."

"You hesitated. You had to think about it. Trying to concoct a story?"

"No, I wouldn't do that."

"So do you, or don't you?" Nakia asked, not taking the pressure off of him.

"I have someone. Yes."

"See how easy that was," Nakia said, taking a sip of her

champagne without her eyes ever leaving his face. "Well it was nice meeting you, Dante..."

"What do you mean nice meeting me?"

"I don't mess with men that are involved in relationships. I don't share. I give my all to my lover, and I expect his all in return. A man that has somebody can't give me his all. I deserve and demand his all...no matter how fine he may be or how attracted I am to him," she added, shaking her head as if it were a pity. "Damn!" she mumbled, finishing off the rest of the champagne.

"So we can't get to know each other?"

"No," Nakia said, signaling to the bartender to bring her check, "It wouldn't be fair to neither of us, nor your woman...especially your woman. I don't want to break up your happy home."

Dante chuckled. "You like that, huh?"

"You were willing to suck my toes and you haven't even seen them: imagine the shit you would do if you get a taste of me. My sweetness will become your weakness."

"You all that, huh? Sugar and spice..."

"Naughty, but nice," Nakia finished, sliding three bills on the check and a fifty dollar tip to the bartender. "It's been nice, Dante, but it's time for me to blow this joint."

"Can I at least get you phone number?"

"Nah. That'll only cause trouble," she said, standing.

Dante gave her a once over. "Well can I at least walk you to your car?"

Nakia smiled. "You're persistent, aren't you?"

"Only when it's something I want."

Nakia arched her brow. "Something, not someone?"

Dante backpedaled. "I didn't mean it like that."

"Mmm-hmmm." Nakia chuckled. "You can walk me to my car. I parked over in the garage and it is kind of desolate."

"I like desolate...I mean I would be happy to make sure you get to your car safely."

"Thank you."

***

"This is me right here," Nakia said, stopping next to her Acura TL. "Thank you."

"I really don't want this night to end," Dante said. "I want to get to know you."

"Let's save ourselves some heartache..."

"Can I at least get a kiss for walking you to your car."

"That's how much you chargin' for walkin' me to my car?"

"Don't say it like that. I just want one kiss."

Nakia smiled. "Kissing is too intimate. One kiss will lead to other things."

"You wanted to suck my toes," she said with a devious smile, "come on, I'll let you suck them," she said, sitting up on the hood.

Dante blushed, staring at his shoes in disbelief.

"Oh, so you're all mouth. You say anything to a woman hoping that you won't have to deliver," Nakia said, getting ready to slide down and leave.

"Where are you going?" Dante asked, placing a hand on her thigh to stop her from sliding down. "I didn't think that you were serious," Dante said, getting down on his knees. He raised her right leg, caressing her shapely calf, all the while staring directly into her steamy grey eyes. He let his fingers skim lightly across her skin, then added soft kisses to her already sun-kissed skin, unbuckling her stilettos as he did so. Dante's tongue traced the straps, stopped and nibbled on her ankle, then kissed and licked each of her toes individually.

Nakia's head rolled back. Pleasurable moans escaped her lips and her hand started caressing his head.

Dante slid his tongue in the spaces between each and every toe, causing her to mumble unintelligibly. He nibbled on her toes making her skin prickle, then he slipped all five of her toes into his mouth.

Nakia gasped. She leaned back on both elbows and let her head roll back: the overwhelming sensations stirring deep into her soul.

Dante made tender love to her toes. He kissed and suckled each toe as if he were sucking on five nipples. His hands tenderly massaged her calf, her instep, and her soft heels, slowly moving up her firm inner thighs toward her temple.

Fire raged within her. This was so indecent and scandalous what they were doing. But, it was exhilarating and saucy.

His hands and mouth made her feel alive. She felt light-headed, tingly all over. He was making her hot. Making her wet. Filling her with passion. Enflaming her with desire.

Dante's smooth hands continued venturing up her leg sending sparks shooting ahead of his heated touch. His wet tongue and soft lips trailed lazily behind, but instead of putting out the fire that his hands had created, it made the fire blaze hotter. His tongue was like gasoline. When Dante's hands reached her warm inner thighs, she trembled in anticipation.

The glorious unexpected. She didn't want him to stop. "Don't stop now," she panted, wiggling closer to the edge of the car.

Nakia's legs parted invitingly. Dante's hand brushed across her naked wetness. His eyes widened when he realized that she wasn't wearing any underwear. He was sure that he hadn't seen any panty lines earlier, but he had thought that she at least had on pair of thongs or G-string. Knowing that she had nothing standing in his way turned him on even more. He was hard as a rock. His manhood strained to get out of his pants. His mouth watered at the succulent flesh at the apex of her perfectly tanned thighs. His heart raced as he wondered if she had a Brazilian wax, a landing strip, or was completely bald.

Dante raised both her legs onto his broad shoulders and kissed her inner thighs. He didn't want his hands to defile her temple, not before his mouth had a chance to sample her sweetness. His tongue made lazy figure eights on her inner thighs: he was preparing her for pleasures to come. Intriguing. Her body responded to his every touch, enticing him on. His lips brushed against, and around the edges of her fleshy folds sending shivers racing up her spine.

Nakia mumbled the sweetest curses. He kissed and suckled her sensitive lips better than he had done her toes. Her body released a sample of her potent nectar. Dante lapped it up making delicious, erotic noises. He craved for more. Now he had an unquenchable taste for her nectar. Dante's tongue licked donuts: clockwise and counterclockwise. Figure eights, starting in one direction then switching to the next. Up and down. Side to side. Top to bottom. He licked, lapped, swirled and twirled, all in an effort to please and get more of her potent nectar.

Nakia rolled her hips like a true island girl: winding and grinding against his mouth. Nakia was moaning and chanting the sweetest string of curse words that he had ever heard. She praised up to the high heavens, then cursed down to the depths of hell. Then her breath caught.

Dante teased her clit, and then moved away from it. He did that repeatedly: had her pleading and begging him for more. His tongue flashed in and out of her temple with the speed of lightning; her guttural growl sounded like thunder. Then he slowed down and made the slowest of circles around her clit, letting his hot, thick tongue linger. Then he did it all over again.

Nakia's body shook and shivered as she gyrated her hips slow and sensuously against his lips and tongue. She sat up—getting up off her elbows—grabbed his head and pulled to force his tongue to go deeper, but she wound up slipping. Her feet were over his shoulders, so he placed his hands under her hip to support her as her entire pelvis pressed against his face. His tongue never stopped darting in and out of her. The sound of his tongue lapping her savory juices brought her that much closer to her pleasure palace.

Nakia's hands latched onto his head, her thighs tightened against his ears as she gyrated her waist and pummeled her hips into his face. His tongue delved deeper into her. Deeper and deeper.

Dante's arms went under her ass and his hands moved up to the small of her back to support her weight. Once he had her cradled, he stood up to his full six-foot height.

Nakia screamed out. She was thrilled and frightened of being up so high. She was getting eaten out sitting up on his shoulders. Emotions overwhelmed her. A sudden barrage of sensations— unexplainable feelings—raced through her body creating waves of new pleasures.

Dante's unyielding tongue licked deep into her while his lips trembled against her clit, bringing on yet another new and exciting set of pleasures. This was a totally new experience for her. Her body twitched as his tongue, lips, and mouth pleased every part of her temple. Every chamber, apse, and chancel: from the nave to her altar. From the pew to the pulpit. Everything was blessed.

Nakia started speaking in tongues. Fire raged through her body. Her body shook and she called out to the Lord, Her creator. She sang out at the top of her lungs as ecstasy descended down upon her. The wrath of her climax: Painful. Pleasurable. Excruciating...yet intoxicating. She cried out. Her body bucked and twitched as her orgasm arrived and spread through her. She surrendered her mind and body to ecstasy, but not her soul. This wasn't love; this was sex with her antagonist's man. She was doing this to get back at the evil bitch. That thought made the tide rise higher. The floodgates opened. Her orgasm ripped through her releasing her sweet nectar. The nectar flowed freely as her body shivered and convulsed violently. Sweat drained down her face as ecstasy took control of her.

Dante drank his reward. Her cup runneth over. Her sweet, potent, addictive nectar flowed.

Nakia was floating. She was sensitive. Her entire body felt alive. All of her senses were alert and being stimulated by the erotic sounds, sight, taste, smell, and feel of sex.

Nakia smiled as her orgasm reached its boiling point, then started to simmer. It was true, stolen fruit was the sweetest fruit. She couldn't help but smile. Jennifer had been right, her boo did know how to eat and treat the coochie right. Did he really know how to beat the coochie too? That she would wait to find out some other night.

Dante was gentle as he lowered her to the ground. "Thank you for the kiss. I guess this means that we can exchange phone numbers now," Dante said with a confident tone.

"What, now you expect to be my little secret? No, now I'm supposed to be yours? I told you I don't share..."

"Let me get to know you, and maybe you won't have to share."

"So we're supposed to continue down this path—in secret—while you decide which woman you want? Now that's funny."

"How about just conversation? None of this for now," Dante

begged, still not willing to give up.

"I don't just want conversation. I want all of what we just did and more...and you can't give that to me, so let's just thank each other and go our separate ways."

"That's cold. Okay, how about I give you my work number and you give me a call if you ever just happen to think about me..." Dante smiled, letting his voice trail off.

"Okay, give it to me, but don't hold your breath."

Dante smiled, whipped out his business card, handed it to her, then turned and left. He turned around and yelled: "Drive safely."

FULL SERVICE MAN

"Harder! Harder!" Destiny yelled, gripping my ass and pulling me up into her.

A voice from the other side of the bathroom stall that we were in, yelled, "Hey, can I join in the fun?"

"You've got to keep it down," I said, giving her all nine inches of my Rough Rider shrouded wood to the slow rhythm of Shabba Ranks, 'Mr. Loverman,' playing throughout the club. It was an eighties party, so all the good, old school reggae classics were being played.

We were in the last stall in the men's bathroom in Casablanca's. My sister, her boyfriend, and my sidepiece, Nicole, were all on the dance floor. Nicole suspected nothing. She trusted Destiny; they're stepsisters, for Christ's sake.

"You better hurry and get yours," Destiny panted. "Why?"

Destiny was standing with her back against the wall, one leg on the ground, the other on the edge of the toilet seat. Her skirt was bunched up around her waist, and her thong was in her purse. We had both decided to run off to the rest rooms after too many bottles of Moet and Hypnotic. Destiny had been sneaking peeks and brushing up against me all evening. As far as I know, Destiny—twenty-two years old—has a man. He's only nineteen or twenty, but he's a man.

Nicole, twenty-five, has a man also. I think he just turned twenty-one. I'm not single either. I'm doing my thing, and doing it well. Every woman that I deal with knows that I have a woman, and they respect that. Destiny's little flirting, though not in front of Nicole, didn't just start tonight. Anytime Destiny was around—which was almost always—she gave me those 'you can get some of this whenever you want' looks. Tonight it came to a head. She had pushed me to the limits with the flirting. She'd been coping feels and giving me those come-hither looks.

Both of us had needed to use the bathroom, and her flirting ended up with us a stall over in the men's room. I learned tonight that Destiny is not one to dare. She's young, but she's not scared.

"Because...mmmm. Yesss," she moaned, "I'm about to get mine, and we really...mmmm...don't have all night," Destiny moaned as she rocked forward into me.

With that, I picked up her foot that she had on the ground and started stroking her to a new rhythm. It wasn't to the music that was playing; it was to my own beat.

Destiny gripped my baldhead and worked her hips feverishly.

Her face flushed and she arched her back to meet my thrusts.

Her pussy was hot and wet. It was young, tight pussy. It was inexperienced pussy: a vagina. But it was new pussy and, it was someone else's pussy. All that made it good pussy. I gripped her ass and spread her cheeks as I drove deeply into her. Her back arched to meet each stroke. I stroked her fast and furiously. But, I dared not cum.

Destiny's mouth closed on mine. It was our first kiss, and it couldn't have come at a better time. Her mouth was cool and sweet from the Moet Nectar. Her tongue slithered into my mouth: exploring; probing; relishing; savoring my flavor.

Destiny exploded. I loved the way her pussy felt as she came. I loved the way she sucked my tongue as she came. I imagined her sucking my wood the exact same way. I made my wood jump in her as if I were about to come. I squeezed her firm cheeks together, closing her lips tight around my wood as I pumped and pounded into her.

My strokes had Destiny climbing up the wall.

"Come with me," she whimpered. "Tell me this pussy sweeter

than Nicole's."

I didn't answer that. I pretended to come with her. "I'm cumming with you," I lied, pummeling her with my rapid strokes as she came. I grunted and made the ugliest fuck- face that I could. I grunted and pulsed as she continued to saturate my wood with her discharge. I stalled out on my strokes, locked up and growled.

She was still spasming. Her eyes were closed as she continued to come.

"That was good, Girl," I grunted, breathing hard as I pulled out of her. Using some toilet tissue, I pulled off the empty condom, dropped the entire wad into the bowl, and flushed it before she had a chance to see it.

Destiny was back on her own two feet. "Whew," she shivered as she opened her eyes and smiled at me. "That was better than good," she said as she gathered herself. She shook off the feeling and took a few deep breaths while she dug in her bag.

I watched as she pulled out a small plastic container, removed a few wet naps, and handed me a couple. She motioned for me to slide over, then squatted over the bowl and relieved her bladder. I cleaned up myself while she did so. When she was done, she cleaned up herself nice and proper, then took her thong out of her bag and put them back on. When we were both fixed, Destiny unlatched the door and stepped out of the stall ahead of me. Heads turned instantly. Guys watched as we casually walked over to the line of basins. Destiny washed her hands, checked her hair in the mirror, turned and kissed me, removed the sheen from her face with a powder sponge, then reapplied her lip-gloss.

Stunned, envious men gawked. I smirked arrogantly, washed my hands, dried them with the towel that the valet gave to me, then dropped a tip in his basket. Destiny did the same, said thanks, blew our audience a kiss, then led the way out; sexy, young ass swishing extravagantly. That shit turned me on: gorgeous, sassy, cool, and confident.

We rejoined our crew on the dance floor. They were all the way in the back against the far back wall. Nicole was dancing with a guy from her job, so Destiny and I engaged in a post coitus dance of eroticism. Nicole dismissed her dance partner and slid behind me. She was in between the wall and me. I backed into her, and she pressed her breast into my back. Her hands snaked around my waist pulling me tight into her body. With her height, she was able to nibble and lick my ear.

Destiny turned her back to me and put her ass right on my wood. Nicole whispered, "You like this, don't you? Look at you...just like a piece of meat between two slices of bread."

"I like one on one action," I lied smoothly while grooving to the island vibes. I had to smile, Shaggy's tune, 'Wasn't me,' was playing. For those of you that aren't familiar with the song, it's about a man being caught by his girlfriend red handed, but he still denies it. How appropriate, I thought.

Nicole and Destiny switched positions. It was like they were playing musical chairs. Nicole took Destiny's previous position, and with her ass centered around my dick, she reached back and put one hand around my head and caressed my baldness. Her body, writhing sensuously against mine, got me hard quickly. She responded favorably as she felt me growing.

Destiny was still doing her thing behind me. She had a hand on either side of my waist with her soft breast rubbing my shoulders. It was the double effect of both of them that had me stiff in my pants again. I was imagining myself with the both of them, but I knew Nicole would never let that happen. She was extremely jealous, even though I wasn't her man. She would never let me fuck someone she knew. She could barely accept me fucking my own woman. She told me that was the way Trini women were. They want their cake and ice- cream too. Shit, so do I.

"You two look like y' all done this before. Y'all work well together," I teased.

"Don't get any ideas," Nicole said over her shoulder, "This if as far as this goes; dancing."

Her face was turned to the side, and it was dark, so she couldn't see what Destiny was doing behind me. Destiny was using her tongue and running it along the back of my neck and on my ear on the other side away from Nicole. I reached behind me with one hand, slid it between Destiny's body and me, and rubbed her clit through her clothes. I felt her body quake. At the same time, I licked and kissed Nicole's cheek. I licked her ear then whispered, "I don't want you two to think it was going any further. I like one on one lovin'," I reiterated, using that good old reverse psychology. "I only have one dick so what I need two pussies in the same bed for?"

"One for your dick the other for your face."

"I tired telling you I don't eat pussy, woman. Pussy make to fuck: breast make to suck."

"You don't know what you missing."

"I know what I ain't missing."

"You missing out on a lot. Fifth base is where you need to go," she said, moving straight up and down on my erection.

My wood was straining to get out of my pants. I felt it slide between her cheeks and I was ready to bend her ass over right there in the dark. She put that Carnival winding on me like only Trini women can do and I had no choice but to scoop down low and come up so I could let her feel me trying to force my wood up in her with my clothes still on.

Destiny spun around so that her ass was to my ass; palms opened and pressed against the wall. She spread her legs and got wicked with her rhythm. The DJ was yelling and pointing to a group of girls dancing down front. "Wicked in ah dance and dead in a bed."

I knew for sure that wasn't the case with Nicole, and from the little quickie in the bathroom a few minutes ago, I didn't think so with Destiny either. I think what she was putting into it, was exactly what she would bring to the bed. She was auditioning for a full-time, part-time position. She might just get it too. With a little training, she could develop into something truly special.

The music changed. A snippet came through the speakers, '…a back-shot mi love.' The selector pulled it up and the DJ yelled, "I want all da gal dem start doggy style. Gal dem love it more dan you! Positioooon! Doggy style!"

The music came back up and the crowd got extra hyped. Nicole bent all the way forward and put one hand on the ground. She was in position when the music started. "Doggy style, no gal can do like you..."

That was her song. The DJ was yelling, "Go head, mi gal. Give it to dem, mi gal. Give dem da wind, gal."

It was too good a feeling to pass up.

I slipped down my zipper, pulled out the good wood, got up under her little skirt, and slapped it up against her pussy. One of her hands was on my wood in an instant. Fingers from that same hand pulled her thongs to the side and guided me to her hot entrance. She backed up and my head plopped into her sweetness.

I continued to wind my waist and get on bad. Nicole took care of everything else. She wiggled and worked her ass until she worked every inch of my wood into her tightness. Experienced lover. She had a slow wind going until I touched the back of her cave. Then she turned it up. My left hand was on the small of her back; the right hand was behind me slithering around, then up Destiny's warm thigh.

Destiny's hand was on top of mine, guiding it to her pussy. Both our fingers pulled her thongs to the side, then fingered her pussy. She was doing to our fingers what Nicole was doing to my wood. Both of them were assisting me to bringing them to a climax.

Nicole's fingers were still between her legs, fingering her clit and massaging my shaft as it slid in and out of her. Her pussy gripped and grabbed my dick as she worked her stomach, waist, and ass together. Her loving was roily and outré.

Nobody was paying us any attention; every man had his hands full during this session. And it was pitch black. My sister and her man were over to our left, and another wall was to our right, so you can say that no one, even if they looked, could see what was going on in our corner pocket.

The music continued to change and the DJ continued to hype up the crowd. The position didn't change, and every girl was bent over delivering or receiving some kind of vicious back-shot from her dance partners. This session would serve as foreplay for many because the dance would soon come to an end.

Nicole's grinding got out of sync with the music. She was coming. Her strokes went from wicked to vicious. Her insides went from tight and wet to almost impenetrable and soaked. It was almost impossible for me to get an inch of movement. I would have had to grip her by the waist and forcefully thrust into her. In my present circumstance, I wasn't at liberty to go ballistic in the pussy; nor did I want to. If I did that, I would come for sure, and I didn't want to come. I couldn't come.

Destiny on the other hand wanted to come. In fact, she was coming. Destiny pulsed around my fingers, so I slipped in a third digit. That took her up another notch. I could feel her fingers patting and working her clit. I felt her arch into me as Nicole wiggled the last of her come onto my dick before straightening up with my wood still in her.

I was still rock hard and working her to the music.

She turned her head to the side, and leaned into my shoulder. My hand slithered around her stomach and I held her close as she slow-grind on me. Our lips touched, and though awkward, it was exhilarating.

Destiny finished coming, then settled into a nice slow groove. The DJ announced the final selection, and a few of the lights came on. Not in the corner where we were, but it wouldn't be long.

Two things happened at once: Destiny wiggled and pulled my fingers out of her, held them as she got a few wet-naps out of her purse, then cleaned them off; Nicole, hiked up her hips and moved forward. My wood plopped out of her like a cork from a champagne bottle.

Destiny turned around, still dancing against me, but now with her back pressed against the wall.

Nicole also turned around, still dancing, and stepped close enough to me to block anyone's view, "Destiny," Nicole said over my right shoulder, "Give me a few of those baby wipes you always traveling with."

I prayed that Destiny had some more. She did. Nicole took the wet naps, cleaned me up, made sure none of her juice was on my pants, reinserted my good wood back into my boxers, then zipped my pants. Then she leaned in and whispered, "I'm heading to the little girls room. I'll meet you guys by the door."

Not long after she had left, the lights came up. My sister and her man—both looking like they had been doing exactly what I had been doing—turned to Destiny and me. "Y'all ready?"

"Yep, Nicole's going to meet us at the door," I said.

We worked our way slowly toward the door with the rest of the crowd. By the time we got to the door, Nicole was on her way out of the rest room. We all walked out together. The sun was mere minutes from rising. My sister and her boyfriend waved and went to the valet stand while we walked across the street to the parking lot where we had parked.

"We don't have time to eat, we've got to hightail it to the airport," Nicole said, looking at her watch.

"And I sure worked up an appetite," Destiny chimed, rubbing her stomach.

"I'm going straight home and jump in the shower...get this smoky scent off of me."

"You got to get more than the smoky scent off of you before your woman smell you and kill your ass," Nicole snickered, unlocking her Audi A6.

"Y'all be safe. I'll see y'all later," I chuckled, sliding into my BM.

I got home and went straight in the shower. Two pieces of pussy, both satisfied and I didn't even bust a nut. Couldn't take the chance of busting the nut. I knew as soon as Sonia walked through this door, she was going to want hers. And she measures every ounce. If I try and slip her seconds, she will know, and I will be dead before she asks me about it. She is crazy jealous: worse than Nicole.

TOP PERFORMERS

"Tom, come over here so I can introduce you to my fiancée," William shouted clear across the room.

Tom, who was standing on the other side of the room, whispered to the group of guys that he was standing with. "He wants to show her off, that's all."

"More like rub it in your face," Chris chuckled.

"She could rub those D's in my face anytime," Tom shot back. "Let me go and play the gracious host. The king has summoned."

"In your own house," Chris snorted.

"The king is the king anywhere he goes," Jeremy mumbled under his breath. "Go on. Mustn't keep the king waiting."

"Just keep him over there. I have enough of his royal, arrogant ass during the damn week," Chris mumbled, giving William, who was watching them, a fake smile.

"Give his fiancée a kiss for me," Jeremy laughed as Tom walked away.

Tom chitchatted and greeted some of his guests as he maneuvered through the packets of people that were standing around schmoozing.

William grinned as Tom drew close. He had one hand in the small of his fiancée's back as he made the introduction. It wasn't a sign of affection: it was a sign of possession. "Tom, I'd like you to meet my fiancée, Brittany. She just flew in from Palm Springs today. Brittany, this is Tom. Tom is on of the top performers that I beat out to get the top position."

Tom smiled, ignoring the dig and shaking Brittany's hand. "It's a pleasure to meet you."

"Thank you," Brittany smiled, looking around. "I like your house. Your wife must enjoy living right here on the water."

William snickered. "Tom's not married, honey."

"No. I don't have any of the luck that William obviously has," Tom retorted, holding her gaze.

Brittany blushed. "I'll take that as a compliment. Thanks," Brittany sang. "William, he's such a smooth talker. No wonder you said he's one of the top performers on your team. Who can say no to a smooth talker like him."

"Thank you," Tom chuckled, giving a discreet once over that she caught, but William didn't. "Well, just make yourself at home, some of the ladies are upstairs changing to go for a dip. Feel free to join them if you'd like. Towels are out by the cabana."

"I might just do that," Brittany chimed with a smile.

A promiscuous smile, Tom thought.

Tom had barely turned when Candy walked up to him. Candy was bubbling: drink in hand; bikini top barely able to conceal her areolas; bikini bottom visible through a sheer, asymmetric wrap mini skirt that revealed her long, slender legs. "Tom, there you are," she babbled excitedly. "I've been looking all over for you. Is it alright if we go in the Jacuzzi?"

"Sure," Tom replied, trying to keep his eyes from wondering.

"This is a pool party, after all," he chuckled.

"You coming in to join us?" she asked playfully, running her fingers down his arm.

"Maybe a little later," Tom blushed.

"Okay. I'm going to put my stuff upstairs," she blabbered, then sauntered off joyously.

William's eyes followed her as he walked away. Tom noticed that Brittany caught him, but her expression remained pleasant. It didn't even faze her. And, Candy was worthy competition. That meant one thing in his mind: Brittany's a player.

The pool party continued on as the sun disappeared over the rooftops, behind the surrounding hills, then below the horizon. Under the cover of darkness, drinks continued to flow. Girls were going wild, taking off their tops in the pool and Jacuzzi. Lewd and frolicsome dancing and behavior was going on. And a rowdy gambling game had the guys going deep into their pockets.

Tom decided to make a round to make sure that the lewd behavior hadn't spread upstairs into any of his bedrooms as it had done at the last pool party that was held over at Chris's house, or the time before that over at George's house.

Tom was passing the upstairs guest bathroom when Brittany came out and nearly crashed into him. "Oh hey, Tom. I really, really like your place," she said, provocatively, sounding almost out of breath. She reached out and touched his arms. "Especially the bidet."

"Yeah," Tom grinned, "that comes in handy."

"It can be rather stimulating, especially when you know how to use it."

The look that she gave Tom could not be misinterpreted. She stunned Tom. Damn! She's licking her lips...and that's a lascivious look if I've ever seen one. Oh yeah, she wants me. She's running her tongue over her dazzling, perfectly white teeth. Those lips. That mouth. Damn! If she keeps looking at me like that, I'm going to fuck her right here in.... Hold on! This is my boss's fiancée. He's a prick, but...shit...he's right downstairs. Fuck him! If she wants to give it up, I'm going to fuck...or at least get a quick blow-job, Tom thought as his eyes took stock of her assets.

"Candy never showed you how to properly use a bidet?" she asked with a devious grin.

Okay, so she just let me know that she caught on to the fact that I'm fucking Candy. It didn't take a rocket scientist to figure that out, though, Candy put it on Front Street. But here's Brittany, looking steamy and whorish to put it mildly. Mmm-mmmm!

"No, she never did," Tom finally answered.

"Would you like me to show you?" she asked, stepping a little closer.

"William..."

"He's wrapped up in that poker game downstairs. He's losing, so he won't get up from there until he's either broke, naked, get tossed out...or he wins. You work for him, so you know how he hates to lose."

Tom looked around. People were moving all around his house. This was risky, but fuck it. William's an asshole...and Brittany was damn sure fine. "Come on. You can show me in my bathroom," Tom said, leading her down the hall. He checked back over his shoulder a few times to see if anyone was watching.

Tom locked the door as soon as they got into his room. He didn't want any surprises. Brittany walked into his bathroom like it was her own. She stopped, spun around and untied her bikini straps. Her perfect D's bounced out. Store bought, but worth every penny. Money well spent. She obviously thought so, too. Her eyes sparkled when she looked down at them. She felt their weight, and caressed them as she slowly plumped and pushed them together. Erotic sounds seeped from her mouth. She was putting on a performance for Tom.

Tom enjoyed watching her, but he knew that they didn't have time for all this foreplay. Time was of an essence. This had to be a quick in and out. He had to get in her, then quickly get her ass out.

Tom stepped toward her. His mouth went directly to hers. He kissed her and rubbed his open palm over her nipples. The direct stimulation made her nipples plop out from their hiding spot. Her nipples were small, but the way they poked out and ripened made Tom instantly hard. Tom's mouth moved down her neck, then went straight for her breasts. His hands bypassed her toned stomach and went straight down and cupped her sex that looked like a camel-toe between her legs.

Brittany pushed him back. "Slow down sailor..."

"Slow down? We don't have all that much time," Tom said, trying to touch her again.

"We have time. Besides, I came in here to show you how to use the bidet."

Tom was getting somewhat impatient, but fuck it, this was her show. "Well, start the show then," he replied, trying to keep the impatience out of his voice.

Brittany sauntered over to the bidet, straddled the fixture in a reverse cowgirl and turned it on. The water was aimed directly between her legs.

Tom watched as Brittany fondled and licked her nipples. She was acting like a porn star. She was moaning and wiggling her hips as if it were the greatest feeling that she ever felt.

Her hand glided from her breasts, over her toned stomach, then slid into her swimsuit bottom and disappeared. Her eyes shot open, then just as quickly, shut tightly as she fingered herself. After a few minutes of self-pleasing and finger fucking, Brittany untied the left side of her bottom and pulled it out of her way. She shifted over, parted her lips, and let the powerful stream of water pound her lips and clit. She cooed and aaaahed to the sweet stimulations. Erotic sounds filled the bathroom as she bounced up and down and on the water stream.

Tom couldn't take it anymore. He had his cock out, stroking it as he watched Brittany's live pornographic show.

Brittany flicked her tongue against her nipples hungrily. She trembled as she squatted lower against the flow: the direct stream and continuous pressure stimulating her lips and clit. Her fingers danced along her thin lips, then slid into her mouth. She began sucking them; making wet noises as if they were a cock.

Tom moaned, then stepped over to her. He removed her fingers from her mouth and let the head of his cock rest gently between her parted lips. He was substituting her fingers for the real thing.

Tom took his time, patiently feeding her his bulging mushroom-head.

Brittany's tongue darted in and out, licking and teasing his rosy-red head. She toyed around with his head, then took it into her mouth. Tongue whisking, swishing, and twirling all around it. Glazing. Polishing. Buffing his head. Teasing him. Pleasing him. Driving him insane.

Tom closed his eyes, bit down on his lips and squirmed. His ass tightened. His stomach clenched. His breathing: sporadic. His hands fumbled recklessly on her stacked rack. He couldn't concentrate on two things at once. His pleasure came first. It was William's job as her fiancé to worry about her pleasure.

Brittany wasn't having any problems getting off. She was mere seconds from ultimate pleasure. Her legs turned rubbery as the steady stream against her clit became almost unbearable. The only thing saving her from cumming was the fact that she was concentrating on making Tom cum. She wanted to taste his precious seed: his natural elixir.

Brittany found it more and more difficult to prolong her orgasm. She kept taking more and more of Tom into her mouth. She used her hands to caress and gently squeeze his balls.

Tom gripped the back of her head and started going deeper. Faster. He kept his strokes soft.

He couldn't help imagining how he was going to feel every time Will tried to belittle him or act all high and mighty...

Tom's asshole tightened even before his thoughts were interrupted. Brittany's finger was rimming his white-chocolate center. His stomach clenched as her fingernail gently grazed his opening. She made a clucking noise with her tongue against his mushroom-head, inundating him with multitudinous sensations that ran through his head, down his shaft, and straight into his nut sack.

He cried out as the sensations tripped the pressure switch in his nut sack. His thick, hot liquid elixir shot up with so much force that he didn't get a chance to warn Brittany even if he had wanted to. But, he didn't want to. He gripped her head tightly as he continued to pour his appreciation down her throat.

Brittany felt him swell, then bulge in her mouth. Knowing he was about to blow his wad, she started sucking and pumping him harder and faster. She felt his elixir rising. It delighted her. A thrilling sensation rushed to her core. Her mouth watered in anticipation.

Then his hot elixir splattered against the roof of her mouth. She didn't swallow the first shot. She savored the sensational flavor of his life giving elixir, letting it flow all over her tongue.

Brittany suffered a sensory overload. Her legs twitched. She found it difficult to maintain her balance. She lost it. She gripped onto his waist for balance as he stroked powerfully into her mouth. Brittany started cumming. Waves of pleasure resonated through her as the stream of water hit her clit with pinpoint accuracy and just the right amount of pressure. Swallowing his liquid appreciation made her orgasm even sweeter: more intense. She had to shift away from the stream of water. Too much pleasure! Too ferocious! Too fucking delicious!

Tom withdrew from her mouth weakened. He moved away from her shaking like he had the willies. He leaned back against the counter and watched as Brittany's orgasm peaked, then tapered.

Her mouth, still formed in an "Orgasmic 0," looked painful. Erotic. Beautiful. He wished that she were sitting up on him staring down into his eyes with that pure, unadulterated look of euphoria etched on her face.

Then Brittany smiled and licked her lips. "You must be one healthy eater, because you sure are yummy."

Tom could barely speak. The head she had given him had been incredible. It was the type of head that you tell your friends about. Fuck that! It's the type that you want your friends to experience. Tom smiled. He couldn't wait. "I eat any and everything," Tom replied as he reached for some towels so that they could clean themselves up.

"You keep talking like that and I'll make you prove it."

"I wish we had some more time..."

"You think they missed us?" Brittany asked, standing up.

"We need to go and show our faces for a..."

"Then can we come back so that I can get some of that there...in here?" she asked, pointing to her dripping pussy.

"Let's go and check, then we'll see," Tom said, already imagining going up in her.

They got cleaned up, sneaked out of his room, then separated.

Outside, Tom went and found Chris and Jeremy. They were parked at the wet bar over by the cabana.

"We were looking for you, Tom. We thought you had carried Candy upstairs for a little taste, but then we saw her getting real friendly with that blonde right there," Chris said, pointing the thong-wearing, breast-revealing blonde out, "in the hot tub."

"Look like you're going to have two times the fun tonight: blonde and brunette."

"Fuck that!" Tom bellowed. "I just got the most incredible blow-job..."

Jeremy's face lit up. "From who?"

Tom laughed and shook his head. "You're not going to believe this..."

"Who?" Chris asked impatiently.

Tom smiled like the devil himself. "William's fiancée."

"Stop lying," Chris barked, almost choking on his beer.

"Toe-curling head. She swallowed and everything.... Look, he's calling her over to the table. You know what would make me laugh right now?"

"What?" Jeremy asked, turning to him, then following his eyes over to where he was looking.

"If he were to kiss her! Oh shit! There it is. He's tasting my nut! She barely rinsed out her fuckin' mouth!"

"Aw, man. That is soooo nasty. Look at him. He's kissing her as if to rub it in all our faces."

"Was she any good?" Chris asked.

Tom grinned. "She polished and shined the knob up real good. I had to put on my Ray Ban's just to look at it."

"Sweet!" Jeremy hooted.

"If you guys can keep him busy, I'll take her somewhere to sample her other holes."

"He's losing now, but if we get the guys to let him start winning a little, we'll probably be able to buy you a little time."

"Work on it," Tom said as he caught her eyes. He poured himself a healthy helping of brandy. He chugged it and growled as it burned its way down. "Now I'm ready."

"If you need some help, I'll be glad to lend my assistance."

"She has three holes, Tom. Don't be greedy," Chris interjected.

"You think she'll go for it?" Jeremy asked.

"We could try her," Tom said, "but if she doesn't welcome it..."

"We know," Chris shot, cutting off his spiel.

"Just keep an eye out. I'm going to take a stroll around to see what's going on and see if she bites."

ISLAND PLAYERS

LOS

"Hello?"

"Your woman there with you?"

"If she was, would I have answered the phone?"

"She on the island or she gone to her other man in Miami again?"

"What other man? Don't even play with me."

"Damn! Le'me change the subject before you bite my head off. You so fuckin' sensitive."

"Chantell, what da fuck you want?"

"What makes you think I want something?"

"It's three o'clock in the damn morning and you sound like you been drinking. And I know how you get when you been drinking."

"So if you know how I get, why you actin' all funny? You want me to beg you for some dick?"

"Where ya man?"

"With your fuckin' woman. Now you ga do to me what he doin' to her...or should I just go and join dem?"

"You tink I does fuckin play."

"What you askin' me where my man is for? Ask a stupid question; get a stupid answer. Now, can I come get me some a da dick or what?"

"Where you at?"

"By your complex. Your lot is full, so I gatta park in the lot over by the other building."

"You don't know how to call first, eh?"

"I callin now, am not I? So talk fast. I could carry my ass home and pull out Pleasure and Pain."

"You probably een gat no damn batteries for dem fuckers."

"Pleasure runs on electricity; Pain, da big boy, is gas operated, premium unleaded."

"Fuck, you een need me den. Go home to ya toys."

"Dey can't hold me or talk back. I hoppin out my fuckin car and on way to your door, so take of dem drawers and have dick ready for me when you open the gat-damn door. Dat's what you do."

"Hurry the fuck up! All that talking gat my dick hard. I ga ram it right down your muthafuckin throat when you get up here. You know I ga punish your ass for talkin all dat shit, right?"

"All you is is mouth," she snickered, ending the call.

I threw my cellphone on the nightstand and leapt out of the bed. I snatched off my wife-beater and boxers. My dick was hard from the second I had heard Chantell's voice. Da girl gat a mouth on her. My nickname for her is Oral Viagra. She'll talk a limp dick into a rock-hard hard on in a second.

On the way to the front door, I stopped in the kitchen. In the freezer was a bottle of Remy VSOP. I unscrewed it and took it to da head. I horse-backed two—okay, three—healthy swigs, closed the bottle, and returned it to its permanent home.

Chantell started knocking as I approached the door.

"Hold your horses," I yelled. "My neighbors sleepin'," I said, opening the door.

Her smile was enough to light up the entire downtown area of

Freeport. It would have been nice if my face had put that smile on her face, but unfortunately it was my dick.

"Oh how I miss dis nice, big, juicy dick," Chantell said, getting down on her knees as soon as she was in the doorway. She took my dick into her hands like it was a treasure to be valued. I mean it is, but damn. She peppered my dick with kisses like it was her long lost child...maybe not child, that would be incest, but you know what I mean.

"You een even say hello to me. You een even in the damn door yet and you just ga grab my dick like.... Well mudda fuck, Chantell! Mmmm, dat feel fuckin good," I cursed as I lost my sense of balance and stumbled back. I had to reach behind me for the comfort and support of the wall. She had chewed up Altoids in her mouth with a little piece of ice. Oh. My. Goodness!

Chantell sucked my head, depositing little pieces of mint, then licked it with her cold tongue. When she blew on it, chills ran all through my ass. After licking, swirling and twirling her tongue over every inch of my dick with her frisky tongue, she gobbled up my dick. She started sucking and licking and doing that thing she do that causes me to forget what the fuck I was thinking...what I was doing...or was it what I was saying? Fuck, I dun forget!

Chantell stared up at me with her big brown eyes as she continued her wickedness.
"You...want...me...to...talk...or...suck...your...dick?" Chantell asked, swirling her tongue around my head, then plopping it in and out of her mouth.

"Just...shut...the...fuck...up and suck my dick...oooooooh! You a fuckin pro. Fuuuuck!" I squirmed, slamming into the wall behind me, then trying to bounce off that fucker and ram my dick down the back of her throat. She liked that shit. She liked when I tried to force it down her throat. I grabbed her head, pulling forward as I thrust forward. "Suck...this...fuckin...dick. All...that...shit you...you was...talkin. Swallow every inch of dis dick," I said, humping her mouth with fervor.

Chantell wasn't even fazed by the hard strokes. She did some crazy shit with her tongue that made me let her head go and lose my stroking power. It made me forget that I was trying to push my dick out the back of her neck. That head was smokin'. It felt so good 'til the only thing I was trying to do was get away from her deliciously, evil tongue. Anything this fuckin sweet couldn't be good. "Chantell!" I managed to get out. "Oh fuck, girl! The fuckin door still wide ass open."

"So! Leave it open!" she shot back, gettin' up. "If a muddafucka up and lookin, let em watch. Deh might learn sumtin."

"So what you stoppin for?" I asked.

"I wanted to taste the dick—das just a lil appetizer—but I came here to get fucked," she said sassily as she stood up and turned her back to me.

Chantell backed into me rubbing her big ass up and down on my dick. She spread her legs, then bent over and placed one hand on the ground in front of her. I know every quarterback wished they had a female center to hike the ball...except no game would ever be played. All I can say is waist like wasp, ass like horse.

I grabbed her waist, scooped down to let my dick get up under her skirt. She was ass out. No drawers. "Where the fuck your drawers at?" I asked, forcing my dick up between her cheeks.

Chantell groaned and her ass jiggled like drug store jelly. She caught herself, then bounced her ass back into me. She started backing her ass up onto the dick like a stripper on a damn pole. "I took em off when I was talking to you."

"You was fingering dis pussy while you was talking to me, eh?" I asked, letting my dick dip under, then rub between her fat pussy lips. My big head plowed through her wetness, curved up, then bumped into her clit.

"Ooooh shit, baby, hit it again!" Chantell cooed.

"Can't miss hitting that big muddafucka," I shot, letting my big head jump up and hit it a couple more times.

Chantell had to put her other hand on the ground to stabilize herself as incredible sensations dispersed from her inch-long bundle of nerves, then spread through her body.

Chantell has one of those clit's that's at least an inch long. Dat muddafucka scare me the first time I "experienced" it. It was an experience. I thought we were going to have to fight. It was so long and hard that I thought she had a dick. Only thing that stopped me from punching her out was that I had a finger in her ass, and two in her pussy when I had felt it. Then she had the nerve to beg me to eat her pussy...I had to ask her if she meant suck her fuckin dick. My mouth wasn't going anywhere near that long-ass clit...not until I realized how sweet the pussy was. She had—still have—some good pussy...and she knew how to work it, too. "Put it...yeah, put it in, baby," Chantell begged, wiggling her hips to try and draw me in.

"Beg fa dis dick," I said, grinding real slow while my shaft rubbed back and forth between her lips.

"Stop fuckin 'round...and give me what I come here for."

I was about to force myself up in her when I realized that the door was still wide-ass open. I reached out and closed it.

"Scary ass," Chantell scowled as she reached back to try and grab my dick.

I didn't give her a chance to get it. I slid my big head back, right to her opening, checked the angle to make sure it wasn't going in clean, pulled all the way out, then rammed forward. Full speed ahead. "Dis what you fuckin want?" I snarled as my head smashed through her outer lips, stretched her inner folds, then plowed through her warm, succulent flesh before colliding and bouncing off her walls and slamming into her womb.

Chantell grunted as she pushed her ass back to get the full force of the impact. "Fuuuuck yeah! Dis what I want. Give me all dis dick!" Chantell started winding her waist and rolling her hips like she was trying to grind my dick off. Round and round. Back and forth. Up and down. Then she rolled that big, juicy ass.

I didn't have to move if I didn't want to. I could have stood stock-still and still get a proper fuck. Fuck is what we do. Plain and simple.

"Work dis pussy! Yeah! Yeah! Das it! Dis pussy sweet, eh?"

"Mmmm-hmmmm!" I grunted, holding her waist and giving her some long, hard strokes. The more I put in to it, the more she gave back. I was doing the old dollar wine on her: cent (left), five cent (right), ten cent (back), dollar (front). She started bouncing up on her tiptoes and I knew what that meant. She was about to get her first one. "Fuck! Pull my hair... I know you could fuck harder dan dat," she growled, picking up her speed.

I gripped her by her hair and wrenched back while delivering nothing but straight shots. No left: no right. Strictly back and front. Straight dollar shots I was giving her. Big money shots. I was hitting her womb. I was trying to force it up and out of her mouth.

Chantell bucked, got up on her toes and froze. She couldn't move. Her orgasm shot through her like a female poodle running from a horny pit-bull. She didn't know if she was going to get fucked to death, or eaten to death. Only thing that bitch knew was that if she got caught, she was going to die.

Chantell's orgasm put her into a state of suspended animation. "Pull it out," she managed to mumble. "Pull it out! Don't fuckin touch me!" she yelled.

Chantell gets extra sensitive when she cums. I pulled out and waited for her to float back down off her orgasmic high.

A minute later, I was back up in her. This time, she was holding onto the back of the couch with one foot on the ground, the other up on the seat. Back-shot queen, that's what Chantell is. Every position is a back-shot. She cums too quickly when she's in any other position. That big ass clit will rub her the right way in a minute. Missionary, and she dead. Two strokes and she's cumming.

I was going up in her deep when her cell phone rang. Ring tone. I knew it was her man. I had heard that ring tone before. "Your man can't be with my woman if he blowing your shit up," I said, punching her in her side as I stroked her.

Chantell winced and sucked in air noisily. "I gat to answer. He een ga stop...ooh yeah! Punch me again. He een ga stop callin till I answer."

"Answer then," I shot, spanking her ass. "Talk to ya man."

"Keep...mmmm," she mumbled, biting her lip. "You gat to keep quiet."

"Okay," I said, grinding her slow while she fumbled for her phone. Then I punched her again just as she pressed send.

She answered on the fourth ring. "Ugh! Hey, baby!"

I bit her on her shoulder and slowed my stroke as I withdrew several inches from her. Her body shook. I could only hear her end of the conversation, but it was enough for me to get the gist of what he was saying.

"I stopped at Ruby Swiss to get something to eat with the girls."

I reached around and fingered her clit.

Chantell slapped my hand and twisted around mouthing, "Stop," then she spoke to her man. "It's quiet because I stepped outside to talk to you."

I fingered her clit again and slammed all the dick back in her. She almost cursed out loud. I could hear her man going off on her. Shit. I was going to get mine before she left. I pulled out and made her lay on the couch as she talked.

"I dun order my food..."

I put one of her feet up on the back of the couch, and the other one up on my shoulder.

"About five minutes ago."

I rest my dick at the entrance of her treasure box and let the head slide in, then out. She tried to wiggle so that my dick would go all the way in, but I kept teasing her.

Chantell's eyes rolled back in her head as I slid in and out of her. "It shouldn't take too long. I soon come."

"You een lie," I whispered, stuffing all my dick into her.

"Fuck!" she cursed.

I didn't hear what her man said, but she was stuttering when she answered him.

"Nut-nut-nutin. Shit! This stupid fucker just swing in the lot and almost sideswipe dis woman car."

I leaned forward and started stroking her good and hard so that I could cum before she had to hurry and leave. My pelvis rubbed against her clit causing her to lock up. Her mouth was open, but nothing came out for a minute.

"Ohhh....ssss."

I was trying my best to make her make some gaddamn noise. I don't like her man anyway. Fuck him, I thought as I continued to whale away.

"I-I...they calling me. My food reach now: I ga call you when I on the way."

I was whaling and shaking my head as she lied to her man. She's the fucking best. Lying to her man and fuckin me back at the same time. She enjoyed living dangerously.

I was so close to her that I could hear her man's voice clear as day when he spoke. I should say yelled: "So you in Ruby Swiss?"

"Yeah...that's what I said. Why you asking me that again?" she asked, in between breaths.

I was stroking her hard and she was making those incredibly ugly fuck faces. I was doing a number on her clit, so I knew she was fighting her orgasm. That made it even more fun for me. I knew she was dying to cum.

"So if you in Ruby Swiss, then this ain't you muddafuckin' windshield that I'm busting up."

Booooooof!

I heard the windshield shatter through the phone.

There were several more smashes before he came back on the phone yelling. "Bring your stinkin ass out here! Right. Fuckin. Now."

Chantell's mouth opened. Her eyes went wide. She froze.

Chantell was cumming. Her crazy-ass man was down in the parking lot busting out her windshield and this crazy-ass bitch was cumming. Without me. Shit! Not a day like it. I started humping and thinking about how sweet her pussy is. I was thinking I was fuckin Halle Berry's fine ass up in there and I only had a minute to get her ass pregnant.

Chantell was trying to push me off, but I wasn't getting off until I got off. Fuck her man! And fuck her car! I needed to get my nut.

Chantell was still cumming, so she dared not talk.

Her man was still going the fuck off: "Bitch, I ga kill you! Bring your fuckin ass out her right dis fuckin minute!"

Chantell's orgasm ebbed, but my nut was rising. I pushed her knees back until they were both touching her head. I braced my foot in the corner of the sofa for leverage, and dug deep into that pussy.

She started humping up and squeezing her muscles around my dick. She was squeezing the nut up and out of me. The first barrage hit her just as she was about to open her mouth to speak. I knew what she wanted. I squeezed the base of my dick as I pulled out of her.

Chantell moved the phone, pressing the mute button as she opened her mouth. I crawled up over her and stuck my dick into her opened mouth. Her warm mouth closed around my shaft. Her lips formed an airtight seal. She cleaned my big head and then caught the second blast with her tongue. She swirled it around and turned on the suction to extract the rest.

My legs straightened out and my back stiffened as I tried to go down the back of her throat again. My nuts were slapping her chin as I deposited the last load. When she ran her tongue over my head, I jumped off of her. I couldn't take it. My shit was too muddafuckin' sensitive.

Chantell swallowed and licked her lips. She brought the phone up to her ear as she got up. She went into the kitchen, peeped out the window at her car over in the next parking lot, then came into the bathroom behind me. I gave her a warm, wet towel to clean herself as she spoke.

Once she was cleaned up and out the bathroom, she was all business. She pointed to my motorcycle helmet and made some hand gestures as she spoke to her man. "What the fuck are you doing1?" she asked, getting her panties from her bag and putting them on.

She kept asking him a string of questions that made him rant even more. She was buying time.

I cleaned myself, threw on some jeans and a t-shirt, got my cellphone, wallet, helmet, and bike keys, then kissed her on the cheek.

Chantell pointed and grabbed the other helmet.

I opened the sliding glass door for her. I got an old sheet, tied it off on the railing, tied it around her waist, and slowly lowered her down to the ground. I dropped her bag and the spare helmet, and then went out the front door, locking it behind me.

I went downstairs, and sure enough, I saw her crazy-ass man sittin on the hood of her Mazda 6 over in the other parking lot.

The windows were busted out and everything. I walked out talking on my cellphone, placing a rush order at Ruby Swiss, promising a fat tip if it was ready in five minutes. He didn't know me, but I knew him. Always know the other man, but try your best not to let him know you.

He took a quick glance in my direction but dismissed me because I had come from the wrong building I guessed. Besides, he was too busy arguing on the phone with Chantell.

I hopped on my Hyabusa, closed the phone, and fired it up. I put on my helmet, and rolled out of the lot.

CHANTELL

I don't believe the fuckin nigga dun follow my ass. He must not have seen me though, 'cause if he did, he would have been shooting through Carlos damn door. Nigga dun bust up my shit in the parking lot. Oh he ga pay. I don't even want that car no more. He ga buy me another one. I don't care how he gets it, but muddafucka ga buy me one.

"I hope you een dun fucked up my car," I said, to get him arguing as soon as I got my ass down from a two-muddafuckin-story balcony like a gaddamn cat burglar. This takes me back to my Tomboy days. The tings a bitch gatta do for some good dick.

Damn! I thought as I ducked and zigzagged my way through the other buildings to make sure I wasn't seen. I heard the bike start up in the distance. Los was coming around the side street to get me and dis stupid mudda fucker was still screaming in my ear.

"Bitch, I sitting on your car, and I een movin' until you bring your stinkin, ho'in' ass out here!"

Well sit right there, then. That'll buy me time to put my plan in action. Here comes Los now. I've got to get off the phone 'for Kevin hear the bike. "Who you calling a ho?" I yelled over his aggravating voice, "Nicca, fuck you!" I yelled, and pressed the end button as the bike's headlights came into view.

As Los stopped next to me, I hopped on the back of the bike. "Get me home before he get there."

"I ga stop at Ruby Swiss to pick up your food first. It should be ready when we get there."

"Okay, let's go." I hadn't even thought about that. I was too busy working on the other angle. "Le'me hold your phone and earpiece. I need to call my girl."

I slipped his Bluetooth in my ear, and dialed my girl, Anna, as we pulled off. My phone started beeping right away. I knew he would call back. I had no plans on answering his ass, though.

Anna answered on the third ring. She wasn't sleeping, but she was busy getting her groove on. I told her what I needed her to do, then hung up and turned the power off on my phone. He'd eventually get tired calling, just as he would eventually get tired waiting.

www.ingramcontent.com/pod-product-compliance
Lightning Source LLC
Chambersburg PA
CBHW071055250626
47159CB00002B/478